Praise for *Esme Cahill Fails Spectacularly*

"Marie Bostwick wows with thabout taking risks, chasing drea places you love most. Set in an i tain resort, it is a vacation in wor and absolutely could not put down. Esme Cahill is a protagonist to root for who will ultimately uncover the true meaning of family, the power of ancestral memory, and how, sometimes, failing spectacularly is the only way to begin again. This is Marie Bostwick at her storytelling finest!"

—Kristy Woodson Harvey, *New York Times*
bestselling author of *The Wedding Veil*

"Marie Bostwick's latest, *Esme Cahill Fails Spectacularly*, has everything I love: a funny, brave heroine who knows how to rock failure so well that she's writing a book after receiving two hundred sixty-eight previous rejections, women helping each other, a lakeside resort in need of some BIG repairs, a loving and dysfunctional family—and caramel cake! And quilts! I read this wise, loving book in one sitting because I simply couldn't stop. And now I want a sequel!"

—Maddie Dawson, bestselling author of *Snap Out of It*

Praise for *The Restoration of Celia Fairchild*

"Perennial fan favorite Marie Bostwick has done something special. This new novel has all the hallmarks readers have come to love about her books. . . . This bighearted tale of redemption, family ties, secrets, tough choices, and happy endings is filled with her trademark warmth and wisdom that will leave readers deeply satisfied."

—Susan Wiggs, *New York Times* bestselling author

"With warmth, heart, and hilarity, Marie Bostwick dazzles with a story about taking risks and letting go of the past to make way for the future of her dreams."

—Adriana Trigiani, *New York Times* bestselling author

"With gorgeous writing, Marie Bostwick has hit new heights with this surprising story of one woman's redemption. *The Restoration of Celia Fairchild* is wise, witty, and utterly compelling."

—Jane Green, *New York Times* bestselling author of *The Friends We Keep*

"There is lots of Southern charm as well as plenty of sweet tea in this wise and funny novel. . . . Marie Bostwick writes with such warmth and generosity and humor that you won't want to put this book down."

—Maddie Dawson, internationally bestselling author of *A Happy Catastrophe*

Esme Cahill
Fails
Spectacularly

Also by Marie Bostwick

The Restoration of Celia Fairchild
Hope on the Inside
The Promise Girls
Just in Time
The Second Sister

COBBLED COURT QUILT SERIES
Apart at the Seams
Ties That Bind
Threading the Needle
A Thread So Thin
A Thread of Truth
A Single Thread

TOO MUCH, TEXAS SERIES
From Here to Home
Between Heaven and Texas

HISTORICAL NOVELS
On Wings of the Morning
Fields of Gold
River's Edge

NOVELLAS
Secret Santa (with Fern Michaels)
Snow Angels (with Fern Michaels)
Comfort and Joy (with Fern Michaels)

Esme Cahill Fails Spectacularly

A Novel

MARIE BOSTWICK

𝓌𝓂

WILLIAM MORROW

An Imprint of HarperCollins*Publishers*

ESME CAHILL FAILS SPECTACULARLY. Copyright © 2023 by Marie Bostwick. All rights reserved. Printed in the United States of America. No part of this book may be used or reproduced in any manner whatsoever without written permission except in the case of brief quotations embodied in critical articles and reviews. For information, address HarperCollins Publishers, 195 Broadway, New York, NY 10007.

HarperCollins books may be purchased for educational, business, or sales promotional use. For information, please email the Special Markets Department at SPsales@harpercollins.com.

FIRST EDITION

Designed by Diahann Sturge

Illustrations © Aluna1; Bright_Design / Shutterstock

Library of Congress Cataloging-in-Publication Data has been applied for.

ISBN 978-0-06-299731-9

23 24 25 26 27 LBC 6 5 4 3 2

*To the Spectacular People, those who figure out how
to keep going when they feel like giving up*

PROLOGUE

Adele

January 1942

Anger tastes like ginger root, sharp and sweet and juicy, a tang that makes your tongue burn.

At least, that's what this anger tastes like, the anger of frustration and betrayal, of being discounted and blocked at every turn, forced from the path I'd mapped out for myself years before, exiled to the outskirts of everything I long for, cast aside, disregarded, sidelined.

So many words. But they still can't fully express all I'm feeling, the taste of this fury.

That's the problem with the English language, with words in general. They have no inherent meaning in and of themselves, and so many are required to explain an emotion, even to yourself. As much as I love books, I sometimes wonder how writers do it, and why. It all seems so wasteful. You can fill a page and still miss the mark of what you meant to say.

But I've never been very good at putting my thoughts into words. I didn't talk until I was four. I don't mean that I couldn't talk, only that I didn't. Even then, I felt the inadequacy of speech, sensed that I experienced the world differently than other people and that trying to explain this could only result in misunderstandings.

I was right.

When my mother told the family doctor that her eight-year-old daughter tasted emotion and felt color, he frowned and muttered and sent us to other doctors—a pediatrician, a child psychiatrist, and finally a neurologist, who told my mother, "Adele suffers from synesthesia, a brain malfunction in which the senses can become confused, eliciting an abnormal connection in response to certain stimuli. For example, seeing a particular color and experiencing an actual sensation of taste associated with it."

I didn't understand what he was talking about. But when he uttered the words malfunction *and* abnormal, *looking at me like a lab experiment, I tasted and saw mustard.*

Now, having lived for twenty-one years as a synesthete, I'm not convinced that the doctor understood what he was talking about either. It's not a malfunction, it's a gift, an extra portion of perception that not everyone gets to experience. Like most other people, I can talk, write, and express myself. But most other people can't do what I do, experience emotions as something tangible and concrete, a sensation that requires no explanation or interpretation. It might not be normal, but I wouldn't give it back.

When I feel the bite of ginger on the back of my tongue, I know exactly what type of anger I mean. It has a color too, this anger that's been simmering during the hours-long ride from Washington and bubbles up again as the bus starts to slow: it's the gray of spent coal shot with ink black and cinnamon.

When I was little, we had a tomcat with fur just that color, a stray who showed up to lick some cream I'd spilled on the stoop and never left. He had six toes on each front paw but only one eye, and his battle-scarred right ear was torn in three places. When I asked if I could keep him—a silly question because nobody can "keep" a cat, they come or they go—my father said, "Why? That's the most miserable cat I ever laid eyes on." The name stuck. So did the cat.

Miserable lived under the steps that led to the alley. He wouldn't come inside, not even if you tempted him with tuna. But sometimes on a summer day, he'd lie on his back to soak in the sun, arms stretched high over his head, and let you rub his belly three, four, or even five times. And then, without warning, he'd collapse into himself like a jackknife snapping into a sheath and pierce your friendly hand with all twelve of his sharp little front claws, often drawing blood, then slink back under the porch with a hiss that said you should have known better.

So maybe that explains the unusual color of this ginger-flavored fury? Because the anger of the moment is coupled with conviction that someday I will have my revenge on those who should have known better than to stand in my way, not by piercing them with my claws but by proving them wrong.

I should be making art, perfecting my technique, working toward the day when I'll see my work hanging in galleries, or even museums. Instead, I've been banished to the mountains to babysit other people's paintings and sculptures for the duration of the war. The fact that my canvas and marble-carved charges are among the finest in the world offers some solace. Perhaps the talents of the masters still cling to the works they've left behind? Perhaps I'll breathe it in somehow, find inspiration by osmosis? But it's still a banishment, a grossly unfair one, my penance for the sin of rebuffing the advances of my married boss.

The bus groans and squeaks and shudders to a stop. The driver calls out, "Asheville! Asheville, North Carolina! Next stop, Montreat!"

I jump to my feet, the only passenger to do so, palming the back of my head to make sure my blue hat is still pinned on before pulling a leather portfolio of my paintings and a wheat-colored suitcase holding more brushes and tubes of paint than clothes down from the luggage rack. The mid-thirties masher in the wrinkled suit, who was offended when I moved to another seat after jolting from sleep to find his hand on my knee, scowls and crosses his arms over his chest, making it clear he has no intention of helping.

I lumber up the aisle, the suitcase bumping against my legs with every step, worried it's going to catch on my stockings and wondering if I'll be able to find another pair if it does. The war is only days old but already there's talk of hosiery being rationed to reserve silk and nylon for making parachutes. I stretch my arm out as far as I can to keep my bag from banging on my legs and get to the front of the bus without incident. The kindly driver, a man with salt-and-pepper hair and a heavy Baltimore accent that marks him as a native of my hometown, who has been at the wheel since Washington and told me he makes this same trip twice a week, takes my burdens from me, sets them onto the curb, then offers his hand as I descend the steps.

"Thank you. Do you know where I can get a cab?"

"Nobody's coming to meet you?" he asks.

I pull a folded slip of paper from the pocket of my best blue jacket, now terribly wrinkled from the journey.

"I've got an address for a boardinghouse on Flint Street."

"Well, you won't find any cabs in this part of Asheville, miss. But if I'm remembering right, Flint is over in the Montford neighborhood." He points. "Go through that alley, take a right onto Broadway, then a left at the next corner onto Starnes. Just keep walking three, maybe four blocks. It's not far but I don't like leaving a lady all alone on the street." He glances at my suitcases, then at his wristwatch and shakes his head. "If I wasn't already behind schedule . . ."

I smile, then purposely put on the accent I'd worked so hard to rid myself of after leaving home and going to art school. "You don't need to worry about me, mister. I'm a Baltimore girl, not a lady."

He laughs. "Well, all right. I guess you can take care of yourself then," before wishing me well and climbing back behind the wheel.

The bus drives off, belching exhaust.

I pick up my bags and march down the deserted sidewalk in my platform pumps, tasting raw ginger, seeing cat fur and the comeuppance to come, a gallery hung with my work and the day I will prove them all wrong.

CHAPTER ONE

Esme

2009

The new used car I bought impulsively in New York and immediately nicknamed "the Toaster" on account of its boxy shape had a sticky clutch, a top speed of fifty-two miles an hour, and air conditioning that smelled weirdly of sauerkraut and worked only intermittently. So, by the time I reached the outskirts of town, I was tired, hot, cranky, and way behind schedule.

But when I putt-putted to the top of the hill and I saw blue-green waves of mountains reaching the horizon in every direction and the city in the center, looking like the only human habitation in the known universe, suspended in an endless sky, irritation gave way to awe. On a perfect day in early June, "Land of the Sky" is more than a tagline; it's a spot-on description of Asheville, North Carolina.

There was a time when this mountain town felt like a kind

of heaven to me, a place of rescue and redemption. But when an injured animal is given refuge and time to heal, there comes a day when safety starts to feel like suffocation. The same thing happened to me. That's why I left Asheville nearly fifteen years before, intent on becoming a writer.

I'd been talking about it since I was twelve, scribbling stories and "honing my craft" while hammering out the particulars of a year-by-year plan to create a happy, secure, successful life as a multi-published, bestselling novelist who had it all—house, husband, family, friends.

Step one was to get myself to New York City.

When I told my grandparents that the time had come for me to begin my career and leave the lakeside lodge where they'd raised me, George couldn't understand what the one had to do with the other.

"Why can't you stay here and write? We've got paper and pens in North Carolina too, you know. Not to mention lots of material to work with. Take Thomas Wolfe," he argued. "*Look Homeward Angel* is a classic, one of the best novels of all time, and the whole story takes place right here in Asheville."

"Yes. And Wolfe got his master's at Harvard, taught at NYU, and wrote most of the book in Europe, George," I said. I'm not sure why but I always called my grandparents by their first names; maybe because I didn't know they existed until I was ten. "New York is the center of the literary universe. If I'm going to be published by twenty-two, I need to start making contacts."

"You're only nineteen," he countered. "What's the rush? You've got plenty of time."

"I'll be *fine*," I said, responding to the look in his eyes and how he was tugging at the buckle of his suspenders, the way he did when something worried him. "It's not like you're never going to see me again. I'll come back to visit all the time, I promise. But now that I've finished college, there's no point in my hanging around here any longer. Besides, if you plan to lead an amazing life, you've got to go where life is amazing."

George hooked a thumb around his suspenders and turned toward my grandmother.

"What do you say to all this?"

Adele fixed her eyes on mine.

"When were you thinking of leaving?"

"There's a bus on Friday morning."

"I see. So you want to be gone before Robyn comes home? You're sure? She's still your mother, Esme. You haven't seen her in ten years."

I bit my lower lip but didn't speak. Adele wasn't much of a talker but when she did talk, she had a way of cutting to the heart of the matter.

"Well," she said at last, reading the resolve in my silence and then looking at George, "I'd say that we have a lot to do before Friday."

Yes, we did.

From the day Adele taught me to sew my own clothes, my closet had been stuffed. My therapist says it stems from childhood deprivations. I just think I like variety. And making stuff. That's the problem with therapists: they turn everything into a diagnosis.

No way would my wardrobe fit into two suitcases, so I just packed my summer clothes and boxed up the rest to be shipped once I found a place to live, along with my books and the portable sewing machine I'd gotten for graduation. It ended up being a pretty big job. However, Adele's most pressing concern was teaching me to cook shrimp and grits.

"The grease adds lots of flavor, so make sure the bacon is good and cooked before you toss in the shrimp," she explained as she stirred a mess of crackling lardons in her favorite cast iron skillet. "New Yorkers probably won't know about it so they'll think you're making something exotic. The best thing about this recipe is it's scalable, perfect for parties."

Oh, Adele.

Any other grandma about to send her teenage granddaughter off to the big, bad city would have been instructing her in the proper use of handheld mace. Adele's big concern was making sure I was prepared to entertain. That fact that I didn't have an apartment, a job, or two nickels to rub together and didn't know a soul in New York was inconsequential—Adele was absolutely certain I'd be throwing a lot of dinner parties.

Of course, that's exactly what happened. Though I'm honestly not that great a cook, shrimp and grits became my signature dish, a recipe that works for a first-date dinner for two or a baby shower for twenty. Like Adele said, it's scalable.

George had a more practical, or at least more grandfatherly, response to my departure. He did, in fact, buy me some mace, and a rape whistle, and taught me a couple of karate throws to use should I ever be attacked from behind.

Back then, I had a halo of brown ringlets that matched my eyes and hung to my shoulders, a sprinkling of freckles on my turned-up nose, and a heart-shaped baby face. The day after I moved in with Yolanda, I borrowed her scissors and hacked my hair into a short, messy pixie cut in hopes it would make me look older and force people to take me seriously, but it didn't really help. I was twenty-eight years old before I was able to order a cocktail without getting carded. So that, along with the fact that I'm five feet tall without shoes and weigh one hundred and seven pounds soaking wet, made George's attempts to turn me into a badass feel somewhat laughable. But I played along to ease his mind and because, well, it was sweet that he worried about me.

I'd never met my own father or even known who he was. On the rare occasions when the topic came up, Robyn referred to him as "the sperm donor," which made me suppose he'd been just another of her many one-night stands. But George was better than two fathers to me, so I never felt the lack.

Now, driving down the highway, I spot the exit that George's battered green pickup had taken when dropping me off so many years before, and the memories come flooding back, as vivid as if they were occurring in real time.

The bus was late. I remembered feeling impatient, wanting to make a clean break, wishing my grandparents would just get in the truck and go because the way George kept pacing and jingling the change in his pocket was making me crazy. I also remembered feeling worried about what would happen if they *did* go and the bus didn't come. What if I'd already missed it? There wasn't a proper terminal in Asheville, just a pickup and drop-off point in front of a gas station. What if this was the wrong gas station?

Finally, the bus rumbled around a corner. The long stretch of waiting gave way to flurry and flutter, the counting of suitcases and hurried inquiries about the packages of new underwear Adele had left on my bed the night before. Then, suddenly, the bus was at the curb, belching exhaust, and the driver was lifting a door on the underbelly of the beast—quickly, so quickly—

and loading my bags into the expanse before closing the compartment door with an impatient clang and saying we had to get moving, that he needed to make up time.

I remembered the jolt of elation that coursed through me, the euphoria of adventure and fresh starts. And I remembered the last round of hugs, and the wet sheen in George's eyes and how he pressed a hundred-dollar bill into my hand, and reminded me to call as soon as I got to New York. And I remembered Adele placing her hands on my cheeks and leaning in until we were nose to nose, saying, "I love you, I love you, I love you," and me saying it back.

I remembered following the driver to the door, putting my foot on the first step, being interrupted by a squeal and a hoot, and turning to see Adele running toward me in her going-to-town shoes with short, stiff strides, her platinum curls bouncing with every step.

"Your lunch! Your lunch! You almost forgot!" she cried, then thrust a paper shopping bag with enough provisions for a week into my arms. "Eat the egg salad first," she instructed, "so the mayonnaise doesn't turn. And then the pimento cheese. Save the peanut butter and jelly for last. Don't forget."

"I won't."

"Sit by the driver," she advised. "And watch out for mashers."

"What are mashers?"

"Men with overcoats and wandering hands."

I laughed. "I love you."

"I love you more."

"Don't worry, Adele. I'll be fine."

"Oh, I *know* you will!" she exclaimed and squeezed my hands. "I absolutely *do*! Big things are in store for you, Esme. Big, big things!"

I found a seat in the back, next to a window. My grandparents stood on the curb, taut smiles signaling their determination not to cry. I waved, dry-eyed, thinking that they were
preciously overemotional. After all, it wasn't like I was never
coming back. When I came to visit, I'd be successful, happy,
and possibly famous, and they'd be proud of me.

But as the bus pulled away, I felt a sudden stab of . . . not
regret precisely, more a wish that things could have been different, that I hadn't lived the kind of life that made me into
the kind of person who would accelerate her exit plan to avoid
her own mother, the mother she hadn't set eyes on in nearly
a decade. Heaven knew I had my reasons. So did my grandparents, which is why Adele hadn't urged me to delay my departure. Because what would be the point? If I stayed on an
extra week, or even two, it wouldn't have made any difference.
Robyn made her choices and now I was making mine, a choice
to forget the past and focus on my future.

I got up onto my knees, pressing my palm against the grimy
window and craning my neck to keep my grandparents in sight
for as long as possible, feeling a shiver of excitement as the bus
picked up speed and drove off. Adele was right, big things were
ahead for me. I was sure of it. All I had to do was work hard
and stick to my plan.

Everything is perfectly straightforward, when you're nineteen.

CHAPTER TWO

New York

1997

Carl Zinfandel, fifty-something and balding, with hands like hams and a 1962 class ring on one of his fleshy fingers, dressed in a short-sleeved shirt and striped rayon tie that floated an inch above his belt buckle, looked more like the assistant manager of a grocery store than a senior editor for a major New York publishing house. In short, he wasn't at all what I expected.

But maybe he was thinking the same thing about me.

I was short and the chair across from Mr. Zinfandel's desk was weirdly tall. I sat there, toes dangling above the floor, while he read my résumé.

Considering how slim it was on actual content, I was surprised it was taking him so long. I'd stayed up all night writing it, padding my skimpy work history with a list of writing awards and using the biggest font I could reasonably get away with.

I looked down at my lap and frowned. Wearing linen was a mistake. When I sat down, my dress pleated into a dozen uneven wrinkles. And I didn't even want to imagine what my hair looked like. After the big brown eyes I inherited from Adele, my crown of chestnut ringlets was my best feature, but they frizzed into a tangle somewhere between Brillo pad and bird's nest when it was humid.

I ran my hand over my hair, thinking about how many of my favorite authors had been published by Dorne and Merrill— E. Foster Llewellyn, Rita Harris-Crown, Oscar Glazier—and how amazing it would be to work here. Or, if I was honest, just about anywhere.

Mr. Zinfandel cleared his throat and laid my résumé on the desk.

"So . . . you really haven't done anything. Have you?"

"Sorry?"

I was prepared for questions about my strengths and weaknesses, not honesty. I tried to recover, mumbling something about being in charge of author events at the bookstore when the manager was recuperating from gallbladder surgery (there'd only been one), but Carl waved a beefy hand through the air and cut me off.

"That friend of yours who works in the design department— the artsy one with purple hair . . ." He fluttered his fingers over his pate as if he were sprinkling fairy dust on his head.

"Yolanda? We're roommates. She said you had an opening for an editorial assistant."

"Yolanda. She said you're a writer?"

"Yes. I mean . . . I was. I've never really published anything."

"Did you *finish* anything?"

"Over the last three years, I've written fifteen novels in

various genres." He raised his eyebrows, waiting for the rest of the story. "And got two hundred and sixty-eight rejections."

His eyebrows reached new heights. *"Really?"*

Yes. Really.

Who'd have guessed I had such an infinite capacity for humiliation? Admitting it was humiliation of a different sort. But for the first time since I'd walked into his office, Mr. Zinfandel looked interested. So when he propped his elbows on his desk and rested his chin on his big knuckles, I did the thing that you should probably never, ever do in an interview—I told the absolute truth.

I told him about growing up as the only child of a single, teenage mom who found her escape in drugs and alcohol and about how Zip, one of the many "uncles" we lived with over the years, taught me how to read before disappearing like all the others, taking all the money from my mother's purse but leaving me with my escape, books. I told him about having our car repossessed, being hungry when Robyn got fired, which happened pretty often, and the run-in with the law that landed her in jail and me in foster care. When Carl started to look sorry for me, I skipped ahead and told him about George and Adele, the grandparents I'd never known I had, and how George had driven through the night to collect me after a social worker called to inform him of my existence and predicament, and took me home to the Last Lake Lodge, a rustic fishing resort outside of Asheville.

"And you lived happily ever after?" Carl asked, rocking backward in his chair, grasping the cracked leather armrests and making the springs squeak.

"Yes and no."

Without going into too many details, I gave him to understand that starting a new school in a small town wasn't easy, especially once your classmates found out about your drug addict, jailbird mother. It's not fair to judge children for the mistakes of their parents but people will do it. That's why it's so important to make a name and reputation for yourself. I knew that from an early age. What I didn't know, not at first, was how to do it.

During a shopping trip for school clothes in Asheville, not long after I arrived in North Carolina, Adele decided we should stop by the bookstore. Oscar Glazier was there, signing copies of *Red Dawn and Cold Steel*. I was agog, awestruck by my first sight of a living, breathing published author. The book was adult action adventure and way over my head, but Adele bought me a copy anyway and made me promise not to read it until I was fourteen. I broke my promise almost immediately.

Of less importance than the book was the man who wrote it. Mr. Glazier didn't even look up while signing my copy, but the encounter changed something in me, opened a door in my mind. I started secreting paper, pencils, and a flashlight inside my pillowcase and scribbling under the covers when I should have been sleeping.

Reading stories offered me escape. Writing them gave me release, and a sense of safety and control, the ability to create worlds in which heroines always triumph against seemingly impossible odds, *always*. My first efforts were shaky, peppered with plot holes and deplorable spelling, but I was hooked. Soon I was writing all the time, under the blankets in the dark of night, in my head during the light of day. Bit by bit, I got better at it.

After winning a countywide writing contest for sixth graders, my teachers decided I should skip the seventh grade entirely. This convinced me of two things: that writing was my destiny and that it was possible to speed the process of growing up. My grandparents were caring, kind, and supportive, but I could never shake the feeling that childhood left a person too much at the mercy of others. Even at eleven, maybe especially then, I hated being dependent and understood that if you didn't take hold of your own destiny, somebody else might.

And so I took every AP class my high school offered, plus community college classes during the summer, graduated at sixteen, earned my bachelor's degree from Appalachian State at nineteen, and moved to New York City a month later, right after learning that my mother had been paroled and was moving back to the lake, "just until she gets back on her feet," as George said. How long that would take was anybody's guess, but even one day was too much for me, so I caught that bus the day before she was due to arrive.

New York was all I'd hoped it would be—bustling, loud, and overcrowded, an assault on the senses, with bookstores in every neighborhood and potential characters on every corner. I spent my second day in the city parked on the stoop of the West Side Y, scribbling notes about the people who streamed in and out, figuring at least one of them would make a good story. But in New York, even the Y was beyond my budget. After spotting a "roommate wanted" ad on a coffee shop bulletin board, I called the number and moved in with Yolanda the same day.

Our apartment, which shared a bathroom with a ground floor nail salon that was probably a money-laundering operation, was really more of a hallway sandwiched between two other apartments, and definitely not legal. But it was cheap and I liked Yolanda, a funny, free-spirited art school grad who crocheted weird and whimsical googly-eyed monsters that looked kind of like those paper and clay animals from the Oaxaca region of Mexico, was forever falling in love with guys who were all wrong for her, and who loved to read as much as I did.

We lived on cheese sandwiches, ramen noodles, and hope. Yolanda was waitressing at three different restaurants until she could find a gallery that was willing to buy her art. I sold books at Barnes & Noble during the day and wrote into the wee hours in every imaginable genre—romance, suspense, young adult, fantasy, steampunk. It was fun at first. Yolanda came from a small town too, and we loved exploring the city, figuring out everything you could do to entertain yourself in New York for under two bucks, telling each other that someday, after we were famous, the stories of our starving artist days would make great interview fodder.

But cheese sandwiches and ramen get old after a while. So does rejection.

When the landlord raised the rent, Yolanda took a job as a junior graphic designer at Dorne and Merrill and ended up liking it more than she'd thought. Maybe I would too?

I cleared my throat and clarified my position on Carl's inquiry about living happily ever after. "What I meant to say is, not yet. But I'm working on it."

"And you think getting a job as my assistant might speed the process?" he asked. I clasped my hands in my lap, saying nothing. "Are you sure you're ready to give up on writing?"

"Absolutely."

I meant it. If you don't take the hint after two hundred and sixty-eight rejections, when will you? And at this point, I just wanted to be *good* at something again.

"Well." Carl paused to slurp his coffee. "You wouldn't be the first editor who started out thinking they were a writer. What kind of books do you like?"

"*All* kinds." I wiggled toward the front edge of the chair so that my toes, which had lost all feeling, made contact with the floor, and listed my favorites by genre. It took a while.

"But . . . ," I said finally, and paused to lick my lips, worried I was about to say the wrong thing. "I'm not all that crazy about literary fiction. Most of it anyway. I mean, I'm not saying that I *hate* it—"

Carl cut me off with an enormous, yawping guffaw.

"Gawd, I do! Pretentious, self-indulgent, word salad most of it. Everybody dies and *nothing* happens!" He slapped his palms flat against his desk and rocked his whole torso forward, as if preparing to leapfrog across the expanse. "What's so smart about writing a book that doesn't have a *plot*?"

Was this a rhetorical question? He was staring at me like it might not be. Before I could formulate an answer, Carl rocked back into his chair.

"If you work with me, you'll be working on commercial titles, the books that people actually *buy*. Publishing is a business. And an editor is only as good as his last year's sales."

If I worked with him?

It wasn't definite but it sounded promising. I scooted forward and moved my hands to the armrests. The jingling of my bracelets drew Carl's attention and a laugh. "Anybody who likes jewelry that much needs to marry an orthodontist."

"Oh, I'm not planning on getting married anytime soon."

This was true. I very much wanted to get married someday, but not until the time was right. If you don't control your life, life ends up controlling you. That's why you need a plan.

Realizing I was going to miss the boat on getting published by twenty-two, I'd recently regrouped. My new plan was pretty similar to the old one, still centered in New York (cramped, illegal, money-laundering nail salon apartments notwithstanding, it was still where amazing people lived amazing lives) but more reality based and with a slightly more generous timeline.

I'd establish myself in a viable, interesting career by twenty-four, marry the man of my dreams by twenty-eight, buy a garden apartment where we could cultivate flowers and a wide group of interesting and accomplished friends by thirty-two, and start a family by thirty-five, leaving open the option to have a second child two or three years later. At the moment, I was way behind schedule, but if Carl hired me, maybe I could make up for lost time?

"I don't even have a boyfriend," I assured him. "And I made the bracelets myself."

"All of them?" he asked, looking mildly impressed.

"Jewelry making is one of my hobbies. And sewing. I made this dress myself."

I ran my hand over my dress. Wrinkled or not, I loved the full skirt, the pink and fuchsia orchids and matching fuchsia belt. Not a conventional choice for an interview but surely people who worked in publishing appreciated the unconventional? Besides, I couldn't afford a suit.

"Yeah." Carl cleared his throat again. "Didn't think you bought it in the city. That's okay, kid. It's good that you've got interests."

"Oh, I do! *So* many! Reading, obviously. Sewing. Jewelry making. Knitting. Gardening."

Since I couldn't seem to master increases or decreases, the only thing I knew how to knit was scarves and my current garden was a rusty coffee can on the windowsill where I grew parsley and cilantro but Carl didn't need to know that. Once my someday husband and I bought that garden apartment together, I would become a certified master gardener. And learn to bake sourdough bread. And make truly amazing Bolognese sauce. Like the outlines I had formerly used for the plots of my writing projects, my life plan included headings and subheadings.

"Oh, and I've been learning origami—"

"Origami?" Carl popped his bushy eyebrows.

"It's very calming."

"Uh-huh." Carl nodded slowly. "So, Esme Cahill, if I asked you to pitch me an idea for a nonfiction book, what would it be?"

"Nonfiction?"

This should have been the easiest thing in the world. Yolanda and I invented a game we called That Oughta Be a Book, where we'd each come up with a topic that we thought would make a good book and then argue about whose idea was better. Most of the time, I pitched plots for novels, but I had plenty of thoughts about real people or situations that would make interesting reading too. However, the second Carl asked me to actually name one, every book idea I'd ever had flew straight out of my head.

"Umm . . ."

"Take your time."

My brain was blank. The only thing that penetrated was the sound of Carl's desk clock, ticking away the seconds and my chances of getting a real job. But then . . .

"Oh! Oh, wait! I've got one!"

"Just tell me. You don't need to raise your hand."

"I . . . I know a woman who feels colors. Tastes them too,

sometimes." Carl leaned in a little so I kept going. "She makes quilts. Every color she puts into them is connected to the emotions she's experienced at a particular moment in life."

"A quilter with synesthesia?" Carl tilted his head to one side. "Can she write?"

"I don't think so," I said, truthfully.

"Huh. Well, it's an interesting idea. You know, editors don't always just sit around waiting for manuscripts to land on the desk, Esme. Sometimes our job is to pick up the phone and convince people to share their stories."

Our job? Was Carl Zinfandel saying what I *thought* he was saying?

"So . . . do you want me to call her?"

My heart dropped into my stomach. Adele rarely talked about herself, deflecting questions with more questions of her own. If getting this job hinged on convincing my grandmother to open up about her life, I was doomed.

"An editorial assistant's job is *assisting*," Carl said. "Answering email, scheduling meetings, keeping the wheels rolling. It's grunt work. But I'd never hire an assistant unless I believed they had the potential to step into my shoes someday."

He went quiet. I held my breath, sensing he was nearing his verdict.

"You are an odd young woman, Esme. But I've got a good feeling about you. You've had to fight for the things you want. Which means you understand what reading is all about: finding connection, knowing we're not the only ones who struggle, or dream. You've got to understand other people before you can understand yourself."

He leaned forward, pressing his palms together. "Publishers create books, but what we really sell is hope. If you've never had to rely on it, never had to figure out how to keep going when you felt like giving up, you'll never understand what story is and why people need it."

The hair was standing up on the back of my neck. Carl Zinfandel was explaining what books meant to people but I couldn't shake the feeling that he was explaining me to myself.

I had to get this job. I *had* to work for this man!

"You're so young. But somehow . . . somehow I think you *do* know." Carl narrowed his eyes and clucked his tongue against his teeth, thinking. "No, Esme Cahill, I do not want you to call the synesthetic quilter.

"What I *do* want is for you to come back here on Monday morning, wearing"—he looked me up and down—"almost anything but *that*, and start working for me."

CHAPTER THREE

2009

*H*ave I ever felt as happy as I did after leaving Carl's office with the promise of a job?

After three years of hearing nothing but no, no, and *no*, somebody in the book world had finally said yes! I returned my visitor's pass to the bored guard at the security desk, chirped "See you Monday!" and practically floated down West Fifty-Eighth Street. I was thrilled, certain that Adele's prophecy was coming true and that big things were ahead for me.

For a while, it seemed like they were. Carl was a skilled editor and supportive mentor, sharing everything he knew with me. Within a couple of years, I started editing books on my own. Thanks to beginner's luck when one of my titles made the bestseller lists, I got my first promotion and raise, and rented a nice (and legal) studio apartment of my own in Queens.

Establishing myself in a viable career by the time I was twenty-four? Check.

Carl retired and moved to Florida five years into my tenure at DM. I missed working with him and worried that my career might stall without his guidance. However, I edited two more bestsellers and was promoted from associate editor to editor the following year, with a pay bump that allowed me to start saving to buy a place of my own. After realizing he hated humidity, bugs, and golf, and wasn't ready to spend his days eating dinner at four o'clock and waiting for death, Carl returned to New York and opened a literary agency. We met for lunch almost every week and I bought a few books from him over the years.

So, yes, my life was good. And on schedule. Which is not to say there weren't setbacks.

Yolanda, my friend and closest confidante for more than eight years, left DM and New York, disappearing without a trace. The fact that it happened just two days before my wedding to Alex and that I never knew why made it worse. I stood on the steps at City Hall holding a bouquet of daisies that I'd bought at a corner bodega, scanning the sidewalk for Yolanda for so long that we almost missed our appointment with the justice of the peace.

It wasn't the wedding I'd envisioned, that's for sure. We ended up paying a lady dressed in red spandex and bedroom slippers, who we found loitering outside the city clerk's office, five dollars to witness the ceremony. But it was done. I was married to Alex, a handsome, charming, athletic, perfectly dressed and groomed man with a Georgia drawl and manners to match. And with only a little prodding, I'd convinced him to tie the knot just a week before my birthday.

Happily married by age twenty-eight? Check.

Well, okay . . . Not all that happily.

Don't get me wrong. Everybody liked Alex, including me. So instead of bemoaning the fact that the romantic side of the marriage was disappointing, I focused on how lucky I was to be married to a man who felt more like a friend than a husband. No marriage is perfect, right? I figured that passion was just one factor in a large, complex equation and while we might not be perfectly happy, we were happy enough.

But math has never been my strong suit. Neither, apparently, is picking up on signals.

The most embarrassing aspect of my divorce is when people lean in, drop their voice to a whisper, and say, "So you honestly didn't know? Or suspect? At least a little?"

Let me state for the record that, no, I did not know my husband was gay. To be fair, I don't think Alex knew either, not in the beginning. Or maybe he was trying *not* to know. Maybe we were both fooling ourselves. All I know for sure is that on a beautiful Saturday, I dragged Alex to an open house for an adorable garden apartment in Queens. It needed work and was a stretch financially but it was the house of my dreams, or would be once we fixed it up. The fact that it had come onto the market six months before my thirty-second birthday felt like an omen. I'd blow out my candles and cross another milestone from my list, right on schedule.

Check!

But just as we were about to go through a door to which a real estate agent had pinned a red sign that read, in a really ugly font, "Welcome to *your* new home!" Alex tugged at my sleeve.

"Esme, there's something I need to tell you . . ."

In case you weren't aware, "there's something I need to tell you" is never a preamble to good news. *Never.*

I should know. In the hellish year and a half since Alex informed me our marriage was a sham, I've had more than my share of bad news. To start with, there was the whole divorce debacle. Four years is just long enough to make disentangling your life from somebody else's a shockingly complicated and pricey procedure. And even if your marriage was built on a lie and utterly devoid of passion, the emotional aspects of divorce are no picnic either.

On the one hand, I was furious with Alex. On the other hand, I missed having him around. Or maybe I just missed having *someone* around? It's hard to say. The bottom line is, loneliness sucks. I'm not mad at Alex anymore, not like I was. I just wish he'd been a little more self-aware; I wish we both had. And when your marriage ends like mine did, quickly becoming water cooler fodder for people to gasp and giggle over, people you *thought* were your friends? Well . . . that's when you start to wonder if you'd ever had any friends. Or ever will.

Work had always been my self-medication of choice, but that wasn't going well either. Some of it was just bad luck. Who could have predicted a breakout of mad cow disease the same week we released *Cookery for Carnivores*? But it wasn't like I was the only editor whose sales had been soft. Books are one of the first things people cut back on in a recession.

Still, if I'm totally honest with myself, it wasn't just bad luck or even the economy. Though I did my best to put on a brave face, I couldn't find joy in my job or anything else.

Then, eight months ago, things got worse. That's when Adele called.

"Esme, I want you to come home for Thanksgiving."

I begged off, saying I was slammed at work, which was true.

"Why don't you and George come here instead? I'll need to be in the office but I can juggle my meetings so we can squeeze in some sightseeing and shopping. We could go to the parade on Thanksgiving and maybe I can get us some Rockettes tickets. How does that sound?"

I thought she'd jump at the chance. Adele and George had come to New York three years previously and she'd loved it, bought so much fabric in the Garment District that she had to buy an extra suitcase to get it all home, and had been so wowed by Radio City's famous *Christmas Spectacular* that we ended up going three times in five days.

"No, no, no," she insisted. "Esme, I understand you don't like spending time around your mother but I need for you to come down *here*. There's something I need to tell you."

Surprising no one, Robyn Cahill never had quite managed to "get back on her feet" after being released from prison, and was still living at the lake on George and Adele's dime.

Though I'd scheduled my initial move to New York purposely to avoid seeing my mother, our paths crossed whenever I went back to the lake for a visit. For the sake of my grandparents, I always made a concerted effort to be polite to Robyn, efforts that weren't always returned in kind. That, coupled with my always slammed work schedule, was why I so rarely made it back home. However, in that moment, dealing with Robyn was less of a concern than the strained tone in my grandmother's voice. Something wasn't right here.

"Adele, what's going on? Are you okay? Is George?"

"I'm fine," she assured me. "And George is . . . George is fine too. But I want you to come home for a few days. There's something I need your help with, something I can't do alone."

"Okay," I said evenly. "But can't you just explain it to me first?"

"If I was good at explaining things, then I wouldn't need your help." She let out a short laugh, sounding more like herself. "Nothing all that terrible or unexpected is happening, I swear. It's just . . . just life. But I need your help, Esme. There are things I need to show you, conversations that can only be had face-to-face." She paused, took a breath. "So you'll come."

I would have. But I never got the chance. Five days later, Adele died of a stroke. I couldn't believe it. She was eighty-three but, somehow, I thought she'd go on forever. Maybe that's why I was able to hold myself together in the immediate aftermath, because it didn't seem real.

George called to tell me what happened but was so distraught that he had to hand off the phone to Robyn. After hanging up, I threw some stuff into a bag and took a cab to JFK Airport. Luckily, there was one seat available on an itinerary that would eventually get me home but I had to change planes twice and spend five hours in the Atlanta airport. But I got there as soon as I could, took a cab directly to the funeral home to meet up with George and Robyn, and spent the next four days dealing with arrangements, so busy I barely had time to think, which was just as well. If I'd stopped to try to process what had happened, I'd have completely lost it and been of no use to anybody.

That part didn't come until later, after I returned to New York.

Sales conference, a quarterly, multiday meeting where editors present their roster of upcoming books to the sales force, is a big deal in publishing. It's an editor's first and best opportunity to get the sales department excited about her titles and start building an in-house groundswell of support for a potential big seller. I had nine books scheduled for publication the following spring, so I threw myself into preparing my presentations as soon as I got back from Asheville, stuffing my emotions into a lockbox and throwing away the key. Initially, my laser focus paid off. My presentations went without a hitch. After

I wrapped up, Stephanie Mandela, the editor in chief, gave a smile and nod that seemed to say, "That's the way to do it, people. The old Esme is back!"

So when I sat down, I was actually feeling pretty good. Then Camille Espinoza stood up to present her book, a story about a divorcée whose emotional wounds are healed after she—somewhat unwillingly—adopts a stray dog. It wasn't a particularly original plot; I've read variations of that story a hundred times. But when Camille described how the dog rushed into the street to save the woman from being struck by an oncoming car, only to be killed himself, I started sniffling, then crying, then sobbing uncontrollably.

The meeting came to a standstill, full stop. For ten seconds that felt like ten years, my colleagues just stared. Then Camille handed me a tissue and Stephanie poured me a glass of water and I pulled myself together enough to drink it without choking, then muttered an apology and left the room.

I took some time off and spent much of it in bed sleeping and weeping. After using up all my vacation days—a first for me—I went back to the office.

When I stepped into the elevator and pushed the button for the eighteenth floor, I felt relieved and thought that everything would be fine if I could just get back to work and resume my normal life. But it wasn't that easy. Though I stayed on top of all my deadlines, the malaise refused to lift. A lot of the time, I was going through the motions. After a couple of months, Stephanie took me to lunch and suggested I "talk to someone."

When I say that everybody in New York has a therapist, I'm not exaggerating. On the Upper West Side, even the dogs have therapists. So I was skeptical. Despite that, therapy helped me come to grips with the scope of my grief. I'd lost so much in the last year—Adele, Alex, and my dreams. Nothing was turning out like I'd thought it would.

However, finding out that Darius Ebersoll was retiring helped more.

Work has always been my antidote to pain. I was certain that being promoted to the senior editor spot that Darius was vacating would ease mine, giving me a chance to get my life back on track and grab victory from the jaws of defeat. Though I knew it was a long shot, I threw myself into work with a vengeance, trying to prove that I could fill Darius's shoes. He'd been Oscar Glazier's editor for twenty years, so when the job of editing Oscar's new manuscript was handed to me, it felt like a sign. And three months later, when Stephanie said she wanted to see me after she got back from vacation, I was certain it was to tell me I'd gotten the promotion. Instead, there was . . .

Well, an event so phenomenally humiliating that I don't like to think or talk about it, and now refer to simply as "The Incident," a failure more spectacular and demoralizing than all my previous rejections combined, which ended, not with my promotion, but with me packing twelve years of memories into boxes under the watchful eye of a security guard, being ousted from the only real job I'd ever held, doing the only thing I'd ever truly excelled at. After a fruitless two-month job search, my lease came up for renewal and I realized I had no choice but to slink back home with my tail between my legs—divorced, depressed, and unemployed, a failure on every level.

"Quit saying that," Carl commanded, dabbing a paper napkin on his tie to blot some soup he'd spilled during our farewell lunch at his favorite Midtown diner. "And quit sounding so pitiful. This is just a setback, kid. A detour, not a banishment. You'll be back."

"Not if I can't find a job," I moaned. "I've applied everywhere and for everything."

Well . . . not *everything*.

For about fifteen minutes, I considered switching industries and applying to be a "Planning Transformation Control Project Lead," who would "support the evolution of transformation initiatives within planning initiatives, collaborating with stakeholders to drive execution and ensure initiative scope definition reaches alignment objectives." However, just before hitting the send button I had a moment of clarity and realized that the only thing worse than being turned down for this job would be getting hired to do it.

Apart from that, I'd applied for every position that I was even remotely qualified for and hadn't scored a single interview.

"It's because of The Incident," I muttered. "I'll never forgive Oscar. *Never*."

Carl stopped slurping his soup long enough to roll his eyes. "Again with the drama. There's no conspiracy here, Esme. Oscar had nothing to do with it. The economy sucks, book sales have tanked, DM had to thin out the herd, and you released a meat cookbook during a mad cow outbreak."

"That wasn't my fault!"

"What's fault got to do with it? This is about timing," he said, then laid down his spoon. "Esme, what did I tell you? On the first day we met, when you marched into my office wearing a homemade dress and carrying your padded résumé, what did I tell you?"

"An editor is only as good as her last year's sales," I mumbled.

"Exactly. I know you're upset but you've been going a hundred miles an hour with your hair on fire for years. This is a chance to catch your breath, take stock."

"Of what?"

"Your life." He held out half a roll, offering to share. I shook my head. "I understand how you feel; I've been in your shoes too, remember? They called it early retirement but the writing was on the wall; take it or get canned. In retrospect, it was the best thing that could have happened. I'd never have opened the agency otherwise."

"It's different for me, Carl. All I've ever wanted to do was be an editor."

"Not *all*," he reminded me.

"Please. That doesn't count," I said, waving him off. "I was a kid. Writing was a fantasy. And lest we forget, I was bad at it. Nobody would publish me, nobody."

"After twelve years of life and editing experience, is it possible that you've improved?"

Carl had always been a lemonade-from-lemons kind of guy. I was too, most of the time. But my temporary exodus from the city was about survival, not reinvention or taking stock. The only reason I was going home was because my lease was up and my severance wouldn't last forever. But as soon as I found another job, I'd drive right back to New York and try to get my derailed life back on track . . . assuming the Toaster hadn't totally broken down by then.

Every time I crossed a state line, I discovered some new issue. Entering New Jersey, I found out the AC smelled weird and only worked sometimes. Between Pennsylvania and Delaware, I realized the shocks were shot. Crossing into Maryland, it started rattling whenever I picked up speed. After spending the night in a motel in Virginia and rising before dawn in hopes of getting an early start, I realized I had only one working headlight.

That was why I needed to get to Last Lake before dark. But I also needed to pick up some toothpaste and hair gel on the way. If I remembered correctly, there was a Harris Teeter nearby where I should be able to get what I needed.

There was a good three hours before sunset, but when I left the highway and took a left onto a surface street, the day became suddenly darker. My car was enveloped in a thick bank of fog. Fog isn't unheard of in Asheville, but it usually burns off in the morning. Even so, it didn't strike me as all that strange in the moment.

Wisps of white and gray vapor swirled through the air. I pressed the brake pedal to slow the car. At the same moment, a big gray bus pulled out of the fog, making a sharp right directly in front of me. I gasped and hit the brakes again, jerking to a full stop. The bus stopped too, just a few feet ahead of me, brakes squealing as it pulled to the curb.

The road was narrow and with the fog I couldn't see what might be coming from the opposite direction. I sat there and waited, heart still pounding as I considered how close I'd come to getting T-boned by a bus, and thinking what a strange coincidence it was. A few minutes before, I'd been reminiscing about catching a Greyhound and heading off to my new life in New York. The next thing I knew, a Greyhound cut me off. Only this bus didn't look like the one I'd traveled on, or like any I'd ever seen before.

The logo on the side was familiar, a greyhound dog with its long legs stretched out front and back, racing to an invisible finish line, but everything else was different. The windows were small and squat, the roofline rounded. It was definitely vintage, maybe from the 1950s. Or earlier? I'd never seen anything like it except in movies. What was it doing here? Maybe some car enthusiast had taken on a grand scale restoration project?

After a few seconds, the bus rumbled and pulled into the street at a snail's pace. I followed behind, wishing the driver would turn or the fog would clear so I could get around him. Passing the spot where the bus had stopped, I saw a woman walking down the sidewalk.

She was vintage too, or looked it.

She wore a knee-length pleated skirt of pale blue and a matching jacket, short-waisted with pads in the shoulders, and a blue felt hat perched at a precarious angle at the back of her head. Her shoulder-length hair was strawberry blond and wavy, swept up and away from each side of her face, stray locks tucked under the hat. She wore silk stockings with seams bisecting her ankles and calves, and navy, peep-toed platform shoes. She had a leather portfolio tucked under her arm, and carried an old-fashioned suitcase, wheat-colored with brown leather trim.

We were traveling in the same direction so I couldn't see her face, but the way she marched down the sidewalk, stacked heels smacking against the pavement at a drumbeat pace, it made me think she was trying to keep her anger in check. I turned my head as I passed, catching a glimpse of her face. My instincts had been right. The young woman was mad as hell. And very, *very* determined.

A short honk from behind jolted me back to reality. Glancing into the rearview mirror, I saw I was being tailed by a green Mazda. I shrugged an apology, then turned my eyes toward the road again, surprised to see that the fog *and* the bus had disappeared. So strange. The road was completely clear. So were the streets to the left and right. I'd been driving very slowly, distracted by the woman with the suitcase, so it was possible that the bus had turned when I wasn't looking, then made another quick turn at the next corner, driving out of sight.

Of course, that's what happened, I told myself. It must have. Big silver buses don't just pop out of the atmosphere like soap bubbles on a summer day. I set my hands on the wheel and picked up speed, embracing the logic of this explanation, and glanced in the rearview mirror again.

The Mazda was still there. But the sidewalk was empty.

THE CLERK AT the store, a woman with snowy hair, ebony skin, and bright red nails that tapped in price codes at lightning speed, didn't know any more about it than I did.

"No bus stop in this part of town. Used to be that they'd drop passengers off a couple of blocks from here. But that was a long, long time ago. Maybe fifty years? I don't know where they pick up now." She called over her shoulder to a cashier at the next register. "Ray? Do you know where the Greyhound bus terminal is? This lady is asking."

Ray, who looked even older than his colleague, the white wisps of his combed-over hair unable to hide the pink skin of his bald spot, shook his head.

"No bus terminal in Asheville. They pick up and drop off at a gas station not too far from the golf course." I knew where he was talking about. It was the same place I'd said my goodbyes to George and Adele. Ray frowned in my direction, looking concerned. "Did you miss your bus?"

"No. I was just wondering," I said, handing my money to the woman. "Let me ask you, are they filming any movies around here right now?"

"What? You mean here in Asheville?" The old man's eyebrows popped. "No. But if they ever do, Shawna and I ought to go audition. It'd be a shame," he said, smoothing a hand across his comb-over and grinning, "letting these good looks go to waste. Isn't that right, Shawna?"

Shawna hooted and handed me my change, long red nails clicking on the coins as she counted it out. "Too true! Honey, I've been waiting my whole life to be discovered."

CHAPTER FOUR

I hobbled through the door of the lodge, limping like a three-legged dog and hauling my suitcases. George looked up and shouted, "Baby Sister!" then tossed aside his book, leaped up from the front desk, and bounded across the lobby in his size thirteen boots.

If George died and came back as an animal, he'd definitely be a golden retriever. At eighty-seven, my grandfather was still a big, gamboling bundle of puppyish enthusiasm, always up for an adventure. Just jingle the car keys and George is ready to roll. And whether I've been gone for five minutes or five months, he acts like I've made his year simply by showing up.

"Lookit you! Lookit you!" he hooted and threw out his arms, ready to scoop me up.

"Careful!" I laughed. "You'll hurt your back!"

"Pshaw! You're no bigger than a minute. And I'm still strong as an ox."

It was true. George's big arms felt as strong and sure as they had on the first day I met him, when he strode through the door of the foster home and carried me away to a new life. He looked the same too, dressed in his standard uniform, a plaid shirt, suspenders, dark blue Levi's, and a hat. George had a collection of hats that he wore year-round—fedoras, porkpies, homburgs, ball caps, bucket hats, and even straw boaters. Today he sported a black beret, worn at a jaunty angle atop his thick mass of white hair. There wasn't a man in a fifty-mile radius who could have pulled it off, but somehow George did.

"That's one of the things that made me fall in love with him," Adele told me once. "Not the hats; the fact that he was comfortable in his own skin. He wasn't trying to impress anybody," she said, then laughed softly. "Well . . . except me."

George set me back onto my feet. "You look about good enough to eat," he said, then frowned when he noticed my broken heel and the dusty knees of my black pants. "But what happened here?"

"Nothing. Picked a fight with the spruce and lost. I'm fine."

George shook his head. "Yeah. I really need to do something about that."

Fifty years before, Adele had planted a spruce in front of the newly constructed lodge, failing to realize that the tree would grow to be sixty feet tall and that the eruption of roots would create a tripping hazard. George had been saying he should "do something" about it for as long as I'd known him. But since cutting out some of the roots would risk killing the spruce, I knew he never would.

"That's what I get for wearing city shoes to the lake. But the real problem is my car. It gave up the ghost a quarter mile up the road. Something with the clutch, I think."

"Why didn't you call me? I'd have driven down in the truck and picked up your bags." I'd actually tried to phone when the Toaster broke down and couldn't get any cell reception, but before I could explain, George slung an arm around my shoulders. "So happy you're home."

I was too, now that I was here. When your world turns upside down, there's comfort in the idea that some things never change.

The Last Lake Lodge sits on sixteen acres that slope toward the water, so every cabin has a view. The land was raw when George and Adele bought it, just after World War II. George cleared the trees himself and used the logs to build four small cabins near the water, renting the extra three to fishermen. Though remote, the setting was gorgeous, the lake was full of fish, and the prices were right—eighteen dollars a week in 1944. A boxed lunch cost fifty cents but iced tea with homemade cake or cookies was complimentary, served on the porch every afternoon.

When the fishermen started bringing their families, George rented a bulldozer to create terraces in the hillside where he could build more cabins. By the late 1950s, there was a marina, a snack shack, a beach area made with trucked-in sand that sported a volleyball net, picnic tables, and an old school bell hanging from a wooden support that was supposed to be rung *only* in emergencies, but which eleven-year-old boys couldn't resist, as well as twenty-five rustic log cabin accommodations connected by meandering pathways.

There'd never really been a plan; George just kept building as need arose and Adele kept planting flowers as inclination struck. All the roofs had green shingles. If you climbed into the hills and looked down, it looked like somebody had tossed a handful of green plastic Monopoly houses into the air and let them land where they would. The only two structures that involved an architect were the café and the lodge.

Built to replace the old snack shack in 1973, the café was essentially a larger version of the cabins, with higher ceilings and a small flagstone patio, plus more and bigger windows that looked out onto the lake. With a view like that, what else did you need?

The lodge was larger and grander, with a roomy second-story owner's apartment where Robyn and I had grown up in turn, and where George still lived. There was a storage room too, where Adele had done her sewing. It was cavernous and high-ceilinged, but a little gloomy because there weren't any windows. As her eyesight got worse, Adele kept adding floor lamps.

The first floor was home to two simple but functional back offices, a game room with foosball, pinball machines, a pool table, and a canteen that was tucked into a corner behind reception. There guests could pick up candy, postcards, playing cards, marshmallows, worms, or fishing tackle, and bring them to the front desk where George rang up purchases and rented boats, serving as clerk, concierge, and raconteur.

But the lobby was the centerpiece of it all, with a beamed log ceiling that soared to a peak thirty feet above the floor, an enormous river rock fireplace, and walls of shelves holding hundreds of books and an array of board games for guests to borrow. The furnishings were comfortable, functional, and timeless. Two mission-style armchairs where Adele and I used to read during the winter flanked the fireplace, just as they always had.

A door leading to the laundry opened. Robyn entered, carrying a stack of towels.

"Look what the cat dragged in!" George hooted. "Esme's home!"

Robyn was only sixteen when I was born, and people had

sometimes mistaken us for sisters. They wouldn't now. She was fifty and looked it. She slid her glasses down her nose, staring at my feet.

"What'd you do, trip over the spruce?" Before I could say anything, she clucked her tongue. "You've ruined those fancy shoes. How much did you pay for them?" Spotting my luggage, she shook her head. "Looks like you brought your whole closet."

"Everything but my ballgowns and burglar tools," I quipped, attempting levity.

"Good," George said, and squeezed my shoulders. "Means you can stay a long time. Maybe we can work in a little fishing while you're here."

"That'd be great."

I hadn't been fishing for four years, not since Alex and I went to Maine and he ended up getting a hook stuck in his cheek. But when I was a kid, George and I used to fish all the time.

"Or maybe, you could do some actual *work* while you're here," Robyn said.

Nope. Nothing had changed. Robyn and I had been breathing the same air for ten seconds and already I felt like smacking her. But I restrained myself.

"Esme's here to rest," George said, frowning at Robyn. "She doesn't have to—"

"It's okay. I don't mind helping. I'm no good at resting. What do you want me to do?"

"We'll talk later, after you've settled in." She shifted the load of towels in her arms. "Well . . . I'd better drop these off. Welcome home, Esme."

Robyn headed out the back door. George reached for one of my suitcases. When I protested, he flapped his hand at me.

"I'm not so old that I can't help my granddaughter with her

luggage. Especially the kind that rolls." He smiled, chuckling at his own joke. "I thought we'd put you in number nine, near the water but off by itself. Unless you'd rather take the extra room in your mother's cabin?"

"Hmm . . . You know, I think it'd be better if I'm on my own. I stay up late reading."

George wasn't fooled by my excuse.

"I know Robyn gets under your skin," he said. "But can't you think about giving her a second chance? For both your sakes? People can change. And I won't last forever, you know. Someday it'll be just you and your mom."

People *can* change. But Robyn was always going to be Robyn.

"Just try to get along with her," George said, as if countering my unspoken thoughts. "I'd have put you up in your old room but I snore like a bandsaw. You'd hear it right through the walls. Adele's always complaining about it. Bought about ten different kinds of earplugs, trying to find some that worked but . . ."

He stopped mid-sentence. His grin faded.

"I mean, she *used* to complain about it."

George looked away. The fact that he'd briefly forgotten that Adele had died gave me a moment's pause. But then I remembered that the same thing had happened to me only a couple of weeks before. While walking through the Garment District, I'd spotted a bolt of this gorgeous nubbly orange fabric that I thought Adele would have loved. It wasn't until I walked through the shop door that I remembered she was dead.

I squeezed his forearm. "It's still hard to believe she's gone, isn't it?"

"Always thought I'd go first. But here I still am," he said hoarsely. "Sometimes I wish—"

"Yep, here you still are," I said, interrupting a sentence I didn't want to hear. "I'm glad."

George took a ragged breath and forced a smile. I held the door open and he wheeled my bags over the threshold. Though the moon was starting to rise, it was strangely dark outside. Hardly any lights were on in the cabins. Where were all the guests?

"Are you hungry?" George asked as we picked our way down the path. "I'll run to the café after we get you settled and order a sandwich. We've got a new chef, Dawson McCormick. Goes by the name of Dawes. Kind of an odd duck. I found him alongside the road."

"Excuse me?" I choked out a laugh, certain this was another one of his jokes.

"No, really," George said. "I was driving into town, saw a cargo van broke down next to the road, and I pulled over to see if I could help. The engine was shot but I stuck around to keep Dawes company until the tow truck showed up and he made me breakfast.

"You've never seen anything like the inside of this van," he continued. "Has a big bed on a platform in the back, with a real mattress, and flip-down benches and a table in front to make a dinette. There's a full kitchen too—sink, stove, slide-out pantry—the works. Even had a pullout drawer with a commode under the bed. Wouldn't mind having one of those myself. After I turned eighty, I started having to get up to pee about ten times a night. Prostate."

I love George but this was definitely too much information. And way off topic.

"Wait. You found this guy camping in his van and offered him a job as a cook?"

"He was *living* in his van," George said pointedly, as if that made it better. "And he's a chef, not a cook. Dawes used to have his own restaurant but now he travels around, takes a job for a while, and then moves on. He made me the best scrambled eggs I'd ever had in my life, had all these herbs in them and some kind of fancy cheese sprinkled on top. I took one bite and offered him the job," George said, wrapping up the story as we reached my cabin. "I advanced him the money for a new engine and he promised to stay through the summer."

"George!" I gasped. "You handed over thousands of dollars to some random hobo? How much did you give him? How do you know he won't skip town in the middle of the night?"

"Because I *know*," he said, glowering. "I might be old but I've still got my wits about me. And I'm still a good judge of people. Even if I wasn't, what I do with *my* money is *my* business."

"You're right," I said. "Sorry."

"Dawes is good people. And he makes one helluva grilled cheese sandwich." George thumped my suitcases onto the porch and turned to face me. "Now do you want one or not?"

"Sure," I said. "Grilled cheese sounds great."

GEORGE WENT OFF to see about my sandwich. I wheeled my bags into the cabin, worrying about him. There were all kinds of people out there who would take advantage of elderly people. Clearly, I needed to find out more about Dawson Mc-Cormick. But as I began snapping on the lights, I realized that one ill-considered hiring decision might be the least of our problems.

If the gold Formica counters in the kitchen said 1970s, then the brick-patterned vinyl flooring positively screamed it. That might not have been so bad—after all, this was a rustic lakeside fishing lodge, not a five-star hotel—had the rest of the decor looked a little less shabby. The scratched dining table had matching pub-style chairs with wobbly legs that made me think about velvet-backed paintings of poker-playing dogs. And while "distressed" furnishings can give off a relaxed vibe, the coffee table with the rubbed finish had crossed the line from homey to homely years before. The braided rag rug had faded from charming and cheerful to washed-out, worn, and just plain sad.

But saddest of all were the throw pillows.

After George found a deal on red sofas, Adele decided to make pillows for all twenty-five of them. My grandmother suffered from a condition called essential tremor, which caused her hands to tremble almost constantly. The only times the shaking stopped completely was when she was holding George's hand or sewing. Though she didn't truly need assistance, she asked if I'd like to help with the stitching. I was fourteen years old and thrilled.

We spent an entire weekend making those pillows. I remember how beautiful they looked, and how proud I felt when we finished the last one.

"Aren't they gorgeous!" Adele exclaimed, plumping a pillow into the corner of a sofa. "That delicious red! Tastes like cinnamon and feels like anticipation, the kind you get waiting to open your presents on Christmas morning. Gorgeous! We did good, didn't we, Esme?"

I'd always struggled to understand Adele's synesthetic links, but that day I felt connected to her in a way I never had. I felt like an equal in her eyes, an adult. For as long as I could remember, that's all I'd wanted to be. Her enthusiasm shed new light on what adulthood entailed, the sublime satisfaction that comes from making your unique contribution, playing your part in the hive of humanity. To this day, whenever I hold the first copy of a book I helped edit, the world still feels like Christmas morning.

The pillows were threadbare now, the once vermillion poppies a sickly salmon, as faded as the rest of the decor. Were all the cabins this shabby? If so, maybe that helped explain the vacancies? I had all kinds of questions, but my immediate concern was getting warm. I cranked up the thermostat, hoping the heater would kick in. When it didn't, I decided to start a fire.

George had a healthy respect for fire, and wouldn't let anyone else light the big logs in the lobby, including me. Consequently, I'd never really learned how to start one. But there was a pressed wood log in the grate. After kneeling down by the hearth and reading the instructions, I lit a match and held it to the end of a wrapper. The waxy, yellow paper started to smoke, then curl away from the log, glowing red before expanding into a flame.

Instant fire! Exactly as advertised!

I rocked onto my haunches, enjoying my small accomplishment and the warmth of the dancing flames. If only I had some food, life would be perfect. Forty minutes had passed since George went to see about my sandwich. Supposing he'd forgotten about it, I decided to take a shower. The water pressure was great and I spent a good ten minutes luxuriating. When I shut off the faucet, the sound of rushing water was replaced by a high-pitched, ear-piercing beeping. I hopped out of the shower, wrapped myself in a towel, opened the bathroom door, and immediately started coughing. The fire was still crackling, but the smoke that had billowed up the chimney after I'd lit the log was now billowing back into the room.

With dripping hair and bare feet, I ran to the hearth, grabbed a poker, and stabbed at the log, which only made the flames flare higher. Someone began pounding on the cabin door. I ran to unlock it, clutching the towel around my body and hacking like a two-pack-a-day smoker. A man too agile to be George pushed past me. After dropping a bag onto the counter, he rushed into the living room, and knelt down in front of the hearth.

"Careful!" I shouted, trying to make myself heard over the whining smoke alarm.

The man pulled off the plaid shirt he wore over a blue Henley and wrapped it around his hand. After a moment of hesitation, he shoved his arm into the fireplace, inches above the flames, and made a jerking motion. The smoke immediately started to billow up the chimney.

"Open the door!" he ordered. "Fan it back and forth to clear the smoke."

While I did that, my rescuer quickly opened all the windows, then stood with his back to me and flapped a tea towel through the air. Between the open windows, my wet hair, and the fact that I wasn't wearing anything but a towel, I was so cold my teeth were chattering. Finally, thankfully, the smoke cleared and the alarm stopped.

"That's enough," he said, then turned around and looked at me.

He was taller than me—almost everyone is—probably six three, and looked to be in his middle thirties. His face was tanned, his complexion almost swarthy, and his eyes were dark brown set beneath thick, brownish black eyebrows. The hair on his head was lighter brown, coarse with a bit of curl. His nose was straight and his jaw was sharp if not quite chiseled.

My type is blond and blue-eyed and clean shaven, tall but not too tall (five ten is ideal for a woman of my stature, tall enough so I feel feminine by comparison, short enough so that kissing doesn't require a stepstool), with an athletic build and a hint of muscle, shoulders broad but not too broad, a kind of guy who looks born to wear a tux. Though undeniably handsome, this guy looked like he was born to wear . . . well, pretty much what he had on.

His hands were grimy too, though that might have been the soot. He had a small scar on the left side of his face, just above his jaw, and one of those stubbly beards that looked like he either forgot to shave or couldn't be bothered.

In short, absolutely not my type.

Then he looked at me, his eyes sweeping over my frame, from dripping hair to bare feet, and my insides turned into fondue. My teeth stopped chattering. My skin started to tingle. Ten seconds before, I'd been freezing. Now there was steam coming through the towel.

The logical, evolved part of my brain, which seemed to be operating in the background, like software that can record events but not incite them, knew this was entirely *il*logical, an involuntary response to biological impulses, the fact that I was healthy, thirty-three, had been unknowingly married to a gay man for years and, therefore, hadn't had sex in basically forever.

My unevolved lizard brain didn't care.

I could breathe just barely and speak not at all. This turned out to be a good thing. Otherwise, I'd have probably told him I wanted to get married and have lots of sex and babies.

"We need to close the windows," he said and stomped toward the kitchen.

"Yes. Right," I said, moving toward a window. "Thank you

so much. I don't know what I'd have done if you hadn't come along. Well, actually . . . Yes, I do. I was going to throw a pitcher of water on the logs. That would have been a mess, wouldn't it? Anyway, thanks."

"I *thought* the cabin was on fire."

The tone of his voice made it sound as if he thought I'd done it on purpose.

"Yeah. For a minute I did too." I laughed nervously. "You must be Dawes. I'm Esme."

"George told me. He said you're a book editor?" I nodded. "So I assume that means you can read?" he asked, glaring and pointing. "Because there's a sign over the mantle, saying you need to open the flue *before* you light the log. Did you notice it?"

In fact, I hadn't. And if I had, it wouldn't have made any difference. What was a flue?

"The flue," he said impatiently, as if repeating a word was the same as defining it. When I didn't respond he grabbed me by the arm and dragged me over to the fireplace, where the fake log was still smoldering. He squatted down in front of the hearth.

"There's a metal bar just inside the chimney. You see it?" I nodded, taking his word for it. "When you pull it, the flue opens and the smoke goes up the chimney. When you push it, the flue closes so cold air can't get inside the cabin. Got it?"

"Got it," I replied without really looking. Since I'd made up my mind to never again attempt lighting a fire, I didn't need to know about flue placement and operation.

"Your dinner is in the bag," Dawes growled, then got to his feet and left, shutting the door in a way that wasn't quite a slam but forceful enough to make a point.

Sheesh! It was just a little smoke. Did he have to be such a jerk about it? But the fact that he was such a jerk was probably a good thing, because falling in lust was the last thing I needed right now. And clearly, it *was* lust, nothing but. I'd get over it.

The cabin still smelled like smoke so I pulled on jeans and a sweatshirt, and took my food out onto the porch. The sandwich had perfect golden grill marks and beautifully crisp edges, a grilled cheese so gorgeous it could have posed in a magazine. The center held gooey cheese, decadent béchamel sauce, paper-thin slices of salty ham, and tasted divine. This was no regular grilled cheese!

I closed my eyes while chewing, practically swooning with happiness. Dawes McCormick was rude and so *not* my type. But anybody who knew how to make a croque monsieur this good probably wasn't a scam artist. Maybe Dawes would grow on me?

Then I remembered how he'd galumphed through the door without saying good night and decided, no, probably not.

CHAPTER FIVE

I have my faults, but an inability to take direction isn't one of them.

Proof that Carl's hints about my less than conventional taste in clothing on the day he hired me had not gone unheeded was on full display when I unpacked the next morning. My closet and drawers contained six blazers, eight pairs of slacks, four pencil skirts, two dozen blouses and tops, and five cocktail dresses—all black. Because as everyone knows, black is the color of choice for New York professionals, at least until something darker comes along.

However, besides three pairs of jeans (one of which was also black), a couple of plain white T-shirts, a gray hoodie, and two pairs of Lululemon leggings in tangerine and plum (New Yorker or not, I still love color), nothing I'd brought was suitable for life at the lake. If my exile lasted more than a week or two, I'd probably have to use some of my precious severance to buy casual clothes. But the immediate problem was shoes. As evidenced by my encounter with the spruce, heels just weren't going to cut it. I'd have to go to Asheville to buy new ones but since driving to town required a car, the first order of business was to deal with the Toaster.

Hoping to avoid spending hundreds on a tow truck, I decided to hike back to the car and attempt to start it one more time. Couldn't hurt to try, right? But when I reached the lodge, I found the Toaster was parked out front, jacked up on one side with the hood raised and two pairs of denim-clad legs sticking out from under the vehicle.

"Hello?"

I bent down, trying to get a look at whoever was down there. George shimmied out from under the car, wriggling on his back like a tipped-over turtle before grabbing the gnarled old shillelagh he'd left on the ground, which he used more as a hiking stick than a cane, and got to his feet.

"Good morning, Baby Sister! Howdja sleep?"

"Fine. How did my car get here?"

"We hooked a chain to my truck and towed it."

"Who is we?"

"Me and Dawes," George said, thumping his shillelagh on the dirt and looking pleased with himself. A muffled voice called out from under the car. "Think that's got it, George. Let's start her up again." Dawes shimmied out from under the car as well, then stood up and slapped the seat of his jeans with greasy hands, trying to banish the dust.

"How were you able to start it without a key?" I asked, holding up my keyring.

"Dawes hotwired it," George replied. "He's real handy."

The guy my grandfather picked up on the side of the road not only knew how to make a terrific cheese sandwich, he also possessed basic car theft skills?

Great. Just great.

George got behind the wheel and fiddled with some wires. When the Toaster roared to life, I blinked my amazement at Dawes, who smiled and shrugged modestly.

"It wasn't anything serious. Your spark plugs were fouled, that's all. We decided to take another look underneath, just to make sure. But everything's fine, you're good to go."

"She's humming like a top now," George said, then climbed out of the car and slapped Dawes a high five. "Good job."

They looked as if they'd dressed out of the same closet that morning—dark denim straight-leg jeans, blue and green plaid shirts, and scuffed brown lace-up boots. Apart from the fact that George was fifty years older, and sporting suspenders and a tweed driving cap, they could have been twins. It was really kind of adorable.

"Dawes, meet my granddaughter, Esme." George swept his arm toward me with the grandiosity of a game show spokesmodel gesturing toward the Grand Prize.

"We met last night," Dawes said. George gave him a quizzical look. "You came by the café while I was cleaning up and asked me to bring her a grilled cheese sandwich, remember?"

"Oh, sure. That's right. Sure," George said. "Cheese sandwich, I remember."

"And it was *amazing*," I said, smiling at Dawes, grateful that he'd seen fit to leave out the part where I nearly burned down the cabin. "Best croque monsieur I've ever had, even better than the ones at Petit Chou, this great little French bistro I used to go to in Brooklyn."

Dawes gave a slow, exaggerated nod. "Petit Chou, huh? Praise indeed."

My cheeks felt warm. *Croque monsieur? Petit Chou?* I sounded like one of those snobs who acts like the greatest compliment you can offer to anything is to say it was as good as you'd get in New York. Why hadn't I just said, "It was the best grilled cheese I've ever had," and left it there? Who was I trying to impress? I'd even put on a French accent, for heaven's sake!

"Well, it was terrific. Thanks. And thanks for fixing my car and . . . you know, everything."

"My pleasure. Always ready to help a damsel in distress."

Now my cheeks were flaming. Not because of the "damsel in distress" line, which was corny and possibly even a little insulting, but because I saw George's gaze darting back and forth between me and Dawes. His interest in our exchange was intense, and way too obvious.

"Where did you get the parts?" I asked, changing the subject. "I'm sure you didn't just happen to have a spare set of spark plugs lying around." I laughed.

"Actually, I did. When you live in a van, you carry a lot of spare parts with you."

"Oh. Right."

My nodding was less to convey agreement than to remind myself what my lizard brain had chosen to ignore, that in addition to not being my type, Dawes lived in a *van*. Of all the types who weren't my type, the most unsuitable was the type who couldn't settle down.

"Well, I'd better get to work," Dawes said, glancing toward George. "Soup of the day is lemon chicken with orzo."

"Sounds good. Save my spot at the bar. Hey, Dawes, you ever been fly-fishing?" Dawes shook his head. "Oh, you'd love it. And Esme here is a terrific fly fisherman . . . uh, fisherwoman. We're planning to catch some trout while she's in town. You should come along."

"Oh. Well . . . sure." Dawes shrugged. "If there's a slow day at the café."

"Good," George said, flashing a grin at Dawes and then at me. "It's a date."

When Dawes was out of earshot, I turned toward George and glared.

"What. Was. That."

"What was what?" he said, blinking innocently.

"That!" I hissed, flinging a pointed finger toward the corner Dawes had just disappeared around. "George, the ink is barely dry on my divorce. The last thing I need right now is to get myself tangled up in"—I windmilled my hands around my head, searching for the right words—"in whatever it is you're trying to get me tangled up in!"

"Don't know what you're getting so upset about," George said. "What's so terrible about me wanting to see you happy?"

"Happy." I choked out a laugh. "You think trying to fix me up with some guy you picked up on the side of the road—and doing so in a humiliatingly obvious way, I might add—is going to make me happy? The man lives in a *van*, George. He's one step up from being a hobo!"

"He's not living in a van *now*," George countered. "I set him up in number twenty-two, that studio cabin right near the café. And what's wrong with spending a couple of years driving around and seeing the country, anyway? He's an adventurer, that's all."

I rolled my eyes. "Apart from the fact that he knows how to make cheese sandwiches and hotwire a car—a mark which is *not* in his favor—you don't know a thing about him!"

"Well, I like him," George groused, tugging the brim of his

hat. "He's a good man. You'd never come home from work one day and find out Dawes left you for his 'personal trainer,'" George said, making air quotes with his fingers, "that I *do* know."

I put my hands on my hips. "Wow. Did you really just go there? That was mean."

"Sorry," he mumbled, breaking my gaze. "I didn't mean that the way it came out. But this whole thing has got me upset. I just want to see you happy, honey."

His cockeyed caterpillar eyebrows were as white as snow and the wrinkles at the corners of his eyes looked like pleats in an unfurled fan. But with his head hanging and his shoulders stooped in chagrin, George looked about seven years old.

"So do I," I said, softening. "But if there's one thing that I've learned since Alex left, it's that there are things you can't push, no matter how much you want them. If I ever do fall for somebody again—and it's a big if—it'll be somebody with no secrets, somebody I know inside and out and who knows me the same way, and loves me in spite of it. Or even because of it."

George nodded. "That's the way it should be. Adele loved me in spite of me."

I smiled. "Remember the time you served yourself some chicken soup from a pot on the stove, only it turned out to be saffron fabric dye? Your tongue was yellow for a week."

George laughed, placing one hand on the crown of his cap and shaking his head. "I remember. She was always getting up to something. And the fabric. Oh, the fabric! There was one stretch of about four years, before she took over the storage room, when I couldn't eat at our table because it was always covered with fabric, and scissors, and thread, and sewing machines, and I don't know what all.

"But I'll tell you something true," he said, his smile fading, "I'd give everything I have not to be able to eat at my own kitchen table again. It's clean as a whistle these days but there's just too much room. That's why I started having my lunch down at the café. Dawes saves me a stool and a bowl of soup. If it's not busy, he comes over and talks to me while I eat."

"That's nice," I said, thinking more gently of Dawes. "What do you talk about?"

"Nothing earth-shattering." George sniffed. "Baseball, the weather. Sometimes he'll tell me how he made the soup. Nothing important, just shooting the breeze. I like him."

"Sounds like you and Dawes have yourselves a little bromance going," I teased.

"What's a bromance?" George asked, drawing the cockeyed caterpillars together.

"Just a word," I said, thinking I'd leave it there but then realizing that George was going to insist on an answer. "It means you two are friends."

"Yeah," George said after a moment's thought. "I guess we are."

"Can't have too many, right?"

"Nope. Especially at my age."

George headed back to the lodge and I got into the Toaster. Pulling out of the parking lot, I glanced into the rearview mirror and saw my grandfather slowly mount the steps, leaning on his shillelagh as he ascended, then stand and stare at the door like a conflicted housecat, unable to decide if he wanted to be inside, or outside, or someplace else entirely.

AFTER FINISHING MY errands and returning to the lake, I went into the lobby and found Vera, a housekeeper who'd worked at the lodge for as long as I could remember, manning the front desk. She told me she was filling in because Robyn had taken George to Asheville for some doctors' appointments.

"Oh. Did she say when they'd be back?"

Vera shook her head. "But I think it might be late. She usually tries to book George's medical appointments back to back. Don't worry, I'm sure it's just routine," she said, responding to my frown. "George is a force of nature. He'll probably bury us all, but at his age, you want to stay on top of things. George grumbles about it, of course." Vera grinned. "He says he doesn't need to be fussed over and gripes about damned doctors buying boats and beach houses on his dime. Robyn just ignores him."

I smiled. That sounded like George all right. And I was glad to know that Robyn was making sure he took care of himself.

"Want to leave a message?" Vera asked. "I can ask him to call when they get back."

"It's okay, I'll check in with him tomorrow. Right now, I'm going for a walk to break in my new shoes. Don't work too hard," I said, tossing her a wave and preparing to make my exit.

"Not much chance of that," Vera replied, coughing out a mirthless laugh. "We don't have anybody checking in this afternoon. I'm only here to answer phones and handle walk-ins."

"Do we get many of those these days?"

"Nope. Not many reservations either." Vera sighed. "I'll be honest, Esme, it's starting to worry me. You know how I started working at the lodge when I was sixteen, lifeguarding at the waterfront, then taking the housekeeping job, thinking it'd just be temporary. George and Adele were so good to me that I just stayed on, never regretted it either. I raised two kids working this job, put one through beauty school and helped

the other pay for college, plus look where I get to be every day."
She swept her hand toward the big picture window facing the
lake, then tsked her tongue, a shadow of worry clouding her
features. "After all these years, it's hard to imagine having to
start over someplace else, but if the lodge closes down—"

"What?" I said, giving my head a single hard shake. "Who
said anything about closing the lodge? Did George tell you
that? Did Robyn?"

"No," Vera replied, shrugging. "But we're getting fewer
guests every year and with all the deferred maintenance around
here, things are going downhill fast. So I just figured that—"

I slashed my hand through the air. "Nobody is closing *anything*," I declared.

"No?" Vera blew out a breath and clapped her hand to her
chest. "I can't tell you how happy I am to hear you say that,
Esme, or how glad I am that you're home. I can't afford to re-
tire for another five years. But I guess there's nothing to worry
about, now that you're here."

The relief on her face was so palpable that I didn't have the
heart to tell her that my residence was temporary and I'd be
heading back to New York the nanosecond I found another job
in publishing. Instead, I just said, "I'm glad to be back," and
waved goodbye.

It had been too dark to see the signs when I arrived and I'd
been too preoccupied with worries about the car to pay much
attention to my surroundings that morning, but as I walked
the serpentine path from the lodge to the lakefront, I started
to understand what Vera was talking about. Conditions at the
lodge had taken a sharp turn for the worse since my last visit.

The flower beds, once Adele's pride and joy, were weedy,
overgrown, and untended. The bluestone pavers along the

pathways were cracked in spots with clumps of crabgrass grow-ing through the gaps. There were dandelions sprouting in the lawn and weeds outside the cabins too. After inspecting the cabins one by one, I found four listing porches, several torn screen doors, and a downspout that was leaning so far from the gutter that a good wind would have knocked it over. I paused to prop it back up, not worried about disturbing the occupants because this cabin, like nearly all the others, was vacant.

No wonder business was slipping. It was too soon to say that the lodge was a total dump, but it was certainly heading that way.

Passing by the café, I saw that the mortar between the patio pavers had worn away and that a section of the stones had set-tled, creating a catch basin for standing rainwater, which, when the weather got warmer, would be an ideal breeding ground for mosquitos. And though the café was built from logs that never had to be painted or stained, the painted trim around the windows and doors was peeling. The dock was in bad shape too, with waterlogged boards that signaled rot and a few planks that were missing entirely. The marina restrooms were less than sparkling and had an invasive, fast-growing kudzu vine crawl-ing up the back wall. I tore it down as best I could, though I knew it would grow right back—kudzu can grow a foot a day.

Coming to the edge of the property, I found the old hiking trail that led to the top of the hills and then circled the lake. I followed it all the way around, questions about the dilapidation of the lodge and worries about George dogging my footsteps.

I couldn't get my head around it. George had always been so meticulous about maintenance, adhering to a detailed, year-round schedule of updates and repairs. What had happened?

And why hadn't Robyn stepped in and done something about it? If she wasn't worried about Vera and the handful of people who worked at the lodge, you'd think she'd at least be concerned about George and Adele's legacy. Did she honestly not care? Was she really that selfish?

The longer I walked, the more I thought about Robyn, the angrier I felt, especially after hiking to the top of a hill that overlooked a verdant valley dotted with houses and barns.

Though the farms looked picturesque and tidy from a distance, I knew from my growing up here that many were in various stages of disrepair. One was close enough that I could actually see the neglect, a slanted porch built on sinking cinderblocks, the patina of rust on a metal roof, an abandoned truck with a missing wheel that was half covered by a blanket of kudzu. Unless someone intervened, the vines would swallow it completely by summer's end. The truck would become another of the involuntary topiaries you sometimes see along southern roadsides, cars, trucks, or even whole houses entombed by invasive vines, absorbed into nature, as if they'd never existed at all.

The hike back to the lodge took two hours. The image of the farm, the truck, and the vines stayed with me the whole way. How was it possible for things, for people, to simply disappear? How was it possible that I was here, at the lake, and Adele was . . . just gone?

The surety of death is probably one of the few absolute truths in life, yet we know almost nothing about it. People have their opinions, but nobody actually *knows* where people go when they're gone, because nobody comes back to tell you.

My wishful thought was to reverse the calendar to my final conversation with Adele. If I could live that day again, I'd have hung up the phone and flown to Asheville that same night and spent the next five days at her side, fulfilling her last request. In her entire life, my grandmother had never asked me for anything, except that one time.

There's something I need your help with, something I can't do alone.

If only she'd come out and told me what it was! If only I'd made her tell me! But she didn't and I didn't. There was nothing I could do to change that now, nothing I could do for the woman who'd meant so much to me.

Was there?

I emerged from the woods a little before sunset, tired and footsore, and made a beeline for the toolshed. After fumbling through the cobwebs and shadowy interior I located a shovel and carried it to the marina.

The root of the kudzu vine went deeper than I'd realized. Digging it out brought sweat to my brow and raised blisters on my hands. But I was determined. I couldn't turn back the calendar. I couldn't alter the past. But I could beat back this incursion and, at least for today, prevent the elements from overpowering the legacy of the two people I loved most. After unearthing the crown, a tuber as thick and long as my arm, by the light of the full moon, I put the shovel aside and sank down on the grass, my arms so heavy I could barely lift them.

And when I turned my eyes to the water, I could have sworn I saw her again, a solitary figure standing with her back turned toward me, gazing at the lake, bathed in uncertain moonlight and dressed in powder blue.

CHAPTER SIX

I woke before dawn with threads of a dream, a conversation with the woman in blue, clinging to my brain like cobwebs but quickly brushed them aside, attributing the whole thing to tricks of moonlight and an overactive imagination. I had more pressing concerns at the moment. Finding employment, a cup of coffee, and the reasons for the lodge's downward slide topped the list. The second problem was solved and the third moved to the front burner when Robyn showed up at my door with two foam cups of coffee and a fat file folder.

"I thought we should talk."

No kidding.

If we'd run into each other the night before, I might have peppered her with a barrage of questions and commentary, if not outright accusations. As far as I was concerned, Robyn had a lot to answer for—though there was nothing new about that. But it was too early for arguments and over the years I had learned that the best way to tackle any problem is to ignore personalities, check your emotions at the door, and focus on facts. I took the cup she offered and waved her inside without saying a word.

Robyn set her burdens down on the coffee table and took a

seat on the faded red sofa, then pulled a pack of cigarettes and a lighter from her pocket.

"I thought you were going to quit."

"Yeah . . . well. So did I."

She lit up a cigarette, then narrowed her eyes and took a long slow drag, as if trying to steady herself before going on.

"George had some doctors' appointments yesterday."

I knew that already. Vera said they were just routine, but the look in Robyn's eyes made my stomach clench.

"Is he all right?"

"Yes," Robyn said. "For now. But he's been forgetting things. Little stuff at first, like not being able to find a particular word, or his car keys. I wasn't worried initially. After all, he's eighty-seven. But it got a lot worse after Mom died. When John and Janis Wilson checked in last month, he couldn't remember their names. They've been coming here for the last forty years."

I remembered the Wilsons. They'd come to the lodge on their honeymoon and returned every year to celebrate their anniversary, becoming good friends with Adele and George. Mrs. Wilson did watercolors and had given my grandparents a painting of the lake that still hung on the wall near the front desk. Mr. Wilson played pool and almost always lost to George.

"George tried to laugh it off as a 'senior moment.' But when I looked in his eyes, I saw this flicker of panic. And then I knew." Robyn fell briefly silent, looking down at her hands and rolling her cigarette between her fingers. "He didn't remember them at all."

"That doesn't necessarily mean anything," I said, wanting it to be true. "Like you said, he's eighty-seven."

"It's more than that. He's having trouble adding up the bills too, the accounts are a mess." She lifted her head and gave me a meaningful look. "Last week, he couldn't remember how to tie the tippet onto his leader."

"You're kidding."

George used to joke that the only reason he'd bought the lodge was to support his fishing habit. If he couldn't remember how to tie the surgeon's knot so he could add a new piece of tippet, the small gauge line used in fly-fishing, something was definitely wrong. I pressed my lips together, swallowing the catch in my throat.

"What did the doctor think? Is it . . . is it dementia?"

"*Don't* say that!" she snapped. "I told the doctor and I'm telling you: we are *not* using that word. I won't allow it!"

The sudden, sharp vehemence of her response took me by surprise. Startled, I grabbed a faded poppy pillow from the corner of the couch and pressed it protectively to my chest. Robyn sprang up from her seat, started pacing and puffing, cigarette smoke coming from the circle of her lips in short, frantic bursts, like distress messages from a signal fire.

"You start applying those kinds of labels to somebody and pretty soon it's all they are! So don't you *ever* say that word and George's name in the same sentence."

She spun around and stabbed a finger in my direction.

"Not ever! Understand?"

"Yes, okay. Sorry," I mumbled, feeling cowed and more than slightly off balance.

I'd spent most of my childhood watching my mother teeter on the edge of self-imposed disaster, bracing for her inevitable plunge from the precipice, the slip that would hurl both of us into the void, which, of course, it eventually did. So, when it came to Robyn and me, the sensation of being off balance wasn't all that unusual. But this . . .

I wasn't prepared for this.

Age and death come to claim us all in time, I knew that. But I had always supposed George's end would come all at once and with power, that he would crash to the ground with a boom that was heard for miles, like one of the towering pines he'd felled to build a cabin for his bride, leaving a colossal void where once he'd stood.

From the first day he'd come into my life, that's how I'd always thought of him, as a mighty, deep-rooted tree—a shade against the sun, a break against the wind, a shelter in the storm. So it was disorienting to imagine him diminished in any way, impossible to accept that he could ever be anything less than he'd always been. I mean, this wasn't just some old man we were talking about—this was George!

George of the size thirteen boots. George who loved hats, and Tennessee whiskey, and Flor De America cigars. George who could recite poetry by Emily Dickinson and discuss the novels of John Steinbeck, Flannery O'Connor, and Pat Conroy, and loved cello concertos as much as country pop. George the raconteur, who regaled guests with endless stories, including the one about the time Willie Nelson's tour bus broke down nearby, and how Willie and the band checked into the resort and sat around the firepit long past midnight, playing guitar and passing around a bottle of George Dickel Barrel Select that their obliging host brought to the bonfire.

How could a man like George, so full of life that he sometimes seemed larger than life, possibly have dementia? I couldn't wrap my brain around it. But it was almost as difficult to reconcile myself to this unfamiliar version of my mother.

Robyn had always been so weak in my estimation, waffling and indecisive, an eternal adolescent, selfish, thoughtless, and shallow as a pan. And yet she'd obviously thought long and hard about the power of labels, what they mean and how they can impact the way people see other people. That was perhaps the most surprising thing of all. I'd never seen my mother as someone who stopped to think.

"Okay, but . . . what are we supposed to call it if not—" I paused, catching myself before uttering the forbidden word. "If not, you know . . . that."

"There is no *it*," Robyn said. "There's only George, a smart, strong, interesting man who forgets things sometimes and needs support to keep being the man he always was. The lodge was always a part of that, but, the way things are going . . ." She shook her head. "I don't know how much longer we can keep the place afloat."

So Vera was right to be worried. This was more than deferred maintenance resulting from George's grief or Robyn's inattention; the lodge's future was at stake.

"How bad is it?"

"Bookings are way down. They've been slipping for years but I didn't realize how much until I started digging into things after Mom died. We're at a crossroads, Esme." Robyn pressed her lips together momentarily. "It's time to think about selling."

"What?" I gasped. "You can't sell the lodge! George and Adele spent their whole lives building it up. This is George's *home*! It would just—"

Robyn let out a huff of exasperation and cut me off with a wave of her hand.

"What do you want me to do, Esme? The lodge is losing money; it has been for years. I just don't see another choice. If George ends up needing . . ." She hesitated. "More care, or even a different living situation, I don't know how else we'd find the money to pay for it." She sank down on the sofa and crushed her cigarette butt into the plastic lid of her now cold coffee, then rubbed her face with her hands. "I know you didn't want to come home but I'm glad you did. I've been chewing on this for months and still can't see another way." She lifted her head. "Esme, I need your help."

"To sell the lodge out from under George?"

She couldn't seriously think I'd be willing to play a part in that, could she? The lodge was George's home. And Robyn's too—apart from the years we'd spent drifting from one cheap, roach-infested apartment to the next and those she'd spent behind bars, she'd never had another home. Didn't that mean anything to her?

I crossed my arms over my chest. Robyn gave an exaggerated shrug.

"Fine," she said. "Then help me come up with another plan, because I've got nothing."

"In case you've forgotten, I read *books* for a living. What makes you think I can help?"

She shot me a glare and snatched a pack of Marlboros from her pocket.

"Because you went to college and I dropped out of tenth grade. Because you're smarter than me, dammit!" She yanked a cigarette from the pack. "There. I said it. Are you happy now?"

Happy? Why would I be? Where did she get the idea that I didn't think she was smart?

"Robyn, I never once said—"

"Stop," she said wearily, lighting up. "Just stop, okay? If there was anybody else I could ask, I would. But there's not."

She took a puff and looked at me.

"So? Are you going to help or not?"

CHAPTER SEVEN

*E*ven if we'd been trying to settle on something as mundane as a pizza order, any negotiation between Robyn and myself was going to be difficult. There was subtext in even the simplest exchange, past hurts, betrayals, and suspicions always lurking in the background.

However, once Robyn opened her file and started walking me though the accounts, I realized two things. First, that she cared about George as much as I did. Second, that the lodge really was in serious financial trouble. We agreed that something had to be done, but couldn't agree on how to do it and argued for more than an hour without getting anywhere.

"Okay, okay, okay," I said finally, shoving my fingers into my hair and cutting Robyn off in the middle of a point she'd made five times already. "I get what you're saying and I don't disagree. It comes down to two problems, declining occupancy and deferred maintenance."

"Exactly," Robyn said. "It's a chicken-and-egg thing. We're losing business because we need to renovate, but we can't renovate because business is down. Or is that a catch-22?"

It was both. And possibly an irreversible death spiral. But I didn't say that out loud.

"Whatever you call it, we should still renovate. Seriously," I said, spreading my arms to encompass the shabby surroundings, "do you honestly think anybody's crazy enough to buy a rundown old fishing resort that's been losing money for years? You'd have to fix the place up to sell it, so why not fix it up anyway, do some marketing, and try to make it profitable again?"

I'd proposed different versions of the same argument before, but this time Robyn actually seemed to be listening. She tipped her coffee cup all the way back, drinking down the last few drops, then wrapped both hands around the empty cup and tucked it under her chin.

"Okay, but . . . how long do you think that would take? Showing a profit, I mean?"

"If everything went right?" I picked a number out of thin air. Really, how was I supposed to know? "Two years?" I said, shrugging. "Maybe three?"

"No. That won't work. We can't wait that long."

"Hang on, what if it was only a year? Or," I said, a little desperately, knowing I had one chance to change her mind, "by the end of the summer?"

"Three months?" She paused. "That's impossible. There's no way."

Though she flapped her hand, dismissing me, there was a questioning edge in her voice that made me think at least part of her wanted to be convinced.

"What if I make you a deal?" I asked, scooting closer to Robyn. "I'll spend the summer, figuring out ways to improve our marketing and boost revenue. And I'll try to get a handle on what we'd need to do in the way of renovations, start getting some estimates and—"

"I already did that," Robyn said, tilting her chin to her folder. "You're right, nobody's going to buy the place as is. I thought we'd better fix it up a little before we put it on the market. I was hoping you'd take it from there? I just don't have the time."

"No problem," I said, bobbing my head and trying to sound agreeable. "I'll take care of everything, but on one condition: you give me the summer to turn things around. If the lodge shows a profit by Labor Day, you won't sell. Oh," I said, thinking of one more caveat, "and you won't talk to George about selling before then either, not a word. Deal?"

"I wasn't going to mention anything until I had to anyway, no point in upsetting him. But . . ." She bit the edge of her coffee cup, leaving teeth marks in the Styrofoam. "I don't know."

"What's not to know?" I asked, exasperated. "Whether you sell it or not, you've still got to fix the place up. It'll probably take most of the summer anyway. So what's the difference?"

Robyn narrowed her eyes. "Okay, but what happens if you get a job offer?"

This was a legitimate question, and one I hadn't fully considered. I wanted to get back to work, and the city, as soon as possible, but this was more important. The lodge was George's home. And even after all these years, I still thought of it as my home too, a kind of emotional anchor, the one constant in my life.

"Either I'll convince them to hold my spot or I'll say thanks but no thanks."

"So you promise you'll be here all summer? Job or no job?" When I nodded, she blinked and shifted her shoulders a little.

"Okay then. Looks like the lodge is going to get a face-lift. Now all we've got to do," she said, reaching for her folder, "is figure out how to pay for it."

THE LISTS OF needed repairs and estimates Robyn had pulled together was thorough, but not very encouraging.

"There's one bright spot," she said. "Number seventeen is booked for eight weeks."

"Two whole months?" If it was true, this *was* a bright spot, a surprising one. According to Robyn's charts, our average reservation was just four nights. "Who made the reservation?"

"A guy named Bob Johnson. He's stayed with us a couple of times in the past. I've never met him but George has. Apparently he's a writer. You ever heard of him?"

"No. Maybe he uses a pen name," I said, then I ran my finger down a column of numbers, wincing when I reached the red circled total. "Seventy-three thousand? Really?"

"Afraid so. And that only covers the most urgent repairs," Robyn said, flipping open a notebook. "We need to talk about replacing the dock and the furnace, repairing the walkways and lighting, putting new asphalt in the parking lot—"

She was right about the parking lot. With all those potholes, it looked like a moonscape and gave a very bad, but sadly accurate, first impression.

"And we've got to redecorate," she continued. "The cabins need new drapes, rugs, towels, bedding, the works. The mattresses are in terrible shape."

I rubbed a sore spot on my lower back. She was right about that too.

"What's this?" I asked, pointing to an entry for electrical upgrades. "The electricity works, doesn't it? I mean, everything's up to code?"

Robyn rocked her head from side to side. "Yes and no. George did some of the wiring himself. Might be smart to have it checked by a real electrician. But most of the budget is for new electrical outlets. According to our online reviews—which are pretty terrible by the way—not having enough outlets is one of our top complaints."

"Wow. You actually went online and read the reviews?"

Robyn set her jaw. "Yes, Esme. You think I'm too dumb to know about the internet?"

"What? No! All I meant is that it was a good idea. You ask somebody how they enjoyed their stay and they'll probably just say it was fine, even if it wasn't. Online reviews are much more honest, and specific. It was a good idea," I repeated. "Really."

She rolled her eyes. "Could we please keep the personal comments to a minimum?"

"What personal comments? All I said was—" Robyn glared. "Fine. Let's just focus on finding the money to do all this."

"We're not completely broke," she said, pulling a bank statement from the pile. "After setting aside money for summer expenses, we'll still have twenty-two thousand in reserve."

"Okay, so we prioritize. The furnace can wait. But the dock can't and the grounds are a mess. We don't need to redecorate the cabins all at once. Let's start with . . . five?"

"Five works," Robyn said. "We should get to work on number seventeen as soon as possible. If Bob Johnson bails on his reservation, we're toast."

We spent another hour crunching numbers, trying to squeeze the maximum bang out of twenty-two thousand bucks. With my severance plus the money I'd been saving for a down payment, I could have financed the rest of the repairs personally. But should I? If the lodge truly was in a death spiral, was deflating my financial cushion trying to save it a good idea?

"There is one way we *might* try to raise some cash," Robyn said, interrupting my reverie. "Probably a long shot but . . . we could try to sell Adele's quilts."

Adele's quilts?

Till the end of her life, Adele made quilts for all the cabins, replacing them on a five-year rotating schedule. I'd slept under one the night before, a log cabin design. It meant something to me because Adele made it, but I could have gone to almost any store and bought something that looked similar, churned out in some factory, for fifty bucks. The quality would have been lousy but if you didn't know anything about quilting, could you tell the difference?

"Not those," Robyn said, reading my confusion. "The weird quilts. With the colors."

Now I understood. In addition to making quilts for the cabins—utility quilts, as she'd always called them, to signify their serviceable nature—Adele had also stitched other quilts, quilts that were never intended for use and very rarely seen, even by me.

They were original in design and very abstract, with no traditional blocks. She often used standard geometric shapes, but in ways that were unpredictable. And sometimes her patches were curved or curled, like undulating waves. No two were alike though they all carried Adele's particular stamp. I remember one that she'd finished when I was in high school, with delicate stacks of fabric, piled one on the other in myriad shades of gold, interspersed with thin strips of clay and chalk. It reminded me of desert cliffs, ancient witnesses to the passage of time.

"People should see this," I said. "Why don't you enter it in the county fair?"

"Oh, Esme," she said, then started to laugh. I told her I was serious, that it was a beautiful quilt and people ought to see it but she just kept laughing. "I'm glad you like it. But nobody would understand, believe me. Besides, it's not about that. I make these quilts for me, to explain myself to myself. The same way you write your stories. Understand?"

My stories were about werewolves, or fairies, or grisly unsolved murders, or anything I thought might get me published. Apart from the longing to see my name on a book cover, they had nothing to do with me. But admitting that was embarrassing, so I had dropped the subject.

"You really think someone would want to buy Adele's quilts?" I asked Robyn.

"Maybe. There's a gallery in Asheville that carries textile art. Actually, it's more like a collective. They teach weaving, spinning, basketry, that kind of thing," she explained. "Seems like the gallery is more of a sideline, to give the students a place to sell what they make.

"I dropped in last month and showed the lady who runs it a picture of one of Mom's quilts. She couldn't say what it was worth without seeing the actual quilt but said to get in touch if we ever wanted to sell. Maybe we should give her a call?"

I wasn't so sure.

After I started working at DM, Yolanda and I rented a booth at a craft fair, hoping to sell her crocheted monsters and my handmade jewelry. After paying for materials, booth rental, and two hot dogs for lunch, we ended the day sixty dollars in the hole. Was I ready to let some Birkenstock-clad collective owner sell Adele's quilts for a pittance in her jumble sale?

"We've got to do something with them," Robyn said, responding to my doubts. "Otherwise, they're just going to sit up there in the storage room and turn into moth food."

"No! Don't tell me the moths got to Adele's quilts?"

"Calm down," Robyn said, pressing the air with her hands. "They're fine. There are tons up there but I only unwrapped the one and took a picture to show the lady at the gallery. See?" She whipped out her phone and pulled up a photo.

The few quilts Adele had let me see tended to focus on a narrow range of colors in multiple shades. But this quilt featured countless small, colorful scraps appliquéd onto a pieced white background. It felt like a party, as if somebody had tossed a handful of confetti into the air and snapped a photo. There was such a sense of movement in that quilt, movement and joy.

My eyes started to fill.

Robyn sighed. "You're right. We can't sell the quilts." She swiped her eyes. "I should go. Vera worked late last night so housekeeping is all on me today."

"Do you want some help?"

"From you?" She coughed out a laugh. "Uh . . . no."

"Okay," I said. "But before you leave, do you really think the doctor is right about George? We talked for quite a while last night and he seemed just fine."

She nodded in the way people do when they understand that you think you're right, even though you're not. "He has good days and bad days. You'll see." She got to her feet. "I'll leave the folder; you'll need the lists. Thanks for doing this, Ez."

"I'm glad to help," I said, taking the folder from her hand. "I like having a project."

Robyn grinned. "Yeah. I remember."

I grinned too. It's true; the only thing I dread as much as empty time is having nothing to contribute. And while I had no illusions about the two of us developing a real relationship, I had to admit that Robyn seemed different. Maybe George was right; maybe people can change.

Robyn opened the door but didn't leave. "I almost forgot. There's a box Adele wanted you to have. She mentioned it the day before the stroke, told me to give it to you."

"A box? What's in it?"

"How would I know? Junk, more than likely. Last week, I opened a drawer and found hundreds of those twisty ties they put on bread bags. She'd probably been saving them since the Nixon administration."

"Hang on," I said, screwing my eyes shut. "Adele told you about this box the day before she died and you're only telling me now? Are you *kidding*?" I exclaimed, throwing out my hands, along with all hope for any reconciliation with my mother. I'd try to get along with her, for George's sake. But I'd been right the first time; Robyn was still Robyn.

Nothing would ever change that.

CHAPTER EIGHT

The next day, I followed behind as Robyn stomped up the stairs to the second-floor storage room, her angry footfalls raising dust motes with every step.

"Because I forgot. Okay, Esme? For the ten thousandth time, I just *forgot!*"

Reaching the landing and then the door, Robyn pulled a heavy ring of keys from the pocket of her jacket and fumbled though the collection, searching for the right one.

"How is that even possible?" I asked when she inserted a key into the lock. "It was one of the last conversations you ever had with her, the very last! How could you just—"

Robyn jerked the key to the left, shoved the door so hard that it smacked into a stack of chairs partially blocking the opening, then spun around and shouted, "Because I did! Because everything isn't about you! In case you hadn't noticed, Esme, I've got a few things on my plate here! While you were swanning around New York, I was stuck here holding the bag, taking care of George *and* the lodge, so busy trying to keep my head above water that I never even had a day to sit down and have a good cry over the fact that my mother is dead!"

Robyn always did have a short fuse, but the intensity of her vitriol, as well as what she had to say, pulled me up short. I flipped the switch near the door, illuminating a dual bulb light fixture that was too small for the cavernous space and did little to banish the shadows.

"I'm sorry. I guess I didn't realize how rough things were for you."

"Well, if you called once in a while, maybe you *would*."

Her comment cut me to the quick, as painfully accurate observations often do.

I'd spent a lot of my energy trying to banish Robyn from my life and thoughts and, by and large, had succeeded in my endeavor, never calling Robyn unless I had to and rarely bringing her up in conversations with my grandparents unless one of them mentioned her first. Though I had good reasons for feeling the way I did, now I wondered if I'd taken things too far.

From the day George brought me to the lake and Adele welcomed me with a smile, a hug, and a slice of caramel cake, I'd embraced them as family and the lake as home—*our* family, *our* home. Robyn didn't enter into it. I held her apart, keeping the memories of the life I'd known before safely separate from the new and better life I found with my grandparents.

But this was her home and her family too, just as much as it was mine. Maybe more. She'd been here first, and stayed last; whereas I'd run off to New York with barely a backward glance and visited far less often than I should have. I'd always accused Robyn of being self-absorbed, but who was the selfish one now?

If I'd any idea how to begin, maybe I'd have attempted an apology. Instead, I did my best to be helpful. And change the subject.

Robyn pulled a tall ladder out from behind a pile of old furniture draped with dust covers. I ran over to steady it as she climbed, then launched into a report on my progress with the renovations. Though Robyn's temper could flare faster than a firecracker, it tended to burn out just as quickly. When I told her about the deal I'd found on mattresses, she twisted her shoulders and peered down at me from the third step with an incredulous expression.

"How much?"

I repeated the figure, explaining that I'd found a twenty-percent-off sale.

"But I was able to get them to knock off another thousand."

"How?"

"Because we were buying five at once. Also, I'm a good haggler."

"Guess so."

She continued her ascent. I closed my eyes, twitched my nose, and sneezed. Hardly anyone came up here anymore and the storage room was full of dust. I couldn't help but wonder what that might do to Adele's quilts. According to Robyn, they were safely wrapped up in acid-free paper. I would have to see them for myself, but since they were stored inside the armoire and Robyn's ladder was blocking the door, it would have to wait. Today's mission was to locate the box that Adele had left for me specifically, which, Robyn believed, was hidden somewhere among a tower of boxes piled on top of the armoire.

I've always had a thing about heights. Even watching her ascent made me nervous, so I maintained a steady stream of distracting talk, trying to keep my anxiety and pulse under control.

"So . . . I called a couple of contractors, tried to get another estimate on the parking—" My nose started to tickle and twitch. My mouth opened wide and I sneezed twice more.

"That's three!" Robyn exclaimed, looking down at me. "You know what that means, don't you? Somebody's in love with you."

"Highly doubtful," I said, and picked up where I left off. "Anyway, one guy suggested we rip up the old asphalt and replace it with gravel. Given our rural location and rustic vibe, I think it'd be okay. And it would save us a big chunk of change."

"Anything's better than a parking lot that looks and drives like the lunar surface. But let me talk to George before we make a commitment. He gets testy if he feels like he's being left out of the loop." She shifted a box to get a look at the one underneath it. "Nope, that's not it."

Robyn let go of the ladder and reached for another box, climbing a step above the one with red lettering, which very *clearly* stated that it was unsafe to go beyond that point. I pressed my lips together to keep from yelping a warning and gripped the ladder even more tightly.

"And I was thinking about ways to bring in more business. Maybe we should advertise on Facebook," I said, craning my neck and looking at the soles of her shoes. "DM started doing it just last year. It's not expensive and you can target the ads to specific audiences."

"Uh-huh," she murmured absently. "Sounds good."

"But I was thinking, we should link it to some kind of special event. People are inundated with advertising, so you need something that will get them excited."

Robyn pushed herself up on her tiptoes and stretched an arm out as far as it would go. "What did you have in mind?"

"Nothing specific. I was hoping you might have some ideas."

"I'm not the one who went to college, kiddo. I'll just leave the thinking to you."

My jaw clenched. What was up with all the snide comments about my education versus hers? The implication that I somehow thought I was better than her, smarter than her, just because I'd graduated from college? That I was too light for heavy work? I'd gone to Appalachian State, not Harvard, taking out student loans and waiting tables to pay my way.

"Adele said it was here," Robyn muttered. "But maybe I heard wrong? I mean, she wasn't much taller than you. How would she ever have gotten it up here in the first place?"

She swayed sideways on the ladder, squinting into the dark recesses created by the towers of boxes and cobwebbed corners of the steep log ceiling.

"Hang on! I think I see it."

She raised both arms high over her head, touching a log rafter lightly with her fingertips, then planted her left foot on the top of the ladder and pushed off with her right.

"Mom! Stop! Are you crazy? Stop!"

"Mom?" Robyn was standing on the very top of the ladder now. She hinged her head downward, grinning. "You haven't called me Mom since you were potty-trained."

"Come down from there! Are you trying to get yourself killed?"

She laughed. "Don't be such a nervous Nellie! It's perfectly safe. See?"

She let go of the rafter and spread her arms out to her sides in a graceful arc, fingers curved, pressing her chest forward and her shoulders down, and slowly raised her left leg, balancing on the narrow ledge of the ladder top in a perfect, heart-stopping arabesque.

I screwed my eyes shut. I couldn't watch. I was sweating.

"Will you *please* come down from there?"

"Hang on a second. I still have to get the box."

I heard some rustling and scuffling noises, the sound of cardboard on cardboard.

"Catch!"

I opened my eyes, saw a box falling toward me, and reached up to catch it a nanosecond before it would have clonked me in the head. Robyn scuttled down the ladder with the bravado and ease of a firefighter sliding down a pole, grinning as she reached the ground.

"You were always such a scaredy-cat, even when you were little."

And you were always so reckless. Careless with your life, and mine.

IT WAS AN ordinary cardboard box, the kind people use to store files. Adele had written "Save for Esme" on the top with red marker, secured it with double loops of string. I carried it down to the lobby and Robyn trailed behind. When we came downstairs, George, who was standing near a wall of shelves in the canteen, stocking a basket with candy bars, looked up.

"You found it? What's inside?"

"I don't know yet. Should we take a look?"

I set the box on the floor. George fished out his pocketknife and handed it to me. I sawed at the strings, wondering what it might contain, certain that whatever it was must be remarkable and important. What could it be?

Family heirlooms? Quilts? A trove of letters she'd penned

but never mailed, explaining the secret of life? Jewelry? A velvet bag of gold doubloons?

Unlikely, but a few doubloons would have come in pretty handy just then. And one of the first stories I'd ever written, when I was eleven, featured just such a circumstance. The characters lived happily ever after, naturally. Wouldn't it be nice if we could do the same?

As George and Robyn looked on, I cut the last string, removed the lid, and peered inside. Instead of gold coins and happy endings, the box was mostly filled with paper.

There was an envelope of yellowed newspaper clippings arranged in no particular order. Another held recipes written on an odd collage of papers and cards. Sorting through them, I found the shrimp and grits preparation she'd taught me before I left for New York, scribbled on the back of an old Christmas card. On a torn sheet of construction paper, the kind kids use for art projects, I discovered the recipe for caramel cake she'd made on my first day at the lake and all my subsequent birthdays. Adele had a habit of grabbing whatever was at hand when she wanted to write something down, and then was forever misplacing the scraps and saying, "Now where is that thing? I wrote it on the back of a Harris Teeter receipt and put it right *here*, I know I did."

Further riffling revealed two old, well-loved copies of books by the Lebanese-born poet Kahlil Gibran, a dog-eared book of art prints, a long paperclip chain, a smooth, pinecone-size rock with copper and black stripes, a dried-out paint box, three brushes, a vintage street map of Asheville, a 1943 wall calendar that proudly proclaimed to be "a gift from Hillyard Automotive, Asheville's Good Neighbor Garage," a plastic bag with hundreds of cardboard hexagons, the kind quilters use for

English paper piecing, and a few spiral notebooks with black covers.

At first, I thought they might be diaries. Adele had indeed written a few words here and there, but most of the entries were really paint splotches. They looked more deliberate than the word *splotches* would imply, though what they meant, if anything, was impossible to say.

Robyn reached into the box and pulled out a paperclip chain, dangling it over my head.

"What did I tell you? Junk. More twist ties and rubber band balls."

"She always was kind of a pack rat," George said, nodding but looking disappointed.

Like so many other people who had lived through the Great Depression, Adele was loath to get rid of anything that might have even a remote possibility of coming in handy. "You never know when you might need it" had been Adele's motto. Was this just more of that?

Coming to the bottom of the box, I felt a yawning sense of disappointment. I'd convinced myself that there was something important inside, that Adele had intentionally left a message for me to find, a continuation of the conversation I had postponed too often and for too long, answers to the questions I should have asked when I had the chance. Answers about her past that, perhaps, might provide some answers for me as well, clues to help me solve the puzzle of my once orderly but now utterly derailed life. Instead of insight and answers, Adele had left me a legacy of old recipes, used notebooks, and unsolved puzzles.

Robyn released the paperclip chain from her pinched fingers. It fell onto the papers with a slithery sort of sound, like a snake skittering toward the safety of its den.

"Well. Sure am glad I risked life and limb to retrieve this for you."

She bent down to reach for the box. I pushed her hand away.

"What are you doing?"

"Throwing it in the trash. Unless there's something in there you've got your heart set on saving. Maybe you're running low on paperclips? Or out-of-date wall calendars? Or rocks? Since you don't really cook, I *know* you won't be needing that folder of recipes."

Her sarcasm felt like a poke, a deliberate attempt to get me to react. I told myself not to take the bait, but when I spoke my voice sounded more defensive than I'd intended.

"I cook. Just not very often. Now that I've got more time, maybe I'll give some of these a try," I said, picking up the folder of recipes and thinking I really might.

Though I'd always intended to take up baking, I'd never gotten around to it. And I hadn't had caramel cake since turning nineteen. For my next birthday, perhaps I could make my own? Adele would have liked that. But it might be smarter to start with Miss Ida's Skillet Cornbread. The instructions Adele had written out by hand made it sound a lot easier than caramel cake.

I reached for the worn, three-by-five recipe card. The back felt slick against my fingers. That's when I realized it wasn't a card at all; it was a photograph. I flipped it over.

The black-and-white photo showed a woman in her early twenties with shoulder-length curls pulled back from her face and tucked under a funny little hat that was more decorative than functional, standing in front of a big house with a wide porch, fanlights flanking the front door, and Tudor-style trim that seemed at odds with the solidly Colonial footprint. It was an indecisive edifice, a house that couldn't quite make up its mind what it wanted to be. The expression on the woman's face, the way she clutched her hands together, as if she were trying to keep them from fisting, told me she was suffering from the same sort of misgivings.

But the thing that made my heart race was her outfit—a pleated skirt under a trim-waisted jacket with big pads in the shoulders, and the vintage suitcase and artist portfolio that was sitting on the ground at her feet.

George bent down to get a closer look.

"I remember that suit," he said. "It was her Sunday best all through the war. Back then, you couldn't just go and buy clothes whenever you felt like it, you know. Things were rationed."

I tilted my head backward, looking up at him.

"George, what color was it? Do you remember?"

"Blue. That real light shade; what do they call it?" He frowned, hesitating briefly, and snapped his fingers when it came to him. "Powder blue!"

"That's right," I murmured, turning my eyes back to the photograph. "That's right."

I knew that color, that suit, the woman standing in front of the indecisive house. And though I can't explain how, I suddenly understood why she'd come to Asheville and how she felt about it, as if the shadows of things that had occurred decades before my birth had come strangely and vividly to life in my imagination.

I understood too, and just as suddenly, the reason my grandmother had summoned me home.

Mustard and Mint

January 1942

Sunday mornings in Asheville are quiet. I am grateful.

Though she was widowed in 1934, Ida Ramsay, owner of the boardinghouse, invited me to call her Miss Ida. Apparently, referring to a married or widowed woman as "Miss" is common in the South, no matter her age. This seems odd to me but I suppose I'll get used to it.

I'd never ask directly, but judging from her gray, finger-waved hair and the loose skin on her neck that gives every sign of soon becoming a wattle, I'd estimate Miss Ida's age to be about sixty-two. She's kind, hospitable, and a good cook. But she never stops talking—ever!

When I knocked on the boardinghouse door, wanting nothing so much as a hot bath and a bed, she insisted I pose for a picture before allowing me to enter. I stood in front of the house with my bags while she stood in the middle of the street, fiddling with her Brownie box camera and chattering away in a high-pitched drawl, a sort of ceaseless gurgle that reminds me of the sound of the cowbirds who used to perch in the tree on the corner of my street back in Baltimore.

"That's fine, Miss Maslow. You can just set your things right down on the sidewalk. I'm glad you arrived while the light was good. It gets dark early and you never know if the bus will be late. But here you are, and right on time! Would you mind stepping a little to the left?

"I've taken pictures of everyone who has stayed with me since I first bought the boardinghouse, back in '35. Well, not the people who're just passing through," she said, slipping the camera strap around her neck, "but everyone who stays for more than a week. I paste the snapshots into the album I keep in the parlor. You'll have to look through it after dinner.

"You came all the way from Washington? I've never been there but I plan to, someday. But I suppose it'll have to wait until this war is over now, won't it? Do you have family in the military, Miss Maslow? Brothers? Cousins? Sweethearts? No? Well, that's a blessing anyway.

"Mr. Chestnut, from the estate, said you're taking some sort of secretarial position, working for Mrs. Vanderbilt? Well, I suppose she's actually Mrs. Gerry now, since she married that senator from Rhode Island. Mr. Vanderbilt died after an appendix operation, poor man."

She sighed, frowning as she tilted her head down to look through the camera lens.

"So young. And such a handsome couple, civic-minded and generous. She'll always be Mrs. Vanderbilt to folks in Asheville, no matter who she marries. But we don't see much of her anymore, so I'm curious as to why she needs a secretary? And why not a local girl? My sister's girl, Elaine, types forty-five words a minute and knows shorthand."

Miss Ida speaks in constant questions but rarely stops chattering long enough to get any answers. But this time she did stop, gazing at me expectantly. I told her what Mr. Finley, the director of the newly opened National Gallery of Art and my boss's boss, told me to say to anyone who asks: that Mrs. Vanderbilt has hired me to catalog the Biltmore's extensive collection of art and antiques, a project that could take months and possibly years.

"Beyond that," Mr. Finley said, fixing me with unsmiling eyes, "you need say nothing. Of course, you will be cataloging the Biltmore collection, or at least giving the appearance of doing so. But this is a *top-secret operation. Our nation's most treasured artworks are entrusted to your care. No one, apart from a handful of staff and the security guards, must know the true purpose for your presence. So I urge you to keep yourself to yourself."*

I've never done anything else, so it was easy to promise that I would.

Miss Ida accepted my cover story with a murmur, saying she supposed that explained it then, that they needed a girl who knew a little about art, and went back to fussing with the camera. I could have painted a portrait in the time it took her to snap a supposedly candid shot. But since I would be living in her house, I said nothing and smiled, attempting to look cheerful, like a young woman who was eager to start a new job in a new town.

I guess I'm not a very good actress.

"Try to smile, would you please, Miss Maslow? I know you must be tired but you look like you got a bad oyster. Have you ever had caramel cake? I baked one this morning. As soon as we're finished here, I'll get you a slice. So perhaps you could think about that? Hold still just another minute. I want to make sure to frame everything just right."

Miss Ida shuffled left and then right, trying to get the framing "just right."

"So you know something about art? And I suppose you paint a little too? I see your portfolio. That's nice. A girl should have some accomplishments. My sister plays piano and paints china and ended up marrying a banker. I knit and stitch quilts, but that's not the same thing, is it? Well, at least you're not a writer. I don't trust them," she said, shaking her head.

"People say that Thomas Wolfe is a national treasure. Maybe he is. But his novel hit a little close to home for a lot of folks in Asheville. If you were planning to write a book about the characters in my boardinghouse, I'd ask you to find other accommodations. Painting is nice, though, as long as you don't drip and clean up after yourself when

you're done. I'm sure you'll like your room. I just had it repainted and it gets the morning sun, so it's nice and bright."

Miss Ida scuttled some more. I tried to look pleasant and think about caramel cake. It must have done the trick because at long last, she cried, "That's it! Perfect!" snapped the photo, and escorted me into the house, chattering all the way. And ever since.

While she was holding forth at dinner that evening, one of my fellow boarders, George Cahill, a tall man who smells faintly of cigar smoke, though not in an unpleasant way, leaned close and whispered out of the side of his mouth, "In case you were wondering what happened to Mr. Ramsay, the poor man was talked to death," then winked and waited for me to smile.

I can't say I wasn't tempted—it was funny—but I just kept my eyes on my soup. I've never painted a teacup in my life, but Miss Ida is right, a girl should have some accomplishments. The only thing I care to do during my exile in Asheville is become a more accomplished painter. So George Cahill can save his winks for some other girl.

This morning, Miss Ida and the others went to church. I begged off with a headache, which wasn't a lie. There are six other boarders and I'm not used to living in such close quarters. As if my "nice and bright" bedroom isn't bad enough, there is always some kind of noise—doors banging, water running, stairs creaking and, of course, Miss Ida talking.

I lay in bed with my eyes closed after everyone left, relishing the silence, tempted to go back to sleep. But then, recalling the task at hand and knowing this might be my only chance to complete it, I climbed out from under the covers, put on a pair of splattered dungarees and an old shirt, tied a blue kerchief over my hair, then went downstairs and into the backyard.

I grew up in a brick rowhouse in Butcher's Hill in southeast Baltimore. The alley was my playground, the only place with room enough for boys to play stickball and girls to skip rope. My only encounters with nature involved occasional trips to Patterson Park and helping my mother plant pansies in the flower boxes every spring, then pulling out the desiccated remains when the blossoms perished from heat and neglect, as they inevitably did, by June. And so, even though Miss Ida's yard was no bigger or grander than others in the neighborhood, it seemed miraculous to me. I couldn't get over the idea of having so much space, and all to yourself!

The January air was cold rather than crisp, the trees denuded of leaves, the rosebushes in the corner skeletal, and the dormant grass brown. Even so, the sleeping garden seemed lovely to me. When I thought of what it would look like in a few months, imagined the color and taste of spring, I could almost feel grateful that I'd be there to witness its awakening. I am still an unwilling exile, impatient to return to the city, but Asheville is more beautiful than I had imagined. During the long walks I've taken to escape the noise and bustle of the busy boardinghouse, I sometimes catch glimpses of distant hills and silver sage mountains so beautiful that breath and words leave me, replaced by the earthy flavor of foraged mushrooms and a poignant, almost painful longing. Each night I pray that the war will be won soon, even tomorrow. But if it's not to be and my exile is extended, I pray for the opportunity to truly know those mountains and see them dressed in colors of winter, spring, summer, and fall.

When I opened the door to the toolshed, it squeaked so loudly that I looked around to make sure no one was watching before going inside, digging through boxes and crates to find what I needed. After carrying everything to my room, I pulled the gallon can that I'd spirited into the house out from under my bed, and got to work.

The mint green paint I'd bought feels like aspiration and tastes like strong tea. As I swept the brush over the wall, covering the awful mustard color with green, my shoulders began to unknot. By the time I finished the first wall—or rather the bottom three quarters of it, because the ceilings in Miss Ida's boardinghouse are tall and I am short, my headache was fading.

I took in a breath, enjoying the piquant, anything-is-possible scent of wet paint, and caught a whiff of cigar smoke. I turned around and saw George Cahill standing in the doorway.

"Better," he said. "But it looks like you could use some help with the top."

"I couldn't find a ladder."

"With me around, you don't need one," he said. He took off his tweed cap, revealing a shock of ginger-blond hair, then picked up a brush and started painting.

What could have felt awkward somehow didn't. There was something nice about working alongside someone and not feeling pressured to speak. We plied our brushes up and down the walls in silence until every inch of mustard was concealed and my headache was gone. I thanked George for his help. He smiled and said it was his pleasure. George has a nice smile.

My mother used to accuse me of being not only odd, but impulsive and maybe I am. Because until I heard the sound of a door opening, footsteps on the stairs, and Miss Ida saying, in a voice even more high-pitched than usual, "What is that smell? Paint?" I never truly stopped to consider how she might react to my painting a recently painted bedroom without prior permission. In the circumstances, seeing her turn pale, clap her hand to her bosom, and then gasp, "Adele Maslow! George Cahill! What have you done!" was not unpredictable.

But the way she swayed on her feet and then crumpled to the floor in a faint was something I never saw coming.

CHAPTER NINE

$\mathcal{F}$or someone who didn't have a paying job, I was awfully busy. My first week at the lodge flew by. But some of my efforts were more productive than others.

Finding that old photo of Adele on her first day in Asheville got the ball rolling. But when I sorted through the old newspaper clippings and found a 1944 story about artworks from the National Gallery, secretly hidden at Biltmore House during the war, being returned to Washington in triumph, accompanied by a grainy black-and-white photo of grinning men carrying paintings to a waiting truck with a woman only partially in the frame, her back toward the camera but her figure familiar, the ball went hurtling downhill and carried me along with it. I've experienced bursts of creativity before but nothing like this.

George confirmed that Adele had worked at Biltmore but wasn't able to recall details of her duties, only that he thought she was some sort of secretary. His vague response concerned me, especially after Robyn cast me a "this is what I was talking about" glance.

But Robyn knew even less about Adele's war work than George did, so maybe Adele had never told either of them?

Also, since the art had been transported to and stored at Biltmore in secrecy, Adele may have been instructed not to tell anyone what she was doing. Perhaps she just kept to the policy, even after the war? I could see that; Adele wasn't a talker.

In any case, it didn't curtail my writing. The images, action, and dialogue were so vivid in my mind that I got swept away. Writing the first two scenes, Adele stepping off the bus in Asheville and then painting the bedroom and sending her landlady into a swoon, was as effortless as turning on a tap to get a drink. Words poured out; all I had to do was hold out my glass to capture them. It was easy. And such fun.

Adele was in her early sixties when I met her. Her hair was gray, the lenses on her glasses were starting to get a little thicker, as was her waistline. At first glance, she seemed like most grandmothers. She read books, baked cakes, stitched quilts, tended her flowers, fussed over her husband, carried family photos in her wallet.

But Adele *wasn't* like most grandmothers, or anyone I've ever known.

The synesthesia was clearly part of it; that "extra portion of perception" illuminated the artistic center of her soul, helping her see what the rest of us missed. But there was more to it. Even in her eighties, Adele had a twinkle in her eye that almost dared people to pigeonhole her, giving you the idea that, at any moment, she might do something unexpected, even outlandish. But apart from making saffron dye disguised as chicken soup, hanging festoons of dripping, freshly dyed fabric from the trees every summer like so much Fourth of July bunting, and the times I'd go outside in the morning, discover a freshly dug flowerbed, and realize that Adele had gotten an idea in the night and roused herself to execute it, plus that one time I went for a walk and discovered her doing a little dance in a clearing of trees, humming to herself and pirouetting for pure joy with the grace of a girl, she never really did. But you always felt that she *could*, sensed she was holding herself back. That's what made her so interesting to me.

Thanks to Adele, I've always been drawn to the odd people, the eccentrics, the artists, the people who are doing their damnedest to act like everybody else but never quite pulling it off. Though I felt certain that the scenes I wrote were reflections of actual events and not my imagination, I couldn't prove it. Even so, writing about that fresh-off-the-bus Adele, a woman who was still hardly more than a girl, now thrust unwillingly into an entirely new world and less skilled at controlling her impulses and concealing her oddities than she would be later in life, was . . . pure magic. And so effortless.

Until it wasn't. As soon as the landlady fell to the floor, the spigot of inspiration closed.

I returned to the storage room the next day, took Adele's quilts from the armoire, and spent hours looking at them, hoping to prime the pump. They were sumptuous, abstract, evocative, and mysterious. I felt certain there had to be some connection between the quilts, the stuff Adele had squirreled away for me in the box, and her story, but I couldn't figure out what it was. When I sat at my laptop to write another scene, my mind was as blank as a new canvas.

It was probably just as well. There were so many more important and pressing things to spend time on, projects that might pay the bills and help the lodge make a profit.

I'd turned the kitchen table in my cabin into my command center. The left side was where I piled receipts, budgets, estimates, and anything else related to the renovations. The new mattresses for the five cabins we were updating had already been delivered. Robyn and I had hung up new curtains. George would install new bathroom faucets later in the week. I was sure we'd finish redecorating before Bob Johnson arrived. But there was so much to do beyond that and our funds were so limited, I worried it might be a case of too little, too late.

Even if we had the money to do everything that needed doing, would the fruits of our efforts bloom by summer's end? You don't need an MBA to realize it takes a lot longer to re-build a reputation than it does to lose it. I didn't have that kind of time. What would it take to get people to visit a rustically charming, off-the-beaten-path fishing lodge within the next few weeks and leave some of their hard-earned money behind? I'd been chewing on the problem all week and hadn't come up with a solution.

The right side of the table was papered with job postings and various versions of my résumé. I had about six at that point, each with a slightly different take on my experience and accomplishments. None of them were working. The night before, I spent three hours preparing my application for an acquisition editor job, only to check my email after breakfast and find a "thanks but no thanks" response, plus two similar emails regarding positions I had applied for weeks before. It felt like the bad old days, back when I was submitting manu-scripts and collecting rejections the way seven-year-olds col-lect Pokémon cards.

After years of success, suddenly nobody wanted me. No matter how hard I tried, I couldn't seem to find the path for-ward. For someone like me, who had always been so certain about the road map to fulfillment, this was more than slightly disorienting.

I remembered being about fourteen and sitting with the grownups on the steps of the covered porch that stretched across the back of the lodge, overlooking the lake, partaking of Adele's daily iced tea and molasses cookie offering. Adele and George and Mr. and Mrs. Thayer were sitting in rocking chairs, listening to me read one of my short stories. When I finished, Mrs. Thayer exclaimed, "That was the best yet, Esme! Honestly, you get better every year."

With no irony and even less humility, I informed her that this was because I worked hard and wrote every single day. "You've got to know what you want from life. You've got to have a plan," I said, then proceeded to outline mine, which would be changed but little when I shared it with Carl in my interview a few years later and again with Alex during our third date.

"*That's* a girl who's going places," Mr. Thayer said, nodding to George, who beamed.

"She certainly is ambitious," Mrs. Thayer said. "And precocious. But, Esme, I wonder . . . With all this planning, aren't you worried about missing out on the unexpected? The serendipitous? I don't know about you," she said, looking toward Adele, "but I've always thought that detours are the best part of any journey."

Adele nodded her agreement. "Life has a way of steering you toward the path you're meant to take, whether you meant to take it or not." She lifted her head from her stitching and smiled at me. "But I guess it's the kind of thing people have to learn for themselves."

Was that what this was? A detour? It felt more like an interruption. Or maybe a test?

If that was the case, I was failing.

I looked at the table, taking in the piles of papers, estimates for renovations we couldn't afford, applications for jobs I probably wouldn't get, rejections for jobs I should have gotten, and heaved a sigh. It felt like this whole day had been a waste.

But then I noticed the box Adele had left for me, sitting on the kitchen counter, and remembered that the day wasn't over yet.

CARAMEL IS BASICALLY melted sugar. Making it should be the easiest thing in the world.

It's not.

I was determined that this attempt, my fourth, would work. It had to. I was running out of clean saucepans. The first pan I'd used, which now contained a pool of burnt caramel turned to sugary blackened cement, was a total loss. But things were going better this time.

After watching a couple of YouTube tutorials, I thought I'd found my mistake. You weren't supposed to stir the sugar, only swirl it in the pan once it liquified. And you had to watch carefully after the melted sugar started to color because the window between brown and burnt is pitilessly brief. The moment was at hand. Another couple of minutes should do it.

And it might have, had I not taken my eyes away from the saucepan at the crucial moment and seen the two cakes I'd removed from the oven and set on the counter minutes before begin to deflate, sinking into themselves, sighing like disappointed spaniels.

"No!" I cried. "No, no, no, no!"

My responses were reflexive instead of considered. The metal serving spoon I'd been holding clanged onto the stove when I let go of it, then bounced off a burner and landed upright in the saucepan. I ran to the counter and started blowing like a bellows

on the two slumped cakes, as if doing so might somehow rein-
flate them. It didn't.

"No!" I cried again, and pounded my fist on the counter.
The cake closest to the pounding fell even farther, one side
sinking to pancake flatness.

"Esme? What are you doing?"

I swore, gave my eyes a quick swipe with my sleeve, and
turned to face Dawes.

"Baking a cake. The café's closed on Monday so I didn't
think you'd mind if I used your kitchen." His kitchen? Why
had I said that? This kitchen belonged to George, not Dawes.
It wasn't my kitchen either, but at least I was family. "What are
you doing here?"

"Salting my chickens." I looked at him blankly. "The roast-
ers. I rub them with salt, pepper, and herbs and let them sit
for at least twelve hours," he explained. "Lets the flavors seep
in. So"—he glanced toward the two sunken cylinders—"what
kind of cake were you making?"

"Caramel."

He sniffed the air. "Yeah. I think you're burning it."

"What? Oh, no!" I cried, and spun around.

The saucepan was bubbling like a cauldron, syrup the color
of dark dirt was foaming up like a witch's brew. Without stopping to think, I grabbed the pan's handle with my left hand and
the spoon with my right and immediately recoiled, yelping in
pain.

"Never use a metal spoon for caramel," Dawes advised.
"Metal conducts heat."

"Ow!" I yelled, shaking my hand and ignoring his helpful
observations.

Dawes strode across the room and grabbed my forearm, then propelled me to the sink, turned on the tap, and shoved my hand into the stream of cold water. "Leave it in there," he said, gripping my wrist when I tried to pull back. "It'll stop stinging in a minute."

When it finally did, Dawes shut off the faucet and examined my hand. "You'll live," he said and tossed me a towel. I dabbed it gingerly over my still-red palm, feeling like an idiot.

"They made it look easy on YouTube."

"Yeah, well . . ." Dawes coughed out a laugh, pulled a tray of chickens from the refrigerator. "Everything looks easy on YouTube. Have you baked a lot of cakes before?"

"Funfetti from the package."

"That's it?" Even after I nodded, he still looked like he couldn't believe it. "What made you want to try it today? Caramel cake isn't exactly for beginners."

"It was my grandma's recipe. I thought it'd be fun to carry on the tradition."

Dawes took some fresh herbs from the refrigerator and carried them to the counter.

"Okay, but . . . You honestly never helped her bake one? Or asked her to show you how?"

"I used to hang out in the kitchen a lot when I was a kid, but I usually had my nose in a book. I always intended to ask her, once I had a real house with a proper kitchen but . . ."

I shrugged, embarrassed by the inadequacy of my excuse. Dawes began stripping rosemary stems, then chopping the leaves at lightning speed.

"Tell you what, you help me with the chicken and I'll teach you to make a caramel cake."

"Are you serious? I'd love that!"

"All right, then. Go put on an apron and wash your hands."

"Oʜ . . . Oʜ, wow. That is just beautiful. *So* good."

When he was cooking, Dawes was all business. He issued instructions unsmilingly, moving quickly from one task to the next, pausing only to ask, "Did you get that?" going over it again if I hesitated in the least, watching me do it myself to prove I could. He believed in learning by doing, so we made two cakes, working side by side. But when we sat down to eat, the smiling and laid-back Dawes I'd met when he was helping George fix my car reemerged.

"Your grandma really knew her stuff," he said, nodding appreciatively.

I licked icing off my fork. "This is amazing. It tastes exactly like Adele's recipe. *Exactly.*"

He took the final bite. "So. Tell me the story of your life."

"Excuse me?"

"Tell me the story of your life," he repeated. "It's called conversation. George says that you lost your job and got a divorce. I figured it had to be something like that. You don't seem like the kind of person who just drops everything and goes off to the woods on a whim." Dawes leaned across the counter to cut himself another slice of cake, and I made a mental note to give George a stern talking-to. "Okay, fine. Just tell me what you've been up to this week. I mean, besides trying to burn down your cabin."

It really wasn't any of his business. But he had taken part of his day off to teach me how to make caramel cake, so I felt like I owed him. Also, I think I just needed to talk. Without going into too many details, I told him a little about how I ended up

at the lodge and a little more about its worrisome financial condition and our attempts to turn it around. Dawes didn't speak
until I was finished, which was nice. Most men are so clueless.
They turn themselves inside out trying to figure out how to
attract women, when what most of us want is just to be heard.

"So that's what we're up against," I said when I finished.

Dawes hadn't touched his second slice of cake, but now he
picked up his fork. "I wondered about that. I keep thinking
business will pick up for summer, but so far . . ." He shook his
head. "It's too bad. George is great. And this is such a beautiful
spot, quiet and peaceful."

"Too peaceful," I said. "That's the problem. We can do the
renovations but if I can't spread the word and keep us afloat in
the short term, it might be too little, too late."

"You know . . ."

Dawes lowered his head slightly, pausing for so long that I
felt the need to prod him.

"You know?"

He looked at me. "It's just that . . . I had an idea. Well, not
really my idea," he clarified. "Something a friend of mine tried
once. It might not be very good."

"It's got to be better than what I've got, which is nothing.
Go ahead," I said, nodding to Dawes and the unfinished cake
on his plate. "I'm all ears."

I STUFFED A pillow into a sham and tossed it to Robyn.

"And you're seriously convinced this will work?" she asked.

The expression on her face said she was seriously convinced
it wouldn't.

"Maybe. Besides, what have we got to lose?"

"Well, the money for all the food to start with," Robyn said, then raised both arms high and snapped open the top sheet, which hovered momentarily, then floated to the mattress. "I don't see how giving people a free dinner—prime rib no less— ends with us turning a profit."

I grabbed the edge of the sheet, making sure it was centered before tucking it in. "Not *free*," I reminded her. "It'd be ten dollars, with proceeds donated to the food bank."

"Fine," she said, sweeping her hand over the sheet to smooth it out. "It's not free to *them*. And it sure as heck isn't free for us. Tell me again how this makes money?"

"If people like the food, they'll be back and they'll tell other people," I explained. "Oh, and everybody gets a certificate for a fourth night at the lodge when they pay for three. If three hundred people come for the dinner and only ten percent of them use those certificates, that's ninety additional nights' oc- cupancy. And if we make a good impression, the word will spread."

Robyn unfolded a new red and blue log cabin quilt we'd bought at a discount store. Adele would have been horrified, but sewing quilts was the last thing I had time for just then.

"That's a lot of ifs," she said.

"Dawes knew a chef from the Boston area who did some- thing similar to help spread the word about his new restaurant. Five hundred people showed up."

"How's it doing now?"

"Closed after eight months." Robyn shot me a look. "I know. I *know*!" I said, throwing out my hands. "But this is all I've got right now. Can you at least *pretend* to be supportive?"

I snatched a pillow from a nearby chair, punched it hard, and threw it in the general direction of the headboard. Robyn rolled her eyes.

"Don't be so dramatic. I'm supportive. I *am*," she said when I coughed out a laugh. "In fact, I think it's great idea, especially the part about donating the money to charity."

"Really? Because if we're doing it, we need to do it soon. I was thinking, three weeks?"

"Sure," she said, propping a pillow on the headboard. "Why not? If it turns out to be a bust and we end up dead broke, at least George and I will have an in at the food bank."

"Ha. Ha."

Robyn gave the pillow a pat and looked around at the new bedding, drapes, and rugs.

"Looks good," she said. "Looks real good."

I thought so too. Hopefully, Bob Johnson would agree. He was supposed to arrive the next day. The truth is, Robyn wasn't the only one who had doubts that this dinner would boost our business. Whether it did or didn't, two solid months of occupancy was nothing to sneeze at. And if I had any hope of getting us into the black by summer's end, we couldn't afford to lose a single penny.

CHAPTER TEN

$\mathcal{D}$o you really think he's a writer?" I asked, looking up at George as I popped another pansy from its plastic pod. I'd gotten up early to plant flowers in front of the cabin Bob Johnson would soon occupy. George was doing his part to prepare for our new arrival by fixing the leaning downspout.

"It's just that it's not a very good name for a writer," I said. "What's he published?"

George tipped his head back, let his jaw go slack, and squinted, trying to wiggle the downspout into position beneath the gutter. "Dunno. Told me he's written quite a few but I never read any. Maybe he writes under one of those . . . What do you call them?"

"Pen names," I offered, plopping the pansy into the hole and patting in soil.

George shrugged. "Could be. Honestly, I don't know much about him except he seems like a good guy and likes to play pool."

"Is he any good?"

"Not as good as he thinks he is," George said, giving me a wink. "He'd be a whole lot better if he laid off the brown liquor. His game goes all to hell after the second bourbon. I took a hundred bucks off him."

George wrapped both hands around the downspout and lifted up, clicking it into place.

"That oughta do it," he said, and took a step back.

The downspout listed to the left, then fell onto the grass with a dull thud. George looked down at the fallen soldier, then sniffed and made a sucking sound with his teeth.

"Think I need some duct tape."

George thought he had a roll up in the office. I came along, thinking this would be a chance for us to talk. As we walked, we passed a few folks who were heading to the café for lunch— word of the new chef did seem to be spreading a bit. George kept stopping to chat but eventually I was able to fill him in on my idea of hosting a dinner to benefit the food bank.

"Well, I've always tried to do unto others as I'd have them do unto me. Your grandma felt the same way. And I've been hungry myself too, from time to time."

Yes, he had. Like Adele, George had lived through the Depression. But, unlike her, he'd been happy to share stories of his early life. His father was a moonshiner who consumed more product than he sold. Young George did what he could to keep food on the family table. But too often, George did go hungry.

"But three weeks seems kind of quick to pull off a big dinner," George said as we trudged up the hill. "How are you going to get the word out?"

"The food bank will send out a press release and I'll start an online ad campaign."

George tugged at the brim of his tweed driving cap. "Well, I suppose you know what you're doing. And if it'll help people who're going through a rough patch, then I'm all for it."

In truth, I had no clue what I was doing. But I appreciated his support, which was far more convincing than Robyn's. Nothing was sure about this, but it was a good cause and, in the long run, I hoped George's generosity would benefit the lodge too. Reaching the top of the hill, we heard the sound of tires bouncing over potholes as a vehicle entered the parking lot.

"I think that's Bob," George said. "I remember the car."

No surprise there. You don't see a lot of supercharged Range Rovers at the lake. Though the windows of this car had a slight tint, I could see that the driver was older, tall, and portly, with a head of thick gray hair. But I didn't recognize him, not even after he climbed out of the car wearing black boots, a buckskin jacket with fringe, and mirrored aviator glasses, then pulled out two black leather duffel bags. But when he started walking toward us with a stride that was really a swagger, I knew.

"Oh, no."

"Bob!" George waved and walked toward the man with an outstretched hand. "Good to see you! I've got the pool table all warmed up. How was the drive?"

"Long." He gripped George's hand, removed his aviators, and groaned.

"What are you doing here?" he asked, then turned to George. "What's she doing here?"

George's gaze swung toward me. "You know each other?"

"You could say that." I reached up to massage a pain in my neck. "George, this is Oscar Glazier, the man who cost me my job."

I HADN'T SEEN him since The Incident. But the memory of everything that happened was burned into my brain, my anger and humiliation heightened by the fact that I'd been so looking forward to our first meeting, stupidly certain that being Oscar's editor would boost my career.

In fact, I'd arrived at the office an hour early to prepare.

I'd already sent Oscar's agent an email with some diplomatically worded observations about his book, then asked her to coordinate a time for him to come into the office so we could discuss it. I wanted to highlight some passages I liked and thought could be preserved in the rewritten version, but hadn't gotten very far when Shauna Brown, a newly minted associate editor who occupied a cubicle down the hall, knocked on my door. "Do you have a sec?" she said, wincing apologetically. "It's about the cover for *Water Waltzing*. Kind of an emergency."

I waved her in. Shauna was still green and a little anxious, but I liked her.

"The art department sent over cover mockups and I need a second opinion," she said, and laid three sheets of paper on my desk, slapping them onto the surface like a croupier dealing out a hand of poker. "Tell me, are these as heinous as I think they are?"

I looked over the options.

Single white rose on a blue background.

Flowered tea service and string of pearls on a tabletop.

Empty Adirondack chairs sitting on a beach.

"Yep. Every bit as heinous," I confirmed. "Tell Zane to start over."

"Can I do that? He said we'll miss the print deadline if I don't pick something today."

I shook my head. "He always says that. He's lazy. Don't be afraid to push back," I said, then remembered that Shauna wasn't the push-back type, at least not yet. "Try appealing to his vanity, tell him you heard me say he's the best designer DM has ever had."

A total lie but worth a shot.

"You think? Thanks. I'll try that." Shauna smiled but made no move to depart. "So. Word on the street says Oscar Glazier's coming in. People say he demanded fourteen revisions of his last cover and that Darius retired early because he didn't want to put up with him anymore."

"Darius retired early because his new wife has a trust fund. And it was fifteen revisions."

And the sales were still disappointing. The world's best cover can't make up for sloppy writing. Darius had been letting Oscar phone it in for years. That was about to change.

"Some writers are harder to work with than others. It's worth it if they're talented."

Shauna popped her eyebrows. "You think he still is?"

At his best, Oscar Glazier could be spellbinding. The problem was, he hadn't been at his best for a long, long time. His latest manuscript *was* sloppy, loaded with tropes and clichés. But if Oscar was willing to work hard and let me help him, I believed his best work lay ahead of him.

"Yes. I still think he's talented."

"But a huge pain in the butt, right?" When I popped my eyebrows, Shauna laughed. "Yeah, everybody says you like taking on the PITAs. Nick even called you the author whisperer."

Knowing Nick, it wasn't intended as a compliment. Everybody has their nemesis and Nick Ferrante was mine. A few years before, he wanted to toss a couple of difficult authors to the curb, but I took them on and pulled some good books out of them. One, a murder mystery titled *Don't Look Now*, had five weeks on the bestseller lists. Nick never forgave me.

"Will this be your first time meeting him?" Shauna asked.

"Who, Oscar? We've never had a real conversation, but I've run into him at company parties. One year, he tried to pick me up. But he was pretty drunk so I doubt he'd remember." I chuckled. "At least, I hope so. Could be an awkward meeting otherwise."

"Ewww." Shauna shuddered. "Isn't he like a thousand years old?"

"Sixty-four. But too old for me, and for the women he keeps marrying and divorcing."

I pulled Oscar's manuscript to the center of my desk. Michael, my skittish twenty-three-year-old assistant, walked in, quivering like a collie, to tell me that Oscar Glazier had arrived.

"What, now? He's an hour early. Did you get him some coffee?"

"No but . . . he's in the lobby," Michael said, eyelids fluttering anxiously. I growled and grabbed my jacket from the back of my chair. "Esme, I don't think—"

"Never mind. I'll bring him back myself." Michael skittered back to his cubicle. I fluffed my bangs, then looked at Shauna. "Excuse me, I've got to go find my author and gently explain that his manuscript stinks."

She grinned. "Yeah. Maybe don't use the word *stinks*."

"Right," I said. "Good tip."

I stepped into the hall and saw a man stagger around the corner. He was big, bearded, and stumbling, and looked like a late model Sean Connery, bloated and dissipated, good looks ravaged, his once eloquent tongue grown thick with drink.

"Oscar?"

He swung his head toward me. "*Mister* Glazier," he corrected. "Who are you?"

"Esme Cahill," I said, sticking out my hand without bothering to mention that we'd met several times before. "Your new editor."

Oscar stared at my open palm as if I'd just tried to hand him a dead fish.

"Oh, I don't think so. You, girl, are *not* my editor."

I pulled my hand back. "Oscar, why don't you come into my office so we can talk? I'm really looking forward to—"

"Are you listening?" Oscar snarled, then shouted, "*You* are not my editor. Anyone who has the *nerve* to suggest that I am repeating myself and to call my main character *flat*—!"

He didn't recall my name but had no trouble remembering that I didn't like his book. Things were not getting off to a good start. Doors opened. Heads popped out, including Nick Ferrante's. The presence of gawkers made the situation more awkward but I kept my cool. It wasn't like this was my first pissed-off author.

"Oscar, I didn't say your character was flat. I only suggested that he lacked depth."

"Well!" he bellowed. "Isn't that the same thing?"

He had me there.

"Look, let's just go into my office and discuss your book. It's got potential, and I'm excited about helping you bring that out." I could see Nick smirking from the corner of my eye but paid no attention. "Oscar, I've admired your work for years. And I can't tell you what a thrill it was to be named your editor."

He cocked a gray eyebrow. "Do you know *why* you can't tell me? BECAUSE YOU'RE NOT MY EDITOR!" He pounded the air with his fists. "No chit of a girl is going to edit an Oscar

Glazier novel! Go answer a phone! Better yet, bring me some coffee. *I'm* going to see Matt."

"Hey!" I shouted, taking two steps forward and getting as up into his face as my five-foot-three-in-heels frame would permit. No way was I going to allow a staggering drunk to barge into the office of DM's top executive, Matt Hardesty. And no way was I going to put up with this kind of abuse, not from Oscar or anybody else. "Mr. Glazier, you are way, *way* out of line!"

"Ah-ha! At last, she remembers my name. *Mister* Glazier!"

He bent down to glower at me. I glowered right back, refusing to be intimidated. He straightened back up and looked around at the audience of astonished and amused editors.

"If anybody needs me," he slurred, "I'll be in Matt's office, choosing a new editor. Maybe one of you lucky people." He stumbled down the hall, toward the executive suites.

"Oscar? Oscar, you cannot go down there."

"Coffee!" he shouted without looking back. "Milk and two sugars!"

"Oscar!" I started after him, arms pumping as I tried to catch up, avoiding eye contact with my colleagues. "Oscar, come back here!"

I broke into a run, hoping to cut him off before he could get to Matt's office. It was no good. Oscar barreled through the door, pushing past Matt's assistant. By the time I caught up, he was in full diatribe mode, raving, hurling insults, demanding Matt replace me with an editor who wasn't "an illiterate in a dress." Oscar wanted me banished from the company and, if possible, from the country. Matt, a bespectacled man in his mid-fifties who looked like a Brooks Brothers model, calmly asked Oscar to take a seat, then looked to me.

"Thank you, Esme. I'll take it from here."

There was nothing I could do but slink back to my office, trying to block out the echo of Oscar's bellowing insults as he maligned my professionalism, sex, height, vocal pitch, and taste in clothing. Everybody on that side of the building heard him. It was the most humiliating moment of my life. Several of my coworkers loitered in the corridor, casting sideways glances as I walked past. Nick Ferrante wasn't that subtle. He crossed his arms over his chest and smirked as I entered my office.

"There she goes, people. Esme Cahill, author whisperer."

I flung myself into my desk chair, ticked off but determined to get some work done, only to be interrupted by yet another knock on my door. Where was Michael? He was supposed to be my gatekeeper; instead, he was probably cowering under his desk somewhere.

"Whatever it is, make it quick!"

Stephanie Mandela opened my door. "Is this a bad time?"

"Oh! Oh, gosh no," I said, gulping. "Sorry, Steph. I didn't realize it was you. Things have been crazy here this morning."

"Yeah, I heard Oscar yelling all the way in my office."

I nodded and changed the subject. "Did you have a nice vacation? How was Bermuda?"

"Fine. I know we weren't scheduled to meet until later, but we might as well do it now." She crossed the threshold and closed the door. "Listen, Ez. There's no easy way to do this but . . ." She sighed. "There's something I need to tell you."

GEORGE GAVE HIS head a sharp shake. "You mean *that* Oscar Glazier? The one whose books you were always reading when you were a kid? You sent me one a few years back, for my birthday. It was okay." When he shrugged, Oscar's eyes smoldered. "I thought you liked him."

"That was before I got to know him."

Oscar glowered at me. "This girl," he said, addressing George but stabbing an accusatory finger in my direction. "This *girl* is a menace; she turned my life upside down. Why is she here?"

George tugged at his cap. "That girl is my granddaughter, Esme."

Oscar hinged his head backward and threw his arms wide. "Well, that's great. That is just great. I drive all the way down here and—" He slapped his thighs, then bent down to grab his bags. A jolt of panic swept through me.

"Oscar? What are you doing?"

"Leaving. If you're staying here, I'm not." Oscar started toward his car.

I stepped in front of him, blocking his path. "You can't do that! You made a reservation for two whole months!"

"Which I am now canceling. You can keep the one-night deposit."

"One night? But—"

When I grabbed Oscar's sleeve, George stepped forward to pull me back.

"Let him go, Esme. We don't need his money."

Except we did. I was counting on it. If Oscar canceled, the financial hole we were in would become an abyss.

"Oscar," I said, spreading my hands, "I realize this comes as a shock but . . . Please don't leave. We redecorated a whole cabin, just for you. Surely we can work something out."

"If I wanted to, I'm sure we could. But I don't." He stabbed a finger in my face. "You said my characters were *flat*."

I did and they were. But none of that mattered right now.

"I didn't mean it. I'm sorry. Let's go inside so we can discuss it."

"That's what you said back in New York. What is it with you and trying to get me alone in small rooms? Do you have a crush on me or something? Honey, you're wasting your time." He inclined his head and glared down at me. "I don't date idiots."

"What did you just call my granddaughter?" Without waiting for the answer, George spat on his hands and started rolling up his sleeves. "Put 'em up, Bob."

Oscar sighed wearily. "George. I'm not going to fight you. You're eighty years old."

"Eighty-seven," George countered. "And I can still take you. Nobody badmouths my family and gets away with it. Put 'em up! We're going to settle this right now!" George crouched down and started shuffling sideways, like a crab skittering across the sand.

"There's nothing to settle," Oscar said, rolling his eyes. "Not like this."

"Oscar's right," I said quickly, jumping between the two of them. "We can't settle it like this. Somebody will get hurt. I've got an idea! How about a game of pool instead? If Oscar wins, he gets to leave. If he loses, he stays and fulfills his reservation, the whole two months."

"What a crazy family," Oscar muttered. "Oscar *gets* to leave? I don't need your permission, you know. I can leave anytime I want to. And I am." He picked up his bags again and started toward the Range Rover. I followed behind, jogging to keep up.

"Oscar! Oscar, wait. Can't we talk about this?"

"Let him go," George called out. "He knows he'll lose. He still remembers that hundred bucks I took off him last time."

Oscar stopped in his tracks and turned around, looking at George through narrowed eyes. My heart was pounding. I could tell he was tempted to pick up the gauntlet my grandfather had thrown. For a moment, I was sure he would. But then he blew out a breath and shook his head. "Forget it," he said, turning away. "It's not worth it."

I clutched at his sleeve.

"Oscar, wait! What if I *made* it worth it?"

CHAPTER ELEVEN

$\mathcal{O}$scar dropped his bags unceremoniously by the door, as if planning a quick getaway, then breezed past the front desk and headed straight to the game room. "One game," he announced, raising a single digit above his head. "If I lose, I keep my reservation. If I win, I'm out of here with five hundred bucks in my pocket."

"Fine by me," George said to Oscar's back, then shot a look that said he really, really wished I hadn't put up the money. "You ready?"

Oscar took off his jacket. "I was born ready."

Fighting the urge to give him the world's biggest eye roll, I stepped forward. "Maybe we should order some food first. Oscar had a long drive. You're probably hungry, aren't you?"

Oscar shrugged grudgingly. "I could eat."

"Great. I'll run down to the café and order some sandwiches. George hired a terrific new chef. What do you say to a croque monsieur? Or maybe the burger of the day?"

"Whatever," Oscar said distractedly, tossing his jacket on a chair. "Hey, while you're at it, order me an old fashioned."

"Bourbon or rye?"

"Bourbon. And no ice. It dilutes the liquor."

"No problem."

GEORGE WAS RIGHT. Oscar wasn't a very good pool player. And after draining the second cocktail I'd so considerately brought to tide him over until the food arrived, he got worse. Unfortunately, George wasn't playing very well either.

He sank a couple of balls early in the game but then started missing more and more shots. His mouth was tense and I noticed that he winced when taking his shot and massaged his hands after putting down his cue stick. Was he in pain? Or was the pressure too much for him? After Oscar sunk a two ball in the side pocket and evened the score, I started to worry. When Dawes arrived with the food and another old fashioned for Oscar, I suggested breaking for lunch, hoping a timeout might help George recover, but Oscar wasn't buying it.

"No reason we can't play while we eat," he said, taking a long sip from his highball glass, then a bite of sandwich. "Wow. This is terrific. Good hire," he said, nodding to George and Dawes in turn. "The girl wasn't kidding when she said you'd found yourself a great cook."

"Esme," I reminded him.

"Doesn't matter. Once I win this game, I plan never to lay eyes on you again."

Oscar wiped his greasy fingers on a paper napkin and started chalking his cue. I walked across the room to talk with Dawes and George.

"Looks like a close game," Dawes said.

"Keep those cocktails coming," I said in a low voice. "The more he drinks, the worse he plays. Not that it matters," I said, patting George's shoulder. "You're doing great."

"Well, we both know that's not true. It's the damned arthritis." George grimaced as he rubbed his gnarled knuckles. "It's bad today."

Dawes shot me a glance. "Maybe you should postpone?"

"He'd never agree," George said, opening and closing his stiff hands. "I'll be okay."

George had a point. Oscar was definitely a winner-take-all kind of guy. I could have kicked myself. Why had I put George in this position? Why couldn't I have just kept my mouth shut and let Oscar walk? I turned away from the table and whispered so Oscar couldn't hear.

"This is crazy, George. Let's just call it off and—"

"No!" George hissed. "We've got too much riding on this. Not just the money, it's a matter of family pride. You should have let me clock him," he grumbled. "One good punch . . ."

I wasn't so sure about family pride but George's pride was definitely at stake. He was an adult. If he wanted to play through the pain, I had no right to stop him. When Dawes gave a small nod, I knew that he understood and agreed.

"I should get back to my kitchen. But keep an eye on this guy," Dawes muttered after a clatter of balls and a whoop by Oscar. "He just tapped the cue ball twice sinking number six."

"Your turn," Oscar said cheerfully, swaying slightly as George approached the table. He turned toward Dawes. "Hey, you wouldn't mind getting me another old fashioned, wouldja?"

"Coming right up."

But instead of leaving immediately, Dawes stood in the doorway and crossed his arms over his chest to watch George take his shot.

George picked up the block of chalk. From the look in his eyes, I could tell that chalking the stick hurt. When he lined up with the ball, then tightened his grip to take the shot, his face contorted and he let out a frustrated bark of pain, dropping the cue onto the table with a hollow, wooden clatter. I walked over and put my hand on his shoulder.

"It's okay, George. Don't worry about it."

"You forfeit?" The glee in Oscar's voice made me want to punch him. The look on George's face said he'd like to do the job himself, if he only could have made a fist.

"What about a substitute?" George asked.

"You either play or you don't," Oscar said. "And if you don't, you forfeit the game and lose the bet." Oscar picked up his glass, grinning at me before taking another swallow.

"What if I sweetened the pot?" George reached into his back pocket, pulled a stack of twenties from his wallet. Oscar sniffed and tilted his head to one side.

"Who'd be your sub?" Oscar looked toward the doorway and Dawes. "Him?"

Dawes lifted his hands. "Can't do it. I've got to get ready for the dinner crowd."

George looked at me. "Well . . . what about Esme?"

"You're kidding, right?"

When Oscar laughed, simultaneously dismissing the idea and me, I realized that George was right. This was about more than money. I stepped forward.

"Put your wallet away, George. I'm covering this bet. And doubling it."

Oscar's smug smile spread into a smugger grin. "A thousand? You sure, princess?"

I picked up George's abandoned stick.

"I'm sure, old man. Now, do you want to play, or do you want to talk?"

DAWES LEFT AND the game resumed.

What Oscar didn't know was that George had taught me the game when I was eleven. I wasn't that good but I wasn't that bad either, which was enough for me to give Oscar a run for his money. Of course, it helped that Oscar kept swilling bourbon the way porch-sitting grandmothers in the South swill sweet tea. The more liquor he drank, the shakier his game got, and the more his tongue loosened.

"So . . ." Oscar hiccupped, then started again. "So, what're you doing here anyway?"

"Seeing my family and applying for jobs. You got me fired, remember? Eleven ball in the corner pocket." I gave the ball a poke but sent it bouncing against the bumper. "Your turn."

When he just stood there, staring at me, I said, "Are you going to play or what?"

"I did *not* get you fired. Don't get me wrong, I would have if I could. Sadly, I don't have that kind of clout anymore. You're not the only one who's out of work, Half-pint."

He picked up his stick and took his shot without calling the ball or pocket. It wouldn't have mattered. He missed by a mile but didn't seem to care.

"What do you mean, you're out of work?"

Oscar looked down his nose, fixing me with his steely blue eyes.

"What part of 'out of work' doesn't make sense to you? It means that, like you, I was shown the door. After you left the office, Matt informed me that my sales were dismal and not only would DM not be offering me a new contract, they were going to pull the book I'd already finished from production because they'd lose less money by letting me keep the advance than printing it. If memory serves, the phrase 'throwing good money after bad' was mentioned." Oscar leaned closer. "*That* is what 'out of work' means. Any other questions, Half-pint?"

"Oh. Well . . . I'm sorry." For some reason, I really was. "But don't call me Half-pint."

"But it fits. What are you—four foot eight?"

"Five foot *three*," I said, including my heels in the equation.

George, watching from the sidelines, shook his head. "That's rough. I'm sorry too."

"Your shot," Oscar mumbled, ignoring our expressions of sympathy.

I sank the nine ball, then the fifteen but, once again, missed the eleven.

"That's not even the worst of it," Oscar slurred, picking up the conversation and his cue. "The same day Matt showed me the door, Matilda dumped me too."

"That's terrible," George said. "Who's Matilda?"

"My wife."

"Hold on," I said, screwing my eyes shut, remembering a company Christmas party a few years back and a tall, busty, twentysomething blonde who laughed like a harbor seal and drank Dubonnet on the rocks. "I thought your wife was named Layla."

Oscar shook his head while tossing back more bourbon. "Layla was wife number three. And, in retrospect, not so bad. She only took me for my Jaguar, my sailboat, and five thousand a month in alimony. All in all, one of my more affordable terrible mistakes.

"Matilda," he said with an exaggerated nod, "was number four. She's smarter than Layla and has a *much* better lawyer, such a knockout that I was dazzled into marrying her without a prenup. She wants twelve thousand a month and half the house

I grew up in, out in Sag Harbor. It's a mile from the beach, just a plain old house with low ceilings and iffy plumbing. Doesn't even have a pool but . . . I've never lived anywhere else. In theory, I could buy her out. But in Sag Harbor, even a plain old house runs into seven figures."

He shrugged, took his shot, missed again.

"So, yes. As if a fourth divorce and getting fired wasn't enough, I'm broke and on the verge of losing the only thing I've got left that actually matters to me, the house I grew up in. Basically, I'm screwed. And so, I came here," he said, sweeping his arm wide, "in a desperate, last-ditch effort to pound out a novel that might get me a new publisher and a big enough advance to buy back half of my own house from gorgeous, heartless, twenty-eight-year-old Matilda. But since we know I haven't written anything that isn't complete crap in years . . ."

He ran his hand through his silver-gray hair and let out a laugh that was half disbelief, half hysteria. "I swear, I feel like I'm living in one of my own novels. Every time the page turns, things get worse for our hero. Of course, if this *was* one of my novels, either a squadron of helicopters carrying heavily armed Marines would appear on the horizon or there'd be some kind of shock-and-awe, bad-guy-eradicating bomb blast about now. But somehow, I don't think I'm going to be able to write my way out of this one, do you, Half-pint?"

He laughed again, more softly this time, and covered his eyes with one hand.

Wait . . . Was he crying?

George and I exchanged looks, unsure what to do. Finally, I reached out and touched Oscar's arm. "Hey. Maybe we should finish this another time."

Oscar shook his head, then lowered his hand from his face.

When he did, I saw the steel had returned to his eyes. He thrust his cue stick into my hand.

"Your turn." I started to protest but he cut me off. "Let's just get this over with."

I leaned down, announced my intention, sank the eleven and then the eight ball. Game over. Oscar nodded slowly, as if acknowledging the inevitable.

"Well, looks like I'm staying put. Probably just as well. Because, as I'm sure we all realize, I am in *no* condition to drive." He thrust his hand toward me. "Good game, Half-pint."

On top of being obnoxious, Oscar Glazier was a lazy writer, a terrible pool player, and drank too much. Everything that was happening to him was his own fault. I mean, after the third divorce to a woman half his age, wouldn't you think he'd have seen this coming? But as he squared his shoulders and made his exit, I was reminded of those movies in which the unrepentant but weirdly vulnerable criminal marches resolutely through the door to where the firing squad awaits, determined to make a good death of it.

He knows he has it coming. So do you.

Even so, a part of you hopes the governor will call with a reprieve.

CHAPTER TWELVE

Three weeks passed quickly and, considering the circumstances, more happily than I'd have supposed. True, logging into my email every morning to face a fresh round of rejections was always discouraging. But a cup of coffee and a walk around the lake helped me shake it off.

I'd forgotten how incredibly beautiful the mountains were in early summer, and how quiet. Apart from my breathing, I heard nothing but the occasional splash of leaping trout, the lap of oars as an angler rowed to a favorite fishing spot, and the twittering of birds who seemed as anxious as I was to start the day. There was so much to do!

When a local drive-time DJ started promoting the benefit on air, the phones began ringing off the hook with people who wanted to make reservations. Reservations? We weren't set up for that. But we needed some kind of head count, so we printed four hundred first come, first served tickets and told people to expect a line. Within three days, they were all spoken for.

Organizing dinner for four hundred and getting the premises spruced up for the big day was a huge undertaking and kept me busy, but in a good way. The difference between busy and frenetic is the difference between living your life and life living you. Somewhere along the way, I'd forgotten that.

Southerners speak, walk, and even eat at a slightly slower pace. The stereotype that many of my former colleagues bought into said that Southerners were, at best, lacking ambition and, at worst, flat-out lazy. Looking back, I wonder if that's part of the reason I worked not just hard but frenetically, because I was trying to prove I was neither?

The stereotype was wrong. Aren't they always? George was very ambitious. And I was coming to understand that Adele had been too, though in a different way. As far as being lazy, well . . . I'd love to drop Nick Ferrante, or Matt Hardesty, or even Carl, into the woods with nothing but a saw and see how long it took them to build a cabin, let alone an entire resort.

If Carolinians moved at a more considered pace, perhaps it wasn't because they asked for less from life but because they appreciated it more. When you fill every moment with frenetic activity, there's no space left for the things that truly matter.

I made sure that my busy days left room for George. But it wasn't always a picnic; like Robyn said, he had good days and bad days.

When we tried to play cribbage, a game he'd taught me as a child, he couldn't remember the rules and got so frustrated that he shoved away the board and stomped upstairs without saying good night. Our two fishing trips were more successful. George rigged his rod on his own, cast like a pro, and caught his limit. He helped with the renovations too, and seemed to enjoy it, humming to himself as he installed new faucets, re-placed rotten porch steps, and helped me spread mulch. George is project-oriented too; maybe that's where I get it.

So, yes. Good days and bad.

I was trying my best to get along with Robyn, and I think she was making an effort too, but we continued to rub each other the wrong way. I'd say something, she'd take it wrong—or vice versa—and we were off to the races. Fortunately, we operated in different orbits. Robyn was handling the day-to-day operations of the lodge, I was focused on the renovations and the dinner, so our paths didn't cross often. And though I walked past cabin seventeen every day, I never saw Oscar. I knew he was in there because he turned his lamps on at night and I'd sometimes see the silhouette of a man on the window shades, pacing back and forth. If not for that, and the empty bourbon bottles on the porch, I might have wondered if something happened to him. It was just as well. Dealing with Oscar was the last thing I had time for.

On the morning of the big dinner, I woke up before the alarm went off, nervous that I'd forgotten to do something, worried that some unforeseen disaster—fire, flood, food poisoning—would ruin everything. But the second I walked outside, my fears were allayed. The mid-June day was bright, clear, and cloudless. A breeze from the southwest perfumed the air with pine and rippled the surface of the lake, making the water sparkle and shimmer, as if a formation of diamond-bright fish was schooling just below the surface. When I was little, Adele would throw her arms wide on mornings like this and exclaim, "The mountains and the hills shall break forth into singing, and all the trees of the fields shall clap their hands!"

I knew it was from the Bible but thought it sounded silly. "Hills don't sing. Trees can't clap."

"Of course they can," she'd say. "Use your imagination!"

I guess my imagination had finally kicked in, because on the morning of the dinner, it felt like all of nature was shouting for joy, cheering us on. If there hadn't been so much to do, I might have cheered right back, giving the day a standing ovation.

I made one last inspection of the grounds, wending my way along the serpentine pathways, now devoid of weeds and cracked pavers, taking in the neatly mown lawn, freshly painted flagpole with its new flag fluttering in the breeze, and the weed-free planters filled with cheerful pansies, snowy white clumps of impatiens, and truckload after truckload of mulch that George had helped me to shovel and spread. Walking toward the café, I saw Dawes on the patio, helping two busboys set up tables.

Replacing the crumbling mortar and old flagstones on the patio had cost two thousand dollars. Installing more outlets and buying strings of Edison bulbs to hang around the perimeter had cost another eight hundred. It was a big investment; I ended up kicking in a thousand from my savings. But there's nothing as magical as waterfront dining on a summer night and, since we didn't have enough seating without the patio, there was no choice.

Dawes looked up as I approached. His usual kitchen attire was jeans and a long-sleeved T-shirt. Today he was dressed in sparkling new chef's whites with French cuffs and a double row of buttons on the jacket. He looked happy, handsome, and sharp. For a second, that melting fondue feeling I thought I'd gotten over threatened to return. But when he flashed a smile as dazzling as his uniform, I just smiled back, not too broadly, and asked if he needed anything.

"Yes. A really good professional sous-chef."

"Nope, sorry. How about a poorly trained scullery maid?"

"Close enough," he said. "Go inside and grab an apron."

He put me to work alongside his two other assistants, washing lettuce, trimming green beans, and peeling potatoes. He prepped the prime ribs himself, stuffing countless cloves of garlic into the meat, then rubbing it with a mixture of butter, salt, and herbs, whistling and working quickly. The kitchen was clearly his natural habitat, the place where he felt most at home. At one point, he stopped to grab a cup of coffee, jerked his chin toward the mound of green beans I was trimming, and said, "We might make a cook out of you yet."

"Think so? Is this how you started?"

"Uh-huh. When I was fifteen, I got a job as a dishwasher in an Italian restaurant. I was raised on fast food and frozen pizza, so fresh vegetables were a revelation. And homemade pasta?" He placed his hands near his temples and popped his fingers open. "Almost made my head explode. I started asking questions, *lots* of questions. One day, the chef tossed me an apron and told me to watch him peel carrots, then he handed me the peeler and said, 'Do a good job and tomorrow I'll teach you to wash lettuce. The next day, maybe I'll let you seed tomatoes. Do everything right, just like I tell you, and someday I'll teach you to make ravioli.'"

"So that's how you learned all this? By watching and doing?"

"Pretty much," he said, then banged his coffee mug down on the counter, clapped his hands together. "Right! Time to bake cookies."

We made over a thousand—chocolate chip, oatmeal pecan, and snickerdoodles—plus a mountain of green beans, another mountain of herbed carrots, and ten huge trays of potatoes au gratin with heart-stopping amounts of butter, cream, and Gruyère. We could barely stop to catch our breaths, let alone take breaks. But when the clock struck five, we were ready.

I WORKED THE hostess station, juggling seating, escorting guests to tables, thanking them for their donations and their patience. George carried paper bags of Cajun-spiced popcorn to the line of hungry guests that stretched from the door to the dock, regaling them with stories, and having the time of his life. When the line finally started to shrink, he went to the lodge so that Robyn, who'd been answering phones and making reservations for diners who decided to take advantage of their "pay-three-nights-stay-four" certificates, could get some food.

The line was gone but the tables were still full. As I was looking for a place to seat Robyn, a tall, bespectacled man in his mid-forties walked in and asked if we could handle two more. "You're just in time," I said, examining a table map to see where I could put them.

"Great!"

He handed me two tickets and stuffed two one-hundred-dollar bills into the donation jar as if it were nothing at all, then looked over his shoulder to address a woman who'd just come through the door.

"We're not too late, honey. They've still got room."

"Oh, good. I'm starving!"

My head popped up like my neck was a spring. That voice! But not until the man draped his arm over her shoulders and kissed the top of her head, at the spot where the platinum blond gave way to a wide streak of purple, did I truly believe my ears.

"Yolanda?"

"Oh, my gosh! Esme!"

Robyn, who had been standing nearby waiting for a table, stepped closer to the hostess station. "You know her?"

"Well, yes. We were . . ." I almost said we were friends but caught myself in time. "We were roommates in New York. And we worked together too. Small world," I said, letting out a genuinely disbelieving laugh. First Oscar and now Yolanda? Would everybody I'd ever had an awkward relationship with eventually find their way to Last Lake, North Carolina?

"Well, I know her too," Robyn said. "I told you, remember? That day I drove to town and showed the lady in the gallery a picture of Adele's quilt? Well, this is the lady."

Yolanda snapped her fingers and pointed at Robyn. "I remember you! *And* that quilt!"

She turned to the tall man, who'd been standing by silently as the scene unfolded, gazing at Yolanda with undisguised adoration. "Honey, remember that quilt I told you about? The one that looked like somebody tossed handfuls of confetti into the air?"

"You couldn't stop talking about it," he said, nodding.

Yolanda looked at Robyn. "You told me your mother made it? I'd love to meet her."

"Adele passed away last year. Stroke," I said. "Very sudden."

"Adele? You mean Adele, your grandmother?" When I nodded, Yolanda shifted her gaze back to Robyn, eyes narrowing as her brain connected the dots. "So you must be—"

"My mom, Robyn Cahill," I said, interrupting before Yolanda had a chance to give any hint of what she already knew about my mother and our relationship. Yolanda didn't miss a beat, just smiled and put out her hand.

"Nice to meet you, Mrs. Cahill. I'm Yolanda. And this is my husband, David Olmsted."

Of course he was. You could tell by the way they looked

at each other. But it was strange to think of Yolanda as married. Not just because she'd always had a gift for falling in love with whatever man was most likely to make her miserable, but because she'd always said that, if she ever did get married, she wanted me to be her maid of honor.

Then again, I'd said the same thing to her. I guess the difference was that I had been serious.

"Congratulations."

"Thanks," Yolanda said, then laughed. "This is crazy! I knew it was your grandpa's hotel but I never imagined running into you here. How long are you in town for? Is Alex with you?"

"I'm not quite sure how long I'm staying, and Alex is . . . well, we got a divorce."

"He turned out to be gay. I always thought he might be," Robyn confided, inclining her head toward Yolanda before turning to me, apparently impervious to the daggers in my eyes. "Hey, can we get a table before the kitchen closes? I don't know about these two, but I'm starving."

"Why don't you sit with us, Mrs. Cahill?" David suggested. "We'd love it if you would."

"Oh. Well . . . sure. That'd be nice. I've never met any of Esme's friends." She looked to Yolanda. "Maybe Esme can take you upstairs after dinner and show you Adele's quilts."

Yolanda's eyes went wide. "Wait. Quilts? As in, more than one?"

"Probably more than forty," Robyn replied.

Yolanda gave David an imploring look.

"Go on." He laughed. "I'll ask them to box up your dinner."

WHEN I BEGAN removing the paper and unwrapping the quilts, one after another, Yolanda's eyes glistened and she raised her

hand to her mouth, murmuring, "Oh, oh, oh," through lat-
ticed fingers, as if so overcome that there truly were no words.
I'd had a similar response the first time I'd seen them. But
looking at my grandmother's work through Yolanda's eyes
heightened my sense of how truly remarkable it was, how remarkable *she* was.

"These are . . . They're stunning," she said at last. "You never
told me Adele was an artist."

The way she said it, almost like an accusation, caught me off
guard, and when I answered, my voice sounded defensive even
to my own ears.

"I know she went to art school for a couple of semesters, but
as far as I knew, the only thing she made was quilts."

"You don't need a paintbrush to be an artist," Yolanda replied, with a tinge of irritation that said I should have known
better. She was right, I should have.

How many tirades and tears had I witnessed back in New
York, when Yolanda returned from visiting a gallery she'd
hoped would be willing to display and sell her crocheted creatures, only to have the condescending owner say that her art
was not art at all but craft, the stuff of dabblers or bored house-
wives. I understood Yolanda's frustration. Anybody with eyes
in their head could see that she was an artist, talented, passionate, and imaginative.

But I hadn't thought of Adele in quite the same light, not
until now.

"The way she combines colors is so unusual, and so skillful,"
Yolanda said, turning the quilts with care, as if handling something fragile and very precious. "This one, for example: mint
green and mustard are two colors I'd never think of combining
but somehow, she makes it work. It's amazing. And look," she

said, pausing to examine another quilt, "she's used the same color green here, looks like it might even be the same fabric, but the feeling is totally different. Pairing the green with different shades of cream, and using a lot of meandering curves gives it such a playful quality. You get the feeling that she's improvising here, and having fun doing it.

"The emotion in her work is palpable," Yolanda said, examining one of the smallest quilts, pieced from dark colors, a background of black, charcoal, and ashen gray, interspersed with angry slashes of cinnamon. "This one is so raw, full of fury. What did she say about it?"

"Nothing. I'd never even seen it until a few weeks ago."

Yolanda frowned, a fold of frustration indenting her brows. "Well, when did she learn to quilt? Who taught her?"

"I don't know, she never said."

"She never said *anything* about her quilts? Nothing at all?"

"We had one conversation years ago, when I was a teenager. She told me they were how she explained herself to herself, but that's all. I'm sorry," I said when Yolanda's face fell. "I didn't press her because it seemed like she didn't want to talk about it."

"Do you at least know when she made it?"

I didn't. But before I could answer, Yolanda flipped the quilt over, exposing faint, faded pen marks, written in a familiar hand. Why hadn't I noticed that before?

"January 1942," Yolanda murmured. "So maybe it had something to do with the start of the war? That would make sense; emotions were running high after Pearl Harbor."

It *did* make sense. Far more sense than my seeing a bus that wasn't there, and a specter in blue, then an old photo, and suddenly knowing with absolute clarity a chapter in my grandmother's history and writing it all down, tapping out the scene with such ease and surety that it felt more like transcription than actual writing. Most people wouldn't have given my story an ounce of credence, but Yolanda wasn't most people. From the very first moment, that's what I liked about her. As I said, I've always been drawn to the oddballs, the eccentrics, the artists. They're the ones who see, and believe, what other people can't.

"Ez, that sounds incredible! And after all these years, you're writing another book! Fantastic! Can I read it?"

"I guess. But . . . it's not a book, just a couple of scenes. I doubt I'll do more."

Yolanda gave me an incredulous look, as if I'd just said I had doubts about the existence of oxygen and my willingness to keep breathing it. "Why not? Why wouldn't you?"

I tried to explain to her about the water tap of inspiration, how it had closed as suddenly as it had opened, but she didn't seem to get it.

"So what? Write anyway."

"I can't. The vi—" I stammered, stopping myself because the word *visions* sounded way too woo-woo. "The images stopped as quickly as they started and now I've got no idea what happens next. Or what any of this means," I said, motioning toward the stack of quilts.

"Okay, then why not just use your imagination?"

"Because this isn't just some story, it's *Adele's* story. I can't just invent something out of whole cloth. If I was going to do it, I'd need to do it right, and know it was true."

Yolanda flattened her lips and made a face. "Excuse me, but are you *sure* you're Esme Cahill? Did you and I not work in the same industry? Ez. Every book is a fiction, you know that, influenced by the author's experience, values, viewpoint, and, yes, imagination. Historians interpret. Biographers embellish. Memoirists only tell their side of the story. And writers *write*. You of all people should know that! Don't stand there and tell me that you can't find inspiration, not when you've got access to all *this*!"

Yolanda reached for the pile of quilts and held them up, one after another: first the piece with the cinnamon slashes; then one that looked like a shattered mirror with a gold rim and countless cracks created by stitching spidery black threads on a silver-blue fabric; another that had dozens of long, thin, colorful triangles colliding in the center; as well as an ominous-looking quilt with dark green rectangles of different sizes that avalanched from the upper left corner, piling up on one another until they blocked out much of the blue background; and finally, a quilt that showed a tree with bare branches on one side and a gorgeous profusion of vivid scarlet leaves on the other. She then swept her hand toward the other stacks of quilts.

"You've got so much to work with here," she said. "Just start with imagination and see where it takes you. So what if your grandfather doesn't remember everything? Or never knew to begin with? Adele spent sixty years in Asheville, she must have left a few bread crumbs behind. Go find them! Your grandmother might have been tight-lipped when she was alive, but she's obviously ready to talk now. Your job is to listen."

WE ARGUED FOR a while, bantered a bit, and caught up on what had happened over the last few years, carefully avoiding all mention of the events that preceded our parting, our conversation comfortable and awkward by turns.

While I was wrapping up the quilts, Yolanda filled me in on how she met David, a history professor who sometimes volunteered to lead walking tours of downtown Asheville.

"It was just supposed to be a side trip on my way to the wedding of a cousin, who was marrying a lawyer from Lexington. I never planned on staying. And I *really* never planned on falling in love," she said, laughing as if she still couldn't believe it. "Heck, I didn't even plan on taking the tour! I was hanging around Pritchard Park, listening to a drum circle, when David walked by with a bunch of tourists who were trailing behind like a column of ducklings. The second I laid eyes on him, that was it; I was *done*. I jumped off the bench and followed along.

"He had his eye on me too," she said, grinning. "At the end of the tour, David asked if I wanted to get coffee and we talked for six hours. I never did make it to my cousin's wedding but, three months later, I had one of my own."

David was a distant relative of Frederick Law Olmsted, the famous landscape architect who designed parks and gardens all over the country, including Central Park in New York and the gardens at the Biltmore estate. He and Yolanda lived in a 1928 brick Tudor in Grove Park, an area generally beyond the reach of starving artists and college professors, so I suspected that a little family money came with the Olmsted name. While David taught, Yolanda ran a gallery that showcased female artists, with an attached workshop where she and others taught fiber arts.

They loved their work and life in Asheville and, as was obvious after we came back downstairs and saw David sitting patiently in the lobby, holding Yolanda's sweater and a catering box with her now cold dinner, they also loved each other, very much.

"Oh, David. I'm sorry. I didn't mean to take so long."

"No worries. I had a nice conversation with Robyn and the

food was great. We're definitely coming back. The chef came out of the kitchen and sat down with us at the end—really interesting guy. George joined us too," he said, smiling at me. "You've got a great family."

"Thanks," I said. It didn't seem worth the effort to explain that Dawes wasn't family.

He turned back to Yolanda. "How were the quilts?"

"*Jaw*-dropping. Thank you for being such a sport while I ran off to see them." She leaned closer, swaying toward him like a willow in the wind, kissed him on one cheek, and rested her hand lightly on the other, gazing into his eyes.

When Yolanda had walked through the door that night, I'd felt a jolt of pure joy, a sensation of having something precious returned to me. Still, just because I felt that way didn't mean the feeling was mutual.

But then David held out her sweater so she could slip her arms into the sleeves, and Yolanda said, "You'll come see me, right? I'm at the gallery every day. Your mom knows where." When I nodded, she smiled. "Come soon. We've got so much lost time to make up for."

I promised I would and said good night, then went back to the café to help clean up. Even with everybody pitching in, it took quite a while. It had been a good day in so many ways. But by the time I got back to my cabin, I wanted nothing more than to crawl under the covers and sleep for a week.

Instead, I made a coffee, booted up my laptop, and started with imagination.

Winter to Spring

1942

George Cahill isn't the man I thought he was.

No, that's not quite accurate. No one could be more wholly himself than George. He's a kind man, sees the best in every person and situation. He's also a jokester, a tease, a teller of tales, a charmer, and a shameless flirt. And thank heaven for it. Otherwise, in the wake of my impetuous, mustard to mint paint job, Miss Ida might well have told us both to pack our bags.

But because George is George, he got around her and all was forgiven. Now, she acts like mint green was her idea all along and is looking for fabric so she can make a quilt to match the walls, all because George couldn't dissemble if he tried and presents as just what he is: an essentially happy human being, the sort of man people can't help but like.

George started work the same day that I did. Since we both work at Biltmore, Mr. Chestnut made arrangements for him to drive me to the estate every day. George took the job at the dairy because he was classified 4-F on account of a heart murmur he never knew he had until he went to the army recruiting station. "My ticker's never given me a moment's trouble," George told me with an uncharacteristic scowl. "I told the doc that but he just said I ought to look into farming because somebody had to stay home and grow food to feed the troops."

That doctor wasn't wrong; the government has asked dairy farmers to increase production to make cheese and evaporated milk to feed soldiers stationed abroad. George's work is essential to the war effort but I know he'd rather be fighting. George has shared quite a lot about himself during our daily drives. I've surprised myself by returning the favor, sharing a little about my past, my ambitions as an artist, and even a little bit about synesthesia.

It was something of a test. Most people look at me like I've got two heads if I mention it, but not George. He asked a lot of questions and eventually said he thought being a synesthete must make life pretty interesting. And he's right, it does. But I didn't tell him everything about myself; I can't. Almost no one, including George, can know that behind the heavy draperies hung to camouflage the entrance of the unfinished Music Room is a secret vault hiding the nation's greatest artistic treasures, and that this is where I spend my days.

I've gotten to like George. But today, I figured out that he isn't what I thought he was. It started weeks ago, with the book.

George goes to a pool hall on Saturdays to have a beer with his old boss, Jimmy, and pocket a little money playing pool. Since servicemen awaiting deployment rotate in and out of Asheville every week, George rarely has trouble hustling up a match. He's invited me to go with him several times but I always say no. I can't picture myself sitting on the sidelines, nursing a beer and watching while the men actually get to do something. Even if I could, I don't want to give George ideas. Besides, evenings and weekends are the only time I have to paint.

One Saturday in early March, George came back from the pool hall earlier than usual. The sun had set so I'd already put my paints away and was reading. When George tapped on my door and asked if he could come in, I put down my book. It's gotten to be something of a ritual, these post pool hall chats. George comes inside, leaving the door cracked so Miss Ida and the others don't get the wrong idea, and

*tells me about his evening, joking, flirting, telling stories, and trying
to make me laugh, which I can tell is something he dearly loves to do.
In addition to being essentially happy, George is essentially generous.
Laughter is a gift you give to others, a means of sharing your happiness
with someone else. George does so easily and often.*

*After revealing that he had actually lost that night, laughing as he
shared a self-deprecating story about having to hand over three dollars to
a corporal from Indiana who'd managed to "hustle the hustler," George
asked what I was reading.*

*"The Prophet. It was written by a man named Kahlil Gibran. It's
poetry. Well, sort of. It's prose poetry. No rhyme schemes," I said in
response to his frown. "The way the words feel and sound and . . . well,
taste, is like poetry but the way it's written out is more like prose."*

*Even to my own ears, the explanation sounded confusing and un-
interesting, though the book was anything but. If I could have painted
what I meant, I might have gotten further. But illustration is a daw-
dling form of communication and this clumsy explanation was the best
I could do. So I was surprised when George picked up the slim volume
and looked at the cover.*

"What's it about?"

*Perhaps because Gibran was an artist too, had worked and studied
in Paris, his writing felt like painting to me, emotional, evocative, and
truthful, the flavors of life pooled onto paper. But I didn't know how to
explain that. Once again, the inadequacy of language tripped me up.*

"It's about life, love, death, faith . . . Just everything really."

"Can I borrow it?"

*George had a two-year liberal arts degree from the junior college, so
I knew he wasn't uneducated or incurious, but the only books I'd ever
seen him with were paperback westerns by Zane Grey. The Prophet
didn't seem like something an amateur pool hustler with a Carolina*

drawl would be interested in, especially after hearing my fumbling explanation of the subject matter. I wasn't convinced he'd actually read it, but of course I said yes.

"But maybe you shouldn't leave it out where Miss Ida can see it."

"Why not? Is it blue? Are there pictures?"

George wiggled his eyebrows, grinning like a schoolboy who'd pinched a pack of cigarettes from his daddy's pocket, making me laugh.

"No pictures. But Mr. Gibran was born in Lebanon and writes his poems in Arabic. I just don't think Miss Ida would understand."

George winked and said it would be our secret, then slipped the book in his pocket before saying good night. And that was that. We didn't speak of it again, until today.

Early May in Asheville is warm and wonderful. Almost overnight, the grass in Miss Ida's backyard turned from dun brown to a bright green that feels like curiosity and question marks and tastes like sour berries. The dogwood tree is beginning to bloom too, showy white blossoms lush and splendid. And so, when George asked if I wanted to take a drive to the mountains, reminding me that gas rationing is set to start on May 15 so it might be our last chance, of course I said yes. From my very first week in Asheville, I'd been longing for just that.

We drove about an hour to the Pisgah National Park, to hike a trail to Douglas Falls. The scenery was breathtaking, majestic in ways that make words small. When we rounded the final bend on a narrow and curving portion of road and George pulled into an overlook, I left the car to gaze at the world from the aspect of angels, staring slack-jawed at the endless tide of mountains and valleys in more shades of green than I knew existed, speechless with awe, urges to clap, or dance, or cry coursing through me in waves. I was so grateful to George for bringing me there. When we got to the trailhead and made our way to the falls, my gratitude increased.

George has a gift for noticing the small things, the magical soft-spoken beauty in nature that other people might miss, things that I certainly would have missed without him.

Padding down a path without speaking, the sound of our boots a dull thud against the dirt and duff of the trail, George stopped suddenly, frozen in mid-step, stretched his hand out to halt my advance, then lifted it to his ear and smiled at the "tea-kettle, tea-kettle, tea-kettle" song of a Carolina wren, perched high in the branches of a tree. Another time, he crouched down low, pointing past a tangle of underbrush to a shy little clump of jack-in-the-pulpits and a nearby patch of lady slippers, pink and perfect. George knew the names of all the wildflowers—Solomon's seal, columbine, and Dutchman's breeches—and had a gift for spying them out, not because he was trying to impress me but because every little discovery brought him such joy, too much to keep to himself.

But I was impressed and charmed. When we reached the falls, I became more so.

We squatted down next to a small pool beneath the cascade and made our hands into cups, scooping water into our mouths. George finished first and rose to his feet, then tilted his head skyward, face lifted to the canopy of trees, and turned in an unhurried circle, his expression full of admiration and a sort of satisfaction, the look of a man who finds life agreeable and knows his own good fortune, then planted his hands on his waist.

" 'Trees are poems the earth writes upon the sky, we fell them down and turn them into paper, that we may record our own emptiness.' "

I lifted my head to look at him, water trickling from my fingers as I waited for him to look back. But he just stood there, staring up at the branches and the patches of bright blue sky.

"That's beautiful, George. Who wrote that? You?"

He let out a guffaw, as if no question could have been more absurd.

"Not me. It was your friend, Mr. Gibran."

It was? The style was Gibran's, but I didn't recognize the passage and I'd read The Prophet *countless times. Seeing my confusion, George shrugged and said, "I liked* The Prophet *so much that I went looking for more. That line is from another book he wrote,* Sand and Foam. *It's not due back to the library for a week. You can borrow it from me if you want."*

George Cahill isn't the man I thought he was. He is more.

CHAPTER THIRTEEN

*I*magination *was* a good place to begin.

I woke up around noon, feet still sore after a successful but very long day, then reread the scene I'd worked on until dawn, and I felt pretty good about it. Adele never quite spelled out all the things she loved about George, who appeared to be her opposite in so many ways, but I'd lived with them long enough to know they had more in common than most people realized.

Adele noticed beauty in the everyday that others often missed. So did George. The other day, he'd joined me for a hike around the lake. We hadn't gone fifty yards when George spotted a stacked cluster of fungus clinging to a fallen tree stump. "Well, look at that," he'd said, squatting down next to the stump. "Beautiful, isn't it?"

The mushroom-like growths were vividly colored, with bands of bright yellow and burnt orange, and shaped like sea-shells with furled edges. Never in my life had I thought of fungus as beautiful but they truly were. I'd traversed that path a dozen times and never noticed the fungus before, but George did. If Adele were still alive, she would have too.

You couldn't explain my grandparents' attraction, or write

Adele's story, without illustrating their shared delight in everyday beauty. Sitting at my computer, I remembered my hike with George and let imagination take it from there. But after reading through the first draft, I felt like something was missing and went searching through the box Adele had left me.

I'm so glad I did. For one thing, after flipping through her old notebooks I put two and two together and realized that the paint splotches and numbers entered in her notebook corresponded to the colors of the quilts and the faded dates on the backs of them. I still wasn't sure if the quilts were somehow related to Adele's story or simply abstract artworks. Considering her emotional connection to colors, I suspected it was the former and that I'd have to learn to think like a synesthete to figure it out. But in the moment, my attention was centered on the two much-read and underlined volumes of Kahlil Gibran. What were they doing in there? Why had Adele decided to tuck them in among clippings, calendars, recipes, and the rest of it?

Gibran's works are classics; the themes are timeless and the writing is so lush, reverberating with truth and longing. Readers in the 1940s would have found Gibran's poetry enthralling and exotic. Imagining how a young Adele might have responded to these books and then remembering that once, when I'd complimented George on his taste in literature, he'd brushed it off, saying, "That was all your grandma's doing. I was just a backwoods boy before she civilized me, thicker than a cold bowl of mashed potatoes," got me to thinking.

What if it was true?

Not the part about him being thick, of course. Though memory might be letting him down now, George was sharp as a tack and always had been. But might Adele have been the one who introduced him to the kinds of books he'd never known existed? If she had, wouldn't it have fanned the spark of attraction between them? Nothing makes the heart thrum quite as quickly as a man who shares your passions, and Adele was nothing if not a passionate reader.

Once again, a clue to my grandmother's past sparked my imagination, filling in what had been missing. But imagination could only take me so far. I needed the facts as well. Yolanda had made a valid point. Adele spent most of her adult years in Asheville, so if I looked hard and did the research, I'd surely stumble upon at least some documentation of her life here.

Obviously, fixing up the lodge and trying to beat the end-of-summer profitability deadline was my biggest priority. Getting estimates, trying to negotiate better prices whenever I could, scheduling contractors, and taking on as much of the work as I could manage myself took up a lot of time. But I enjoyed it, especially cleaning up the grounds and restoring Adele's neglected flower beds.

For years I'd been saving up money in hopes of someday being able to afford the silver unicorn of New York real estate—a garden apartment. Scratching my gardening itch was easy now and so satisfying. I loved working outside. Things were looking so much better already; just getting rid of the weeds had made a huge difference. Guests noticed. It felt good when someone would see me digging in the dirt and stop to say how nice everything looked. Also, two different women had come over to ask where I'd bought my flowered shorts and were impressed when I said I'd made them myself. My all black, all the time, New York wardrobe was too hot to wear while gardening. The shorts and skirts I'd sewn at Adele's old machine, using a stash of bright floral prints I'd found in the storage room, were cool, comfortable, and pretty darn cute. They'd been fun to make and I loved wearing colors again.

So yes, between general contracting, trying to think what direction our marketing should take, plus gardening, sewing, submitting job applications, and filling in at the desk when George needed a break, I was very, very busy. But in the coming weeks, I would also carve out time to dig into Adele's past, dredging up facts that would lead me in new directions or provide illuminating details to graft on to what I'd already written, like adding shading to a painting, small touches to give the picture depth, contrast, and context. Sometimes I'd discover the bread crumb clues to events in Adele's past among my own memories, sprinkled into conversations or events I'd nearly forgotten.

Three days after the big fundraising dinner, I delivered nearly seven thousand dollars in donations to the food bank's grateful executive director, then drove to the Biltmore estate, the two hundred and fifty-room French Renaissance chateau that George Vanderbilt had built, which was completed in 1895.

Though the family still owned the house, they hadn't lived there since the 1950s. Biltmore was one of the most popular tourist destinations in the state, welcoming a million visitors annually. I'd been doing a little research over the last couple of days, finding out more about what had happened there during World War II.

Even before Pearl Harbor, David Finley, the director of the recently opened National Gallery of Art, had worried about the safety of his gallery's collection. He needed a secure place to store the most valuable pieces, in a location that was unlikely to become a bomb target. Edith Vanderbilt had the perfect hiding place: the Biltmore's never-completed Music Room.

Under conditions of great secrecy, the room was turned into a vault. The gallery's most important pieces, including Gilbert Stuart's portrait of George Washington and works by Raphael, Van Dyck, Goya, Titian, and Vermeer, were quietly shipped to Asheville and stored there until the danger had passed. The exterior walls of the Music Room were concealed behind heavy drapes, so nobody suspected millions of dollars' worth of precious artwork was hidden there.

According to my research, round-the-clock security guards were hired to protect the art. But surely David Finley would have wanted someone else watching over it as well, wouldn't he? Someone who knew something about art, was associated with the National Gallery, and would remain on-site to be responsible for it and to make sure conditions were safe? But because the operation was top secret, that person would have needed a cover story to explain their presence, perhaps that they were there in some kind of administrative role, hired to catalog the existing Biltmore collection?

George's recollections about Adele's employment during the war were a little vague. Whether that was because he was holding back, or because Adele had decided the secret nature of her work should remain secret even after the war, or because George's memory was failing him, was impossible to know for certain. However, I feared it was the latter.

In former days, George had taken pride in greeting every guest by name. Now, he tended to address all the men as "Big Guy" and all the women as "Young Lady." He was as friendly as ever, and none of the guests seemed to take any notice of his reliance on generic monikers, but I did. There was no ignoring the fact that George was forgetting things, a lot of things.

Still, he was able to confirm that Adele had been employed

at the estate and that her job had "something to do with art," even going so far to say that she'd been making "some kind of list" for Mrs. Vanderbilt. This was enough to convince me that I was on the right track. Deep down, I was sure of it, and that Adele, then a young and frustrated artist, had come to Asheville at David Finley's behest to watch over the gallery's collection. Still, I wanted my story to be based on more than gut feelings, inexplicable visions, and shaky recollections from a grandfather whose memory was fading. And so I went to Biltmore and bought a ticket for a self-guided tour, in search of bread crumbs and inspiration.

I'd been to the estate before, during a school field trip. Adele had also taken me on a personal tour when I was thirteen or fourteen. I still remembered being amazed that she knew so much about the place, especially the artwork. During our visit, the other tourists were gawking at the opulent furniture and architecture, just as they were on the day I visited on my own. How could you not? There's no house in America that compares to Biltmore.

My first stop was the Winter Garden. It was glorious. The soaring arched ceiling was composed of countless framed windowpanes, arranged to look like flower petals blossoming in the sun. Sunlight spilled onto an indoor garden, lush with flowers and trees from the tropics, transforming what could have been a gloomy interior into a bright and breathtaking oasis. Every one of the two hundred and fifty rooms was thoughtfully designed, decorated with the best available materials and meticulous attention to detail. The breakfast room, the library, Edith and George Vanderbilt's separate bedrooms—each was unique and expressive, an art installation unto itself. Most impressive of all was the Banquet Hall, with seventy-foot, vaulted barrel ceilings, a table that usually sat thirty-eight, a cavernous fireplace, and even a pipe organ. It was stunning, as was every room. As I wandered, I saw people craning their necks, gazing with open-mouthed awe.

Yet, when I'd come here with Adele all those years before, she'd strolled through the rooms with a nonchalance that, even at the time, seemed odd to me. Now I understood why. She'd seen it all before, day after day for years. The artwork was a different story.

She was completely tuned into it, could rattle off the title of every painting, drawing, or print, as well as the names of the artists, tidbits about composition, style, and influence without so much as glancing at the guidebook or posted placards. I was fascinated, and impressed.

George Vanderbilt was a passionate art collector and was supportive of modern, progressive artists of the day, including Renoir, Monet, and Pissarro. When Adele asked me which piece I liked best and why, I pointed to a Renoir hanging in the breakfast room, *Young Algerian Girl*, saying I liked the colors.

"Me too," she said. "Some of the yellow shades in the head-scarf reminds me of one of my favorite paintings, Vermeer's *The Lacemaker*. She's an old friend. But you won't find her here, not anymore. She's hanging in the Louvre, in Paris."

At the time, I didn't think to ask when it had hung at Biltmore, or how she knew about it, or why it had been moved to Paris. And I didn't think twice when she referred to the painting as an old friend. Adele was always saying things that seemed odd to me, like the thing about the trees clapping their nonexistent hands. I took them at face value and moved on.

"Well, then, what's your favorite painting here at Biltmore?"

"My favorite isn't a painting, it's these," she said, turning toward three huge Flemish tapestries, *The Triumph of Prudence*, *The Triumph of Faith*, and *The Triumph of Charity*, made in the 1500s.

She laid her hand on her neck as if searching for a heartbeat, gazing at the tapestries with a wistful sort of reverence. There was joy in her eyes, and a kind of familiarity, the quiet elation of an unexpected reunion with someone dear. I asked why they were her favorites.

"Because unlike nearly every other work of art in this house, it's possible they were created by women. Probably not the design but it's likely they helped with the weaving."

"Is that true?" I asked.

"It *should* be true," she said. "Isn't that what matters?"

Later, while walking along a tree-lined boulevard and ascending a brick stairway that led to the parking lot, I paused to take one more look at the Vanderbilts' fairy-tale chateau. How strange it must have been for Adele, a soft-spoken girl from a family of modest means, to spend her days in such a palatial setting, surrounded by unimaginable wealth and the greatest artwork in the nation, curator to a collection no one ever came to see.

It had to have been lonely at times. Still, as I thought back to our long-ago conversation, I felt sure that she'd found inspiration here too, a way to lay claim to the things that *should* be true. No matter how much research I did, I would never know the whole of my grandmother's story, and that was all right. When it comes to our lives, the absolute truth is less important than the truth we absolutely believe. For good or for ill, what we believe about ourselves is what shapes our life, our future, our legacy; *that* is our story. I didn't understand why Adele had entrusted her story to me, but I wanted to tell it well.

After leaving Biltmore, I drove to Montford to search for Miss Ida's boardinghouse.

When George saw the photo of Adele standing in front of a big house with her suitcase at her feet and confirmed the color of her suit, he also said that the boardinghouse was where they'd met and lived during the war. He couldn't recall the address, or tell me much about their lives during that period. When I pressed him, he hemmed and hawed and tugged at his suspenders, and Robyn shot me a look so I let it go. But he did remember that the house was in Montford so I just kept driving around the neighborhood, hoping I'd find it.

Asheville isn't one of those places where people just bulldoze old houses without a second thought; it's a city that cares about its history. So finding Miss Ida's house still standing didn't come as a huge shock, but finding the structure so utterly unchanged was a surprise. The trees were taller and the sidewalk a bit more cracked but, apart from that, the house looked exactly as it had in the picture.

George told me that there'd been a horseshoe pit in the side yard where they'd sometimes play a few games on Sunday afternoons and a stone birdbath too, near one of the trees. Neither had been visible in the photo but when I got out of the car and started looking around, there they were. Standing on the sidewalk, I took my phone from my purse, intending to snap a few pictures. I pulled up the camera app and zoomed in on the birdbath. While trying to compose the shot, I suddenly saw a flash of blue gingham, heard the laughter of two voices.

I lowered the phone. Miss Ida's yard was empty and the neighborhood was perfectly quiet. I was the only person on the street.

The hair rose up on my neck. Once again, I knew. I just *knew*.

I went back to the lake and then straight to my cabin, rushing to write it all down before the shadows could fade.

At Last

August 1942

Though the redundant catalog of Biltmore artwork I'm creating will likely be discarded at the end of the war, I've made my notes as thorough as possible, learning everything I can about the artists, the themes, and the intent behind each piece, and the techniques used to create it. If I have to put in the time and make a show of working, I might as well get something out of it.

And I am. Far more than I got out of art school.

Though they had no problem taking my tuition, the instructors there didn't take me, or any of the female students, seriously. Sometimes their indifference was subtle, but one teacher, who was young enough that he might have been a little more enlightened, was very frank. "Why waste time trying to teach women? You'll all end up married, and spend the rest of your lives making babies and casseroles, so what's the point?"

I dropped out of art school the next day. With instructors like that, what was the point?

Why do so many men go out of their way to make you feel small, shamed, worthless? When my married boss put his hand up my skirt and tried to pin me down on the desk, and I slapped him and pushed him off, why couldn't he apologize, or even laugh it off, pretending it had all been some big misunderstanding? We both knew it wasn't, but

I'd have been willing to play along. Why did he have to glare at me with such hatred and say, "What is it you think you're good for? You're nothing. You're a frigid, useless nothing."

And then, just to drive the lesson deeper and throw one more roadblock in my way, he shipped me to Asheville, saying male staff couldn't be spared for such a menial task.

I've decided that menial is in the eye of the beholder. Though this isn't the job I signed up for, I intend to do it well and learn as much as I can in the process.

Besides cataloging the collection, I've spent quite a bit of time in the Music Room this week. Even in the mountains, August heat brings humidity, so I've been taking readings to make sure the air isn't too moist, emptying the water pans in the dehumidifiers every three hours. And, as long as I'm in the neighborhood, taking time to chat with the charges in my care.

George Washington, painted by Mr. Gilbert, is as regal as you'd expect, but not much of a conversationalist. I find myself drawn more to the company of women, though not all of them. A Woman Holding a Pink, *by Rembrandt, shows a dour and dark matron.* Girl with the Red Hat, *by Vermeer, is more colorful, but that shade of red is aggressive and tastes like bitter chocolate, and the girl beneath the brim of the hat always seems surprised, and not especially happy, to see me.*

Also, she seems indolent. I prefer girls who keep their hands and minds occupied.

Velázquez's The Needlewoman *is a buxom, industrious country girl and seems pleasant enough, but I'm more intrigued by the woman in Carpaccio's* The Virgin Reading. *I'd like to know what her book is about and if she's enjoying it. My favorite by far is the woman depicted in* The Lacemaker.

Her hands are busy and her work is precise, she takes pleasure in it, and even pride. Her bodice is a yellow egg yolk creamed with butter, tastes like caramel and serenity. And the lace on her collar is lovely. Did she make it herself? I've decided she did, and that we're friends.

Though I'm grateful that the heat has given me an excuse to spend more time with my charges, the air outside the mansion's stone walls is stifling. My second-floor bedroom at the boardinghouse is like an oven, so hot I can't paint there, even with the windows open. And so, after church on Sunday, I changed into my coolest frock, a blue gingham picnic dress with a loose bodice, and set up my easel in the yard, near the birdbath.

Maybe I should try to paint birds? Nothing else has been working—my landscapes are amateurish, my attempts at still life are worse, and my painstakingly wrought self-portrait was too revealing, the woman looking back from the canvas anxious, wondering what is happening to her and how much longer she'll be able to conceal her shaking hands in pockets before people start asking questions.

Birds will be easier. And the tremors aren't bad today. A yellow bird perched on the bath.

Just when I have mixed the paint on my palette, achieving the perfect egg yolk and butter shade, George shows up with a folding table, two chairs, an extension cord, and Miss Ida's radio. When I shoot him a look, he holds up his hand like a Boy Scout. "It's okay. I asked." Then he goes inside the house and returns with a tray, two glasses, and a frosty pitcher.

"I bought a bag of lemons. Our sugar ration is used up for the month but a friend gave me a jar of honey. It tastes just as good," he says, then pulls out a chair so I can sit.

How can I refuse?

George pours the lemonade and turns up the radio. Soon I've forgotten all about my painting, and my worries, and the heat. George pulls a flask from his pocket and pours a little brown liquor into my glass and a little more into his.

"*Better not let Miss Ida catch you.*"

George jerks his chin toward the window.

"*I checked before I poured. Nobody's watching.*"

I don't much care for whiskey but it's not too bad mixed with lemonade. Soon we're talking easily, or rather George is talking and I am mostly listening. Someday, after the war, he wants to open his own business, but not in Asheville, somewhere out in the country. Since that day at the falls, I understand. Though I don't think of Asheville as the city, certainly not the way Baltimore is, it's not the place for George. He's happiest, and most himself, when he's in nature.

I like George, so very much. I hope his wish comes true.

A funny new song from Spike Jones and His City Slickers, "Der Fuehrer's Face," comes on the radio. George starts singing along, sticking out his tongue and giving Hitler a great big raspberry on the choruses. I start laughing, I can't help myself. George leaps from his chair and reaches for me. "Come on, Adele! Let's cut a rug!"

Instead of joining the dance, I fish an ice cube from my glass and throw it at him. Then I kick off my shoes and start running across the lawn in my bare feet. George chases me and I squeal, pretending I don't want to be caught. When I run toward the birdbath, the little brown wrens flap their wings and fly off in alarm. I run behind the bath and George catches up. We crouch down, circling left and right with scuttling little steps. When George shoots out his big arm, trying to grab me, I squeal again and smack the water, sending a wave splashing over the front of his shirt.

"*That's it!*" *he roars, his smile as wide as the open sky.* "*I'm gonna get you, girl!*"

We chase around the trees, shouting and laughing and running, until we're out of breath. I see Miss Ida come to stand at the window. Another song, a softer more romantic tune, plays over the radio. When

I run around the trunk of the big poplar, gasping for breath, George is lying in wait on the other side. He steps closer.

"George, don't."

"Why not?"

Because I don't want that teacher to be right. Because I want to create more than casseroles and babies. Because I don't want to be nothing.

But I don't know how to explain that to George, so instead I say, "Miss Ida is watching."

He pulls me around to the other side of the poplar, away from prying eyes, and tosses his hat to the ground, then lifts my hands toward his lips. They start shaking again, worse than they ever have. George hasn't seen this before and looks into my eyes, his frown silently requesting an explanation. I don't have one. The shaking starts or stops and I never understand why.

He presses my small hands together, as if in prayer, and covers them with his own. The shaking stops. George smiles gently, leans close, whispers Gibran in my ear.

"'Love is trembling happiness.'"

A man on the radio croons that his love has come along, his lonely nights are gone, at last. George takes me into his embrace. I drape my arms over his shoulders, clinging like a vine.

I don't want to be nothing. I don't want to love him. But how am I to help myself?

George presses his lips to mine. I am undone.

CHAPTER FOURTEEN

*B*ack in the day, Haywood was the hub of the city's shopping district, home to millinery shops, haberdashers, jewelers, and elegant department stores. The advent of malls in the 1970s squashed scores of independent merchants and threatened to turn downtown into a ghost town but, unlike in most American cities, Asheville's commercial center had bounced back.

The renaissance was fueled by civic pride, historic preservation, and a rising creative class who opened bookstores, cafés, restaurants, and galleries, plus scores of boutique shops selling everything from yarn and ceramics to hand-dipped chocolates and hot sauce, mostly small-batched and locally sourced. Downtown Asheville was a magnet for shoppers in search of the unique and even quirky. Yolanda's gallery, called Gender Specific, fit right in.

The 1920s brick storefront was actually two storefronts, connected by interior doors, with two large display windows facing the street. Through the first window, passersby could see the workshop, home to floor looms, spinning wheels, and sewing machines of every era, plus vats and tubs for dyeing fabric. My first thought was "Adele would have *loved* this."

The second window was for the gallery. Most of the pieces offered for sale and displayed on movable white walls were fiber-based, produced by women who taught or took the workshops. Paintings, sculptures, and even a couple of mobiles were exhibited too. But it was Yolanda's crocheted creatures with their fanciful mishmash of animal elements—lions with wings, zebras with chicken feet, leopards with horns—that really grabbed my attention.

The way she displayed them, on clear glass shelves attached to the window at different levels, was ingenious. The shelves were nearly invisible, so the monsters appeared to be floating, staring out at the street and the people passing by, who frequently stopped to stare back.

As I approached, a little late for our lunch date, two preteen girls were standing at the window and giggling at the monsters, pointing to their favorites. But the gallery itself was empty, except for Yolanda, perched on a counter stool, crocheting at an almost blurring speed.

"Sorry I'm late!"

"No worries," she said. "I can't leave until the UPS guy shows up anyway, so I pushed our reservation back. I thought we could walk over to Early Girl."

"Great!" The Early Girl Eatery served breakfast all day—French toast, pancakes, scrambles, omelets, and some of the best biscuits in town. I glanced around the empty gallery. "Quiet day?"

"I don't schedule workshops on Tuesdays. Gives me time to work on my own projects. This one is for you, a present," she said, smiling. "Or maybe a peace offering. Either way, it's a voodoo monster."

I laughed. "Voodoo monster? I can't think of anybody I need to voodoo just now."

"Are you sure? What about your mom? Or Oscar?" Yolanda snapped her fingers. "Nick Ferrante!"

"Now *there's* an idea. If there's anybody who deserves to have a curse put on him, it's Nick. He was just named senior editor. Can you believe it?" I asked, my smile fading as I shook my head. "Nick gets *my* promotion and I can't so much as score an interview. I don't get it."

Yolanda exchanged a nubbly orange yarn with streaks of red for the lime green.

"What I don't get is why you'd want to go back. The lake is gorgeous but still close to Asheville, and me." She looked up from her work, fingers flashing. "Don't desert me now, Ez. We only just found each other again!"

"I'll keep in touch after I go back. Promise. It was a crazy coincidence though, wasn't it? Running into each other after all this time?"

Yolanda's hands had been busy ever since I'd come through the door, twisting and turning and pulling her yarn. Now they became still.

"Things don't just happen, Esme. They happen for a *reason*. Especially if you give the cosmos a little nudge."

Was she trying to be funny? I tilted my head to one side.

"Are you saying you planned all this? Boy, that better not be true. Because if you're the one responsible for upending my entire life . . ."

Yolanda rolled her eyes. "Obviously, I didn't *plan* it. But

I also don't think it's a coincidence that, after leaving New York and floating from town to town for two years, I ended up visiting Asheville for a weekend and falling in love. I truly believe that David is the man who'd always been meant for me, and that our meeting was inevitable, written in the stars. But part of the reason I made that trip," she said, her voice turning hoarse, "is because I knew Asheville was your home. Somewhere in the back of my mind, there's always been hope you'd find your way back, that someday I'd walk into a room and . . . and there you'd be. I've missed you, Ez."

When her hands went limp and her eyes started to glisten, I felt myself tear up as well.

"Well . . . Me too. You big goof."

I swiped at my eyes, feeling such relief. The awkward part was behind us now. We could put the past on the shelf and start again, pick up where we'd left off. Yolanda hopped off the stool and gave me a quick hug.

"And I just have to say it: I'm so, so sorry about the whole thing with Alex. Please forgive me."

"What's to forgive?" I asked, dismissing her apology with a flap of my hand. "We both had too much to drink that night—I have never, *ever* ordered another Long Island iced tea—but I'm the one who flew off the handle and blew everything out of proportion. You were just trying to be a good friend.

"Okay, sure," I said, shrugging, "your timing could have been better. If you are going to tell someone you think her fiancé is all wrong for her and that marrying him is a mistake, maybe bring it up *before* the bachelorette night, not that it would have made any difference. When it came to Alex, nothing you said could have made me see reason. You were just trying to look out for me. But instead of recognizing that, I went ballistic in front of the whole bar, and accused you of trying to ruin my wedding and steal my fiancé. It was awful, Yolanda. I was awful! The whole thing was my fault. I'm sorry."

Yolanda was listening intently, her eyes growing wider the longer I talked. When I got to the end, she clutched the turquoise pendant she was wearing and blinked.

"Ez. Is *that* why you thought I disappeared? Didn't Alex ever say anything to you?"

"What are you talking about? What has Alex got to do with it?"

In all the years I'd known Yolanda, I'd never seen her blush. But now, embarrassment bloomed in her cheeks like poppies on a sunny day. "Um. So. The thing is . . ." She looked at her hands. "I kind of *did* have a thing for Alex."

"What? Yolanda!"

She lifted her head and made a sheepish, wincing face, raising her shoulders toward her earlobes, as if bracing for a richly deserved slap. "I know, I know. But everybody did, didn't they? I mean, can you blame them? He was just *so* gorgeous."

She wasn't wrong about Alex's looks. But still . . . I crossed my arms over my chest.

"In my defense, I honestly did think your marrying Alex was a mistake. And even though I kind of had a crush on him, a little one," she said pinching some air between her thumb and forefinger, "I was trying to warn you, *not* steal your fiancé. But then you started yelling and everybody in the bar started staring, and I felt so humiliated that I stormed out."

After three Long Island iced teas, there were many things that I couldn't recall about that night. But I clearly remembered Yolanda grabbing her coat from the back of the barstool, slamming some money down on the counter, and stomping off. I also remembered thinking that I should go after her. But I was too drunk and too ticked to follow through. Also, in *my* defense, I never dreamed that six years would pass before I saw her again.

"Anyway," she said, flipping her hand and going on with the story, "when I got onto the street and started heading to the subway, Alex was coming from the opposite direction. He saw me, waved, and asked how the party had gone. And then I—" She stopped mid-sentence, gave me a stricken look, and blushed even brighter. "Don't hate me. Remember how sloshed I was. Then I grabbed Alex and planted this huge, wet lip-lock on him, like a starfish trying to suck the guts out of a sea anemone. It was awful, Esme. The poor guy didn't stand a chance."

"Yolanda!" I gasped.

"I know, I know."

She lifted her hands. I stood there for a second, trying to picture the scene.

"What did Alex do?"

"Nothing," she said, making a slashing gesture with her hand. "Absolutely nothing. He didn't kiss me back, he didn't push me away, or tell me to knock it off, or ask for my phone number. He just *stood* there. It was like trying to make out with a piece of lumber."

I believed her. When it came to Alex and romance, her description was spot-on.

"Then what did he do? After you let go?"

"Walked away," she said. "Didn't say a word, just walked off and went into the bar. That's when I panicked. I was sure he'd tell you what I'd done, that you'd hate me forever and disinvite me from the wedding, and everybody in the office would find out and they'd hate me too. So, I left," she said, shifting her shoulders. "I packed my stuff, emailed my resignation, gave my keys to the super, took a cab to Penn Station, and bought a train ticket home to Spokane. That's it."

Yolanda fell silent. I fixed my gaze on a mobile hanging in the corner, with tiers of plastic birth control pill dispensers, spray-painted with gold. They bobbed in the breeze of a nearby air duct as I tried to sort through what she'd said, and how it made me feel.

"How could you do that?"

"I don't know," she said softly. "I've asked myself a million times and I still don't know. You were my best friend! What kind of person makes a play for the fiancé of her *best* friend?" She was looking at me as if I might actually know the answer.

"No. I wasn't talking about that. Kissing Alex—that was nothing. You were drunk, and mad. I *made* you mad. It wasn't your best day, Yolanda. But it wasn't mine either. We were both stupid. And stupid happens.

"But how could you just leave?" I asked, incredulously. "I was getting married in three days! You were supposed to be there for me. Not just for the wedding but for all of it, for life. There were so many times when I wanted to talk to you, when I *needed* to talk to you. But you disappeared without saying anything. And I thought it was my fault!"

Yolanda grabbed my hand. "It was *my* fault. I was scared, convinced that you would hate me, that you'd never forgive me. And I couldn't bear it so—"

"You left." I pulled my hand away. "Well. That was stupid, Yolanda. Really stupid. Because I *would* have forgiven you."

"I believe you. But . . . what about now?"

I took in a breath, then let it out slowly and narrowed my

eyes. She stared at me, still but alert, like a famished puppy hoping for a biscuit.

"Would it help if I promised never to do it again?"

I thought for a moment. "Possibly."

"What if I reminded you that I was right about Alex?"

"Yeah, but you didn't know *why*."

"So what? Neither did you. Face it, Esme. We were the two greenest turnips that ever tumbled off a truck. While everybody else was hitting clubs and going to raves, our idea of a big weekend was baking brownies, making friendship bracelets, and playing forty-six rounds of That Oughta Be a Book. So, say you forgive me. And that we'll stay friends forever. You know you want to. You have to! Who else is going to hang out with a couple of losers like us?"

I laughed. I couldn't help myself. Then I hugged her.

"I really hate you, Yolanda Olmsted."

"I really hate you too," she said, and hugged me back.

After a few minutes of teary laughter and mutual apologies, we dried our eyes. "Okay," I said at last, "but you're never allowed to desert me again, Yolanda. I'm serious."

"I won't. Never again," she replied, raising her hand as if swearing an oath, then looking at her watch. "Hey, we'd better get going. I told Sylvia to meet us at twelve-thirty. I'll just drop the package off at the UPS store on the way back," she said, taking a boho-style bag out from under the counter and stuffing the delivery box into it.

"Who's Sylvia? And why can't you just leave the package outside the door with a note for the UPS guy? I mean, it's Asheville."

"Sylvia is a surprise. And even in Asheville, I'm not going to leave twelve hundred dollars of merchandise on the doorstep and hope nobody decides to steal it."

"Twelve hundred dollars?" The box in her bag was maybe eight inches square. Unless she was smuggling drugs or stolen jewels, I couldn't imagine how the contents could be worth twelve hundred bucks. "What are you mailing?"

"A monster," she replied absently, searching the bag for her keys. "It's a commission piece for a Japanese collector."

"*A* monster? As in *one*? Of yours?"

Yolanda pulled out the keys and smiled quizzically. "Esme, my monsters are pretty popular. I've sold fourteen to museums and ten times that many to private collectors. Prices in the gallery start at four hundred, but I charge as much as two thousand for a commission piece."

"You're kidding. Wow. I just . . . I had no idea. All out of your little gallery in Asheville?"

She grinned. "Yes, Esme, all out of my little gallery in Asheville. What did you think? That David was financing all this?"

Yes, that's exactly what I'd thought, that sweet David Olmsted, a besotted history professor whose well-heeled people had lived in Asheville forever and had ties to Frederick Law Olmsted, the famous and very successful landscape architect, was funding his bride's feminist art gallery hobby job out of family money and the kindness of his heart.

"You know, it *is* possible to make a living as an artist outside of New York. Manhattan isn't the center of the art world. It only thinks it is." Yolanda threw an arm across my shoulders.

"Don't go, Ez. Stay in Asheville. We'll do crafts, and eat food fried in pork fat, and get into trouble, and be best friends till we die. Come on. Say you'll stay. Please."

"Yes, to the friends forever part. But the rest of it?" I shook my head. "I can't. New York may not be the center of the art world, but it is the center of the book world. That's what I do, Yolanda. That's what I love."

"You could learn to love other things," she reasoned. "What about your chef?"

I pushed her arm off my shoulders. "Stop. Dawes isn't *my* chef, he's *the* chef."

"Well, maybe he oughta be your chef. The only thing sexier than a man in uniform is a man in an apron. The first time David made me a Caesar salad, that was it. I was *done*," she said, opening her mouth and hooking her finger into her cheek. "If Dawes had baked *me* a caramel cake, I probably would have laid down on the floor and offered to have his children."

Dawes hadn't baked me a cake, he'd taught me how to bake one for myself. There was a difference, but I suspected this would be lost on Yolanda.

"Can we talk about something else?"

"Fine," she said, but in a way that suggested the topic was only postponed. She switched off the lights as we headed out the door. "What's the news from New York? I mean, besides Nick getting promoted. Hear anything from Alex?"

"I know this probably comes as a shock but we haven't really kept in touch."

"Maybe you should," she said as she locked the door. "If he and the personal trainer get engaged, they could have the wedding at the lodge. That could bring in as much revenue as the whole place makes in a month. Maybe you should call Alex and float the idea, offer to give him away."

"Maybe." I laughed. "Or not."

CHAPTER FIFTEEN

Sutton Barnett, Sylvia's daughter, was a perky and petite twenty-five-year-old who was almost as short as me. She had bright blue eyes, auburn curls that barely brushed her shoulders, a sprinkling of freckles across her nose, and a ready smile. I liked her.

I was less enamored of her fiancé, thirty-three-year-old Martin Waddell, a not very handsome and not very nice financial analyst who specialized in emerging European markets and whose salary with bonus was "mid six figures." Why do I know this? He told me within ninety seconds of our introduction.

Sutton and Martin had been engaged for a year and planned to be married on the second Saturday in August. After a honeymoon in Bermuda, they would fly to London where Martin held a position at an international investment bank. Two hundred and fifty guests had accepted the invitation. It was meant to be a grand and glittering affair.

There was only one problem.

Ten days before Yolanda had introduced me to Sylvia, a water main burst at a private club where both the wedding and the reception were supposed to take place. The ballroom, meeting spaces, and grounds were destroyed in the flooding. Renovations would take months. Until they were completed, all events, including the Barnett-Waddell wedding, had been canceled. Sylvia, who was a regular participant in workshops at Gender Specific, had been searching frantically for an alternative wedding venue ever since, with no success. But Yolanda had an idea.

"David and I were at Last Lake Lodge a few days ago," Yolanda told Sylvia, "at a benefit for the food bank. Did you hear about it? No? It was fabulous. We were so impressed. How many people did you serve, Esme? Over five hundred, wasn't it?"

"Umm . . . I think it was more like four hundred," I said, twisting my neck so Sylvia wouldn't see the look I was shooting Yolanda.

After the benefit, we'd booked a few more stays and seen increased business at the café. It was all good but not quite the game changer I'd hoped for. A big wedding banquet might be, but could we really handle that? I didn't want to overpromise.

Sylvia seemed nice, if a little anxious. The way she kept clutching at her pearls worried me. I kept thinking they were going to break and get lost in her salad.

"Five hundred, four hundred," Yolanda said, dismissing the difference with a wave. "The service was excellent. The lodge is so charming, rustic but in a good way. Sylvia, I think it's a lucky thing that the country club isn't available. They're always so generic, aren't they?"

When Yolanda wrinkled her nose and dissed the country club, I had to look away. Who *was* this woman?

Yolanda had a purple streak in her hair, a zirconium stud in her left nostril, owned a feminist art gallery, and had grown up in Spokane. But if you closed your eyes and listened, she sounded exactly like a Lilly Pulitzer–clad club woman. It was hilarious! More hilarious was the way that Sylvia kept nodding, buying the whole thing. When Yolanda's vowels got longer and she slipped into a subtle but weirdly convincing Carolina drawl, I grabbed a biscuit and feigned deep interest in making sure the butter was spread evenly to keep from cracking up.

"If Martin's people are coming all the way from Massachusetts," Yolanda said, leaning closer, "you'll want to give them a taste of real Southern hospitality in a setting that they won't find in Boston. You can have the ceremony on the lawn, just steps away from the water. That lakeview is amazing. And the food!" Yolanda pressed a palm to her chest and closed her eyes in rapture. "You *must* serve the prime rib. It was divine! And the cookie plate. Delicious. It'd be nice to serve something a little different, don't you think? I mean, *everybody* does cake."

"Oh, well . . . I don't know," Sylvia said, twisting her pearls. "You'd really have to work the menu out with Martin." She looked left and then right and dropped her voice to a whisper. "Of course, Howard and I always planned to pay for Sutton's wedding. But it's gotten to be such a *big* affair. And with this recession . . ." She picked up her salad fork, leaving the sentence unfinished. "Fortunately, Martin is willing and able to pay for everything. Sutton's a lucky girl; he's quite a catch. But very particular."

She looked to me. "Martin is flying in from London next weekend. I realize it's short notice, but would it be possible for Sutton and Martin to drive out to the lake on Saturday for a tour of the facilities?" She laughed nervously and grabbed her pearls again. "I'm sure it's lovely, but, as I say, Martin is *very* particular."

He certainly was.

However, my initial concerns were centered on Dawes. Booking this wedding could help us pick up a lot of yardage in our drive toward the September profit goalpost. But without Dawes, we didn't have a prayer.

He'd opened up more in the last few weeks, telling the story of how he learned to cook and describing his travels in the van, sites he'd seen and characters he'd run into. But whenever I asked about his personal life, he'd clam up or change the subject. It was strange, and worrying. I kept imagining him as a character in one of Oscar's novels, a seemingly ordinary man whose identity was hidden until he disappeared in the night and Interpol agents showed up the next day, hot on his trail and asking questions. Clearly, I was letting my imagination get away from me, but taking on a wedding was impossible without a firm commitment from Dawes, so I pressed the issue.

"George advanced me the money to fix my van and I promised to stay until Labor Day," he said, setting his lips into a line. "Do I look like the kind of man who goes back on his word?"

Not really, but how was I to know? Dawes wasn't exactly an open book. And so many things about him confused me. Ever since Yolanda and the "your chef" conversation, I had a sudden, surprisingly vivid vision of him grabbing me and kissing me whenever I saw him. "It's nothing personal," I said, banishing the image from my brain. "I just need to know we can count on you."

Dawes crossed his arms over his chest. "If I make a promise, I keep it. Period. End of story. Besides, I'd never let George down."

The way he said it made me believe him, and when Sutton and Martin came for a tour, Dawes pulled out all the stops. He

prepared a wonderful tasting menu—appetizers, three different salads, prime rib and roasted herb chicken with scalloped
potatoes and green beans almondine, and white chocolate cake
filled with raspberry mousse. Everything was delicious and
Sutton couldn't have been more delighted. But Martin's response was basically "meh."

"Feels less like a wedding dinner and more like the buffet
line at Golden Corral," he said, and laughed out loud at what
he apparently thought was a funny joke. Sutton giggled but
with obvious discomfort, her eyes beaming an apology. Dawes
took it in stride. Like me, I think he'd already figured out the
Martin/Sutton relationship dynamic, probably better than Sutton had.

"We can kick things up a couple of notches," Dawes said.
"What did you have in mind?"

"Instead of prime rib, what about bacon-wrapped filet mignon with hollandaise sauce? And chicken—" Martin made a
face and laughed again. "It's what you serve at a chamber of
commerce silent auction, not a wedding."

"Filet mignon for that many people could be a problem,"
Dawes said. "But I could do pepper-crusted beef tenderloins
with a mushroom and cognac cream sauce. And instead of
chicken, how about roasted Cornish game hens with an apricot
glaze?"

"Better." Martin shrugged. "The salads are okay. But the
side dishes—green beans and scalloped potatoes?" Martin
rolled his eyes. "Please."

"If you'd rather, I could make haricot verts and gratin dauphinois."

I'd had enough high school French to know that haricot
verts and gratin dauphinois were just fancy-sounding names for

green beans and scalloped potatoes. At first, I thought Dawes was trying to lighten the atmosphere and get Martin to laugh. But when the groom-elect nodded grudgingly and said that would be an improvement, I realized Dawes was toying with him, confirming that Martin was just as big a poser—and just as big a jerk—as I'd thought.

Dawes caught my eye for a moment, and I had to look away and pretend to cough to keep from laughing. A part of me wanted to grab Sutton by the shoulders and beg her to call off the wedding. If I'd had the least hope that she'd listen, I would have. But as I knew from personal experience, some things people have to figure out on their own. I could tell that Sutton had made up her mind, and nothing and nobody would convince her to reconsider.

She clutched Martin's arm. "It all sounds delicious. Don't you think so, Gummy Bear?"

Martin made a grumbling sound. "I told you we should have gotten married in Boston."

"I know. But it's too late now; the wedding is only six weeks away," she said, giggling anxiously. "Maybe this isn't quite what we'd planned, but I'm sure the food will be fabulous. And really," she said, gazing toward the lake, "could we ask for a prettier spot?"

Even Martin was willing to concede the perfection of the setting. "But the rest of it . . . I don't know. If I hadn't already cleared my work schedule, I'd say we just postpone."

Sutton, who looked like she was holding her breath, waited. Martin drummed his fingers on the table, keeping everybody in suspense. About the time I thought Sutton might pass out, he sighed and said, "Well, I guess we'll go through with it. What's the price per head?"

Dawes, Robyn, and I had worked up some figures the day before. But before I had a chance to hand over the paperwork, Dawes answered for me, quoting a figure that was nearly double what we'd discussed. What was he thinking! I let out what I hoped was a convincing laugh and turned toward Martin, ready to say that Dawes was just joking and giving him the real estimate. But then Martin popped his lips a couple of times and said, "Okay. But that includes a full bar as well as taxes and gratuities, right?"

The price Dawes so casually threw out there wouldn't have raised an eyebrow in New York, Boston, or Miami, but in this part of the world, it was astronomical. As a guy who supposedly specialized in emerging markets, you'd have thought Martin would be better informed about what the local market would bear. But apparently not.

I looked at Dawes, assuming he'd take it from there. Instead, he rested his chin on his elbow, his mouth twitching into a sort of "the ball is in your court" smile.

"Umm . . . well. Yes. Bar included. Taxes and eighteen percent service charge are extra."

Martin grumbled a little but, miraculously, didn't balk. I couldn't believe it.

There was no doubt in my mind that this wedding would be a day that Sutton would live to regret. But if things worked out, the second Saturday in August would not only help us reach profitability in a single day, it could open a path to a new business model that could secure the future of the lodge, ensuring it stayed in family hands and that, no matter what happened, George could live out his days at home and in comfort. Our problems were solved!

When Martin agreed to the terms, I felt like jumping up and doing a dance. Fortunately, I restrained myself. Our "very particular" groom wasn't finished negotiating.

ROBYN HELD UP her hand, interrupting my story.

"Wait, wait, wait. Let me make sure I'm getting this straight: this stuck-up Yankee won't book a wedding at the lodge unless we pave the parking lot, double the size of the patio, update the bathrooms, create an outdoor chapel, buy two hundred and fifty folding chairs, and a ginormous white tent?" She started laughing. "I am *so* sorry I missed that meeting. I'd have loved to see you tell him where to catch the next bus back to Boston."

"Yeah," I said. "Except I didn't. I took his fifty percent deposit and said we'd see him in August. We're going to use his money to turn the lodge into a first-class wedding venue."

Robyn stared at me for a second, as if she was waiting for the punch line.

"You're serious, aren't you? Wow. Will the deposit really cover everything?"

I took a breath. "No. I'm putting up the rest myself."

"What?" Robyn gasped. "You were saving for a down payment. And you still don't have a job. Esme, you can't. That money is your security! Your future!"

Her reaction pulled me up short. I wasn't used to Robyn saying something that sounded . . . well, so much like what a mom would say. Her concern for my welfare was unfounded, but also kind of sweet. For a second, I was filled with unfamiliarly warm and fuzzy feelings toward my mother.

"Everything's going to be fine," I assured her. "With Alex out of the picture, I can't afford to buy a place anytime soon anyway, so I might as well put my savings to work. Not only will this event put us in the black, it could open up a whole new business model so you'll never have to sell the lodge. Weddings can be very profitable."

"*This* one won't be. You're spending the profits before you even start."

Robyn made a scoffing sound and I felt my jaw clench. So much for warm fuzzies.

"For once in your life, just once, could you *not* be the person searching out the cloud in every silver lining? This could turn out to be a *good* thing," I said, urging her to envision the possibilities. "Everybody knows you've got to spend money to make it. And it's not like I'm just throwing my money down a hole. I'll get it back after the wedding. It's just a loan."

"It could be a hole," Robyn said, crossing her arms over her chest. "I sure don't think it's a business model. How many people will want to get married at an old, rundown fishing resort? The *only* reason Martin Moneybags and his bride are having their wedding here is because the country club got flooded. You can't count on that kind of thing happening all the time, Esme."

"By the time I'm done, it won't *be* rundown," I said, sweeping my arm toward a flower bed that I'd spent all morning weeding, frustrated by her constant negativity. "And maybe I won't need it to happen all the time, maybe once is enough. Is there a little risk involved? Sure," I said, though I didn't honestly think so. "But this is our chance to turn everything around. Things don't just happen, you know. They happen for a reason."

Robyn dropped her chin. "Who *are* you? You're one of the most cautious people I've ever met, always had to have a plan, even when you were little. Now, all of a sudden, you want to risk everything and just jump headfirst into the wedding business? I swear, you're starting to sound just like Adele." She shook her head and pulled out a cigarette. "A pipe busted, Esme. It was an accident, not an opportunity."

I threw out my hands. "Sometimes an accident *is* the opportunity! Don't you get it?"

I'm pretty sure that the next thing she planned to say could have catapulted the conversation from heated dispute to raging argument. Fortunately, George exited the café and walked across the grass to greet us before things got out of hand.

"Hey! I was just talking to Dawes. He says we're having a big wedding next month?"

"That's the plan," I said, jumping in before Robyn could say anything to the contrary.

"Sounds like fun. You know, Adele wanted to have our wedding by the lake, but her mother was set on her getting married in Baltimore so we did it there. But I proposed to her here, right there under that tree," he said, pointing out the window to a red maple that stood on the crest of the hill. "Did I ever tell you?"

Robyn smiled and took his arm, our argument forgotten for the moment.

"No, Dad. You never did. What did you say when you popped the question?"

He grinned. "Oh, you know. The things a man usually says at times like that. I can't recall the exact words now, only that they weren't very convincing. She turned me down."

Robyn tilted her head to one side. "What? I never knew that."

"Yup," George confirmed, bobbing his head. "Obviously I had better luck the next time, otherwise you two wouldn't be here. Practice makes perfect, I guess."

"What did you say the second time?" I asked.

George's forehead pleated into a momentary frown, then he flapped his hand. "Oh, who wants to hear about ancient history? Anyway, I'm busy. We're running low on candy for the canteen so I need to go to town. Can you keep an eye on the desk while I'm gone?"

Robyn nodded. "Sure, Dad."

"Thanks," he said brusquely and started toward the lodge, leaning on his shillelagh as he ascended the hill. But he stopped and turned after a few steps. "Oh, Esme, do you want to go fishing in the morning? I hear they're biting pretty good right now."

"Sure. Sounds great, George."

"See you at five," he said, turning abruptly and walking away. When he was out of earshot, Robyn closed her eyes, her unlit cigarette dangling from her fingertips.

"He doesn't remember," she murmured. "And he *knows* he doesn't remember."

"Not necessarily. He's busy, probably wanted to get to town before it gets dark. You know his eyesight's not what it used to be."

She opened her eyes and looked squarely into mine. "You know that's not true. All his life, he's been a storyteller. But now he's too busy to share what must have been a really great story?" She moved her head from side to side. "The only thing that's not what it used to be is George."

Robyn pulled a lighter from her back pocket and lit the forgotten cigarette, looking at me through narrowed eyes as she inhaled.

"I've seen you through your window at night sometimes, typing on your computer and digging through the box Adele left. Are you writing it down? Their story?"

"Yes. I mean . . . I'm trying to."

She bobbed her and sucked on the cigarette, making the tip glow red.

"Good. Don't stop."

CHAPTER SIXTEEN

*R*obyn hadn't taken a lunch break, so I said I'd watch the desk until George returned. Since I hadn't eaten either, I grabbed the last PayDay bar from the canteen and ate it while doing research on wholesale prices for folding chairs and thinking about our conversation.

Apart from Yolanda, I hadn't told anyone I was writing, not even Carl. He'd called to check in with me a couple of days previously, walking on West Fifty-Sixth as he rushed to a meeting.

"Things are crazy," he said. "Two years ago, I couldn't give away historical fiction. Now, everybody wants it. Enough of that—what are you up to?" I told him about the dinner, the job hunt, the hikes around the lake and fishing excursions with George, but not a word about my writing. I just didn't want to talk about it yet, not until I knew what it was, if anything. And if I wasn't ready to tell Carl I might or might not be writing a book, why would I tell Robyn? Still, a part of me was glad that she'd figured it out on her own.

Things were different between us now, very different. "Who *are* you?" she'd said. I could have asked her the same thing. It was as if we'd suddenly traded roles, Robyn becoming cautious and protective, me turning into someone who leaped before looking.

In the extreme, planning is less about organization than it is about staying in control. And if there was anything I'd learned in the last year and a half, it's that control is an illusion. I hadn't taken the decision to use my savings to make the renovations Martin demanded lightly. But the more I thought about it, the more I felt like it was the right choice. Was it? Time would tell.

I crumpled up my candy wrapper and took a plastic bag of fabric scraps from my purse.

My initial response when opening the box Adele had left for me wasn't very different from Robyn's. It really did look just like a lot of junk. But now I felt like everything in the box had been put there for a reason, including those cardboard hexagons used for English paper pieced quilts. There were hundreds of them, enough to make a whole quilt if I wanted to. But hand-stitching hexies is slow work, so I was thinking more about a wall hanging. Or maybe a beverage coaster.

Folding the little scraps over all five template edges and stitching them down was fiddly at first but got easier with practice. While I sewed, I started thinking about Yolanda's question, wondering when Adele first started quilting and who had taught her.

An entry in Adele's notebook suggested that the mint green quilt with the cream background and meandering curves may have been her first. The technique pointed to that as well. As Yolanda said, it looked like she'd had a lot of fun with it, but the curves weren't as smooth as they could have been and the construction not nearly as polished as her later pieces. The green quilt was pretty but when you compared it to the others, you could see Adele had had a learning curve, kind of like I was having with these first few hexies.

Why had she taken up quilting in the first place? And how had she developed her particular style, creating art quilts that were so unusual, especially for the 1940s? As I stitched, my needle dipping and pulling and dipping again, creating tidy, colorful patches, possible answers and explanations started to take shape in my mind. Just as I was about to reach for a pen and jot down some notes, the desk got really busy.

In a little over an hour, I answered a dozen calls; checked in three new arrivals; made change for two teenagers who wanted to try their luck on our ancient Pac-Man machine; sold three containers of worms, a postcard, and a box of Junior Mints; rented a boat to a couple who clearly knew nothing about boating; and gave directions to the café, the bathrooms, and Catawba Falls, sketching a map for a hiker. It was a little crazy. I kept glancing at the clock, calculating how long it might be until George returned. But it was also fun.

Every guest I dealt with was smiling. Without any prompting, several told me they were having a great time. Two made specific mention of the food at the café, one commented on the beautiful grounds, and one person, who was staying in one of the redecorated cabins, said that the accommodations were first rate. It was such an affirmation. The lodge's financial viability was still an open question, but in terms of guest satisfaction, we'd earned five stars. So, yes. I was feeling pretty good.

That is, until I looked up and saw Oscar standing in front of the desk.

He looked awful, like he hadn't slept in days. His shirt was wrinkled and sported coffee stains, his hair was unwashed and sticking up at weird angles, and there were bags the size of steamer trunks under his bloodshot eyes. Had it been anybody but Oscar, I'd have been concerned. For a second, I was.

Then he smacked a dollar on the counter and demanded to know where the hell I was hiding the PayDay bars, and I remembered that I couldn't stand him.

"What do you mean you're out?" he said when I informed him of the situation.

"I mean just that: we are out. The current supply of PayDay bars is zero."

"Looks like there was at least one until recently," he said, narrowing his eyes and scowling at the crumpled candy wrapper I'd left on the counter.

"That is true," I said, adopting the self-satisfied tone of an officious bureaucrat, enjoying the small power I had to deny him. "Until a few minutes ago, there was one PayDay bar. But I ate it. Now there are none. How about some M&Ms? We have plain and peanut."

"No!" he bellowed, pounding a fist on the counter. "It *has* to be a PayDay!"

His response was disproportionate. I mean, really. We were talking about a candy bar.

"Oh, come on, Oscar," I said, dropping my sarcastic tone. "There must be something else that'll work for you. Snickers? It's practically the same thing."

"You don't get it! I *just* finished my manuscript and sent it to my agent. And now I—"

I put up my hands. "Hang on. You *finished* the manuscript? How is that possible?"

"I'm a fast writer."

"Okay. But . . . four weeks?" I've known a lot of writers, some faster than others, but I'd never heard of anybody who could write a decent manuscript in a month. For a second, I honestly thought he was joking. I started to laugh, but Oscar just looked at me.

"That's . . . that's amazing," I said, recovering. "Were you always that fast?"

"No. But I figured it all out about ten years ago. Once you start, just power through and get it done," he said, making a fist and punching the air. "And I did. So now I need a PayDay."

Though this clearly made perfect sense to Oscar, I was still in the dark.

"What does a candy bar have to do with finishing your manuscript?"

Oscar gave me a glare that said his patience was running thin. I crossed my arms over my chest and glared right back, so he'd know I could do this all day.

"Fine," he said at last. "Not that it's any of your business, but thirty-seven years ago, I was living in Sag Harbor, hanging dry wall during the day and writing on a rented typewriter at night. The second I finished the manuscript for *Death Comes for Mr. Fox*, I went straight to the post office and sent the manuscript to DM Books. On the way home, I used the last fifty cents in my pocket to buy a PayDay."

"And DM bought your book," I said. "I remember *Death Comes for Mr. Fox*. Your debut novel, right? It was terrific." I paused, leaving space for him to say thank you, but he just stared at me with a sort of what-did-you-expect expression. "How long did it take you to write it?"

"Three years."

And now he wrote books in four weeks? In my mind, this explained an awful lot about the downward trajectory of his career, but Oscar obviously hadn't connected the dots.

"So now, you think about having a PayDay as soon as you send off your manuscript as a kind of . . . talisman?"

"Thirty-seven years, thirty-seven books, thirty-seven Pay-Days," he said smugly. "When you find a formula that works, don't mess with it."

I was tempted to ask when he'd started messing with the formula that involved actually investing the time required to write a really good book but thought better of that too. Why bother? It wasn't like he was listening. Oscar cast another withering glance at my candy wrapper and then at me, as if he suspected me of deliberate sabotage.

"So now I'll have to drive all the way to Asheville," he said petulantly. "For a *candy* bar."

"So it would seem. Drive safe," I chirped, waiting until Oscar stomped out the door to add, "Or, you could wait for George to come back from his candy run. He should be back any time."

Sure enough, ten minutes later, George walked through the door with a great big smile on his face and a great big box of candy in his arms, including three dozen PayDays. I turned over the desk duty and went to my cabin to write.

Detour

October 1942

I wasn't sure I liked quilting, not at first.

Miss Ida said that the sawtooth star blocks were easy. But when I finished my first and handed it off, she looked at my mismatched points and frowned, then flipped it over to examine the back and tsked her tongue in a way that belied her next sentence.

"Not too bad."

When I gave her a look that said I knew better, she amended her statement.

"For a beginner. I don't think you're ready to tackle a whole quilt yet, but you'll improve with practice," she said, then told me I was welcome to use her sewing machine whenever she wasn't and could help myself to the fabric scraps in her bin as well. After she left for her Wednesday quilt circle, I decided to take her up on the offer.

Every bedroom in the boardinghouse is full, so Miss Ida does her sewing in the attic. The ceilings are low in spots and I bumped my head into a rafter while fumbling around for the light switch. After pulling the string to illuminate the bulb, I sat down at Miss Ida's machine.

The trembling in my left hand gets worse if I'm pressured. Pausing to close my eyes and take some deep breaths definitely made a difference. But it didn't take long for me to realize that no amount of practice would turn me into someone who enjoys sewing stars with matching points, or any of the patterns Miss Ida draws so precisely with her pencil and ruler, making sure that each shape is perfectly even, perfectly placed, and perfectly predictable.

I backstitched a block, took it out from under the needle, and laid it aside, feeling disappointed. The fabrics were so colorful, pretty and promising, but stitching the same blocks other women have been sewing for the last hundred years was dull.

When I was in art school, some teachers would make us reproduce the paintings of other artists, grading the canvases according to how closely they matched those of the old masters. What was the point? I still don't know.

Don't misunderstand me; studying the work of other artists can be educational. In these last months, wandering the hallways of the mansion on the pretense of cataloging Mrs. Vanderbilt's already catalogued art collection, and slipping into the fortressed Music Room to gaze at the works of Stuart, Raphael, Rembrandt, Bellini, and Vermeer has been an education and an inspiration. Often, I'll skip dinner to paint, trying to draw on what I've seen in hope of creating something unique and original. Isn't that the purpose of art?

But my attempts always fall short. Many are spectacular failures. The harder I try, the more my hands shake. Maybe it's the war; there's so much to worry about. Every time we hear news of another battle, I can't help but think about the lives lost. When we sit around the radio in the evenings, listening to Edward R. Murrow's broadcasts, I look at George's face and know that he wishes he was in the fight. It's selfish, I know, but I'm grateful he's not.

Fabric is harder to come by these days, but Miss Ida managed to find two and a half yards of mint green cotton and offered to teach me to sew. I was excited, thinking that making a quilt might help take my mind off the war and reignite my creative spark. Quilting is a good *distraction—as I sit alone at her machine, the only thing I'm focused on is trying to make the seams match. Still, it doesn't seem very creative.*

But . . . what if?

I take a scrap of mint green from the bin, a long and somewhat narrow piece, cut it into thirds, then find three other scraps about the same size, a bright snowy white, a creamy vanilla, and a slightly yellowish scrap that looks like a piece of old parchment. I layer them into pairs, cutting gentle curves along the edges before stitching them.

An hour flies by before I know it, then two. My mind is free of worry as I sew and my hands are steady, I'm having such fun! Yes, sewing curves is more difficult than stitching straight edges. For one thing, there's the problem of making the pieces lie flat when you're done. But in spite of the lumps and bumps, when I am finished and examine what I've made, I like it much more than the best of the practice blocks I made from Miss Ida's pattern.

The colors make my tongue tingle with the flavors of clove, black pepper, and, strangely, rhubarb. That's a new combination for me, but I suddenly realize they're the flavors of discovery, that giddy, exciting, fearful sensation that comes over you in the moment between summiting the heights on a roller coaster and plummeting down the hill.

I don't know if my feelings are connected to the colors or simply to the joy of creating. I do know that it's possible for quilting to be creative, unique, and even artistic, and that, in time, I could end up being very good at it.

But only if I do it my way.

CHAPTER SEVENTEEN

When my alarm jangled at four the next morning, I smacked the snooze button and rolled over, repeating the cycle twice before finally crawling out from under the covers and trudging to the lodge to meet George for our fishing trip.

"You've heard the phrase 'ungodly hour'?" I asked him when I entered the lobby. "Four in the morning is what they're talking about."

"I'm always up by four," he replied. "Just after sunrise is the best time to catch fish. They're hungry and looking for breakfast."

George was right. But geneticists could probably make a lot of money by engineering breeds of fish with a more cosmopolitan mindset, fish who liked to linger in bed on weekends, perusing the book and style sections of the *Times*, and preferred brunch to breakfast.

"So," I said, stifling a yawn, "should we drive to Dillsboro or try our stream?"

Scott Creek wasn't really ours but George and I had always called it that because it was the nearest good trout stream to the lodge. But getting to the "secret spot" George had discovered years before required a hike that I wasn't sure he'd be up for.

"Uh . . . yeah. About the fishing," George said, looking suddenly sheepish. "I don't think I'll be able to come. My stomach's bothering me. Nothing terrible but I think I'd better stay home."

"What? Why didn't you call and let me know?"

"Well, just because I'm not going fishing is no reason you can't."

"George, I am not going fishing by myself," I said, a whining edge creeping into my voice when I thought about the sleep I'd missed for no good reason.

"Oh, you won't be alone. I wouldn't do that to you," George said, chuckling. "I invited Dawes. You kids just go along and enjoy yourselves. Don't worry about me, I'll be fine."

"Me and Dawes? George, noooo," I said, transitioning from whiny edge to full-blown whinge. "He's going to think you're trying to set us up. And do you know why? Because you are!"

"I'm not trying to set you up with Dawes," he said with unconvincing innocence. "Come on now, Baby Sister. It'll be fun! Tell you what—I'll lend you my lucky fishing hat."

He pulled the favorite of all his hats from his head, a battered bucket hat with a dark brown band and three caddis fly lures stuck in the crown. I waved it away.

"This is *not* going to be fun and I don't want your hat! Why did you—"

Before I could finish, George jerked his head up and waved an arm over his head.

"Good morning to you, sir! You're right on time. Ready for some fishing?"

I turned around. "Hey, Dawes."

"Hey, Esme." He yawned, then looked at George. "So. Are we ready?"

THE PROBLEM WITH people trying to fix up other people is that most of them are so bad at it, don't you think?

I'd been rehearsing that sentence in my head for twenty silent miles. Because if I just came out and said what both of us were thinking, and then laughed, that would make things less awkward, wouldn't it? Unless, of course, Dawes had *no* idea that George was playing matchmaker. In which case, drawing attention to the situation could only make things worse.

The problem with Dawes was that I could never tell what he was thinking.

If he'd been less inscrutable, or if I'd been braver, I might have risked it. As it was, I took another bite of a blueberry muffin that Dawes had brought and said, "These are good."

He yawned. "Thanks. They were left over from yesterday. How much farther?"

The Toaster wasn't built for gravel roads, so Dawes had volunteered to drive his van, which was less rough and ready than I'd imagined. There was a platform bed in the far back with two short, squat benches in front of it and a flip-up dining table between them. There was a small closet and storage area on one side, and a kitchen with a refrigerator, two-burner stove, and open wooden cubes holding baskets of cookware and food on the other. The walls were light gray wood paneling and the counters were white. Everything looked light and bright and tidy, without an inch of wasted space. Dawes had designed the layout and done the conversion himself.

I swallowed my muffin. "Should be a pullout pretty soon. We'll park and walk."

"How far?"

"About a mile."

Dawes shot me a doubtful look. "Kind of a long way to go fishing, especially since we started out at a perfectly good lake stocked with perfectly good fish."

"Fly-fishing in a stream is a whole different animal," I said. "It'll be worth it, trust me. If we get to the end of the trip and you tell me I was wrong, then I'll . . ." I bit my lip, trying to think of something he might enjoy. "I'll bake you a cake."

"Caramel? Because that's my favorite."

"Yeah? Good thing because that's the one I know how to make."

I smiled. Maybe this day wouldn't be as awful as I'd thought.

THE TRAIL WAS more of a deer path. If you didn't know where you were going it would be easy to get lost, and I'll admit that I took us off track once or twice. But Dawes followed along gamely, trekking through the underbrush and climbing over logs without complaint. In fact, he didn't speak at all. In the car, his silence had felt awkward. Now, I was grateful for it.

When encountering something that inspires genuine awe, the only authentic response is silence. And the woods, the mountains, the sun shafting through the treetops truly was awesome. I don't know if Dawes felt the same or if he was just too involved with hauling his backpack and gear through the woods to waste energy on words. Either way, I appreciated it.

Alex had hated the outdoors, *hated* it. First there was the disastrous fishing trip when he hooked his own cheek, then that hike in the Hudson River Valley. He pretended to enjoy it, but it was obvious that he didn't. And he talked the *entire* time, which ruined it for me. After that, our encounters with nature were limited to strolls in Central Park. Nice but not the same.

About the time I figured Dawes had to be wondering if I'd gotten us lost, I heard the sound of rushing water. The trees thinned out and we stood on the pebble-strewn bank of a wide stream that gurgled over rocks and through twisted tangles of branches. The water was so clear you could see the colors of the stones scattered along the streambed—amber, and charcoal, and sandy gray. Dawes dropped his backpack on the bank, next to the rod and waders that George had loaned him, and stood there for a long moment, taking it all in—the music of water and birdsong, the scent of pine, the kiss of the morning sun on his face—before finally saying, "Wow," which was really the only thing *to* say.

He got it. That made me happy.

I pulled out a tackle box and gave Dawes a short lesson on fly-fishing, explaining the different types of flies and how they're made to resemble insects that fish feed on. Then we assembled our rods and I talked him through the rigging procedure, showing him how to feed the tippet and line through the guides and how to secure his fly with a simple clinch knot.

Most men chafe under the instruction of a woman, especially when the curriculum centers on skills traditionally considered to be within the masculine domain. Dawes was the exception to the rule. Instead of blowing me off or dismissing me halfway through the demonstration with an "Okay, I've got it," he listened attentively, accepted instruction, and asked questions when he needed clarification. In short, he treated me with respect. It was nice.

Once the rods were rigged, I showed him how to cast.

"Start with the tip pointing down, hover it low above the

water. Keep your grip firm but relaxed. The movement should come from your forearm. Bring the rod behind you with a quick, smooth motion, pause just for a moment so the line can unfurl, then flick the rod forward so the line sails out over the water and your fly drops in where you intended it to go," I said, delivering the same speech George had given me the first time he'd taken me fly-fishing.

It sounds easy but it's not. It took me years of practice before I was able to duplicate the graceful, balletic arc of the line that George achieved with every cast. Even though I'd been fishing with George twice this summer, my cast was still a little rusty. But after a few minutes of practice on the bank, my rhythm returned, and Dawes was doing well enough that I thought it was time to do some actual fishing.

Of course, you can fly-fish in a lake. But fishing in the middle of a river is so exhilarating. Even though I was wearing my felt-soled boots, the rocks felt slippery as I waded into the stream, and keeping my balance wasn't easy. Until I got in past my knees, it felt like the rushing water was trying to knock me down at every step. But then the pressure of the current dissipated and I regained my center of gravity, moving confidently through the water.

For over an hour, we waded up and down the stream, casting our lines into spots near rocks or branches with calmer, deeper water, where fish might hang out and rest. We saw several trout swimming beneath the surface, as well as countless birds, chattering squirrels, and a mother deer with twin fawns. When I waved at Dawes to get his attention, then pointed silently to the little family, he let his line go slack and watched until they retreated into the safety of the trees, a huge grin on his face.

It was a beautiful morning, so pretty and peaceful that I don't think either of us cared that we weren't getting any bites.

But then, just as I was thinking it might be time to head back, Dawes got a hard tug on his line. He whooped and jerked his rod upward. I whooped too, crashing through the current with big, clumsy strides to reach his side.

"That's it! You've got it! Reel him in! Don't let the tip drop, keep it up high!"

I doubt Dawes even heard me, but his instincts were good. He reeled as fast as he could, keeping the line high and tight, moving the fish unwillingly closer. Spotting a flash of silver, I pulled my net from my belt and dipped it into the water, scooping up the fish.

"Nice job!" I said, handing the net to Dawes.

"Whoa!" He bent down for a closer look. "He's a beauty. Brown trout?"

"Rainbow," I said. "About fourteen inches. Do you want to keep him? Or release him?"

After I snapped a quick picture of Dawes holding the trout, he released the fish and picked up his rod, eager to try again. Over the next hour, I caught and released three more beautiful rainbow trout. Dawes caught two, releasing the first and keeping the last.

We waded upstream to the place where we'd left our backpacks. I wriggled out of my waders and put on my hiking boots and then headed off into the woods to relieve myself. By the time I returned, Dawes had built a fire and was squatting down next to it, pushing a chunk of butter around a skillet with the blade of a Swiss Army knife.

"Well, aren't you the well-prepared scout," I said, sitting

on a nearby rock and stretching my hands out toward the fire. Dawes pulled a lemon, two forks, and several paper packets of salt and pepper out of his jacket pocket. "Hungry?" he asked.

That trout, fried in butter over an open fire, served with a squeeze of fresh lemon, and eaten straight out of the pan, was better than any fish I'd ever had in any fifty-dollar-a-plate restaurant in New York.

"The atmosphere's hard to beat too," Dawes said, lifting his head and looking out toward the stream, before picking up a stick and poking at the fire, stirring up red embers.

"What is it about boys and fires? Every man I've ever known was a pyromaniac."

"Not me," Dawes said, drawing his brows together and nodding toward the blaze. "About seven years ago, I had a restaurant in Northern California, in an old 1930s gas station out in Humboldt County. Somebody had turned it into a donut shop years before, so there were a few tables and the start of a commercial kitchen. It needed a lot of work but the price was right so"—he shrugged—"I bought it, remodeled it, and named it the Black Dog Diner.

"That first year was rough," he said, kicking a smoldering branch toward the center of the fire with the toe of his hiking boot. "But I was very popular with the staff at the homeless shelter. I'd bring them all the meals I hadn't sold, which was a *lot*. As it turned out, that was the thing that saved me—for a while.

"The director of the shelter called the local paper and told them about me. A reporter came out, took a bunch of pictures of the restaurant and of me, cooking and loading my car with food for the shelter. Suddenly, people started showing up. Eight months later, for the first time, I turned a profit—one hundred and fourteen dollars and sixty-eight cents."

"Wow," I said. "You're quite the tycoon."

"I know, right?"

He picked up a stick and started poking at the fire again. I watched him, resisting the urge to say, "And then?" partly because I knew he'd get there in his own time but also because a part of me wanted the story to end right there, on a note of hope, freezing his future at that moment when his dream came true.

"There was a fire," he said, lowering his gaze again.

"In the kitchen?"

"No. I mean . . . yes. It started in the kitchen but . . ." His voice trailed off. "No one was hurt. When I opened the door and smelled smoke, I ran inside and grabbed the fire extinguisher but it was a lost cause. By the time I turned around, a wall of flame was blocking my exit. Luckily, I was able to climb out a window, but the building was a total loss."

"That's terrible. Did you have insurance?"

"Not enough," he said. "I used what there was to pay off my debts, buy the van, and convert it for full-time living. At that point, traveling light and not planning too far ahead seemed like a smarter way to live."

"Dawes, I'm so sorry."

"Don't be. No, really," he said, countering the doubt in my eyes. "It could have been a lot worse. I'm not looking for sympathy. But I wanted you to know my story because when I delivered your dinner to the cabin that first time we met, I was kind of a jerk to you. The truth is, I was scared. I thought the cabin was on fire and so I kind of . . . reacted."

I pressed my lips together, so stunned by his admission, and his bravery, that I was momentarily at a loss for words. In spite of all he'd been through, he ran through my door anyway, and even stuck his hand into the flames, pushing aside his fear to rescue a stranger.

"Dawes, you are a good human."

He barked out a laugh. "Or a dumb one. That's twice I've run toward a fire instead of away from it. Anyway, I'm sorry," he said, and started gathering his stuff, putting the dirty pan in a paper bag before placing it in the backpack along with his knife, then getting to his feet. I stood up too, and put on my backpack.

"Nothing to be sorry about. You fixed my car the next day, so believe me, all was forgiven. Plus, George is crazy about you and—"

Just before blurting out that I was crazy about him too, or thought I might be, I did something fairly uncharacteristic: I stopped to think.

Six weeks had passed since Dawes had pushed past me and run into the cabin. It wasn't like we'd seen each other on a daily basis, but if he had any feelings for me, he'd surely have mentioned it by now. We'd baked an entire cake together, for heaven's sake! And fed a crowd of four hundred. If that didn't foster intimacy, what would?

So why hadn't it?

I wasn't deceiving myself about who Dawes was, the way I had with Alex. I was sure of it. So, it had to be me, didn't it? Mutual attraction ought to be the simplest thing in the world. I mean, biological forces were at work here. Unless, of course, they weren't?

There was only one way to find out. I proceeded with caution, pumping the brakes on any potentially embarrassing declarations but leaving the door open in case Dawes felt like making one of his own.

"You've been such an incredible help, first the dinner and now the wedding. The lodge wouldn't stand a chance without you. And I just want you to know that I . . ." My eyes fluttered closed briefly. "I really appreciate all your hard work. We all do."

"It's been fun," he said, ducking his head. "I mean that. And you've worked hard too, Esme. I can't believe what you've accomplished in such a short time." He paused, as if weighing his words. "What I'm trying to say is, I think we'd make a pretty good team."

He did? Hearing him say it out loud made my heart leap. But I clamped my lips closed, determined to stay silent until I was sure he was saying what I thought he was saying.

This turned out to be a wise move.

"I know you're putting your own money into renovating the lodge for the wedding. So, I was wondering if I could do the same thing." The blank, possibly stunned look on my face must have told him that I wasn't tracking. "You know," he prompted, "come in as your business partner?"

An icy splash of romance-killing reality was accompanied by a dropping roller-coaster sensation that left me feeling off balance and hugely disappointed, as well as hugely grateful that I'd kept my mouth shut. After all, there's only so much humiliation a person can endure in a given calendar year before they spontaneously combust. You've heard the phrase "I thought I'd die from embarrassment"? I'm convinced that's an actual thing.

"Um . . ." I licked my lips and bobbed my head a couple of times, trying to shake off my disappointment and focus on the issue at hand. "So . . . you're saying you want to invest some money to help with the renovations. And become a partner in the lodge?"

"A minority partner. Five percent, two, one. You and George can decide what's fair."

"Okay, but . . . do you actually have any money?"

I didn't want to be rude but the reason he'd ended up working for George in the first place was because he'd been too broke to buy a new engine.

"I can raise it," Dawes said, lifting a hand as if to assure me of his honesty. "Somebody offered me fifty-five for the van, but I didn't want to sell until we talked. I'd keep some of the money to buy a used car and invest forty thousand in the lodge."

"You'd sell your van? I thought you were one of those guys who doesn't like getting tied down to one place?"

"I was," he admitted. "For a whole bunch of reasons that are . . . well, too complicated to explain. When people hear I've been living in a van and traveling from place to place for years, they always ask when I plan to settle down. My stock answer is 'when I find something that makes me want to.' It's my way of telling them to mind their own business.

"But something changed for me this summer. I've finally stumbled upon a place that feels like home, work I feel proud of, and people—" He smiled and shook his head, almost as if he was laughing at himself. "People I can't stop myself from caring about. So, if it's okay with you, I'd like to stay."

The roller coaster surged again, climbing toward the pinnacle of the hopes I'd begun to believe had passed me by, and I said the only thing I could say.

"I'd like that too."

Dawes took a step toward me. The strains of an old, old song played in my head, a crooner who's grateful that after so much time, so much loneliness, love has come along at last.

I closed my eyes, waiting for his kiss.

CHAPTER EIGHTEEN

The second I'd gotten back to the lodge, I called Yolanda to see if she and David wanted to meet me for dinner that evening. Sometimes, friendships between formerly close girlfriends fade after one of them marries and the other feels crowded out of the relationship by the new, often unlikable, and sometimes overly possessive husband. But I didn't feel that way about David. I think we could have been friends even without the Yolanda connection. He was a kind and genuinely interesting man, as well as a fount of historical knowledge.

Thanks to David, I'd been able to confirm Adele's connection with both Biltmore and the National Gallery. He'd taken on a consulting project for the estate, documenting the history of the gardens. This granted him access to all kinds of historical documents, including some of Edith Vanderbilt's letters. Among them, he found a letter from David Finley to Mrs. Vanderbilt, dated December 8, 1941. It contained an oblique reference to "the packages" scheduled to arrive on January 12, the same date the artwork was delivered to Biltmore. Mr. Finley also wrote that Miss Adele Maslow, the gallery employee he'd recommended, was taking a "leave of absence" and would arrive in Asheville the following week to begin cataloging Biltmore's art collection.

Though David wasn't permitted to show me the actual letter, when he told me about the contents, the hair along my arms stood up straight. I mean, what were the odds? My dear friend just happened to be married to one of the only people who was in a position to provide factual confirmation of events that I shouldn't have known about but somehow did.

Could it have been a coincidence? Possibly. But I honestly couldn't see how.

David had a faculty party that evening and couldn't join us for dinner. But he insisted that Yolanda go and suggested we make a reservation at S&W Steak and Wine, a downtown restaurant housed in a 1920s art deco building that was listed on the National Register of Historic Places and had once been home to the S&W Cafeteria. Growing up near Asheville, of course I'd seen it but had never been inside. "You really should go," David advised. "If George and Adele were dating during the war, they'd definitely have gone there."

The building was beautiful, so perfectly preserved that it was like stepping back in time. Yolanda and I followed the hostess into a hall with a soaring, gold leaf ceiling, our footsteps echoing as we crossed the green and gray checkerboard floor to a booth near the back.

"See any ghosts?" Yolanda asked, giving me a sidelong glance. "I mean, any that seem familiar?" I rolled my eyes, then sat down and ordered a bottle of Merlot, launching into the story of my fishing excursion as soon as it arrived. When I got to the part about where Dawes stepped close and I closed my eyes, Yolanda interrupted, pressing her hand to her heart.

"Aww . . . I'm so happy for you, Ez. You deserve someone

nice, you really do. And Dawes seems better than nice." She impaled a cherry tomato, then tossed back a generous slurp of wine. "So? Then what happened? I need details here, the juicier the better."

I picked up my wineglass. "What happened next was nothing. Absolutely nothing."

"What?" Yolanda gasped. "That's not possible. He was just about to kiss you!"

"Yeah, well . . . I thought so too. But then he didn't. I stood there with my eyes closed, waiting . . ." I took another drink, shuddering with embarrassment as I thought about how idiotic I must have looked. "And nothing happened. I opened my eyes and he was just looking at me. His lips were inches from mine, but then he frowned, said, 'I'm sorry, I can't,' and backed away."

"Wow," Yolanda said, sounding disappointed. "That's . . . that's awful. What did you do?"

"What *could* I do? I pretended to laugh it off, said something about it being okay because it was probably a dumb way to start a business relationship. Then we hiked back to the car and made painfully awkward small talk during the drive home. That's it."

"You didn't fire him?"

"Fire him? For what?"

"Well, I don't know," Yolanda said, clucking her tongue. "Harassment?"

"Yeah, except he *didn't* harass me. You can't fire somebody for just not being that into you. Even if you could, where would I find another chef?"

"So you mean . . . Dawes will just keep working for you? Like nothing happened?"

"No," I said, draining my glass. "Dawes will be working *with* us, as a partner. We're giving him a five percent stake in the lodge and an equal claim on the profits, assuming there ever are any. I talked it over with George and Robyn; it's all settled."

"You're kidding. Even after you told them about the kiss?" Her eyelids fluttered closed briefly as she corrected herself. "I mean . . . the not-kiss?"

"I didn't tell them about that. Why would I?" I refilled my glass. Forget George and Robyn, at this point, I was beginning to regret telling Yolanda.

"What else could I do? Yes, the whole not-kiss thing was embarrassing. But the rest of it is actually *good* news," I said in a voice that sounded like I was trying to convince us both. "From day one, my biggest concern about Dawes was that one morning we'd wake up to find that he'd packed up his stuff and disappeared. If we're serious about doing weddings and banquets, we can't afford to lose him. Now that he's got a stake in the business, I *know* he'll stay. If rejection with a side of humiliation is the price I have to pay for peace of mind, so be it."

Yolanda sighed heavily. "Well . . . you deserve better, Esme."

Did I? Sometimes I wondered. Maybe some people just don't have soulmates, maybe some people are better off on their own. Besides, it wasn't like I was completely alone. I had George, and Robyn. Nobody would be nominating her for mother of the year anytime soon but it was kind of sweet, the way she'd fussed about me putting my savings into rescuing the lodge. And now Yolanda was back in my life. And when I returned to New York, I'd have Carl, and . . . well, really just Carl. Alex was out of the picture, obviously. And none of my old friends from DM had been in touch since I'd left. But once I found work, I'd make new friends. Better friends.

"So, listen," Yolanda said in a sort of "next item on the agenda" voice as she topped up her glass. "David has a friend at the college, Ryan Chrysanthemum—"

"Ryan Chrysanthemum?" I snorted and took a drink. "Please, *please* tell me he's a botany professor."

"Actually, he is."

I swallowed as fast as I could to keep from spitting out my wine but didn't quite make it. When I started laughing, Yolanda grinned and rolled her eyes.

"I know, I know. But he really is the *nicest* man, and smart. Reads books, appreciates art, loves to travel. I know you'd like him if you met him. Esme, stop. Will you grow up? It's just a name," she protested before giving in to giggles herself. "He's a great guy! And cute. And kind of famous, wrote a ground-breaking paper on ginkgo biloba that was published in *Botany Today*."

"Wow! And just think! If we got married, I'd be Esmerelda Chrysanthemum!"

Yolanda's eyes went wide as she slurped more wine and considered the possibilities.

"*And* you could give all your kids botanical first names— Peony, Aster, Daisy—"

"Yucca!" I exclaimed, pounding the table. "Wait! Wait! Wait! How about Quackgrass?"

"Stinkweed!" Yolanda howled, totally losing it.

Turns out that there are tons of botanical names out there and that a lot of them are hysterical, so things went on like this for quite some time.

"Thanks," I said finally, gulping air and swiping away tears. "I needed that."

"You're welcome. But . . . I really do think you'd like Ryan."

"Maybe I would. But even if I did, what would be the point? Long-distance relationships never work out. I'm going back to New York at the end of the summer."

Yolanda made a pleading, pathetic face. "Are you *sure*?"

I was, very. Yes, there'd been moments when I'd toyed with the idea of staying. But toying was all it amounted to. Though my career was momentarily sidelined, my life was in New York. If I'd ever had doubts, that silly scene with Dawes had put them to rest.

But I was glad I'd come home. In addition to reconnecting with my family, and Yolanda, there was satisfaction in knowing that—assuming the wedding came off well, and with Dawes now truly on board I saw no reason it shouldn't—I was helping to preserve a vital piece of my family's legacy, as well as my grandmother's story.

The more I wrote, the more I was discovering my story in Adele's, themes that felt familiar and rang true. She was driven like me, had dreams not so different from mine, ran up against one obstacle after another in her quest to fulfill them. Though I would never truly understand why she'd chosen to keep her history hidden during her lifetime, and found it inexplicably sad that she'd chosen to hide her talent away, I knew that Adele wasn't sad and never had been. In spite of everything, she'd found her way, a happiness that added to the happiness of so many others, including mine. Knowing that gave me hope, helped me believe I'd find my way too, eventually.

Had that been her intention all along? Was that why she'd called when she did, because she sensed that time was short and knew I needed to hear what she had to say? Was that why a part of her seemed to be lingering still, pointing to the bread crumbs she'd left for me to find?

If such a thing were possible, if Adele had the ability to breathe upon the veil that separates the temporal from the eternal, fluttering the shadows of time to help the people she held dear, I know she would have. My early life had been rocky, but from the moment I came through her door, carrying everything I owned in a pillowcase, carrying scars, and Adele bent down and said, "Esme, I'm so glad you're here. I've got a caramel cake in the kitchen. Would you like a slice?" I knew that I was home, and loved. Though I would never stop missing her, I knew that a piece of her would always be with me, even after I returned to New York to pick up the threads of my unraveled dreams and find *my* way, *my* happiness.

"I'll be back to visit all the time," I said, knowing it was true.

"You'd better," Yolanda replied, scowling a little. "Because not only do I crochet voodoo monsters, I know how to use them."

"Believe me, I'm not that easy to get rid of. You're stuck with me for life now."

"Well," she said hoarsely, lifting her glass, "I think I can live with that."

If I'd trusted my voice, I'd have echoed the sentiment. Instead, I touched the rim of my glass to Yolanda's, sealing the deal.

Yolanda had to meet David at the college, so I told her I'd pay the bill and we'd settle up later. I sat at the table alone, waiting for the server to bring the check. The restaurant wasn't crowded, only five or six tables were occupied. When I looked across the room, I noticed a couple at a table next to one of the enormous columns.

Even sitting down, I could tell that the man was tall. He had ginger-blond hair and was eating a slice of egg custard pie, an item I hadn't seen listed on the menu. The petite woman sitting opposite him had her back partially turned, so I couldn't see her face. But she wore a Sunday-best suit of powder blue. When she picked up her water glass, her hands trembled so that I thought it might spill.

"There's no rush but if you'd like I can take care—Oh, I'm so sorry!" the server exclaimed when I gasped. "I didn't mean to startle you!"

I told her it was all right, that I just hadn't seen her standing there.

"I get like that too," she confided. "Sometimes I start thinking about something and it's like everything else disappears. My husband will ask me a question and I don't even hear him. I'm just lost in my own little world."

She smiled and went off to run my credit card.

When I looked across the room again, the table next to the column was unoccupied.

CHAPTER NINETEEN

$\mathcal{G}$eorge was lying on the bathroom floor on his back with his head stuck under the vanity, fiddling with tools and water supply lines prior to removing the old faucet and installing a new one. Judging from his frustrated muttering, it wasn't going very well.

Just as I was thinking about putting the shower curtain I was hanging aside and going to see if I could help, water began to gush and George started cussing.

It wasn't that big a deal, the gush was really more of a whoosh that ended as quickly as it began and left an easily mopped-up puddle on the floor, but George was furious. He let out a yowl, unleased a string of expletives, and whacked his forehead on the vanity when he got up, then flung his wrench across the room as hard as he could, coming inches from hitting me and leaving a dent in the wallboard above the toilet.

"George!" I exclaimed. "It's nothing! Just a little water and a stupid faucet."

"It's not the faucet that's stupid!" he cried, slashing the air with one arm, as if he wished he had another tool to hurl, then covered his eyes with one big hand. "It's me! *I'm* stupid! And useless, completely useless."

I closed my eyes and took a deep breath.

All the cabins had to be redecorated before Sutton and Martin's wedding, just four weeks from now. But with the summer season in full swing and our occupancy rates up, we had to juggle reservations and sandwich the work between guests, completing each renovation in a single day. Robyn was taking care of logistics as well as her regular work, so the actual remodeling fell to George and me. It wasn't easy but we were managing, or had been until now.

Two days before, we'd completely redone cabin twelve, replacing the mattresses, bedding, rugs, and curtains, hanging new pictures, painting the bathroom, installing towel bars, shower rods, and faucets, finishing in one busy, long day. I couldn't have done it alone; George was a huge help. But today he couldn't handle a task he'd had no trouble tackling before.

I blamed myself. As soon as we started, I realized this wasn't one of George's good days. He was grumpy and looked tired, and had trouble finding words, for example, pointing to an object and saying "that thingy" instead of using the correct name. I should have invented some reason that he was needed at the front desk; interacting with guests was the job he enjoyed most and continued to do well. But I didn't know how to install the faucets, so I just hung in there and hoped for the best. Bad idea.

"George," I said softly, coming to stand next to him. "It's okay. Really."

I gently pulled his hand from his face. George looked at me with wet eyes.

"It's not. *Nothing* about this is okay. I hate what's happening to me."

"You're just tired. There's so much going on, first the dinner, now this wedding, all the renovations . . . We just pushed too hard the other day, that's all. Tomorrow will be better, you'll see. You're not a spring chicken anymore, you know."

"Spring chicken? Hell," he said, a hint of a smile tugging at his mouth, "at this point, I'm not even an autumn turkey. But maybe you're right. Maybe tomorrow will be better."

I hoped so. But even if it was, I knew there would be other days like this one, days when George was not better. And possibly worse. Robyn didn't want to talk about it and still wouldn't use the d-word. But after today, there was no denying that George knew.

I hate what's happening to me.

I hated it too. But it was what it was.

Though he'd balked a bit when he found out I was fronting some of the costs, George was excited about restoring the lodge to its former glory and wanted to be a part of making it happen. And I wanted that too but needed to be careful not to overtax him going forward.

After convincing George to go home and take a nap, I went looking for Dawes.

"Sorry to bug you on your day off," I said after knocking on his cabin door and explaining the situation. "We can't afford to fall behind schedule and I've got no clue about faucets."

"No worries," he said, yawning and reaching for a shirt. "Lemme get dressed and get my tools. I'll be right down."

In the wake of the whole "not-kiss" weirdness, I'd worried that having Dawes as a business partner, albeit it a minor one, would make our relationship even more awkward, but it turned out to be just the opposite. Not only did focusing our attention on the wedding, the renovations, and other business matters help sweep the remaining weirdness under the rug, it helped me get over him, and myself. The sight of a shirtless, boxer-clad, bed-headed Dawes did nothing for me now. My lizard brain was either dead or hibernating. It was a relief. As I had told Yolanda, my life was complicated enough without adding a soon-to-be-long-distance relationship to the mess.

Besides eliminating the tension between us, letting Dawes have a stake in the lodge reduced the pressure I'd been feeling. Knowing he was in it for the long haul helped me sleep better at night. Also, his financial contribution meant I didn't have to sink *all* of my savings into the renovations. And having someone on board who knew things I didn't—like how to install plumbing fixtures and cook beef medallions for three hundred—was a major stress reducer.

"Once you close the shutoff valve," Dawes said as we stood in the bathroom a few minutes later, "just make sure to open the faucet and release any water that might still be in the lines before you remove the fixture. I think that's where George made his mistake."

"Okay," I said. "Seems simple enough."

It really did. Which made the fact that George had struggled all the more disturbing.

"I don't mind helping," Dawes said. "But it's good for you to know how to do it yourself, in case you run into problems on a day when the café's too slammed for me to give you a hand."

I nodded. With word of our new chef spreading, there definitely were days when Dawes was too busy to leave the kitchen.

"Well, I'm sorry I had to bother you. I know this is the only day you can sleep in."

"Don't worry about it. There won't be any days off for a while, not until the wedding is over and we've cashed Martin's check," he said, pulling a wrench from his tool belt and squatting down in front of the vanity. "If you need help, just ask. I'll be here as quick as I can."

WORKING TOGETHER, DAWES and I were able to finish the redecorating but, once again, it had been a very busy and very long day, with the promise of many more to come. Until the wedding was over, I'd barely have a minute to call my own. Maybe that was just as well because, once again, my writing had hit a roadblock.

After meeting Yolanda at the S&W and seeing the woman in blue with the trembling hands, I hurried back and sat down at the computer, eager to ride the wave of inspiration I felt certain would come. But nothing happened. I hadn't written anything worthwhile in a week and that night was just more of the same. After saying good night to Dawes around ten, I went back to my cabin and tried to write, only to delete it all a couple of hours later. After giving up and going to bed, I had a dream about George.

He was doing construction in the lobby, trying to build a wall. When it was almost finished, he picked up a hammer and slammed it into the wall over and over again, destroying all his hard work. It wasn't until I woke up, gasping and with my heart racing, that I realized the hammering was actually someone banging on my door. I thought it had to be Robyn. Who else would bother me at that hour? Worried that something had happened to George, I threw on a robe and stumbled to the door. Oscar was standing there, holding a big stack of papers tied together with string.

"Oscar?"

I blinked to bring him into focus. He pushed past me without waiting for an invitation.

"I need to talk to you."

He plunked the papers down onto the kitchen table, then strode into the living room and started pacing back and forth in front of the fireplace, rubbing his hands together, like he was trying to grind grain between his palms. I was a little more awake by that time, but still confused about what was going on.

"Oscar, what are you doing here? What happened?"

"It's Claudia," he said, still pacing.

Claudia. Who was Claudia? Another ex-wife? An old girlfriend? A pet? I had nothing. Oscar, perturbed by my cluelessness, fixed me with frantic eyes.

"Claudia! My agent!" He shoved both hands into his gray mane and scrubbed at his scalp until the hair was standing on end. "She hates my book. Hates it!"

"Wait. What?" I shook myself awake. "You woke me up because your agent doesn't like your book? Are you *kidding* me?"

Glowering, I opened the door and pointed, literally showing him the way out.

"No, no, no. You don't understand," he said in a panicked voice. "This is more than not liking it. She *hates* it. She hates *me*!"

At that moment, I had no trouble believing this.

"Oscar, I don't care. You've got to leave. I'm not kidding."

He ignored me.

"She fired me, Esme. After twenty-two years together, Claudia *fired* me! She said I'm an arrogant, egocentric, ungrateful, misogynistic prima donna—"

Again, totally believable. If asked to describe Oscar, I would have used all those adjectives and a few more. But . . . was that a reason for an agent to fire a long-term client? I mean, it wasn't like Oscar was the only arrogant prima donna writer on the face of the earth.

"—and she said that the book was absolute crap, that there was no way to salvage it, and that whatever talent I'd once had had disappeared."

"Seriously? She said that?"

I closed the door, frowning. Some writers, like Oscar, are crazy-making pains in the butt. But editors and agents and publishers put up with them because, at the end of the day, talent trumps everything. If Oscar's agent had decided he no longer had any, his panic was starting to make sense.

"You've *got* to help me," he said, shoving his fingers into his hair again and resuming his pacing. "You've got to read my manuscript."

I laughed. He had to be joking. Except he didn't seem to be.

"Oscar, that's crazy. You think if I like your book, then your agent will decide to take you back? Why would she listen to me? I'm not your editor. I'm not *anybody's* editor anymore."

Oscar spun around, fixing me with a piercing blue stare.

"But you could be. Look, I know our initial meeting in New York was . . . well, less than ideal. But, believe it or not, a part of me was actually excited about the prospect of working with you. I mean it!" he exclaimed, raising a hand and holding it flat when I rolled my eyes. "I was just nervous, that's all!

"More and more, Darius just signed off on my manuscripts without giving me any real feedback. I knew I needed a change, an editor who was willing to do the job, push me harder, help me write books that are actually worth reading. But, at the same time, I was scared. Darius was my editor for thirty years; I'd never worked with anybody else. Then, on top of everything else, Matilda decided to dump me and . . ." Oscar spread out his hands in a sort of you-know-the-rest gesture.

Oh, yes. I knew. How could I ever forget?

But a lot of what he was saying rang true. More than one of my colleagues at DM had said they thought that Oscar had started "phoning it in," which is another way of saying he'd stopped giving a damn. But I'd often wondered if Darius wasn't at least partially at fault. Writers aren't the only ones who sometimes phone it in. I couldn't shake the sense that if somebody had pushed Oscar to polish his initial drafts with a second, third, or even fourth round of revisions, the brilliance of the story might have come through.

Still, the way Oscar talked to me that day, belittling me in front of my colleagues, wasn't something I could easily forget, or forgive.

"If you were so excited about working with me, why did you disrespect me in front of every editor at DM? Why did you barge into Matt's office and try to get me fired?"

Oscar threw out his hands. "Because I'm an ass, that's why! Because I'm a deeply insecure but talented ass! Or I was. Maybe Claudia's right about me," he said in a pathetic voice. "Maybe now I'm *just* an ass, an insecure, obnoxious, talentless has-been."

He sunk into a nearby chair and buried his head in his hands, a picture of defeat.

"Oscar, go home."

He didn't budge, just swayed back and forth like a keening widow. Was this an act? Or was he actually crying? I didn't care. I didn't *want* to care.

"I'm not kidding, Oscar. You have to leave."

"Esme, you've got to help me," he moaned. "I'm dying here!"

"You are not *dying*. You've lost your agent. It's not the same thing as losing your life."

"It is for me. Writing isn't just what I do, it's who I am."

When he stood up, his eyes were clear and perfectly dry. It *had* been an act. The jerk!

"Well, it's not who you are anymore," I snapped. "And do you know whose fault that is? Yours! You're arrogant, and obnoxious, and rude, but do you know what your real problem is, Oscar? You're lazy. You have a gift and you've wasted it. And *that* is unforgivable."

"People can change," he said urgently. "*I* can change. Esme, you've got to help me!"

When he grabbed my sleeve, clutching like a penitent desperate for absolution, I pulled away and let out a laugh. "Let's get something straight, *Mister* Glazier," I said, spitting out the honorific as if it were a curse. "Of all the things I don't have to do, helping you tops the list."

"Fair enough," he said, opening his hands, his tone even and more believable than before. "I mean, why should you help me? You barely know me. But I know something about you, Esme Cahill. You love books. And you have a talent for helping writers transform good ideas and mediocre manuscripts into something memorable, and magical, and fine, a book that's worth reading. That's *your* gift.

"You don't like me?" He shrugged. "Okay. I respect you for it; proves you have some standards. But let me ask you something: On that day in New York, when you said my pages had potential and you wanted to help me bring it out, were you lying? Or were you just telling me what you thought I wanted to hear?"

I wasn't lying. Oscar's book had been pretty terrible on the whole. But every now and then, I'd come across a paragraph so perfect that I'd go back to read it again, or a minor character with intriguing contradictions that made me want to know more. Good books are written; great books are rewritten. That was one of the first things Carl had taught me back in the day. Realizing he was right was what turned editing from a job that would pay my bills to a career I loved. I mean, what could be better than helping talented people craft great books?

"Were you lying?" Oscar asked again. "Because if you genuinely believe the book has potential but aren't willing to help . . . Well, then I'm not the only one wasting their gifts, am I?"

Touché.

Dialogue like that was what had made Oscar Glazier a great writer. Could he be great again? Was he willing to put in the work it would take to make it happen? More to the point, was I? After deciding the answer was no, I walked wearily toward the door and opened it again.

"I'm sorry for your problems, Oscar. But they really are *your* problems."

"But I'm not the only one with problems, am I? You're trying to write a book, aren't you? And it's not going well, is it?"

I frowned. How did he know that?

"I've seen you through the windows late at night, pacing. That's what I do when I'm stuck too, only I close the shades. Maybe try that next time," he suggested. "So, how about this," he said, as if I'd agreed we should enter some negotiation, which I absolutely had not. "You read my book and I'll read yours. Then we'll try to help each other fix them, one blocked writer to another. What do you say?"

A decade of editing had taught me that only one writer in

one hundred has the ability to dispassionately critique their own work. It was like trying to look at a painting from three inches away; they couldn't see the big picture because they were just too close. Had I fallen into the same trap? Was my nose too close to the canvas?

"No," I said, shaking my head. "It'd never work."

"Why not?" he asked.

"Because you're obnoxious and I can't stand you."

"So what? I feel the same way about you. Doesn't mean we can't work together."

"You don't *listen*, Oscar!"

"That's not true. I listen," he said, then paused, thinking better of his claim. "Well, okay. But I *could* listen. And I will, I promise." He got down on his knees in front of me, clasping his hands together in supplication. "Help me, Obi-Wan Kenobi. You're my only hope."

"Oscar, get up."

He hopped to his feet. "See? I can take direction. If you'll help me fix my book, I'll listen, I'll work hard, I'll do anything you tell me to do. I swear. And do you know why?"

"Because you're desperate?"

"Yes. But also because I respect you, as an editor and as a person."

"You *respect* me?" I laughed. "Oh, please. Go jump in the lake."

It wasn't a command, just something that Adele used to say, and not meant to be taken literally. But as soon as I said it, Oscar nodded, then sprinted out the door, toward the waterfront, and into the night. I followed him as far as the porch. What an idiot. Did he seriously think I'd be charmed by his theatrics?

As I turned to go back inside, I heard a splash and someone thrashing in the water.

"Oscar! Oscar, are you okay?"

My question was met with more splashing, curses, and a strangled cry.

"Crap!" I raced across the grass in my bare feet, running toward the sound of Oscar's voice. Just as I reached the shore, the moon emerged from behind a cloud, shining brightly on the black surface of the lake and the gray, leonine head that bobbed and cursed in the water.

"Hang on, Oscar! I'm coming!"

Bare feet pounding across the wooden dock, I tossed my robe aside, stripping down to pink cotton underpants and camisole, and dove in. The water was freezing! My body felt like it was being pricked by ten thousand ice-cold needles. Coming up for air, I gasped for breath, then yelped an expletive and started paddling my frozen limbs, swimming toward Oscar, who suddenly stopped thrashing and began calmly treading water.

"What are you doing in here?"

"S–S–Saving you!" I said through chattering teeth. "You were screaming. I thought you were drowning!"

Oscar shook his head, tossing droplets of water into my eyes. "I wasn't screaming, I was yelling because the water's so cold!"

"Are you kidding me?" I swam off, wishing he *had* drowned.

Oscar quickly overtook me, cutting through the water with long, powerful strokes while I shivered and gasped, paddling slowly and painfully toward the shore, like a waterlogged rat abandoning ship. Moving my frozen limbs required a superhuman effort. But then, when I was still about fifty feet from the bank, I simply ran out of gas. My legs were still kicking feebly but my arms felt like two dead weights. In retrospect, I should have just flipped onto my back and tried to float but I was exhausted and so panicked that I wasn't thinking clearly.

Instead, I sank like a stone into the dark, frigid water, a feeling of pressure growing in my chest. I'm sure I was only under for a few seconds but it felt like more, as if not just my body but time itself had frozen between the breath I was depleting and the one I had to take soon or perish. And just about the time it felt like I might, I sensed a presence above me, felt an open hand claw at my arm and drag me up through the water and into the night air. I broke through the surface and gasped, sucking air into my lungs.

Oscar hooked one arm across my chest, and used the other to swim to shore, pulling my body closer to his as we reached the bank, wedging himself behind me. For a moment we just sat there trying to catch our breaths and summon the strength and will to get up, like two exhausted members of the same bobsled team. Then Oscar took in a huge breath and exhaled through his mouth, and patted my shoulder with a tired, heavy hand.

"See, Esme? Maybe there's a reason we both ended up here. Maybe we're meant to save each other."

CHAPTER TWENTY

Adele could and would read just about anywhere—in the bathtub, at the dinner table, under the hairdryer at the salon when she got a perm. But when the weather turned warm, her favorite reading spot was on a wooden bench that sat under the shade of a big scarlet oak, not far from the water's edge.

I used to join her there on a regular basis. We'd sit side by side and read for hours, stopping only when the light became so dim that we could no longer see the print on the pages, so immersed in the story that the splashes of swimmers cannon-balling off the dock and the shouts of kids playing Marco Polo became white noise in our ears. I made some lifelong friends while sitting on that bench; it's where I met Pippi Longstocking, Anne Shirley, and my favorite girl detectives, Nancy Drew and Trixie Belden.

Time had not been kind to Adele's bench. Wind, weather, and insects had softened the wood and split one of the armrests. When it came to essential repairs and renovations, replacing the bench ranked pretty far down on the list, but I did it anyway, with my own money. When the new teak bench arrived, I took it for a test drive almost immediately.

Within five minutes, the world melted away as I became completely absorbed in Oscar's awful book, until the unexpected weight of a hand on my shoulder jolted me back to reality.

"Don't sneak up like that!" I gasped. "You almost gave me a heart attack!"

"Who's sneaking? I said your name about four times but you didn't hear me, too wrapped up in your reading." Robyn walked to the front of the bench. "The landscaper called to say there isn't any matching stone for the patio available locally. They're ordering some from Atlanta but it's going to put us behind about a week on expanding the patio."

"Well"—I shrugged—"as long as it's in before the wedding, I guess that's okay."

"Also, Sutton phoned to say Martin thinks cotton napkins look cheap. He wants linen."

Of course he did. I sighed.

"I'll call the rental company tomorrow."

"Yes, see that you do," Robyn said, looking down her nose at me. "Because, as everybody knows, if you only have cotton napkins at your wedding reception instead of linen, you're probably not even married. Any children they have could be declared illegitimate."

I grinned. When not directed toward me, I enjoyed Robyn's acerbic wit. She plopped down on the bench, pulled out her cigarettes, and tilted her head toward Oscar's manuscript.

"Must be really good."

"Sadly, no. But it turns out that an incredibly bad book can be as riveting as an incredibly good one, just in a different way. It's like when you're driving by the scene of a car accident. You know you should look away but you can't because you keep wondering how it happened."

Robyn flicked her lighter. "I thought he was supposed to be some bigshot bestseller."

"He was. But he hasn't had a hit in a long time."

"And you're going to help change that?"

For a moment I thought this was one of her barbs, another instance of her trying to take me down a peg. But her expression was genuinely curious, without a hint of mockery.

"If I can," I said. "I know what to do. The question is, will Oscar be willing to do it?"

"Must feel good though, helping somebody write a bestseller."

"Bestseller is a long shot. The first goal is getting him on board to write a book that doesn't totally suck." I read a paragraph and sighed. "He's *not* going to like what I have to say."

Robyn took a drag on her cigarette, holding the smoke in for a good ten seconds, looking past the kids wearing floaties and the mothers who stood knee-deep in the water to shout warnings to their offspring, gazing toward the distant shore. "Adele used to sit here for *hours*," she said, exhaling. "I think I finally get why she liked it so much."

"Wait. You mean you've never—?" The way she'd said it, in a voice distant and deeply lonely, the voice of someone who'd spent the whole of life with her face pressed against the window but had never entered inside, made me sad. "You never came out here and . . . just sat with her?"

"It was her reading bench," Robyn said, blowing cigarette smoke toward an insistent fly. "Anyway, I'm not like you. Or her. I don't like to read, so sue me. When you're dyslexic, it's a lot of work."

"You're dyslexic? Since when?"

Why had she never told me before?

"Since always," she said, chuckling. "It's not like a virus. You don't catch dyslexia, you're born with it. Of course, back when I was in grade school, they just thought I was stupid. I thought so too. But I didn't know why until I went to . . . you know."

I nodded, knowing she meant prison. Like the d-word, there were some things Robyn just didn't talk about. If she mentioned it at all, she'd simply refer to having been "inside."

"There was a continuing ed teacher, Mr. Kinney. He figured out what was going on. And he helped me get better at it—reading, I mean. It's easier, but it's still not easy, not like it is for you," she said, nodding toward Oscar's manuscript. "Even if it was, I never saw the point."

"The point?" I gave my head a shake. "Of *reading*?"

"Well, obviously not *all* reading," she said. "I'm not an idiot. Some books have information you need. There was this one I really liked; accounting for dummies? That's how I taught myself how to keep the books. But numbers have always made more sense to me. You don't have to try to figure out what they're saying; they are what they are, every time.

"I don't see the point of stories. Real life is hard enough. Why should I waste time reading about imaginary people with imaginary problems? I know you and Adele got something out of it, but for me . . ." She shrugged. "All those books they used to try to make us read in school? The people would talk and talk and talk . . ." She rolled her eyes and took another drag.

There were about fifty things I wanted to say just then. The editor in me really wanted to give a speech about how powerful, even life-changing fiction can be. But the daughter and woman could have said even more.

Robyn was a lot of things, but she definitely wasn't stupid. Knowing she'd spent her childhood thinking she was made me sorry, so did knowing that she'd felt unworthy to join her mother on this bench, just because she wasn't into reading. Adele wouldn't have cared if Robyn brought a book; she'd have loved the company. How could Robyn not have known? How could Adele not have told her? How could two people spend years living in the same house and never talk about the things that mattered until it was too late?

Then I remembered that maybe it *wasn't* too late.

"Hey, do you remember Adele's confetti quilt, the one with all the colors?"

Robyn nodded and took a quick puff. "That's my favorite. Looks like a party."

"Do you know why she made it? Because you were coming back home and she was so, so happy, happy and excited."

"You mean when I came home from . . . the inside?"

When I nodded, Robyn's expression hardened, becoming almost flinty. I'd seen that look on her face before. As soon as anyone tried to say something nice about her or praise her abilities, she withdrew behind a veil of suspicion, regarding the speaker from a skeptical distance, as if trying to ascertain what they really meant or wanted before they could get close enough to wound.

"Why would you say that? How do you know?"

"Because she wrote it down. Not in words exactly," I said, rushing to explain when Robyn's frown deepened. "But the date in her notebook and on the back of the quilt coincides with your release. And the colors are those she associated with excitement, delight, love, longing, relief, anticipation. A little anxiety too," I admitted. "It had been such a long time. At that point, I don't think either of you knew how things were going to work out.

"But the most prominent color is that gorgeous, luscious raspberry, remember?" Robyn nodded, but barely. "That color always represented intense joy to her. And the free-floating way she did the arrangement, as opposed to her usual linear composition? That meant she couldn't contain all her feelings. She was so overjoyed by your homecoming that she wanted to throw a party, but worried it might overwhelm you so she made the quilt instead."

"That's just a story," Robyn said, and huffed out a laugh. "You made it up."

"Everything is a story," I said. "The stuff that happens to us is just . . . stuff. The only reason it means anything is because we attach stories to it, declarations of what we've decided is true and worth passing on. Without stories, there aren't any memories. Or art, or history, or faith . . . Almost everything that matters is connected to stories, large and small."

"And you think these quilts are Adele's stories?" Robyn looked at me through narrowed eyes, but I could tell she was listening.

"Yes. For all that she loved books, I don't think Adele trusted the accuracy of words, or her ability to use them. Maybe that's part of the reason she read so much, maybe she was trying to crack the code of what words really mean. Color felt truer to her, like numbers do to you. When she wanted to tell a story well and preserve a memory that mattered, that's the language she used."

Robyn leaned back against the bench, wrapped her arms around her body, the stub of her cigarette pinched between her fingers.

"Maybe, maybe," she mused, staring sightlessly across the water for a long moment. "Or . . . maybe it's just a story." She sighed. "Either way, it's nice out here."

She swung her arm out toward me. I plucked the cigarette from her fingers, took a puff, and handed it back.

"So . . . can I read it?" she asked. "The story?"

"About the confetti quilt? I haven't written anything about that one yet. Right now, I'm just writing stories about the quilts from the war years."

"Well . . . I'd like to read whatever you've got so far. I mean, if that's okay with you."

"Sure. But not yet. I'm fine with you reading it. Really," I assured her when I saw that shut-door look come into her eyes. "It's just that, I don't want anybody to see it until I've finished and done a couple rounds of editing. Well, except Oscar. But that's different. I just want his opinion, writer to writer, before I show it to anybody else."

My gaze drifted up the hill to cabin seventeen and Oscar's closed door. He hadn't emerged for four days, not since he'd fished me out of the freezing water and we'd agreed to read each other's work. Did he like what I'd written so far? Had he even read it?

He should have by now; his manuscript was more than twice as long as the scenes I'd handed to him. I was working long days juggling the renovation logistics and redoing cabins, but I had already read through his book three times, working late into the night and taking copious notes. I didn't expect him to be as thorough as I'd been, but I was anxious to know what he thought. Criticism was fine, and even welcome, as long as it was constructive. However, I doubted that Oscar shared my opinion.

I chewed my lip, wondering how he'd respond to my notes. My guess was, not well. Even so, I knew my assessment was right and my ideas for revision could help him salvage the book and possibly his career. How could I get him to check his ego and hear me out?

Robyn crushed her cigarette butt under her foot, then tossed it into a nearby trash can.

"I should get going. But listen, if you're still worried about what you're going to say to Oscar, I'd just lay it out there plain. Don't pull any punches."

"You think?"

"Definitely. I mean, I don't really know him but something tells me that's how he rolls."

"Kind of like you?" I asked.

"Yeah, kinda." She laughed and got to her feet. "Hey, hate to cut into your reading time but don't forget that cabin five is checking out today. It'll be full from Friday on so . . ." She tapped her watch, signaling that the twenty-eight-hour redecoration window was about to open.

I said I'd be on it soon, but sat on the bench for a few minutes after she left, soaking in the sun, watching the ducks bobbing near the bank, smiling when they popped their fluffy tails into the air to forage for food, listening to the happy giggles of two little girls who were wading near the waterfront and watching tadpoles with pure delight, like I used to when I was little.

I needed to get to work, but it was good to take a moment to enjoy the beauty of the day, to notice the people who were outside doing the same thing, and to be reminded of how special this place was, and what I was working for. The lake, the lodge, the lush green grounds dotted with tidy cabins, this lovely little world my grandparents had created was a place where memories were made.

But thinking about the lodge always brought me back to Adele, and why a young woman who supposedly set out to be a painter ended up making quilts instead—beautiful, evocative, works of art—only to hide them away. The more I wrote, the clearer Adele became in my mind but answers to this question continued to evade me. It didn't make sense.

Just as I was getting ready to rouse myself, George came along, wearing a smile and a wide-brimmed Panama hat. He sat down next to me. "Gorgeous day, isn't it? Just finished my lunch. Dawes made gazpacho. It was good; you should try it. I couldn't eat my roll, so I thought I'd share it with the ducks."

He started tearing off pieces of bread and tossing them into the water. The ducks arrived within seconds, quacking and squabbling as they gobbled the scraps. When it came to George and questions about the past, I'd learned to tread lightly. He got flustered if he couldn't remember, and sometimes even angry. But his smile and relaxed demeanor told me that this was a good day, so I decided to test the waters and post a few questions.

"Adele started out as a painter, right?"

"Yes, and she took it very seriously, worked real hard."

He tossed another chunk of bread to the ducks.

"Well, then where are her paintings? She was such a pack rat that I thought for sure she'd have saved them. But I've looked through the storage room and haven't found any."

"No, and you won't. She burned them," he said, matter-of-factly. "Every single one."

"What? Why would she do that?"

He sighed heavily. "Honestly, I still don't understand it myself. *I* thought they were good. But you know, your grandmother could be so hard on herself sometimes." His voice was regretful but he didn't seem agitated, not like he'd been on other occasions. "Remember that quilt you were asking me about before? The one with all those dark green rectangles? I think it was about that, the night she burned the paintings. I wasn't there when she did it, so I can't claim to know the whole story, or understand what she was thinking."

I felt a tingle on the back of my neck.

"That's all right, George. Just tell me what you do know."

Anger and Ashes

October 1943

"I sure wish you'd have come to see me sooner."

When the doctor shook his head and clucked his tongue, I felt a clutch in my heart and braced myself for the worst, wishing I had not come at all. But then he continued . . .

"Because you could have saved yourself a whole lot of worry, young lady."

When the doctor explained that I didn't share my father's future or his illness, the wave of relief that washed over me brought tears to my eyes. What I'm suffering from is essential tremor, a malady the doctor says can sometimes be misdiagnosed as Parkinson's disease, the condition that began with shaking like mine but eventually and cruelly robbed my father of health and happiness. However, essential tremor is associated with no health problems and, apart from the trembling I'm already experiencing, will have no impact on my day-to-day life.

The eyes of the doctor, the kind weight of his hand on my shoulder, say I should be grateful. And, of course, I am. It could have been so much worse.

But there is no treatment. The tremors will continue. The doctor couldn't possibly understand how this news impacted me. I am a woman, after all, and so he cannot imagine that my ambition could extend beyónd the usual confined borders of womankind, or that trembling hands could thwart me from fulfilling my purpose.

Late in a sleepless night spent thinking of all the things I can never be, I rise from my bed and examine the portfolio of paintings I brought with me to Asheville, then open my closet, filled with canvases I have created since my arrival.

Even before the shaking started, my work never measured up to my aspirations. For years, I have been striving for more, planting my hopes in the deep soil of determination, having faith that if I studied enough, wanted enough, worked enough, the seeds of talent would take root and become fruitful, and my dreams would be realized at last.

Some days are better, or worse, than others. But the trembling is almost constant now and controlling my pencil or paintbrush is always a struggle, and sometimes a pointless exercise. Now I know that it will always be that way.

The truth is not as terrible as I had feared. And yet it is somehow worse, a confirmation of the unspoken fears that have lain dormant inside me since long before the first tremor, blooming to hard, cold reality. No matter how much I work, or study, or strive, I will not become a great painter. My best work is behind me, and my best is not enough.

I am not enough. I never will be.

And so I gather it all up in my arms—sketchbooks, canvases, portfolio—and creep quietly down the stairs of the sleeping boarding-house and into the backyard.

The sky is silky and smooth, black as panther fur, but the stars are bright and the moon is full, lighting my way to the shed in the back corner, and a rusty barrel for burning leaves. I place my burdens into the black, charred maw of the barrel, then strike a match and stand there, watching my dreams flicker and flame and turn to ash.

CHAPTER TWENTY-ONE

*D*awes coated the roller with a thick layer of latex before painting a stripe of pale, buttery yellow from the center of the wall to the ceiling in a single, effortless stroke.

"I'm jealous," I said, swiping my brush on the edge of the pan to wipe off the paint drips. "You don't even have to push up on your toes to reach the top."

"Height has its advantages. But look at it this way," he said, glancing at the lower half of the wall, which I'd painted on my own, "between the two of us, we've got it covered."

He had a point. Painting the entire interior of the café was a big job. But with him handling the upper section and me the lower, we would be able to finish that night. The more I got to know Dawes, the more apparent our differences became. But that wasn't always a bad thing; we made a pretty good team. Though I'd had mixed feelings about his investment in the lodge, it had turned out for the best, and not just because of his cooking, painting, and plumbing skills. By now, I felt like I could talk to him about almost anything. And though I did most of the talking, I was sure he felt the same way.

I knelt down on the floor and started painting the bottom-most portion of the wall, careful to keep the color from seeping under the tape and onto the woodwork.

"I'm just sorry you ended up working on your day off again."

"Nothing to be sorry about," he said. "That's the difference between being an employee and an owner, right? You don't mind putting in extra hours when you know you'll reap the benefits. Anyway, feels good to have something of my own again." Dawes bent down, sloshing his roller back and forth in the paint pan. "So tell me, were you finally able to talk to Oscar? How'd he take it when you told him to start again from scratch?"

"Not *completely* from scratch," I clarified. "There's this one character, Oliver, who's definitely worth saving. In fact, he's terrific."

"Fine," Dawes replied, in a "let's not split hairs" sort of tone. "You're not recommending that he trash the entire book, just ninety-nine percent of it, along with a character he's been writing about since probably before you and I learned to read. So? How'd he take *that*?"

I laughed. "Pretty much like you'd expect."

"But *WHY*?" Oscar had cried, screwing his eyes shut and snarling in frustration. "Why throw Tony out completely? I get that you like Oliver but can't we just give him a little more to do and leave it at that? The story revolves around Tony. If you get rid of him, I'd have to—"

"Write a whole new book," I said, spelling it out for him yet again, "with Oliver Gardner as the protagonist. Yes, Oscar. That is exactly what I'm suggesting you do."

"But *why*?" Oscar cried again, fisting his hands and screwing his eyes closed. "Tony Acierno is gritty, mysterious, handsome. Women want him and men want to be him. Tony is a *man*— adventurous, reckless, with nerves of steel. I picked the name because *acierno* means 'of steel' in Italian," Oscar said, grabbing his glass and tossing back some scotch. "That's who Tony is, a man of steel."

"He's a cartoon character," I said. "A predictable, emotionally stunted, less interesting, less skillfully crafted version of a character Ian Fleming created more than *fifty* years ago. Oscar, you're no Fleming," I said, making it as plain as I could. "And Tony is no James Bond."

I drained my own glass and waited for the explosion. It didn't take long.

"Tony is the hero of my last *twelve* books! I've spent a *decade* writing about him."

"And your sales have been sinking for most of that decade. Face facts," I said, refilling our glasses, "Tony is a tired, testosterone-fueled trope. He's not real, Oscar!"

Oscar snatched his glass off the table. "Oh, I see," he sneered. "And Oliver Gardner is?"

"Yes. He's you."

Oscar made a face and took a drink, as if trying to wash a bad taste from his mouth.

"Think about it," I implored, placing my hands on my knees and leaning in. "Oliver's about your age, tough on the outside but insecure underneath, a man who was at the pinnacle of his profession but has been on a downward slide for a while, who wonders where the time has gone and worries about how little is left, a man who's afraid of becoming irrelevant but self-sabotages every plan that might create any kind of lasting meaning in his life.

"Oliver Gardner is you, Oscar. He's you!" I exclaimed, throwing out my hands. "Why can't you see it? You even have the same initials. Why would you do that unless, at some subconscious level, you were writing about yourself?"

Oscar stretched out his legs and crossed them nonchalantly. "Uh . . . You're reading way too much into this, Dr. Freud. Oliver's nothing, he's a throwaway character."

"He's fascinating," I countered. "Or could be. But you're not even willing to give him a chance. And you know why?"

Oscar smirked. "No, Doc. Do tell."

"Because you're afraid of failure. I get it," I said as an image of a young Adele feeding the paintings into the flames came to my mind. "Wrestling with the fear of failure is something every artist has to deal with. But since your publisher and your agent fired you, you've kind of failed already, haven't you? So what's the harm in trying something new?"

Oscar glowered. And I didn't blame him. That last part seemed more diplomatic before I said it out loud. I tried another tack.

"Oscar, have you ever thought about why writers write? It's because every time you type 'Chapter One,' there's just the slimmest possibility that you're about to do the best work of your life. People who've never done it will never understand how hard this is, how much it costs you. But for someone like you, it's worth it. Oscar, when you're at your best, there's barely a novelist alive who can top you."

Oscar lifted his glass in a mock toast. "Nice try, Esme. I'm too old for your mind games."

"I was not trying to play mind games with you." This, of course, was a bald-faced lie. "I genuinely believe that Oliver's story could be amazing and that you're the only writer who could do it justice." This part was one hundred percent true.

"But, hey, if you're not willing to take my advice . . ." I shrugged and got to my feet.

"Wait. Where are you going? Hold on!" He jumped to his feet, trying to block my exit. "We had a deal. You said we would try to help fix each other's books."

"And you said you'd listen and do whatever I said."

"I'm listening. I am!" he exclaimed when I shot him a look. "But instead of writing a new book about some sad, washed-up cop nobody cares about, why not help me fix the book I already wrote, about an undercover operative who saves the world from nuclear annihilation?"

I shook my head. "Claudia was right; the book's beyond saving. I don't think your career has to be but, hey . . . I understand. I'm sure it feels like too big a risk. And at your age—"

"My *age*?" He laughed. "Just how old do you think I am?"

The sparkle of conceit in his eyes told me he was used to asking this question and hearing a number that was five or even ten years less than the truth. Didn't he realize that people always guess low when asked to estimate somebody's age? To irritate him, I considered tacking on a couple more years. But reporting the actual number was wounding enough.

"Sixty-four is *not* old," he growled.

"Definitely not. I mean, not *old* old. But you know what they say about dogs and new tricks."

Oscar's eyes became slits. "And am I the dog in this stunningly clichéd observation?"

"Of course not!" I gave his arm a patronizing pat. "But at your stage of life, it's understandable if you don't feel up to tackling something new, coming up with a fresh storyline, a character who's nuanced, and deep, and . . ."

I let my voice drift off and my eyes go dreamy. Oscar frowned, interested but suspicious.

"And what?"

"Well, you know . . ." I dropped my voice to a lower register. "Sexy. And powerful. But vulnerable and flawed. There is something irresistible about a character with a dark, mysterious past who's taken some knocks but somehow manages to keep standing."

"Well," Oscar said gruffly, "there's a lot to be said for a man with experience."

"Exactly. Especially if that experience involves an accomplished but tortured character who has come to the end of himself and feels ready to give up—"

"—due to external forces. Circumstances and secrets beyond his control," Oscar said, taking over the sentence, his tone musing and gaze faraway, focused on an imaginary landscape.

"There's a new chief of police," he murmured, "a young, political appointee. He's on the take, but Oliver doesn't know that yet. He's been put on desk duty after a civilian shooting that's really a hit job they're trying to pin on him. But then, Oliver runs across some paperwork that helps him realize the whole administration is corrupt—maybe with ties to an international drug cartel? Not Mexico, that's been done to death. Somewhere exotic . . . Shanghai? France?"

"France," I said. "It'd give Oliver the chance to go to Paris—"

"Which is where the love of his life lives," he added, not missing a beat. "A woman he met years ago who married someone else. Oliver finds her but it's too late, she's dying from . . . I don't know . . . some incurable disease. But she has a grown daughter—"

"Who Oliver suspects might actually be his?" I suggested.

"And whose life is in *danger*," he added, stabbing the air. "She's engaged to the heir of an old Parisian family, never realizing that their wealth comes from the international drug trade."

The faraway look fled from Oscar's face, replaced by a bemused expression, as if confused by my presence. He grabbed me by the arm and propelled me toward the door.

"Go away, Esme. I've got to write."

DAWES LAUGHED WHEN I finished my story. "A little manipulative on your part maybe but sounds like it did the trick. Do you really think this book will be better?"

"Absolutely," I said, pouring the last drops of paint into the pan before opening the second can. "Sometimes, a writer gets this look in their eye and you know, you just *know*, that they're about to create something amazing."

When he did, I'd have the satisfaction of knowing I'd helped make it happen. If there's a better feeling in the world, somebody should bottle it. I tilted the paint can, smiling as I watched thick ribbons of yellow pour out like cake batter.

"Well, good for you," Dawes said, casting his eyes upward as he rolled paint toward the triangular peak of the ceiling. "And for Oscar too, I guess. What did he say about your book?"

"Nothing. He pushed me out the door so fast that I didn't get a chance to ask."

"And you're going to put up with that? After all you did to help him?"

Dawes had a point: what was supposed to have been an even exchange had somehow turned into a one-way street. Not all that surprising, considering who I was dealing with, but still.

Dawes gave the wall a last swipe, then put down his roller and stepped back.

"Not too shabby," he said, then looked at me and grinned. "And only three more to go."

"Oh, is that all?" I laughed, one of those punchy, slightly overwrought laughs that says you're shortchanged on sleep, then let out a sigh. "I don't know, Dawes . . . Three weeks to go, three walls to paint, eleven cabins left to renovate, plus the patio, and the landscaping, the dock, an anxious bride, a picky groom, and nearly three hundred wedding guests to feed . . . Do you honestly think we can do it?"

"Quit worrying; I've got you. August 15 will be a great and historic day, the start of two partnerships—the Waddells' and ours." He winked. "And I'm pretty sure that at least *one* of them is going to last."

THE LAST THREE walls went more quickly than I'd thought. I headed back to my cabin a little after nine, looking forward to my bed. However, judging from the number of illuminated cabin windows, the clusters of people lounging, laughing, and talking on front porches, as well as the packs of hooting barefoot children chasing fireflies and each other across the grass, it looked like I was the only one. I smiled, lifting my hand to wave at people who wished me a good evening as I passed, thinking how much had changed since that day when I'd first arrived and found nearly all the cabins vacant. Now, nearly all of them were occupied. Dawes was right; everything was going to be all right.

When I approached cabin seventeen and the lights were still on, I decided Dawes was right about something else too. Oscar owed me and it was time to collect.

I knew he was in there because I could hear him typing. When he failed to respond, my polite knock turned to insistent pounding. Finally, he opened the door, scowling at me as if he were a diabetic and I was a Girl Scout bent on selling him a box of Thin Mints.

"What?"

"I came to ask about the pages I gave you. Did you read them?"

"Yes. They were good. Keep going."

I waited for more. Oscar just looked at me.

"So, you hated them."

"No," Oscar said slowly, pulling his bushy brows into a line and moving his head from side to side. "I said they were good, and they are. If I hated them, I'd have said so."

"But . . . You're sure you liked them? You're not just trying to spare my feelings?"

"I am not. In case you hadn't noticed, Esme, I'm not some-body who pulls his punches."

Fair point. Still . . .

"Okay, but can you give me a little more? In what *way* were they good? Were there some parts you liked more than others? Things you think I should change? Or maybe add?"

"Well, if it were me, I'd have put in more sex and explosions. But, you know." He shrugged. "Apart from that . . ."

"Come on, Oscar. I'm trying to be serious! Just tell me—did you like them or not?"

He cast his eyes to the ceiling and spread out his hands. "Why do women have to talk everything to death? Why can't they take yes for an answer? Esme," he said in a flat voice, "the pages were good. How many more times do you want me to say it?"

"None," I assured him, suddenly realizing that I sounded like one of those writers who make editors crazy, the insecure kind who need buckets of affirmation. Oscar said he liked what he'd read and to keep going; shouldn't that be enough? On the other hand, I'd invested a good ten hours reading his manuscript and two more in giving him a very detailed, thorough critique. Reading my half-finished manuscript and saying "good" didn't seem like a fair exchange.

"Couldn't you give me a little more feedback? Some specific advice on what to do now?"

"Specific advice," he said, in that same flat voice. "Sure. No problem. Go back to your cabin, boot up your computer, put your butt in the chair and your hands on the keys, and keep doing what you've been doing until the book is done. That specific enough for you?" he asked, then took a step back and closed the door in my face.

In my face! The jerk! I hammered the door with my fist.

"Oscar? Oscar!"

"Go away! I've got work to do!"

"Do you know *why* you've got work to do?" I yelled, pressing my face to the wood. "Because I told you how to save your book! Are you ever planning to thank me?"

A muffled voiced echoed from the opposite side of the door.

"Too soon to say! Now go home and type something!"

I banged on the door a few more times, not because I thought he'd answer but just so he'd know I wasn't through with him yet, then stomped across his porch and down the path toward my cabin, still smoldering.

But when I flicked on the lights and spotted my neglected laptop sitting on the table, I realized that, when it comes to writing, "Go home and type something" is pretty good advice.

Ordinary Triumph

July 1944

It's hard to feel sorry for yourself with a war going on, at least not for long. In a world embroiled in conflict, with suffering on all sides, shedding tears over the loss of a career you never truly had seems small and self-indulgent.

In the moment when the blaze flared, I admit to feeling a flutter of panic, wondering if I had made a mistake and would come to regret my actions. But once the flames had done their work and died away, leaving ash and the charred splinters of canvas frames, relief replaced regret. I was just like everybody else now, released from striving, free to be ordinary.

"But you're not ordinary," George told me. "You couldn't be ordinary if you tried."

The sentiment is sweet but I think he's wrong. Besides, what's so terrible about being ordinary? Other people don't seem to mind. And for once, wouldn't it be nice just to fit in? I've been working hard at doing just that.

My job is just my job now. No more imaginary conversations with painted virgins reading books or making lace. No more research on the lives, influences, and techniques of dead artists. I do what I'm paid to do but nothing more, ticking off boxes and watching the clock.

Now, instead of painting in the evenings, I go to the pool hall and watch George play—turns out I am one of those women who can nurse a beer and sit on the sidelines after all—and sometimes we go to a movie, but not very often. With more workers leaving the dairy to enlist, George has been taking extra shifts to help the war effort. I know he wishes he could enlist too, but with his heart keeping him out of the fight, he does all he can to make up for it. If there is a rubber drive, metal drive, clothing drive, or war bond drive in Asheville, George is probably running it. I'm trying to do my part too.

Following Mrs. Roosevelt's example, I've taken up knitting, making socks for servicemen. The tremors in my hands make it more challenging, but I manage; the shaking isn't as bad if I'm holding something. I serve donuts in the USO canteen too, and sometimes go to the dances so there are enough partners for the servicemen temporarily assigned to Asheville, waiting for their orders to come through. I'm not a very good dancer but some of the boys just want to talk, and I've always been a good listener.

As time goes on, I find that I am not as different as I had feared, and that I enjoy the company of other people more than expected, including the company of other women. The other female boarders, Betty Rae, a nurse, and Edith, an elementary school teacher, joined Miss Ida's quilt circle and invited me to do the same. I'm the youngest but they welcomed me eagerly, happy to share what they know. I still find sewing the same blocks women have been stitching for a hundred years dull, even constricting, but it feels good to be accepted and fit in at last.

When the circle voted to sponsor a raffle for the Red Cross, I volunteered to make a log cabin quilt and spent my Sunday afternoon up in the attic, at Miss Ida's sewing machine. My hands don't shake at all when I am quilting, perhaps because of the vibration of the sewing machine. The log cabin pattern is simple so the sewing went quickly, almost too quickly.

With George still working an extra shift and the empty afternoon yawning before me, I decided to keep going. But instead of making more tidy, predictable blocks, I dug into Miss Ida's scrap bin and started pulling out fabric at random, pieces that vary in color, size, and shape, snipping and stitching and ripping, creating an unpredictable collage, and having the best time.

Eschewing patterns, blocks, and expectations, I am sewing my way again, learning what the fabric will and won't do, how to make curves lie flat, how to combine colors, create composition, achieve balance, solving problems as they arise, starting over when I must, loving even my mistakes because making them is how I discover what works. The process is slow, painstaking, and oddly satisfying. After three Sundays, I have a completed, very small quilt to show, just twenty inches square. It reminds me of ocean waves piling up onto a beach, but in all the colors I love best—azure, amber, raspberry, saffron. Each color has its own feeling and flavor but the combination equals happiness and I love every inch of it.

Happiest of all is that, for the first time since lighting that match, I feel like myself, perhaps more than ever before. Painting often brought me pleasure, especially in the beginning. But it also brought anxiety, the ever-present sentinels of insecurity and doubt.

Fabric is not like that. It is my muse and my medium, a means of creation that makes me feel centered and certain. It is communication, a way of explaining myself to myself and letting the world in on the secret. Or it will be, after I show my friends what I've made.

When I returned to work at the estate on Monday, I spent an hour standing in front of three Flemish tapestries, The Triumphs. *I've walked past them almost every day, often to admire them, and even spent time researching their provenance, which, as they're so very old, is a bit murky. But when I stopped to look at them on Monday, it sud-*

denly occurred to me that, while the design was likely created by men, the actual weaving may well have been done by women.

What was that like?

Did they relish the texture of fiber in their fingers? The way the colors taste, and feel, and tell a story? Did the act of creation make them feel centered and satisfied, proud to pour their talent and days into creating something so beautiful? Proud of their artistry? Proud to be artists?

The fact that there is no sure answer to my questions has sometimes made me feel the injustice of their anonymity more profoundly. But today I have stopped what I am doing to simply admire and seek inspiration in the work their fingers wrought.

Standing there, it suddenly occurred to me that names are like words, possessing no inherent meaning in and of themselves, and easily forgotten. It's action alone that makes the lasting mark, and things we do or create that reveal what we believe and care about, that testify to our presence long after we're gone.

In the end, is there a better way to be remembered?

CHAPTER TWENTY-TWO

$\mathcal{D}$id you ever go through one of those seasons when you feel like you're on a hot streak? Like all your plans are coming together more perfectly than you could have dreamed and you couldn't put a foot wrong even if you tried?

Yeah. Me neither.

But for most of the first part of August, those two weeks leading up to the Barnett-Waddell wedding, it felt pretty darned close.

No, everything didn't go perfectly according to plan. Hiccups happen. For example, taking delivery on two hundred and fifty black folding chairs instead of the white ones we'd ordered and fighting with the vendor to have them replaced. Or having nickel-size hailstones rain down just four days before the wedding, right after I'd spent half a day planting six flats of flowers. But mostly, things went well.

Dawes and I handled the rest of the cabin renovations. I'd do all I could during the day and then he'd come help with the heavy lifting after the café closed. That meant we could put George back on front desk duty full-time. The routine of checking people in and out, handling boat rentals, and ringing up purchases from the canteen was familiar so he didn't have any more meltdowns, and, of course, the guests loved him. There were a couple of instances when he over- or under-charged for rooms, though, so Robyn started totaling the bills at night and taping the invoices to the counter so George could find them easily. It added one more task to her already long days but, as she said, "If it helps George keep being George, it's totally worth it."

I agreed. We were taking things one day at a time. Every time I cruised through the lobby on some mission and saw George telling stories or shooting the breeze with an obviously charmed guest, I felt grateful for this day and said a little prayer, asking that George be just as happy and just as much himself as he'd always been, all the days of his life, amen.

In spite of a few delays and the hassle of doing renovations with an almost full house, which sometimes meant offering guests a discount or free meal to make up for the inconvenience and noise, we were on track to get everything done in time for the wedding. The lodge had never looked better. And it looked like our investments were already paying off.

Sylvia had told some of her friends about Sutton's wedding plans and Yolanda was spreading the word too. Thanks to them, brides-elect had come out for tours and tastings and two had put down deposits for weddings the following year. They would be smaller affairs, around seventy-five guests each, but it was an encouraging sign.

Also, after dozens of demands for changes and upgrades, the menu for Sutton and Martin's wedding was finally set. The café was doing a brisk business as well, the profits adding a little more to the bottom line every week, so Dawes was busier than ever.

Yolanda called every few days, trying to set me up with some guy or other, but even if I'd been interested, there wasn't time. Any spare time I did have, I devoted to writing.

After the door-in-my-face incident, Oscar actually sought me out and offered something that sounded sort of like an apology but not quite. He spoke to me in a fairly civil tone, and suggested we start exchanging pages more often and grabbing coffee in the mornings so we could discuss them. Oscar's feedback continued to be brief, stark, and to the point, but largely positive, which fueled my desire to keep writing. Oscar wasn't pounding out pages as quickly as before, but I thought it was the best work he'd done in years and maybe ever. His cabin was already booked to accommodate wedding guests, so we couldn't extend his reservation, which meant he'd have to finish his manuscript at home. I told him he could call or email if he needed help, but I wasn't concerned. The story was really coming together and he was on a good trajectory. Also, thanks to my recommendation, he had an agent again.

Carl had been hesitant at first, but I pressed the issue, saying he'd thank me later, which he did. After reading the first hundred pages of Oscar's manuscript, Carl was completely on board. Since Oscar already knew Carl from their days at DM, and since Carl had been pulling together some nice deals of late, so was Oscar.

"He's still a complete PITA," Carl said when we talked on the phone, "but the book is fantastic. I've already started calling the right people, letting them know that the old Oscar Glazier is back and better than ever. I don't want to shop the book until he finishes the draft; his reputation proceeds him so editors are going to be cautious. But if the last two-thirds read as well as the first, they'll be lining up around the block to bid on it. Thanks, Esme."

"I'm just happy it's working out for everybody. You're right, Oscar's still a pain but the book is going to be terrific. I've had fun working with him."

"Excuse me?" I heard a thumping noise as Carl tapped his finger against the phone. "It sounded like you just came very close to saying that you *like* Oscar Glazier."

"Yeah. Well. Oscar has the emotional IQ of sharp cheddar, but you get used to him."

"Funny, that's exactly what he says about you. Watch it, kiddo, or you might end up being the next future former Mrs. Glazier."

"Oh, no. Not a chance. We already worked through all that. He tried to plant a lip-lock on me a couple of weeks back."

"And you slapped some sense into him?" Carl asked.

"Worse. I laughed," I said, grinning as I recalled the stricken expression on Oscar's face when I broke from his embrace and doubled over in hysterics.

"Then I explained that I was not now and never would be interested in him romantically and suggested that he'd be a lot happier, and a lot richer, if he quit trying to hook up with women half his age who were on the hunt for their next divorce settlement."

"And he didn't storm off and never speak to you again? Wow. Either Oscar Glazier is turning into an adult or you really are the author whisperer. I'm thinking the latter. Seriously, Ez, if things work out the way I think they're going to, I'll owe you, big-time."

"Glad you feel that way. Any chance I can collect now?"

Carl said he'd be happy to read what I'd written so far and tell me what he thought. Though I didn't want to jinx myself, I really did feel like the scenes I'd written up to this point were pretty good, but I wanted to give the pages one more polish before I sent them along.

It took a little longer than I'd thought—after all, writing was just my night job—but three days before the wedding, after a very long day spent redecorating the last cabin and replanting the hailstone-hammered flowers, I read my chapters through one more time, then attached the document to an email message that read:

Dear Carl,

Here it is, such as it is. Be kind.

Esme

After rereading my note, trying to decide if it was too pointed or just pithy enough, I settled on the latter, took a deep breath, and hit send. And though I'm sure nobody saw it but me, the air was suddenly filled with confetti—sapphire, violet, goldenrod, lemon yellow, and lots and lots of bright, brilliant, joyous raspberry.

I laughed, casting my eyes upward to where I supposed Adele must be. "Well, that's it. I've done all I can, the rest is on you."

INVITING SOMEBODY TO critique your writing, especially somebody you know and whose good opinion you crave, is an audacious act. But if you've given it your very best, a certain measure of fatality takes hold once you've sent it in. Pacing the floor and checking your watch does no good and makes no difference. It will be what it will be; the best thing to do is just accept that and return to your regularly scheduled life. Besides, with the wedding only two days away, there really wasn't another option.

I slept surprisingly well that night and I woke up feeling energized and eager, mentally reviewing my to-do list, excited that we were so close to the finish line, certain that everything would go according to plan.

That is, until I padded out to the kitchen to make coffee and saw the envelope.

Someone had written my name on the front and slipped it under the door while I'd been sleeping. When I opened it, I found a half dozen or so recipes written out on index cards and a note.

> Esme, I'm really sorry. I know I'm letting you down and I'd explain if I could, but there's just no time and no other choice. I have to go.
>
> Dawes

I read it three times, and still couldn't believe it.

He wouldn't just up and leave town, not two days before the wedding that was supposed to save the lodge, he *couldn't*!

It wasn't just me, George, and Robyn he was leaving in a lurch—not to mention the bride and groom; he was hurting himself too. He'd invested everything he had into the lodge, sold his van because he wanted to be part of the business. For Dawes, selling the van was basically like selling his house. He wouldn't walk away from that.

Would he?

No. It was a joke, a cruel, dumb, terrible joke. It *had* to be. The second I found him, I'd give him an earful about how incredibly *not* funny this was. Then I'd smack him upside the head with a cast iron skillet to make sure he got the message.

I threw on some clothes and ran to the café, my panic subsiding when I saw that the lights were on and that a few of the booths by the windows were occupied. But when I went inside, Jamie, a teenager who lived nearby and had been hired as an extra pair of hands when the assistant cook took another job, told me that Dawes hadn't shown up for work.

"I can make scrambled eggs, bacon, and pancakes but that's about it. Dawes did all the omelets and stuff. I've just been telling people that we're out of everything else. Is he sick? Do you know when he's coming in? I can hold down the fort for a little while but . . ."

The poor kid looked like he wanted to jump out the nearest window. For a second, I thought he was going to cry. I squeezed his shoulder.

"You're doing *great*," I assured him. "Eggs, bacon, and pancakes is perfect. Nobody's going hungry. Just keep doing what you're doing, I'll find Dawes. He probably overslept."

After flashing what I hoped was an encouraging smile, I ran out the door and started searching. George hadn't seen him, and the beat-up 1999 Honda Civic Dawes had bought after selling his van wasn't in the parking lot. But it wasn't until I walked through the unlocked door of his cabin and found the dresser drawers open and empty that it really sank in.

Dawes was gone. Really gone!

At six o'clock on Saturday, just two days hence, Miss Sutton Elizabeth Barnett would exit the back door of the lodge dressed in a strapless gown by Vera Wang, proceeding between rows of white folding chairs and dewy-eyed wedding guests to the strains of Pachelbel's "Canon in D Major," played by a string quartet, meeting her groom at the lakeside arbor that cost more than three thousand dollars to build, there to recite the vows that would make her a wife to a truly terrible man. About eight minutes after that, two hundred and fifty hungry guests who had come to witness this blessed event would be looking for food. And if we didn't figure out how to provide it, Martin Waddell was going to make my life a living hell.

What were we going to do? We had fifty-six hours, a handful of recipes, and *no* chef.

For a couple of minutes, I just stood there and stared at the empty room, panic-fueled adrenaline flooding my brain and body, my heart pounding like the hoofbeats of a racehorse on the final stretch. Good thing I hadn't eaten breakfast because if I had, I'd have unswallowed it. But there wasn't time to vomit. Or panic.

As I stood there, fighting back both, I suddenly realized that this wasn't about Sutton, or Martin, or the wedding, or the money we hoped we'd make from it, or even proving to Robyn and myself that I could turn the fortunes of the lodge around.

The lodge was more than a business or a balance sheet. It was the place we'd lived our lives and made our memories, it was our history and home, the common thread that bound us together and made us a family. I had to protect that, and them.

But I couldn't do it alone.

CHAPTER TWENTY-THREE

When a social worker called to alert George and Adele to the existence of the grandchild they never knew they had, George drove eleven hours through a rainstorm to rescue me. When Adele slipped on gravel during a hike and broke her ankle, George climbed down a ravine to get her and carried her three miles to find help. When another storm came years later and Last Lake flooded its banks, George lit a lantern and went out into the gale, guiding guests to higher ground and standing guard through the night, until the danger had passed. He'd always been larger than life, a mighty oak, the guy you'd want on your team in an emergency.

And he still was.

Honestly, I'd been worried about how George would react when I told him that Dawes had disappeared. Only weeks before, he had thrown a wrench across the room in frustration, agonizingly aware of his diminishment but powerless to prevent its advance, so I worried he'd blame himself. After all, he was the one who'd hired Dawes. Also, I knew how much he liked Dawes, and since this felt like such a betrayal, I thought it might trigger another meltdown.

He was upset, we all were. But when faced with a crisis, George rose to the occasion, leading the charge like he always had, a proverbial phoenix and family patriarch. Of course, a leader is nothing without followers, and George wasn't the only one who came running when I sounded the alarm.

As soon as I called, Yolanda closed the gallery, dropped everything, and jumped in the car. David found somebody to cover his afternoon classes and showed up too, not long after. Oscar had to check out of his cabin on the morning of the wedding but said he'd delay his departure until after the banquet and, in the meantime, put aside his writing to lend a hand in the kitchen.

Mr. and Mrs. Wilson, who spent a week at the lodge every June but had tacked on a late August visit this year, said they'd do whatever they could to help and so did a few other guests, people who'd been staying with us year after year.

The staff was terrific, canceling their days off and taking an "all hands on deck" attitude. Jamie, who still looked a bit like a deer in the headlights, was all in to help and so was the rest of the café staff. Vera called her sisters, Vonelle and Ruth, and recruited them to help with the housekeeping so she could take over the desk, freeing up Robyn and George to help with the banquet. By eleven o'clock, the cavalry had arrived and assembled in the kitchen. George stepped to the front, cleared his throat, and addressed the troops.

"When I was in my twenties, an army doctor gave my heart a listen and found a murmur that's never caused me a moment of trouble, before or since. So, I never had the chance to serve in the military. But a lot of my friends did, and they told me that the first thing you do before launching any field operation is conduct situation and status reports.

"Now, it seems to me that the situation is pretty straightforward. We've got a wedding banquet to put on. But our chef has scarpered and he was the only one who knows how to make . . ." George frowned and looked toward me. "What was it?"

"Basically everything we're serving," I said, then launched into my report. "We start the evening with Sutton Place martinis, a gin and elderflower syrup signature cocktail that bears no resemblance to an actual martini but works as wordplay with the names of the bride and groom. The cocktail hour menu also includes a selection of passed appetizers: truffle macaroni and cheese bites, pea pods stuffed with herbed cream cheese, Moroccan lamb skewers with mint sauce, and seared tuna mini sliders with red pepper coulis. For dinner, we're serving a salad of mixed Asian greens with enoki mushrooms, roasted macadamia nuts, and lilikoi dressing—"

Mrs. Wilson lifted her hand. "Lilikoi?"

"Passion fruit," I explained. "To be followed by pepper-crusted beef tenderloins with mushroom and cognac cream, roasted Cornish game hens with apricot glaze, accompanied by homemade Parker House rolls, haricot verts, and gratin dauphinois. For dessert, Dawes had planned to serve a three-tier wedding cake. The first layer was to be lemon filled with raspberry, the second was chocolate with hazelnut cream, and the third was coconut with pineapple custard. Plus," I said, remembering the final touch, "little boxes of French macarons for each guest to take home."

"Man," Robyn said, smirking. "Good thing they tacked on those take-away cookies to the menu. I was worried people might go home hungry."

A ripple of laughter ran through the room and I gave Robyn a grateful smile. Judging from the looks on their faces, our vol-

unteers were starting to wonder what they'd gotten themselves
into, but her wisecrack had broken the tension.

Oscar, who'd been standing next to me, leaned closer and
muttered out of the side of his mouth, "Your mom's kind of a
smart-ass."

"You don't know the half of it," I muttered back.

"Okay," Oscar murmured to himself, gazing across the
room to where Robyn was standing.

"All right," George said, clapping his hands together and
tugging his Panama hat a little lower on his brow. "That's the
situation. Let's move on to status. Does anybody here know
how to cook any of that?"

After a brief silence, Jamie slowly raised his hand. "I can do
the macaroni and cheese bites and the pea pods. Dawes taught
me before he left."

"Great! Now we're getting somewhere! Anybody else?"

I stepped forward.

"Dawes did leave recipes for everything on the menu, but,"
I said, thinking back to my first failed attempts at following
Adele's instructions for caramel cake, "without having made
them before, I think they're just too complicated. You learn
to cook by watching and doing, not by reading recipes, that's
what Dawes always said."

Nobody argued to the contrary and I saw more than one
person nod in agreement, including George. When I stepped
back, he tugged his favorite fishing hat lower on his brow,
pulled an unlit cigar from the breast pocket of his flannel shirt,
and scanned the silent assembly.

"All right, gang. Looks like we're pivoting to Plan B."

CHAPTER TWENTY-FOUR

Though none of us had a clue about preparing cognac and mushroom sauce or Moroccan lamb skewers, we were not entirely without skills.

Using her charm and talent for negotiation, Yolanda talked the food wholesaler into canceling our order so we weren't stuck with a bill for a hundred pounds of beef tenderloin and fifty Cornish game hens we had no use for. Then she haggled to get us a good price on the ingredients we did need and called Sylvia Barnett to let her know of our predicament, assuring her that the revised menu would be amazing. Considering the circumstances, Sylvia was extremely understanding.

"No matter what we feed people, come Saturday night Sutton will still be Mrs. Waddell, that's all that matters. Don't worry about telling the kids," she said. "I'll handle it. The last thing you need right now is to have Martin show up and start making a fuss."

Sylvia had more insight into her future son-in-law than I'd given her credit for.

Yolanda also volunteered to head up a team to make dates

wrapped in bacon, the world's easiest and most delicious appetizer, as well as her grandma Iona's Italian meatballs. Rolled to bite-size and stuck on toothpicks with a mozzarella ball and basil leaf, they were tasty, attractive, and easy to eat while standing up.

And if all that wasn't enough, later that day she handed me the last piece in the puzzle that was my grandmother's life, answering the question that had bothered me from the first: Why had Adele put so much effort into making such beautiful, artistic quilts, only to hide them away where no one would ever see them?

"I know you've got other things on your mind," Yolanda said, chopping basil leaves and tossing them into a bowl as we stood at a counter, making the meatballs, "but I have to tell you about a woman who just started teaching tatting at the gallery, Elizabeth Reynaud. She learned from her mother, Betty Rae, who must be about ninety.

"Liz brought her mom into the gallery last week because we had an exhibit of her students' classwork. Betty Rae is a little deaf now but we got to talking and she was telling me about Asheville back in the day, and that she'd lived in the boardinghouse over on Flint Street during the war . . ."

"You're kidding!" I gasped, feeling that familiar tingling on my neck, the feeling I got whenever I stumbled upon another of Adele's bread crumbs. "Was it the same boardinghouse? Did she know Adele?"

"*And* George," Yolanda confirmed, nodding deeply. "Her memory is amazing, Esme. You should interview her when you have time. Although, I'm not even sure that you have to. She confirmed so many of the stories you said you've written about. She remembered about Adele and George painting the room, and how mad the landlady got. Honestly," she said, her eyes growing wide, "it was kind of spooky. But, also *really* cool."

Yolanda plunged her hands into the bowl, squishing the meatball ingredients together with her fingers. "And here's the part that's really going to blow your mind. In 1944, Adele, Betty Rae, and one of the other boarders, Edith, joined Miss Ida's quilt circle. One night . . ."

By the time Yolanda finished telling the story, it wasn't just my neck that was tingling. It felt like that time I'd gone to get a manicure and the massage chair went haywire, as if little bursts of electricity were running all over my body.

"Yolanda, that is *amazing*! And it makes perfect sense. Thank you! Thank you so, so much! If I didn't have meatball all over my hands, I'd give you the biggest hug right now!"

She grinned. "You're welcome. But instead of a hug, why don't you give me something I'd like almost as much: the chance to read your book?" She tilted her head to one side. "Please?"

I smiled. "Okay. Sure. I'll email the file to you tonight."

David came through the door carrying a huge crate of romaine. George, who came right behind him, was carrying *three*.

"Esme!" George barked, his voice a happy bellow. "If you're not too busy gossiping with Yolanda, maybe you can help David wash this lettuce? These salads aren't going to make themselves, you know!"

I wiped my hands on my apron, snapped him a salute, and marched over to the sink.

"Sir! Yes, sir!"

OVER THE NEXT two days, it really did feel a bit like I'd joined the army. But that wasn't necessarily a bad thing. Everybody pulled together, offering whatever they had for the good of the group, acting like a team.

Lilikoi dressing was way beyond his pay grade, but David's Caesar salad lived up to its reputation. On top of that, he was a cheerful and willing set of extra hands in the kitchen, and gifted at the chopping, sprinkling, and placement of fresh herbs to garnish plates.

Mrs. Wilson supervised much of the baking. Having grown up in South Carolina, she knew how to make beautifully light biscuits, which tasted fantastic served with a honey butter. She also had a recipe for Mexican wedding cookies, which seemed like a good stand-in for macarons. Mr. Wilson and George helped her roll the dough into balls and then into powdered sugar, making five hundred cookies in four hours.

One of George's many odd jobs in his youth included flipping burgers and Mr. Wilson had a recipe for chili that took third place at his church cook-off, so the two of them put their heads together and came up with a modified café menu of hamburgers, grilled cheese sandwiches, chili, hot dogs, chili dogs, apples, oranges, and potato chips. It wasn't exactly gourmet fare but it kept the lodge guests from going hungry.

There were a few grumbles initially, but once they understood the reason for the limited menu, most guests were really nice about it. Upon hearing of our predicament, a surprising number offered to lend a hand. That's where Robyn came in. She'd been managing the staff ever since Adele passed, so she put her organizational skills to work, making sure that everybody had a job to do and the resources to do it properly. And though I'd never have suspected it, she also knew how to pipe a pretty passable buttercream rosette, which was a lucky thing. My caramel cake tasted delicious, but when it came to decorating, I was hopeless.

"Where'd you learn to do that?" I asked, watching open-mouthed as she created a flower with frosting and a perfectly steady hand.

"Food Network. *Ace of Cakes*," she said, keeping her eyes fixed on the cake and an even pressure on the piping bag. "Duff Goldman is my spirit animal."

Who knew?

Less surprising was the fact that Oscar had a recipe to make old fashioneds by the gallon. They looked beautiful when served in cocktail glasses and garnished with cherry and orange peel, so that became the signature cocktail. There was some discussion about calling them something besides Sutton Place martinis. But then George said that nobody cared what you called them as long as they had a kick and tasted good, which seemed like a valid point.

People *did* like them. A *lot*.

When Oscar said we needed to order six more bottles of bourbon than I'd planned on, I had doubts. But then he laid his hand on my forearm, looked me in the eye, and said, "Trust me on this." Though our relationship had improved a thousand percent since the day he'd called me an illiterate in a dress in front of my boss, I'm not convinced that trusting Oscar is always the smart move. But this time it worked out.

Thanks to Oscar, the party got off to a rollicking start. But as tasty and potent as those Sutton Place martinis were, I think some of their appeal was due to the fact that he grabbed a tray and started serving the drinks himself. He can be very charming when he feels like it, and it wasn't long before a wedding guest who was also a rabid fan recognized him. Word of Oscar's presence spread quickly. Soon, he was surrounded by admirers and was telling stories and passing out drinks like a pubkeeper buying a round for the house.

If Carl ever did manage to pull together a deal for Oscar, he really needed to make sure the publisher sent him on tour. Slumping sales or no, Oscar still had a following and knew how to work a room. Of course, I was in the kitchen the whole time Oscar was holding court so I only heard about it after the fact, but according to all the reports, he was the life of the party.

With the dinner hour approaching we needed every pair of hands, so I sent Robyn to bring Oscar back to the kitchen. When they returned, Oscar started helping David plate the salads and Robyn came over to the sink to help me snap stems off the haricot verts, the only item from the original menu that I actually knew how to make. Maybe they taste better in French but in my opinion green beans are green beans are green beans.

Anyway, when Robyn joined me, she had a really weird look on her face so I asked if she was feeling all right. The way she turned her head, stretching it lengthways and sideways at the same time, like a turtle assessing oncoming traffic before crossing the road, made me think something was wrong with her, that she'd pulled a muscle or something.

"He asked for my number," she muttered from the side of her mouth.

"Who did?"

"Him!" she hissed.

"Oscar? Really?"

She leaned her torso to the left, looking past my shoulder toward the salad station, like a kid hiding behind a tree who hopes somebody will come looking for her. I followed her glance and saw Oscar grin and give her a wink. Robyn blushed like a teenager.

"He's been divorced about seventeen times, you know that, right?"

"He's asking for my number, not my hand," she hissed, then peeked around me again and heaved a sigh. "Geez. He's *so* handsome."

I looked across the room, trying and failing to see what she saw.

"Um . . . okay. If you say so."

"And he's smart too, don't you think?" Robyn asked. "Remember that day we were sitting on Adele's bench and you told me about him? I found one of his books in the lobby library the next day and started reading it."

"Which one?"

"*Death Comes for Mr. Fox*. I'm only about halfway through but it's *really* good," she said, sounding simultaneously surprised and impressed.

"It is," I agreed, twisting the stem off the last green bean and tossing it on the mountain of beans that had already been trimmed. "I think his new book will be even better."

"Really? Wow," Robyn breathed. "So? What do you think? Should I give him my number?"

I turned on the sprayer and gave the beans a rinse. "Do you want to?"

"Maybe. It's been so long since anybody asked. And he's *so* handsome."

"Yeah. You said that already."

"I bet he's a *great* kisser," she said, then giggled.

Yep, that's right. My smart-aleck, hard-as-nails, ex-convict mom speculated about kissing Oscar Glazier and then giggled like a schoolgirl. When she did, I clamped my eyelids closed and took a breath, trying mightily to erase the image that had just popped into my mind.

"If you ever find out, promise me you'll keep it to yourself, okay? Also, could we *possibly* postpone discussing your love life to a time when I'm not quite so busy? I've got to make shrimp and grits for two hundred and fifty people."

Yes. I was in charge of the main course. And it was making me really, really nervous.

Adele's recipe was a classic as well as a crowd pleaser and I'd cooked it so often that I could practically make it in my sleep. Still, cooking for a handful of friends is a whole different animal than feeding an actual crowd, especially if your dish is meant to be the star attraction at a wedding banquet. The pressure was intense.

Seafood allergies being what they are, we did have to provide an alternative entrée. Jamie said his mom made a good beef brisket with cola and cocoa powder but that didn't seem quite elegant enough for a wedding. David, who speaks fluent French, suggested we call it "bœuf braisé au chocolat et aux épices" on the menu cards and serve it over mashed potatoes, otherwise known as purée de pommes de terre. Thirty-six people ordered it, which meant two hundred and fourteen people wanted shrimp and grits for dinner.

Two hundred and fourteen!

I'm still not quite sure how we pulled it off but, somehow or other, we did.

The entire day was organized chaos tinged with panic, but that last twenty-five minutes was a flat-out, leave-it-all-on-the-field sprint to the finish. Or maybe I should say a relay, because getting that food out of the kitchen and onto the banquet tables was a team effort.

Shrimp cooks quickly but gets cold in a flash, so we had to work fast and cook in batches, with all eight burners on the big commercial stove going at once. Robyn knew Adele's recipe as well as I did, so the two of us did the cooking, juggling four skillets each. But an assembly line of helpers made it happen.

One group ferried prepped ingredients from the counter to the stove. When the cooking was complete, we handed off skillets to another group for plating and serving. It was loud, and crazy, hot and something of a blur. Every time one of the servers came through the door and shouted, "I need a brisket and nine shrimp!" my blood pressure kicked up a couple of notches.

The worst moment came at the end when somebody at the prep counter yelled, "We're out of shrimp!" But it didn't last long because somebody else immediately shouted, "It's okay, the last order just went out the door! All the tables have food! We're done!"

The best moment came later, after a whoop of triumph rang through the kitchen and the score of volunteers who had worked to make it happen finished a round of handshakes and high-fives, and everybody squeezed together in front of the stove and yelled "Cheese!" as one of the servers captured the moment on his cell phone.

"You know what this reminds me of?" George asked. "That one Thanksgiving when the cook quit and all the guests pitched in to help Adele make dinner."

"That's right! I've still got the picture."

George smiled, looking at me and Robyn in turn.

"Come on with me," he said. "There's something I want you to see."

THE MOON WAS full. Strings of twinkling white lights that hung over the dance floor sparkled against the night sky, like diamonds displayed on black velvet, or clouds of fireflies. The flickering light from the hundred table candles reflected against the still, dark waters of the lake, making the scene twice as bright. Music and soft laughter from the clutches of people huddled in conversation filled the air and echoed through the trees, carried by the breeze.

Dashing men in black tuxedoes and white dinner jackets rested light hands on the waists and bare shoulders of dazzling, bejeweled women in chiffon gowns that fluttered like butterfly wings as they swayed and twirled and floated to the music. It was magical.

Everywhere I looked, I saw people enjoying themselves and each other, collecting memories. And none more than the beautiful, besotted Sutton, who positively beamed as she glided across the dance floor in the arms of her groom, who beamed back at her with adoration, as if he couldn't believe his good fortune at having won her. They looked perfectly, incandescently happy together; I hoped they always would be.

George stretched out his big arms like a pair of sheltering wings and draped them over our shoulders. "What do you think?"

"Adele would have loved this," I said, swallowing back a catch in my voice.

"She would have," George said. "She loved seeing people have a good time."

"I wish she was here," Robyn said softly.

George pulled us closer. "I think maybe she is, in a way."

That was the best moment.

Because when I looked at the faces of my mother and my grandfather, I could see we were thinking and feeling the same thing, deep satisfaction and a touch of pride, knowing that we'd pulled together to accomplish something good against very long odds.

And in that moment, for the first time in my memory, we were a family.

CHAPTER TWENTY-FIVE

The party was going strong but our work was far from done, so when the servers started bringing out the cake, George, Robyn, and I hurried back to the kitchen. Oscar was getting ready to leave.

"I'd stay to help clean up," he said, "but I've got a long drive ahead and if I don't—"

"Go. You've done so much and we've got plenty of help," I said, gesturing toward the remaining volunteers, who were scurrying around the kitchen, scraping plates and wrapping leftovers. "But are you sure you're okay to drive? Those 'martinis' of yours were pretty potent."

He set his lips into a line. "I know you may find this hard to believe, Esme, but I'm not a complete knuckle-dragger. I was serving, not drinking. I *never* drink and drive."

"Good. Because I'd hate it if something happened to you. Against all odds, Oscar, it turns out that I kind of like you."

"Well, I kind of like you too, Half-pint."

"But you know I'd like you more if you'd stop calling me that, right?"

"Yeah, I know. Not going to happen though." Oscar put his

arms around me and hugged me tight, lifting me off the floor for a second before setting me back on my feet. "Give me a shout when you're back in New York."

"I will. Call me if you need any help with your book," I said. "I think you're in good shape at this point, but feel free to send me the pages if you get stuck or want a second opinion."

"Right," he said, putting on his jacket. "And you do the same."

"Why? So you can tell me they're good and to keep going?"

"Would you rather I told you they were bad and to stop?"

I laughed. "Good night, Oscar. Drive safe."

"Good night, Half-pint. And thanks."

Oscar announced his departure and headed toward the door. Just before he made his exit, I saw Robyn brush past him and slip a scrap of paper into his pocket.

People are always more excited about setting up than cleaning up, so I wasn't surprised when volunteers started peeling off after Oscar left, nor did I blame them. It had been a long day, and they'd run their feet off out of the kindness of their hearts, with no more pay than our sincere thanks and a slice of leftover caramel cake.

The paid staff stayed longer but most of them had worked a ten-hour shift—Jamie had been on the clock for thirteen—so I started sending them home too. Near the end, it was down to me, Yolanda, and David, plus Robyn and George, and finally just me after I shooed them all out of the kitchen so I could mop the floor. After two days of chaos and crowds, I appreciated the quiet and the chance to decompress.

By the time I shut off the lights and locked the door, the band had packed up, the bar had closed, and the wedding guests had either driven back to town or retired to their cabins shortly thereafter—except for one couple.

They were sitting on a stone wall we'd built on one side of the new patio, legs hanging over the side, looking at the lake and talking. He wore a tuxedo with the bow tie dangling loose around his neck, like a lounge singer at closing time. She wore a gown of wine-colored satin and chandelier earrings. A pair of discarded silver stilettos sat next to her on the wall.

Their voices were too low for me to understand what they were saying but it was clearly an intense conversation. They only had eyes for each other and took no notice when I padded across the grass. I couldn't see the woman's face but the look in the man's eyes and the way he hung on her words told me that at least one of them was in love.

Had they been seated next to each other by happenstance at the banquet and been hit by a thunderbolt during the salad course? Or had they been friends for years and, as they watched Sutton and Martin repeat their vows, realized that there was more to it than friendship? Could be. People are forever falling in love at weddings. Would they look back on this day as the starting point for their own trip down the aisle? Would they decide to have the wedding here, at the lake?

I hoped so. They couldn't find a better place to begin a new life.

Arriving at my cabin, I kicked off my shoes and turned on my laptop. The story Yolanda had told me kept buzzing around in my brain.

Until I wrote it down, there was no point in trying to sleep.

Shattered

September 1944

There were only twelve women in the quilt circle and no elected positions, but Miss Ida was a sort of self-appointed president, so after Hazel Miles resumed her seat at the boardinghouse's big dining room table, Miss Ida rose and led a brief round of applause.

"Thank you for that presentation, Hazel. That's a very clever technique for mitering corners. I'm sure we all appreciate learning your secrets."

Miss Ida pulled a pale blue notecard from the pocket of her dress, a letter from Mrs. Walter Fisher, head of the local chapter of the Red Cross, thanking us for our one-hundred-and-five-dollar donation, raised through our quilt raffle. After reading the letter, Miss Ida beamed a smile at the circle of faces. "Well! I think that's something we can all feel very proud of!"

I did feel proud. Since the D-Day invasion in June, the Red Cross was more important than ever. Earlier that week, George and I had organized a group of volunteers from the dairy to go assemble care packages for POWs, small comforts to sustain them as they waited for the war to end, as it surely would soon, probably by next year.

That morning, I had received a letter from Mr. Finley, informing me that my charges would be returning to the museum soon. The decision *on a date was yet to be made, but I planned to go to the storerooms during the next week to make sure that the shipping crates that had been used to transport the pieces from Washington were still in good condition.*

Mr. Finley's letter made no mention of what would happen to me after the art was returned to the museum, but almost three years had passed since the kindly Greyhound driver helped me down from the bus; I was ready for something new, excited to find out what the future would bring. Could the folded quilts lying on the floor beneath my chair be a part of that future? When Miss Ida asked if anyone had a quilt to show, my hand shot up.

As I pushed back my chair and carried my quilt to the front of the room, I felt my cheeks go pink and hot, not from embarrassment but from anticipation. I'd been perfecting my technique for months but tonight would be the test, the first time I'd let anyone see my work. I had decided to show my two favorites, the small, square piece with the azure, amber, raspberry, and saffron waves—and the quilt I had completed last Sunday.

It was large, four and a half feet wide and three feet high. Some of the patches were long, thin rectangles but more were long, thin triangles, no two the same size or color, colliding into one another at the center, exactly as my emotions have been doing these last days. Though the composition was designed to look random, creating that effect required hours and hours of painstaking work. I'd lost count of how many seams I'd ripped out to achieve the perfect balance of color, line, shape, and position but I felt that the end result was worth it. I was so eager to show it to my friends.

Whenever anyone showed a finished quilt, the others always clapped. Sometimes their applause was enthusiastic and sincere, other times it was rote and tepid, but there was always some sort of response, always.

My quilts were met with stares, and silence.

For a moment, I thought the women were simply speechless, stunned, to encounter something so unique, a quilt unlike any they've ever seen. Then the silence broke.

Edith leaned over the table, head hovering over the larger quilt, the emotional collision, and frowned. "Your points don't meet at all here."

Her comment jarred the logjam, clearing the way for everyone else's opinion.

"And the colors clash. I don't mind a scrap quilt but this is too much."

"What's it supposed to be? It looks like there might be a heart in the center but . . . not really."

"Looks like my migraines feel," someone mumbled to her neighbors, who snickered. The sound of their laughter was careless and cutting, like haphazard shards of shattered glass.

Now, lying in my bed, awake in the sleeping house, chewing on pewter-colored emptiness that tastes of gravel, I think of the burn barrel in the backyard, and climb out from beneath the covers to gather the quilts from the chair where I left them before turning out the light. Opening the door to my room, I hesitate on the threshold.

The paintings were different, oil and watercolor imitations of work of my betters, and no great loss to anyone, not even me. My quilts are more. They are my thoughts and words, my story. They are my art. I love them too much to burn them, or to share them with people who can never understand.

I turn in the doorway, take the suitcase from under my bed, then place the quilts inside and close the lid, turning the lock with a small silver key.

CHAPTER TWENTY-SIX

Though I only got four hours of sleep, I woke in a surprisingly good mood.

The wedding had stretched me to the limit. Pulling it off in such style was a huge weight off my shoulders. In spite of the bumps, it had been a beautiful affair. And though we'd need to work up the figures after cashing Martin's check and repaying my loan to the lodge, I was pretty sure that, by the end of August, the lodge would post a profit. A small one, it was true, but with the renovations wrapped up and two more weddings already booked for next year, the future was looking bright.

Of course, we still needed to get through the last two weeks of the summer season, and hire a new chef. Also, now that the wedding was over, I really needed to step up my job search and figure out where I was going to live when I went back to New York. But for some reason, I felt sure it was all going to work out. The post-wedding high probably had something to do with it. I'd just pulled one rabbit out of my hat, so why not two? And if Carl liked my book and got me a publishing deal, that would make three. It could happen, right?

I got dressed and headed to the lodge, humming a song the

band had played the night before, wondering if Carl might be reading my pages even now, and thinking about the first things I'd do when I got back to New York. Finding a really good bagel topped the list.

It was a beautiful day, sunny and bright. The anglers were up early as usual and I saw half a dozen boats bobbing around the lake. An older gentleman with white hair and a hobble and a little girl of about seven or eight with brown braids, probably a grandfather and granddaughter, were down at the dock, loading their gear into one of our rental boats. I smiled to myself, thinking about the first time George had taken me fishing, then smiled even wider when I realized a boat in the center of the lake was carrying a familiar figure.

I waved my arm over my head and George waved back, then cast out his line with as much expertise as ever. I made a mental note to fit in one more day of fishing with George, or maybe even two, before I went back to New York. Though the anglers were out in force, the grounds were quiet, which made sense. The wedding guests were probably still sleeping off all those cocktails they'd downed the night before. Lucky for them, Sutton and Martin had requested a late checkout for all their guests.

Turning a corner, I spotted the happy couple exiting the honeymoon cabin, towing two rolling suitcases, and remembered that they were flying to Bermuda that day. I waved and called out to them but not too loudly, mindful of guests who were still sleeping.

"Mr. and Mrs. Waddell! Good morning! I was so busy that I didn't have a chance to say so yesterday but congratulations. It was a beautiful wedding and I hope your honeymoon is just as wonderful."

They looked a little grim but I really didn't give it a second thought, chalking it up to the early hour. Like a lot of other people, they'd probably over-imbibed at the reception. It wasn't until they came close and I saw the look in Sutton's eyes that I realized something was wrong.

"Honey," she said, giving Martin an almost pleading glance, "it wasn't Esme's fault. And the wedding *was* beautiful. Everyone had such a good time. Don't you think that—"

"Sutton, please go wait in the car," he said, cutting her off. "I'll handle this."

"But, Martin—"

"Go," he commanded, in a voice as icy as his stare. "Esme and I have business to discuss. This won't take long."

ROBYN'S PACING WAS making me crazy. I shut my eyes and turned away slightly, pressing the phone closer to my ear as Venita Benedict, David's lawyer friend, delivered the bad news.

"Here's the problem: the contract you signed was very specific when it came to the menu. I'm not saying it's absolutely hopeless. It's possible you might come across a sympathetic judge," she said, though her tone of voice indicated otherwise. "But even if you did, I'm not sure it's worth the trouble. From what you've told me, the groom sounds like one of those guys who love dragging people to court, the kind who'll spend more on lawyers than they'll ever gain in a judgment, telling themselves it's about 'principle' when it's really about power. I'm sorry, Esme. I wish I could be more encouraging."

"It's okay," I said. "I understand. And I appreciate your help. Can you send a bill to me in New York?"

"No charge for a consult," she said, "especially for one of David and Yolanda's friends. If you can send me a copy of your current contract, I'll work up some language to protect you going forward. Shouldn't cost more than a couple of hundred dollars."

"I'll do that." I sighed. "Live and learn, I guess."

"Unfortunately, that's the way these things tend to work out."

I ended the call. When I turned around, Robyn was practically standing on top of me.

"What did she say?"

"In a nutshell? That no matter how much people enjoyed the food, we fell short of serving the meal that was outlined in the contract so he doesn't owe us anything."

"What? Nothing?"

"Not one more dime. Venita didn't come out and say so, but I had the feeling she thought it was lucky he didn't ask us to return the deposit."

Robyn started pacing again. "Wait . . . So after all that work, after the way we killed ourselves to pull together an absolutely gorgeous wedding, this joker can just decide he doesn't want to pay the rest of his bill and there's nothing we can do about it?"

"Pretty much."

This had started out to be such a good day, brimming with hope and possibility. Now I felt both draining away. Robyn had left her cigarettes sitting on the desk. I almost never smoke but now I tapped one out of the packet and lit up. I guess there's a first time for everything if you're desperate enough. And today must have been the day for it. Because as soon as I took that first puff, Robyn sunk into the chair opposite me and did something she never does—tried to look on the bright side.

It was really annoying.

"Well, we learned a lot," she said, "so there's that. And at least we didn't lose any money on food or payroll. The deposit covered that, plus a lot of the renovations. We'd have had to do those anyway, so in a way, we're ahead."

"It didn't cover the extra forty grand that Dawes put in," I reminded her.

"But he's not here to collect it so, you know . . . ," she said, spreading her hands. "Maybe it's better that he disappeared?"

It was *not* better that Dawes had disappeared. If he'd stayed none of this would have happened. And yes, breaking even on food and staffing was unquestionably better than not. But since the profits that we now weren't getting would have repaid the money I'd been counting on to tide me over until I found another job, it definitely wasn't better for me.

"Did you ask the lawyer what we do if Dawes does come back?" Robyn asked.

The immediate crisis had pushed concerns about Dawes to one side, but Robyn was right. I did need to tell Venita about him. Because if Dawes walked through the door anytime soon, the chances of my needing a lawyer were extremely high. Would Venita be able to defend me for an assault with intent to inflict bodily harm? Seemed like contract law was more her thing.

"I'll ask her about it later."

Robyn stretched out her hand and wriggled her fingers. I handed over my cigarette. She took a puff, then passed it back and continued her recitation of upside.

"Look," she said in a practical tone, "Martin might have been unhappy but everybody else loved it. This nice couple from Charlotte who checked out just before you showed up said it was the best wedding they'd ever been to. Word's going to spread, you'll see. We've already got two weddings booked for next year. I'll bet you ten bucks that eventually, we'll get at least one referral from yesterday."

"Can we not talk about it right this minute? I'm wallowing."

"Yeah, I know. Stop it." She shrugged. "Okay, so maybe things didn't turn out quite the way we planned. It's not the end of the world. I mean, things could always be worse, right?"

"Are you crazy? Don't say that! Don't *ever* say that!"

Robyn frowned. "Why not?"

"Because! Things always *can* get worse," I said, planting both hands on the desk and leaning toward her. "Saying it out loud is just . . . It's tempting fate!"

Robyn rolled her eyes and wriggled her fingers to signal her need for another drag, saying something about how people who went to college should be too educated to give into superstition and basically blowing me off.

Maybe it was superstition. Maybe it was coincidence. Or maybe it was tempting fate. All I know is that, before the day was over, things got worse.

Much worse.

CHAPTER TWENTY-SEVEN

I was in the café, talking with Jamie, who'd shown up to cook for the breakfast crowd after working until midnight the day before.

"Don't worry, Miss Esme. As long as you don't mind sticking to the menu Mr. Cahill and Mr. Wilson worked out, I think I can handle things until you find a new chef. The only thing is," he said, looking apologetic, "I've got to go back to school after Labor Day."

A wave of relief washed over me. "Absolutely. Not a problem. I just need to buy a little time. Jamie, I don't know what we'd have done without you these last few days. If you ever need a recommendation for a job, or school, you can count on me."

Jamie's face lit up. "Thanks! I've been thinking about trying to get into culinary school after graduation and—"

The clanging of an old bell that George had mounted on a log frame years before to serve as an alarm in case of fire interrupted Jamie's sentence. I turned toward the sound, then walked quickly to the door and hovered on the threshold, looking for signs of smoke or flame. For a moment I thought it was a false alarm, that some smart-aleck kid had ignored the placard saying the bell was to be rung only in the event of an emergency. But when I saw a clutch of agitated guests standing near the dock, I knew something was wrong and ran toward the lakefront as fast as I could.

Jamie ran faster. He passed me on the way and was pushing through the crowd by the time I arrived, creating a pathway through the assembly of gaping bystanders. There were so many that I couldn't tell what was happening until I emerged from the crush of bodies and saw a small fishing boat, not much bigger than a dingy, chugging slowly and riding low in the water. A heavy-set man sat in the rear with his hand on the tiller, ferrying his passengers—George, plus the grandfather and granddaughter I'd seen loading their gear earlier that morning—to the dock. All three of them were soaking wet.

"George!" I called as they approached. "Oh my gosh, George! Are you okay?"

"Don't worry, Baby Sister, we're fine," George said, his face splitting into a grin. "I lost my lucky hat at the bottom of the lake but, apart from that, everything's okay."

The heavy-set captain turned off the motor. George tossed a line to Jamie, who quickly tied up the boat and lifted the little girl onto the dock. George and the captain went to assist her grandfather, who seemed a little dazed.

"That's it, Jerry," George said, placing his arm under the old man's elbow to steady him as he climbed out of the boat. "Take your time. No rush. You're doing great."

Robyn arrived on the scene, carrying an armload of blankets.

"Somebody said a boat capsized and that three people ended up in the—Dad!" she cried, realizing that George was one of the three. "Dad, are you okay?"

"I'm fine. Just worry about them," he said, waving her off and pointing to Jerry and the little girl. "Might want to call for a doctor, just to be sure."

"Got 911 already on the way," she said.

Robyn wrapped blankets around the shoulders of the girl and her grandfather, Jerry. Someone found a bucket and turned it over so Jerry could sit down. He seemed fine but looked very pale. I thought he was probably just scared but hoped the EMTs would arrive soon.

George stepped onto the dock. I handed him a blanket.

"What happened?"

"Nothing worth getting worked up over," George said. "Jerry got a little confused, accidentally put the motor in reverse and ended up hitting a rock. I got him and Louise out of the water is all."

"There's a little more to it than that," the portly captain said, coming forward and clapping George on the back. "I'm Chuck," he said, introducing himself. "And your granddad is a hero. Well, you are," Chuck said when George began to protest.

"That rock was jagged and Jerry hit it *hard*," Chuck told me. "Tore a big hole in the hull. The boat went down fast. George saw what was happening and got over there as quick as he could, but Jerry panicked while George was trying to help him into his boat. Next thing you know, George's boat capsized and all three of them were in the water. I was a long way off, but I saw the whole thing," Chuck said, lifting his hand.

"Jerry kept trying to climb on top of George—honestly, I thought he'd end up drowning the both of them. But somehow George got him to calm down and hang on to the capsized hull. Thank God the little girl could dog-paddle but she wasn't a strong swimmer. I think she was starting to panic too, but then George swam over and got her, brought her back to the boat. I picked them up as quick as I could. But I'll tell you," Chuck said, shaking his head and looking toward Jerry and little Louise, who were being tended to by Robyn and some other bystanders, "if George hadn't been on the scene, this could have ended up being a real sad day."

"You're making way more of it than it was," George said, flapping his hand in Chuck's direction. "Never believe a fisherman, Esme. They're always telling stories."

The whine of sirens sounded in the distance, becoming louder with each passing second. I put my arm around George's shoulders and gave him a squeeze, partly to show my affection and partly to help warm him up. He was starting to shiver a little.

"In this instance I'm inclined to believe him. You deserve a medal, George."

"At the moment I'd settle for a cup of hot coffee. And maybe a nap," he said, looking suddenly fatigued. He let out a breath and wiped at his brow. "That's about as much excitement as an old codger like me can take in a day."

The ambulance arrived. Two uniformed medical workers jogged down the hill toward the lake, one carrying a big first aid box. Robyn, who was kneeling in front of Louise, speaking softly to the little girl, looked over her shoulder toward me.

"Why don't you take George up to his place and help him change into some dry clothes? I'll take care of things down here."

"I've been putting on my own pants for more than eighty years," George retorted. "I don't need Esme's help."

"How about I just go up to the lodge with you?" I suggested, moving to one side to allow the EMTs to pass before escorting George down the dock. "And you can tell me the story again, from your perspective."

"Nothing much to tell. Chuck mostly got it right. But I was pretty scared there for a couple minutes, I don't mind admitting it."

I linked my arm in his as we walked up the bank. "Sure am glad you decided to go fishing this morning."

"So am I," George said. "Only one thing I do regret. The fish I caught went over the side when the boat capsized. Biggest bass you've ever seen. Hand to God," he said, lifting his as he unlinked his arm from mine, "that sucker was thirteen pounds if he was an ounce. Would have broken my old record, but I've got no way to prove it now. I'll just be one more fisherman telling stories about the one that got away." George sighed. "He was a beauty."

"There'll be other records."

"Nope. My record-breaking days are behind me," George said, his pace slowing markedly as the hill became steeper. He sighed again. "Would have been a good way to go out though, catching that fish."

"Oh, you're not going anywhere," I said, rolling my eyes. "And if it had to be a choice between Jerry and his granddaughter or the fish, I'm glad it got away."

"Me too," George said.

"Besides, how many fishing resorts can say they've got their very own eighty-seven-year-old lifeguard? You are a force of nature, George. A force of nature."

I smiled and patted him on the arm, wondering briefly if I should tell him about my unpleasant encounter with Martin Waddell, ultimately deciding it could wait, and asked what he'd like for lunch, joking that he could have his choice of chili or chili dogs.

Instead of answering the question, George suddenly stopped in his tracks. His face contorted with pain, and beads of sweat popped out on his brow. I reached for his hands.

"George? George, what's wrong?"

"I don't . . . I don't . . ." George winced in anguish, his teeth bared in a silent scream. He clutched his left arm and crumpled to the ground.

"George!"

I knelt down next to him, my heart hammering. He didn't respond but he was still breathing. I jumped to my feet and turned toward the crowd of people still on the dock, cupping my hands to my mouth and shouting.

"Help! We need help!"

CHAPTER TWENTY-EIGHT

*H*ospitals are worlds unto themselves.

In the four days since the emergency room doors opened with a soft whoosh and I crossed the threshold into this world, I have been immersed. Across the border, in that other world, news breaks as it always has, pinging countless millions of phones to alert countless millions of eyeballs to the latest crisis, or scandal, or outrage. Here, none of that matters. The things I once thought I cared about don't penetrate these walls.

Now there is only this world, this room, this day, this moment, this breath.

Even as I dream and hope and pray—pray with a fervency that was foreign to me until now—of returning to the old world with George by my side, a part of me is strangely grateful for this exile, this time set apart.

Everything here is beige and background, remarkably unremarkable—wallpaper, curtains, carpets, food, the music in the elevators—chosen specifically for its inability to draw attention. Attention is precious here. And though minutes sometimes seem like days and days like minutes, time is precious too. Not a droplet of either is to be wasted in attending to anything apart from the beloved in the bed, the cherished companion hovering near the next border to the next world, struggling to breathe, or to heal, to stay, or to go.

Attention is precious. Time is precious. For four days, I spend all I have on George.

People enter and exit, bringing pills and syringes, fresh bags of fluids, flowers and cards, good wishes or grim reports. I know they are there but, like the curtains and the wallpaper, they're so much white noise and background. For me in these days, there is only George.

He sleeps and I watch him. He wakes and I talk to him. He tires and I read to him. I start with a novel I found on a shelf in the waiting room, then articles from magazines. Neither holds his attention.

Robyn is splitting her time between the hospital and the lodge, keeping an eye on everything, dashing from one spinning plate to the next, doing what she can to keep them from crashing. She always brings things with her, fresh clothes for me, George's favorite pillow, a tiny container of butter brickle ice cream she hopes will tempt him to eat. When she brings my laptop, I turn on my computer and start reading the book aloud.

It soothes and settles him. His face and limbs relax and his breathing is more even. That would be enough, just to see him peaceful. But before long, he becomes engaged in the story, laughing at the funny moments, swallowing hard or even tearing up at the sad parts, urging me to keep reading even when I know he is tired. He hangs on every word, engrossed in every scene.

Sometimes it seems he remembers it all so well. Two or three times, he even finishes a line of dialogue for me, speaking the words almost exactly as I've written them. At other times, it seems entirely new to him. When I break to drink some water or insist that he get some sleep, he clutches my hand and asks, "What happens next, do you think?"

But always, he wants more. The moment he wakes, or the doctor leaves, or the nurse removes the blood pressure cuff, he looks at me and says, "Read the story." Not *a* story, *the* story. For George, there is only one now.

Attention is precious here. Time even more so.

Whenever George reluctantly gives in to his body's demand for rest, I sit in a corner and write, typing as quietly as I can, working on the chapter I know he is waiting to hear, hoping there will be time to finish. George is in a hurry. He needs to know what happens, there's no time to waste.

He is weaker on the fourth day. The doctor doesn't have to tell me; I can see it in George's eyes. The spark is still there but the flame is flickering. "Read the story," he commands, so I do, for hours, until we come to the last chapter, the final scene.

He's so still as I read that, for a moment, I wonder if he's fallen asleep. But when I say, "The end," and look up from the screen, he is gazing at me with liquid, shining eyes.

"What a wonderful story," he says. "Wonderful. Whose is it?"

I reach for his hand, my eyes filling.

"It's yours, Grandpa. Yours and Adele's."

His lips stretch into a smile and for a flickering moment, his visage seems lit from within, incandescent. Then he exhales deeply, settles into the pillow, and closes his eyes.

"That's right. That's right. I remember now. What a wonderful story. All of it, every moment, was . . . wonderful."

CHAPTER TWENTY-NINE

Adele used to say that George could go through a toll booth and come out with a relationship. She was exaggerating of course, but not by much.

Just about everybody who ever met George considered him a friend. I'd always known that. But I didn't understand how large his shadow loomed until that day.

The chapel service was private, just Robyn and me and a handful of others in attendance, mostly long-term employees of the lodge and a few of George's closest friends. But the reception was open to everyone.

Hundreds of people came to pay their respects, some driving hundreds of miles to attend, friends he'd known for years as well as those he'd made only recently. Mr. and Mrs. Wilson, who'd celebrated fifty-three anniversaries at the lodge, were there. So was Jackson LeRoy, a twenty-something clerk from the local fly-fishing shop, who'd gotten to know George when he came in to buy a new reel the summer before.

Nobody loved a good party as much as George and that's what we gave him, a send-off that was part testimonial dinner and part celebrity roast. We closed the café and brought in food from a local smokehouse so the staff could attend, a meal that George would have loved—baby back ribs, smoked turkey, cornbread, cheese grits, and collard greens—served with iced tea, beer, and old fashioneds, the latter supplied and personally mixed by Oscar, who'd flown down from New York as soon as he heard and was a huge help.

Without my even having to ask, Oscar and Jamie rose early to set up twenty-five tables and two hundred and fifty chairs on the patio, in the same configuration we'd used for the Waddell wedding. Nearly every chair was filled.

At our request, guests eschewed black and dressed in bright colors—purple, pink, turquoise, lime green, fire engine red, taxicab yellow, and a hundred other vivid hues. The sight of them, and the way I was feeling, made me think of Adele's show-and-tell quilt, with its myriad colors, "colliding into one another at the center, exactly as my emotions have been doing these last days."

That about summed it up.

But I think George would have approved. The party lasted for hours. It felt like everybody George ever met had come, nearly all with a story they wanted to share. I lost count of the people who came up to offer condolences, then said, "Did you ever hear about the time that George . . . ," which was wonderful. The stories I'd heard before were worth repeating, those that were new to me only added to my memories, so it was all good.

Well, almost all.

Dawes didn't show up. That came as no surprise; he probably didn't even know George was dead. I started to text him at one point but stopped halfway through and deleted the message, feeling a fresh flush of anger as I remembered walking into his empty cabin after finding nothing but a bunch of recipes and a note. If he cared about George the way he claimed to, he wouldn't have left, would he?

Even so, part of me kept expecting to look up and see him in the crowd. If he had made an appearance, I'd have been hard pressed to decide what I should do first: spit on his shoes or slap his face. It was undoubtedly better for everyone that he stayed away, but still . . . his absence felt like the one wrong note of an emotional but poignantly good day.

A little before sunset, Mr. Wilson passed out cigars. People lit them up and stood on the beach and sang George's favorite Willie Nelson song, "My Heroes Have Always Been Cowboys," which seemed like the exactly right note to end on.

I would have wished for George to stay with us for many more years. Robyn felt the same way. We were with him at the end, holding his hands, assuring him that it was all right to go if he needed to, trying to be brave, promising we'd be all right and take care of each other. When he stopped breathing and slipped away, we broke into sobs, but our tears were for ourselves, not George. Robyn and I have talked a lot in these last days, maybe more than we ever have in our lives. And though we know we're going to miss George every day and forever more, we know he left exactly when and how he was supposed to.

Hard as it is to say goodbye, there is a painful gratitude in knowing that our most fervent wish for George has been granted, that he was who he was until the end and left life as he had lived it, heroically, a mighty oak that crashed to the ground all at once and with power, leaving a colossal void in the place where once he'd stood.

My hero has always been George. For the rest of my life, that's how I'll think of him.

CARL HAD BEEN listening for a long time, not commenting at all but just letting me talk, which is what I needed to do. When I finished, he let the silence sit between us for a few moments before speaking.

"That's beautiful, Ez. I know you're not ready now but, at some point, you should write all that down. You are such a good writer, Esme. I mean that."

Carl is one of my very dearest friends and always will be. He's never once steered me wrong or told me a lie. When he said he thought I was a good writer, I knew he was sincere. But because I've known Carl so well and for so long, and can accurately read his every pause and vocal inflection, I knew that concern for me in the wake of George's death wasn't the only reason he'd called.

"You read the pages."

"Yes. You're *such* a good writer, Esme."

"You said that before," I reminded him. "So why do I feel a 'but' coming on?"

"You've done some fine, fine work here. But."

I couldn't help but smile at his pregnant pause, a nod to the shoe we both knew was about to drop.

"It's an awfully quiet book, Esme. What's selling right now is all high-concept stuff, books you can explain in a single sentence, with huge plot twists, exotic settings, bright lines between good and evil."

"Like Oscar's book," I said.

"Like Oscar's book," he echoed. "It's just not a big year for subtlety. And your story is—"

"Quiet," I said, saving him the trouble of repeating himself, feeling almost more pained for him than disappointed for myself. Telling a writer their work doesn't quite measure up is never easy, especially when the writer in question is also a friend.

"It's okay, Carl. I get it. And I understand. I mean, it's not like this is my first rejection, right?" I said, smiling. "But you know what is a first for me? This time, I wasn't writing to make money or a name for myself, but only because there was a story that needed to be told and because I was the one meant to tell it. *This* time, I'm proud of what I wrote."

"You should be," Carl said. "I think your grandmother would have been proud too. And who knows? In a few years, quiet may be in fashion again, and then we'll be able to find an audience for this book."

"Maybe. But you know something? I think Adele's story already found its audience—George." I paused, reflecting on those final days in the hospital, my grandfather's eagerness to know how the story turned out, the way he hung on to every word.

"It's not something I can prove, but I'm convinced Adele knew that George's memory was fading before the rest of us did, maybe before George knew himself, and that she wanted me to write her story so that he would never forget it, even after she was gone."

"Huh. Well . . . who knows? True or not, it's a good story," Carl said. "And you tell it well."

"Thank you. I appreciate that," I said, then shifted into a brighter, back-to-business tone. "Now, if you'll excuse me, I need to go hire a new chef and fill out more job applications."

"Right. But before you do," Carl said, "there's something else we should talk about."

CHAPTER THIRTY

*Y*ou're kidding."

For a moment, I honestly thought Robyn's comment was a prelude to encouragement, as sometimes happens when you're sharing good news and the person you're talking with says, "You're kidding. Wow! Good for you!"

But after looking into her eyes, I knew this was not that. Which was irritating.

Because this *was* good for me, really good.

The benefits weren't quite as generous but the salary Carl was offering was the same as what I'd made at DM, and I'd get an extra week of vacation. And though working as a literary agent probably wouldn't have been my first career choice, it was a job in the book world that would pay my rent. The fact that I'd be working with Carl again was another huge plus.

I'd also be working with Oscar, which, depending on the day, could be good or bad. But he was part of the reason Carl wanted and could afford to hire me. Though Oscar hadn't completely finished the draft, a well-regarded editor loved what she'd read so far and made a preemptory bid, offering him a very lucrative three-book deal. Once the word got out, even more authors would be beating a path to Carl's door, wanting him to represent them. So it wasn't like he was doing me any favors. In fact, the way he presented it made it sound like I'd be doing him one.

"I've got more business than I can handle now," Carl said. "Once we announce Oscar's deal, it'll get worse. It's a good problem to have, but it's still a problem. I need somebody who can hit the ground running and handle Oscar. I need *you*, Esme. Please, say yes."

Of course, I said yes. How could I not? It was Carl.

Also, when Carl said we should talk, I'd been about to send in an application for an associate editor position at a small publisher focused on new age nonfiction—a lesser title and salary for editing books on topics I knew and cared nothing about. So, Carl's offer *was* a good thing for me, a godsend. Any other mother would have been thrilled.

Not Robyn Cahill.

"You're kidding," she said again and stared at me, as if actually expecting me to burst out laughing and say that I was and it was all a big joke. "So, you're leaving. Just like that."

Just like that? Was she serious? How much longer did she think I was going to stay?

"I've been here for three months, Robyn. Three *months*."

"And now that George is gone, you'll just disappear, erase me from your life, like I'm some minor character who doesn't fit the story you want to tell or the life you wish you'd had—"

I closed my eyes and shook my head. "Robyn, what are you talking about?"

"You!" she snapped. "I'm talking about *you*! You cutting me out of your life, not coming to visit me when I was inside, taking off for New York just before I got out! *You* never coming home unless you had to because it would mean seeing me too, which was just one more reason for them to be disappointed in me," she cried, her tone almost hysterical.

"Because of *me*, they didn't get to see *you*. You made the choice but somehow it was all my fault! I'm talking about never, *ever* feeling forgiven, no matter what I do or how hard I try, and you just . . . just wiping me out," she said, swiping the air with both hands, "like I don't even exist. Like you never even had a mother—"

Until Adele came into my life, I *didn't* have a mother, not one I could count on. The trauma of my childhood left marks that even my grandparents' love and security could never completely erase, but this was not a conversation I wanted to have right now, or ever. The thing to do was focus on the here and now, deal with the facts and respond in a rational, adult manner. As usual when it came to interactions with my mother, the task fell to me.

"Robyn," I said calmly as I interrupted her tirade, "three months ago, you asked me to get the lodge on a secure financial footing. Even though I was dealing with a bunch of my own problems, that's what I did. Excuse me, that's what *we* did," I said, correcting my mistake.

"George didn't live as long as we hoped, but everything we wanted for him happened. He went out at the top of his game, happily and peacefully—happily because the lodge is looking as good as it ever did and peacefully because he knew that *your* future was secure."

Yes, and wouldn't you think she'd have given me a little credit for it? Been just a teeny bit grateful? Her current financial security was a direct result of my current financial insecurity. Which was a big part of the reason I needed to get back to New York as soon as possible.

"You're safe now," I reminded her.

Her laugh had a bitter edge. "Safe to do what? Spend the rest of my days alone in the boonies, cleaning toilets and selling worms? Having no life? No family?"

She reached into her pocket, pulled out a pack of cigarettes.

"I know you didn't want to come down here," she said, lighting up. "That you only came because you were broke and couldn't afford rent. And the truth is, I didn't want you to come. I'd gotten used to the way things were, gotten over giving a damn if you cared about me or not."

She paused to take a quick puff from her cigarette.

"This summer wasn't a picnic, but it wasn't as awful as I'd thought it would be either. I felt like maybe you and I were starting to get to know each other again, that we'd finally reached a truce and would be able to have at least some kind of a relationship. And I was glad. It felt good, you know? Working on something together, I actually started to think you respected me, maybe even liked me a little bit."

As surprising as it was to find myself agreeing with Robyn on anything, my feelings had been almost identical. Or would have been if she'd stopped right there.

"But now I wish you'd just stayed put. You come down here, get us knee-deep into the wedding business, which I know *nothing* about, and then, the minute George dies, you abandon me, tell me you're going back to New York and leaving me holding the bag!"

"Abandoning you? Abandoning *you*?" I laughed, but not because it was funny. "There is only one person in this room who's abandoned somebody else, and it isn't me."

"I *never* abandoned you," she said, stabbing the air. "They *took* you from me."

"Yes!" I shouted. "Because you abandoned me! You left me with that neighbor lady who watched game shows all day and had an apartment that smelled like fried fish, went out to score some drugs, and never came back!"

"Because I got arrested!" she cried. "And I went out to *deliver* drugs, not score them."

I let out another incredulous laugh. Did she honestly think that made it better?

Robyn put her cigarette to her lips and took an enormous drag. "It was a stupid thing to do," she said, after exhaling. "If I could go back and change it, I would. But at the time, it felt like my only choice. I was two months behind on the rent and we were about to get evicted."

"So why didn't you just get a job?"

"I had a job," she countered. "Maybe you don't remember, Esme, but I had *lots* of jobs, dead-end minimum-wage jobs. Because if you didn't graduate from high school and can barely read, those are the jobs you can get. Say what you want about me, but I've never been lazy."

This much was true. Even when I was little, Robyn had always worked. She didn't seem to hold on to a job for more than a few months, but she's always had one. And over the summer, I'd come to appreciate how hard she worked and to realize some of the things I'd believed about her were wrong, that I'd been unfair in my opinions. But was that somehow supposed to balance the scales for everything she'd done and all that happened because of it?

"If I hadn't had to go to prison to get the kind of help I needed, maybe I'd never have ended up there in the first place," she said. "We were already behind on the rent, and then you got a stomach bug and I had to skip work to take care of you so I got fired, again. A job wouldn't have dug me out of the hole we were in. I had to make some real money, and quick, or we'd be homeless. I was desperate. They offered me a thousand dollars, Ez. A thousand dollars just for picking up a package and dropping it off!"

"A package of *drugs*," I reminded her.

"Yeah, but I didn't know what was in there."

I crossed my arms over my chest. If this was the defense she'd used at her trial, I could see why it failed. Nobody pays you a grand to deliver a pizza.

"Okay, fine," she said, shrugging. "But it's not like I was looking for a career as a drug runner. It was supposed to be one time, one drop that would clear up all my debts and that would be that. Benny made it sound easy."

Sure. Because if your twice-convicted, drug-dealing ex-boyfriend says something is easy, you should totally take his word for it, right? I rolled my eyes. Maybe I had misjudged her in some areas, but this was the Robyn I knew all too well, the one who always had an excuse, pretending she didn't have any choice when we both knew that wasn't true.

"Why didn't you just come home? Why didn't you just catch a bus to Asheville and ask George and Adele to let us live here with them? You know they'd have taken us in. Why didn't you give them the chance? Why did you never even tell them about me?"

She pressed her lips together and looked away. For a minute, I actually thought she was going to cry. Instead, she took another drag on her cigarette. It seemed to steady her.

"You want easy explanations, Esme. You always did, ever since you were this high," she said, holding her hand flat at a spot halfway between her hips and her knees. "All I can tell you is that I was fifteen, pregnant, and scared. Not scared of how they would have reacted," she clarified, "but scared of disappointing them—again. George and Adele were good parents. But the more they tried to be supportive and tell me I was smart, the worse I felt and the less I believed them.

"Look, I know what you think of me when it comes to men. Given what you saw when you were little, I guess I can't blame you, but it wasn't like that, not at first." She looked me in the eye, took a breath, blew it out. "Your father's name was Roger Ainsworth. He was nineteen years old, the cousin of a girl I knew in school who'd come to spend the summer. I thought I was in love." She paused again and swiped at her eye. "At least as much as a fifteen-year-old can be. When I told him I was pregnant, we made a plan to run away to Mississippi and get married, because we wouldn't need parental consent.

"On the night we were supposed to go, I packed my stuff, snuck out of the house, and hitched a ride to the bus stop in Asheville. I waited for hours." She pressed her lips together, then shrugged. "He never showed up.

"I could have gone back home; I wanted to. But the thought of having to tell George and Adele how stupid I'd been was too much, so when another bus drove up, I got on it. I just couldn't face them . . ."

She shifted her gaze from mine, as if she couldn't face me either.

"I always had it in my mind that I would go back, you know? That someday I'd get a good job, buy new dresses for both of us, a car. And I'd come back to the lake with my gorgeous little girl and they'd be *so* happy to see us, and proud of me. And I'd be proud of myself." She let out a wry laugh and took another puff. "Guess we all know how that turned out."

I can't say that her explanations were entirely satisfying. But some of what she said made sense. Thinking back to all the dumb things I'd done as a teenager, I could understand, in the abstract, how she might have believed that running away was the only option. But she hadn't always been fifteen . . .

"Why didn't you ever tell them they had a granddaughter? If not when you got pregnant, then at least after you were arrested."

"I did," she said, leaning forward, an urgent tone creeping into her voice. "When the police put the cuffs on me, I told them my little girl was at a neighbor's apartment, and that you had grandparents in North Carolina. I gave them the phone number for the lodge too. They told me that social services would take care of it. I watched them write everything down."

She lifted a hand, as if swearing to her words. But I had a hard time believing her.

After an entire day had passed with no word from Robyn, the game-show-addicted babysitter next door took a break from her programs long enough to call social services herself. I still remember the conversation, the stink of fried fish in the room, her stringy gray hair, the way she talked about me as if I wasn't standing right there listening to every word.

"She dumped the kid with me and never came back. That's right. Abandoned her, I guess. Well, I don't know. Had a lot of boyfriends, that one. Maybe she got a new one that don't like kids. Or maybe she just got tired of being tied down. Anyway, you'd better send somebody over to get the girl. I can't watch her no more."

A social worker showed up and took me away. I was shuttled to three different homes in the five weeks before George found me, five weeks in which I'd come to believe that the bad babysitter's words were true, that I was a burden my mother had tired of and abandoned.

When you're ten and all alone, five weeks is an eternity.

But what if Robyn's story was true? What if her message had gotten lost in the bureaucracy, or if, among all that shuttling, the bureaucracy had lost track of me?

Robyn dropped her hands to her sides and locked her eyes onto mine.

"I never abandoned you, Esme. You've got to believe me."

I wanted to. But only if it was true.

"If that's really what happened, why didn't you tell me until now?"

She drew back a little. Her eyes became steely, and her expression hardened, looking like the Robyn I'd encountered during my first weeks here.

"Why didn't *you* give me the chance?"

"I was angry," I said. "And hurt."

"Well, so was I."

She put her cigarette between her lips but didn't inhale, just looked at me for a long moment, as if she was trying to make up her mind about something.

"I should have tried to explain, to apologize. I wanted to. But then, after I got out, you refused to see me unless you had to. Maybe I deserved it. Maybe I didn't. After a while, I decided to hell with you. You didn't talk to me, so I wouldn't talk to you either. If you can figure out a way to be angry with somebody, rejection doesn't hurt as much. So I wrote you off, the same way you did me, and never said how sorry I was."

She turned away briefly, blinking back her emotion, then looked at me again.

"If I told you now, I wonder if it would make any difference?"

I closed my eyes briefly, trying to conjure the scene in my mind but coming up short.

"Truthfully? I'm not sure."

CHAPTER THIRTY-ONE

Yolanda turned her fork around backward, put it in her mouth to scrape off the last of the frosting, and raised her eyebrows.

"And did it?"

When I popped into the workshop to say goodbye, drop off a caramel cake, and let Yolanda know I'd be back at Thanksgiving, I told her I had only ten minutes because there was still so much to do before I left—pack, go over the new catering contracts with the lawyer, and, of course, hire a new chef. That was crucial. But somehow chai was brewed, and cake cut, and ten minutes stretched to thirty as I told her about Carl, and the job offer, and the scene with Robyn.

"Did it what?" I asked.

"The apology," Yolanda prodded. "Did it make any difference?"

Robyn was always going to be Robyn. I was always going to be me. No amount of apologizing could change that or entirely erase all the hurtful things we'd said and done to each other. But if you mean it, "I'm sorry" is an amazing conversation starter.

A lot of the things Robyn and I had said to each other over the last couple of days were hard to share and even harder to hear. But it was a more honest conversation than I'd had with my mother since . . . forever. Apologies aren't an end. But for Robyn and me, they might be a beginning. Time would tell.

"Yes. A little," I said honestly.

"But not enough to make you change your mind about going back to New York?"

Yolanda blinked pathetically. I rolled my eyes and took another sip of chai.

"Would you stop? It's not like I have a choice here, Yolanda. I've got to work."

"Yeah, well . . . I didn't notice you lying around without anything to do this summer. Seemed to me there was plenty of work for you at the lodge."

"Fine," I said, conceding her point. "I amend my statement. I've got to work *and* pay my bills. Since I sunk all my savings into the lodge and don't expect to get paid back for at least a couple of years, I need a *real* job. Unlike you," I said, gesturing toward the display window, which held an almost entirely new population of monsters since I'd been there last, the others having been sold, "I lack the kind of artistic skills that people will put down good money for."

Yolanda tilted her head to the side, twisted her lips, and squinted at me.

"Boy . . . there are so many points where I disagree with you here that I'm having a hard time deciding where to begin. But let's start with these bills you mention. I assume you're talking about rent, food, utilities, that sort of thing?"

"Well, yes. There are a few others but those are the biggies."

"Okay," she said in an even, practical tone, "but when you're living at the lake—in a cabin that's much bigger than your old Manhattan apartment, I might point out, and with a view that a hedge fund manager couldn't afford—you're not paying for rent or utilities. So if you stayed here and helped run the lodge, how much money do you really need to make?"

The situation wasn't quite as cut-and-dried as Yolanda made it sound. But yes, I could live on considerably less here than in New York. I'd proven that to myself over the summer.

"So why not stay here, give up the rat race, and be happy?" Yolanda asked. "Asheville's got a lot going for it—art, culture, clean air, recreation," she said, ticking the selling points off on her fingers, "and, of course, me."

"And of all the reasons I wish I could stay, that tops the list," I said sincerely, knowing how much I was going to miss her. "But there's more to work than paying bills. Running a hotel and organizing weddings isn't a bad way to make a living but, for me, it's not enough."

Yolanda cocked an eyebrow. "And being a literary agent is? Esme, the business aspect of editing was always your least favorite part of the job. Now you're going to do it full-time?"

Carl assured me that I wouldn't be spending all my time negotiating contracts and going over royalty statements with a magnifying glass, that I'd also be working with writers and polishing manuscripts. But yes, much of the focus would be on the business side of publishing, probably much more than I'd like.

However, Yolanda had forgotten one crucial thing.

"From the first moment I realized it was possible to make a living creating books, that's all I've ever wanted to do with my life. Is becoming an agent my dream job? No. But in five months, it's the only job in publishing that's come my way. Who knows, maybe I'll end up liking it more than I think I will. Besides, I'll get to work with Carl again."

"I get that," she said, nodding. "Carl is great and thinks the world of you, and I know you'd be miserable in any job that didn't involve books. But when you say that you lack artistic skills that can actually pay your bills, you're not giving yourself enough credit."

Yolanda pushed her plate aside and leaned across the counter, fixing her eyes on mine.

"Esme, I thought your book was wonderful. And no," she said, anticipating my response, "I'm not saying that just because you're my friend. From the second Adele stepped off that bus, I became completely invested in her story. I loved seeing how her quilts became her biography. I mean, ultimately, that's the point of art, isn't it? Art is how we communicate when words aren't enough. As an artist, I found Adele fascinating. But as a woman? Trying to thread the needle between accomplishment, achievement, and happiness, there was so much in Adele's story that I could relate to, that *anybody* could relate to.

"And her voice!" Yolanda thumped her hand to her heart. "It was so strong, so intimate. *You* gave her that voice, Esme. The story is Adele's, but the words are yours. I never met your grandmother but I know she'd be thrilled. Your book is beautiful. And important."

Yolanda's words caught me off guard, made my throat feel thick and a spot in the middle of my chest ache, but in a good way. That she'd read it so carefully and had seen what I'd seen in Adele's story meant more than I could say, though I tried my best.

"But Carl is right. It's too quiet."

"He's wrong," Yolanda said. "Ten thousand percent wrong. Your book's not quiet, Esme. It's powerful. It might not be a bestseller, or a movie. But there are plenty of people out there who will want to read this book, who *need* to read it," she said.

I opened my mouth to speak, to thank her again and change the subject, but she put out a hand before I had the chance. When she spoke, it was as if she knew what I was going to say and understood the things I couldn't say, and perhaps wasn't even fully aware of.

"Don't do that, Esme. Don't discount the work. Don't discount yourself. I know you have a lot of respect for Carl, but he doesn't get it, not this time. If you let his opinion become your excuse for not publishing this book, then you're doing exactly what Adele did, stuffing your story in a suitcase and turning the lock because you're afraid of what people might say, because you're afraid of being rejected—again."

I didn't like the direction this conversation was taking. As a friend, Yolanda meant well but she was coming very close to overstepping the mark.

"Stop. Just stop, okay? Don't try to make me out to be a quitter, because I'm not," I said, stabbing the air with my finger. "Nobody knows that better than you because you were there for all of it, all two hundred sixty-eight rounds of rejection roulette. I'm not setting myself up for that again," I said with a small, mirthless laugh, thinking about all the pointless misery I'd put myself through. "Carl's right. Nobody in New York is going to buy a book about an old woman from North Carolina who made art quilts and hid them in a cupboard for fifty years."

"And for once I agree with Carl," Yolanda said. "There's not an editor in New York who'd be willing to take a chance on your book. But I am."

When I laughed, she just stared at me.

"No joke," she said, shaking her head. "Esme, I want to buy the rights to your book and publish it, the way it *should* be published, with gorgeous four-color photos of Adele's quilts accompanying every chapter, putting in the time, care, and budget to make this book be all it can and should be. But that's just the beginning. I'm going to publish a lot of books, with stories that other publishers might overlook or underestimate."

She pulled herself up taller. "Esme, I am going to become a publisher and I am going to make money doing it. And so are you."

She was dead serious. Yolanda wasn't spinning a dream, she was making a declaration. She had a vision, to publish small- to medium-size runs of beautifully produced books, all hard-covers, all extensively illustrated, and sell them through select bookstores and nontraditional retailers, museums, galleries, historic sites, and the like.

"No cutting corners," she informed me. "The books will be works of art in and of themselves, as beautiful as the stories inside, which you'll curate and edit, working with the writers to polish each manuscript until it absolutely shines. Like other works of art, there will be a limited availability for each title— think of it as numbered prints, or small-batch vintages of wine. Scarcity makes them more valuable, so is the fact that they're intended for connoisseurs, people who value books the way art collectors value paintings—or limited-edition crocheted mon-sters," she added. "That's why we'll be able to charge more for our books than standard titles, and why some people, enough people," she assured me, "will be happy to pay."

Having worked in commercial publishing for so long, I had a few doubts and many, many questions. But Yolanda had an-swers. This wasn't some kind of whim; the idea had come to her fifteen years before, while we were both still working at DM. But she'd never said anything to anybody, not even me.

And though she'd thought about it many times over the years, she'd never taken any steps to turn her dream into reality, not until now.

"I had so many excuses," she said.. "Some of them were pretty convincing. Then I started reading Adele's story and the light bulb came on. There was only one thing holding me back: the fear of failing. *That's* what your book did for me, Esme, helped me push through the fear and decide to take a chance on what I really want. That's what it's going to do for a lot of people.

"When I turned the last page," she said earnestly, "I knew—I just *knew*! Your book was supposed to be the first book published by Loblolly Press, and that you were supposed to be my business partner and the editor in chief. Here, take a look."

Yolanda handed me a blue binder with a twenty-page business plan that included operating budgets for years one through five, with profit and loss projections for the same period. The plan showed losses for three years, a breakeven in year four, and a decent profit in year five. It was very well thought out, at least on paper. And, thanks to the monsters, she had the funding to pull it off.

"Man," I said after looking at the figures. "I *really* should have taken up crocheting when you offered to teach me."

"Not too late," Yolanda quipped. "Grab a hook and some yarn, I'll show you right now."

"Thanks. But I doubt my efforts would end up paying off like yours have. You take yarn and turn it into art."

"You take words and turn them into characters, plots, and imaginary worlds," she said. "And you know how to help other writers do the same thing. Crocheting monsters seems pretty tame by comparison. I need a new challenge, Esme, something that stretches me. Don't you?"

Before I had a chance to express an opinion one way or the other, Yolanda fisted her hands and thumped them on the counter. "*This* could be that something! With me in charge of art direction and production and you overseeing acquisition and editing, I know we could pull it off. But I can't do this without you, Esme, and I wouldn't want to try."

For months, nobody had wanted me. Now, all of a sudden, I was in demand. But being in demand isn't all it's cracked up to be, especially when the demands are coming from two close friends, both of whom say they need you. How could I possibly choose between them? Flip a coin? Whether it was heads or tails, I'd be disappointing somebody.

"I'm sorry," Yolanda said. "I didn't mean to put you on the spot. Take your time. I realize that it's a big decision." She laughed. "I'm not going to pretend that I don't really, *really* hope you'll say yes.

"But yes or no, stay or go, we're still friends. Nothing's going to get in the way of that, Esme. Not ever again."

CHAPTER THIRTY-TWO

There were things I needed to think through. So when Robyn caught up with me in the lobby while I was checking up on Brian, the new desk clerk, and told me I shouldn't worry if I went to the cabin and saw some of my clothes were gone, I didn't mention Yolanda's proposal.

"I was dropping off some towels in your room," Robyn said, "and saw the open suitcase and a bunch of your outfits on the bed. You were missing buttons on a couple of your blazers, so I just thought I'd sew them on for you. I'll bring them back tomorrow."

"Which blazers?"

She shot me a you've-gotta-be-kidding grin. "Uh . . . the black ones?"

"Thanks. But . . . you don't have to do that."

She shrugged. "I know. I just wanted to. Hey, don't forget that we've got two potential chefs coming to interview in the morning."

"Nine and eleven," I said. "I remember."

"Where are you off to?"

"Nowhere special. Just thought I'd take a walk."

"Take a jacket. The sun is out but it's going to get cooler."

Since Robyn and I had cleared the air, or at least started the process, either she'd unearthed a maternal side I'd never known existed or she was trying to make up for lost time. She headed off toward the back office but then, instead of going inside, turned in the doorway and faced me.

"Esme? One more thing. I read your book—I mean, the chapters you've finished so far. I think it's wonderful."

When I started to say thank you, she put up a hand to cut me off.

"No. No, listen to me, Esme. I mean it. It's *wonderful*." She stared at me for a long, unblinking moment, leaving space for her words to sink in. "No matter what happens, promise me you'll finish. Because, Esme? You are a *very* good writer."

Funny thing, isn't it? How a person can say something so simple and so unexpected, and it isn't until they do that you realize it's what you've been waiting your whole life to hear?

I swallowed hard. "Promise. Thanks, Mom."

She stretched out her hand, hesitated momentarily, then curled her fingers around my forearm and gave me a stiff, clumsy pat.

"Don't forget your jacket," she said abruptly, then closed the office door.

It was going to be like this between us for a while, awkward, inelegant, unnatural. We were starting over, or maybe from scratch. Robyn was learning how to be a mother and I, at long last, was learning how to be a daughter. No matter how hard we tried, we'd never be quite like other mothers and daughters. We had to find our own way of being.

But we'd get there eventually. We just needed time.

AFTER STOPPING BY my cabin to drop off the half caramel cake Yolanda had insisted I take back home with me, I grabbed my jacket and went for a walk.

The leaves were beginning to turn, and some had already fallen to the ground and crunched under my feet as I traveled the well-worn trail around the perimeter of the lake. In a few more weeks, the trees would be painted in vivid, flaming color.

And when that happened, I would be here to see it.

Yolanda was right—this *was* a big decision. But it was also an easy one.

Though I'd made up my mind even before I left the gallery, I didn't tell Yolanda. Not because I was trying to be coy or keep her in suspense, I just needed some time to sort out my thoughts, coming to terms with an altered image of myself, a new way of being.

Carl's job offer had felt like a lifeline, akin to that feeling you get when your car breaks down on a remote road at dusk and you sit there for a long time without seeing a single vehicle, and finally spot two headlights coming your way just after dark. You're giddy with relief, so thrilled to be out of trouble that you don't think about the condition of the approaching vehicle or where it might take you. You just want to get out of the mess you're in, to get unstuck.

In short, it seemed like a rescue, and the answer to everything.

The prospect of a paycheck was undeniably appealing. So was the idea of working with Carl, and even with Oscar. However, almost nothing about the actual work excited me. The more that I thought about it, the more I wondered if Carl's offer of rescue would leave me stuck again. Everything would be new—apartment, job, relationships—but it felt a lot like I was retracing my steps, trudging along the same lonely road where I'd gotten lost to begin with. And though I'd told myself otherwise, I knew I'd be settling.

Robyn was a consideration too. Our explosive exchange had blasted a hole, albeit a small one, in the rubble of miscommunication, misinterpretation, and missing facts that had separated us for years. Leaving the lake could put our fragile reconnection at risk. But what else could I do? In the last couple of days, even Robyn came to accept that since the Waddell wedding setback had shredded my safety net, I had to accept Carl's offer. There was no other choice.

But now, thanks to Yolanda, there *was* a choice, and it was very nearly perfect.

I took a familiar turn on the trail, looping back toward the resort, and emerged from the woods, walking toward the big scarlet oak and Adele's reading bench. I brushed away a sprinkle of brilliant red leaves and took a seat, gazing out at the still blue-gray water. The last time I'd visited the bench, there'd been at least close to a dozen ducks bobbing in the water and browsing among the reeds. Now there was only one, a long female with dull brown feathers, paddling and bobbling a few feet from the bank.

I tilted my head back and closed my eyes, soaking in the silence and autumn sun.

Going into business with Yolanda, publishing the books *we* wanted to see in print and doing it the way we'd always wanted to, would be endlessly creative and so, so satisfying. There was no one I'd rather work with, not even Carl, and seeing Adele's story become a real book with my name on the cover was the definition of a dream come true, a dream I'd given up. If things went the way we hoped, this book could be the first of many we'd publish together.

It wouldn't be easy—nothing in publishing is ever easy, or certain—and we'd never get rich. But between the modest advance I'd receive for the finished manuscript, free rent, salary from two part-time jobs—editor in chief for Loblolly Press and event coordinator for Last Lake Lodge—I'd make a living. And since my continued presence at the lodge should help our event-planning business go more smoothly, maybe my loan would be paid back sooner.

Also, I loved my little cabin, loved the view from the porch and the dripping-honey color of the log walls, loved the sound of birdsong outside my window every morning and the crackle of the fire on a chilly evening, loved sleeping in my cozy room with Adele's quilt covering me, loved sitting at the table, tapping out a chapter on my laptop, loved cooking in my little kitchen, filling the air with homey scents of baking butter and simmering soup. And yes, I loved Robyn. Even when I felt like smacking her, I still loved her. And as time went on, I knew I would love her more and be loved in return.

I loved living at the lake too, loved seeing anglers catching fish, kids splashing in the water, lovers paddling canoes, and families playing volleyball on the beachfront. I loved seeing people make memories and knowing I was part of it. I loved meeting new people and welcoming returning guests, talking to employees I'd known forever and getting to know the new ones, like young Jamie.

If you thought about it, it was really kind of amazing. Almost everything I'd left home to find, the boxes I'd been trying and failing to tick off for so many years—home, family, friends, career, stability—had been here all along. In the time it took to eat a slice of caramel cake, almost everything I'd ever wanted was mine for the taking.

So why wasn't I happier?

At first, I wasn't sure. But then, as I was thinking about the unticked boxes, it hit me.

I *had* tried. And I had failed, failed spectacularly on almost every count.

And not only had I failed myself, I'd failed other people too, damaged a lot of relationships, wasted so much time. For what? I'd left North Carolina with three suitcases, high hopes, hubris, and a plan. Now I was right back where I started. For fifteen years, I'd convinced myself I was progressing, moving steadily toward the goals I'd set and the life I wanted.

Was I wrong? Had it all been one long, pointless detour?

Life has a way of steering you toward the path you're meant to take, whether you meant to take it or not.

That's what Adele had said years ago when we were sitting on the porch with the Thayers. At fourteen, I'd barely listened, convinced I knew better. Now I *did* know better, and that I should have paid closer attention.

Adele had known failure too. No matter how hard I tried, I'd never fully understand why she chose to keep her quilts and her talents hidden away. But I did know that, in spite of everything, she'd come out on the other side and found a happy, fulfilling life. And I remembered something else she'd said, just a couple of months before I left home for New York.

I was studying for my finals and Adele was working on a quilt, the confetti quilt she'd made prior to Robyn's return. Though I didn't understand its significance at the time, it was obviously a complicated project because she kept tearing out seams and starting over.

"Seems like such a waste of time," I said. "Why not just leave it?"

"Because I'll do better next time," she replied, squinting as she worked. "And because that's why God invented seam rippers."

When I rolled my eyes, she laid the patchwork down in her lap and looked at me.

"Anything worth doing takes longer than you think. Mistakes are a gift, the way we discover what actually works. You probably won't believe it until you're older but starting over serves its purpose. As long as you learn, no lesson is ever a waste."

Well, I was definitely starting over, right back where I'd begun. I couldn't quite see a purpose in that but at least I wasn't lost anymore. And wasn't that what detours were supposed to do? Take you the long way around, then put you back on the right path, heading in the right direction, on the path you were always meant to take?

Home, family, friends, career—it was all right here. Everything I'd always wanted.

Well . . . almost everything.

The lone lady duck bobbed along, doing the occasional half summersault, head below the waterline and tail feathers in the air, trying to either attract attention or find an afternoon snack. Like me, she was single and likely to remain that way. There wasn't a male mallard for miles. When she noticed me watching, she paddled to the bank, then stared at me expectantly.

"Sorry, girlfriend," I said, turning out my empty hands, "I got nothing."

The disappointed duck swam away. I pulled my phone from my pocket and did a little Googling. The results were not encouraging. There were a million and a half single men in New York City but only fifteen thousand or so in Asheville. I sighed.

Not a male mallard for miles.

My phone started to vibrate, the screen informing me that Last Lake Lodge was calling.

"Miss Cahill? This is Brian, at the front desk. Sorry to bother you. I would have talked to Miss Cahill . . . I mean, Miss Robyn, but she went to run some errands."

Brian sounded nervous. He'd only been with us a couple of days and I wasn't sure he was going to work out, but finding qualified applicants who were willing to work so far from town wasn't easy, so I hoped I was wrong.

"That's okay, Brian. What do you need?"

"There's a man here," Brian replied, speaking more loudly to make himself heard over the sound of voices talking in the background. "He said he's come to interview for the chef job. I didn't think you were interviewing until tomorrow, but I wasn't sure so I put him in the office and told him I'd call you. I hope that was okay."

"It's fine," I assured him. "Good call. Either he's an eager beaver or he's got the wrong day. What's his name?"

"Oh, gosh. I didn't think to ask. Sorry." He laughed nervously. "It's a little . . . it's just a little busy right now. But do you want to hold for a second while I go find out?"

"Never mind," I said, getting to my feet. "Sounds like you're busy. I'll be right up."

CHAPTER THIRTY-THREE

*B*rian really did have his hands full. Three couples were lined up at the desk, waiting to check in. Three kids were hanging out by the fireplace. Two blond, preteen boys were sitting on the couch elbowing each other while trying to watch a video on the same iPad, and a four- or five-year-old girl with curly brown hair was sitting in one of the armchairs, staring at the flames with her big brown eyes.

With Brian looking a bit overwhelmed, I considered popping behind the desk and taking over for him, but decided against it. He had to learn sometime and I didn't want to keep the candidate for the chef job waiting. We had to find a replacement before Jamie left. I breezed past the desk, ignoring Brian's pleading glance, and stepped into the office.

"I'm Esme Cahill. I understand you're interested in the chef position?"

"Yes, if the job is still open."

The man sitting opposite the desk turned around in his chair. "Dawes?"

"Hey, Esme."

After a moment of slack-jawed disbelief that stunned me into silence, the justifiable anger that had been simmering inside me ever since Dawes's disappearance frothed and boiled over.

"What the hell are you—? I can't *believe* you came back! I can't believe you . . ." I closed my eyes, so furious I couldn't bear to look at him. I fisted my hands, grasping empty air and crushing it between my fingers. "What are you doing here? How do you have the nerve to show up after—"

Dawes raised both hands like a defeated combatant suing for surrender.

"I know. I'm sorry. But I want my job back. If you'll just give me a chance to explain—"

"Your old job back? Where do you get the nerve . . . No!" I cried. "Absolutely not! There is no explanation that can excuse what you did! The only thing I'm giving you a chance to do is clear out right now and never, *ever* come back."

George's old shillelagh was propped up in the corner. When I grabbed hold of it Dawes got to his feet but made no move to leave, staring at me like he was trying to decide if I was going to take a swing at him or not. I was asking myself the same question. Honestly, it could have gone either way.

"Esme, I need a job."

"Good! Go find one! You've never had any trouble getting work before and I'm sure you won't now. But there's nothing here for you, Dawes. And there *never* will be, not after what you did. Go!" I commanded, pointing the shillelagh at the door. "Get out of here and don't come back!"

Anger flared in Dawes's eyes. For a moment, I thought he might try to snatch George's stick from my hand.

"In case you've forgotten," he said. "I *own* part of this place. I don't have to go anywhere."

"Five percent. Five," I sneered. "And in case *you've* forgotten, the only reason we let you buy your piddling percent was to make sure you wouldn't do exactly what you ended up doing—walk off the job when we most needed you!

"I told George not to trust you, but he wouldn't listen! What was he thinking? He picked you up by the side of the road, gave you money, a place to live, a job—he didn't know anything about you. *None* of us knows anything about you! You show up out of the blue, pretending you actually care, and everybody falls in love with you, and then you—"

"Wait a minute! Wait a minute!" Dawes raised flattened hands and leaned forward, as if my words were a battering ram and he was the last man standing guard at the gate. "Esme, is *that* what this is about? The day we went fishing and I said I couldn't kiss you?"

"No!" I shouted. "Are you kidding? It's about people who make promises and don't keep them. It's about letting everybody down when we needed you most!"

Dawes stepped forward and started talking over me, as if he hadn't heard a word I'd said.

"Esme. Esme, listen to me. I wanted to kiss you; you have no idea how much I wanted to kiss you. I'd thought about it ever since I first saw you, when I thought you'd set the cabin on fire. Esme, you . . ." His eyes traveled up and down my body. "Even with your hair dripping wet, you look *amazing* in a towel."

What? Was he such a clueless, egocentric asshat that he honestly thought I was mad because he hadn't *kissed* me? I gripped the shillelagh so hard my knuckles went white. Never in my life had I despised anyone as much as I despised Dawson McCormick at that moment.

"But the reason I couldn't," he continued, apparently having zero clue that I was wrestling with a lower order impulse of my own at the moment, fighting back the urge to smack him in the head with George's stick, "is because I'm *not* a guy who breaks his promises. If I make a promise, I keep it. That's just who I—"

"Oh, no. Don't you dare," I said, slashing the air with George's shillelagh, then stabbing a finger at Dawes. "Don't you *dare* tell me what a stand-up guy you are. Because I've heard that one before, Dawes, when I was worried that you'd skip out on us with no warning and no explanation. You said it would never happen. You said you'd never let George down. Except you *did* let him down, Dawes. You let *everybody* down. And now George is dead!"

"What? George is—"

He stopped mid-sentence and gave his head a hard, disbelieving shake. When I nodded, he took a deep breath. "What happened?"

"It was his heart," I said, my grip on the shillelagh loosening as Dawes swallowed back tears. "He's always had problems with it, that's why he couldn't enlist. George went fishing that morning and hooked a huge bass, and when a little girl and her grandpa ended up in the water, George jumped in and saved them from drowning."

"He did?" When I nodded, Dawes sniffled.

"Good for him," he murmured. "Good for George."

Yes. Good for George.

"But it was too much. His heart couldn't take it. The EMTs revived him and he lingered for a few days, but . . ." I stopped, reminding myself that George had lived and died well, and that he had hated seeing me cry. "We were with him the whole time, Robyn and me."

"Esme, I'm sorry. I had no idea. If I'd known, I'd have—"

He took another step closer. I stepped back.

"You'd have what? Never left?"

Dawes dropped his arms to his sides.

"No," he said softly. "I'm incredibly sorry about George. I liked him so much. But even if I'd known what was going to happen, I still would have left. I had to, there was no other choice."

As Dawes spoke, there was no word or combination of words to fully express my fury. But when he finished, I saw and tasted mustard, and clutched at George's stick again, wishing I was the kind of woman who really was capable of hitting another human being.

"Well, good. Then you can go now," I said at last. "Nobody here will *ever* miss you."

"Esme. Don't be like that. Give me a chance to—"

The explanation I had no interest in hearing was interrupted by a soft knock, two tentative taps. The door opened a few inches. A little girl with curly brown hair, the one I'd seen staring at the flames when I came through the lobby, peaked in.

"I'm hungry."

Dawes walked to the door and squatted down.

"I'll be done soon. Then we'll find something to eat, okay?"

She nodded at Dawes, then looked at me.

"Esme, this is my daughter, Hannah. Hannah, this is Esme."

The child lifted her hand but said nothing, just stared at me with those enormous eyes. Though I'd never seen her before today, I knew that look, those eyes, the eyes of a child who has seen things children never should. It was like looking into a mirror from twenty-five years ago.

Something inside me cracked.

"Hi, Hannah."

Dawes turned back toward his little girl. "Can you go sit back down by the fireplace, honey? I won't be much longer, I promise."

Hannah nodded solemnly and closed the door. Dawes got to his feet and turned to face me.

"Look, I don't blame you for hating me, Esme. But before you have me arrested for trespassing, or hit me over the head with that thing," he said, nodding at the shillelagh, "let me explain. The reason I couldn't kiss you, even though I really wanted to—"

I rolled my eyes. This again? Did he honestly think he was that irresistible? So what if he hadn't kissed me; I didn't care anymore. Didn't he get it?

"Just let me talk," he said, responding to my groan. "I want you to understand what happened. The reason I couldn't kiss you is because I'm married. I mean, I *was* married. To Maggie, Hannah's mother."

Given the circumstances, this wasn't a hugely shocking revelation, but it pulled me up short. About fifty different questions bubbled up in my brain, but he'd asked me to let him talk so I did.

"Maggie and I married right out of high school. We were way too young, and totally broke," he said with a small, wry smile. "But we were happy. At least in the beginning.

"Our apartment was the size of a phone booth and we were working two or three jobs each, trying to save money to open a restaurant. I was going to cook and Maggie would work front of the house, that was the plan. One day, Maggie slipped and fell at work, and did a number on her knee. It was bad," he said, wincing at the memory. "They gave her a prescription for painkillers and pretty soon, she was hooked." He paused. "If I'd known what was going to happen—"

Dawes pushed his fingers into his hair and rubbed his scalp hard, as if he was trying to scrub away the mistakes he'd made, the things he'd always feel he should have seen coming.

"When she couldn't get more prescriptions, Maggie started using street drugs. By that time the marriage was . . . things weren't good. Maggie was in and out of rehab. People kept saying I should divorce her but I wouldn't. I still loved her. Even if I hadn't, she was my wife. I couldn't just give up on her. People can change."

He said it earnestly, as if he were trying to convince me. But I was already convinced. People can change. If I didn't believe it before, I did now.

"Things went on like that for about five years," he continued. "Somehow or other, I scraped up enough money to open the restaurant, and to get Maggie into rehab. She was gone for four months. In a way, it was a relief because I was working so hard, trying to get the restaurant off the ground. When she came home, things were good for a while, like they'd been before. I was cooking, Maggie was handling the front, business was picking up. And I thought, okay. We're past it now. We're going to be all right."

Relating that season of renewed happiness, his tone was wistful and his gaze faraway. Now he shook his head, telling me what I'd already guessed: it hadn't lasted.

"After a few months, she started using again, and stealing money from the till to fund her habit. We had a huge fight one night, *huge*. Maggie packed her stuff and took off. I didn't think much of it. She'd done it before but had always come back in a couple of days. Maybe I should have gone after her but, honestly"—he sighed—"I was just so tired of it by then.

"When I went to work in the morning, the restaurant was

on fire. I thought Maggie might be in there, so I ran inside. Thankfully, she wasn't. But I knew she'd set it. I saw her sweater lying on the floor by the stove."

He took a deep breath and blew it out.

"Anyway, the reason I got the van is because I was looking for Maggie, at least for the first few years," he said. "I figured she had to be living on the streets, but I couldn't find her. Whenever I'd take a new job, I'd go to the roughest part of town and leave her picture and my phone number with people at shelters and free clinics."

Dawes pulled something that looked like a business card from the pocket of his blue plaid shirt and handed it to me. The front of the card had a picture of a woman with blond corkscrew curls and laughing eyes. The back was printed with Dawes's name, cell phone number, and a request that he be called day or night if Maggie needed help.

"She's pretty," I said, turning the card over again and holding it out to him.

"She was."

He took back the card and stared at Maggie's face. He still loved her. He would always love her.

There was more to Dawes's story, but he didn't have to spell it out; I understood what had happened. His phone rang in the middle of the night. A voice he didn't recognize told him Maggie was in trouble, had overdosed, and that there was a child involved, a daughter he'd never known he had. Dawes did the only thing he could do. He dashed off a note and drove through the night, hoping to rescue them both, his wife and his child.

Maggie hadn't made it. But Hannah was here, with Dawes.

What I'd said before was true: Dawes could have found a job anywhere. But for Hannah's sake, he needed a safe, secure place with stability, good food, and fresh air and love, a place where she could heal from whatever she'd been through, and learn how to be happy again, a home. And so, he'd brought her here.

Dawes had only been a father for a matter of days, but his instincts were good.

"I know I should have called you," he said. "But there were hospitals, and police, and social workers, and . . . the truth is, I didn't know how to explain, especially not over the phone."

"No, I get it," I said, then took a step back, crossing my arms over my chest and dropping my voice to a more businesslike tone. Just because I understood his story didn't mean I still wasn't mad and wanted to see him suffer, at least a little. "But I have be honest with you, Dawes . . ."

He frowned. I moved my head slowly from side to side, then sighed.

"That was, far and away, the *worst* job interview in history. Seriously terrible!" I said, swiping the air with my hand. "Like, negative fifty on a scale of one to ten."

Dawes tried not to smile.

"That bad, huh? So—I didn't get the job?"

"Uh . . . actually, no. You're hired. We're pretty desperate."

I shrugged. There was another tap on the door. Hannah peeped inside.

"Daddy? I'm hungry."

"Right," he said, looking apologetic. "What do you want to eat?" Dawes took a step toward the doorway but I got there first and waved him off. "I got this," I assured him, then squatted down to kid level and looked into those big brown eyes.

"Guess what, Hannah? I've got a caramel cake in my kitchen. Would you like a slice?"

Completion

October 1944

The men assigned to guard the artwork were given two directives: protect them at all costs and make sure nobody noticed them doing it. A big part of their job was to become wallpaper, blending into the background as much as possible.

But today, all that changed. Today, they are celebrities.

After thirty-three months of secrecy, the whole world may soon know that priceless works of art were cleverly hidden and zealously guarded at the Biltmore estate. The government is eager to spread the news that the war is waning and victory is close at hand, so the grinning guards carry crated art out of the Music Room through Biltmore's echoing hallways, emerging through the arched double doors to great fanfare.

Bystanders applaud and flashbulbs pop as the crates are loaded into waiting moving vans that will soon drive away, escorted by a phalanx of police motorcycles with flashing lights and sirens wailing in triumph. As the guards exit the building, photographers shout orders. "Hold it! Look this way! Smile!" The guards oblige, delighted by their temporary notoriety.

I don't care for cameras. When a reporter asks me to stand near the guards and smile, I quickly turn and walk away, hurrying out of the shot so I can remain safely anonymous. When the press has had their *fill, I go over the manifest with the driver one last time, collecting his signature and the necessary paperwork, then stand on the steps with the guards and watch as the trucks drive away. After the vehicles are out of sight, we shake hands and say farewell, milling about like actors on the closing night of a long-running play, a little reluctant to see it end, a little confused about what comes next. Elmer, the guard I know best, mid-fifties, a father of three daughters who has always been kind, asks about my future plans.*

"I'm catching a train to Baltimore this afternoon. Mr. Finley offered me another job."

When the war ends, most working women, clever and credentialed though they may be, will be asked or forced to step aside, yielding their positions to returning soldiers. But Mr. Finley wants me to be his secretary, typing his letters and answering his telephone, making appointments and coffee and order. I will be surrounded by art and I will earn a living. It's not the life I'd hoped for, but I am luckier than most, so I know I should be grateful. In time, I'm sure I will be.

Elmer frowns. "I don't understand, I thought you'd stay in Asheville. George told me he was going to propose. He showed me the ring."

George did propose.

He took me for a drive on Sunday, down a narrow and winding country road, crowded close with maples, oaks, hickories, and sweetgum trees, adorned with leaves of scarlet, copper, saffron, and bronze, a canopy of colors that made me think of pavilions in faraway lands. Collectively, they taste of exotic spices and feel like reverence, awe in the presence of sacred things.

We drove and drove, bouncing over potholes until the road abruptly ended and we got out to walk. The trail was so narrow it was more like a deer path, but George knew the way, happily in his element, as he always is when we go to the woods. I had given him a copy of Walden *for his birthday and said I was going to start calling him Thoreau, the man who went to the woods and lived deliberately and who, like George, knew more than a little about the marrow of life. I was teasing, of course, but there are similarities. I love George so dearly, but even more seeing him here, so happy and so utterly himself. He's at least as wise as Thoreau, far more handsome and has, I am sure, a better sense of humor.*

As we hiked up hills and climbed over fallen logs, or stepped from stone to stone to cross a creek, George saw and eagerly shared things I might have missed—the beautiful tangle of an abandoned bird nest, an orange-and-yellow-striped tree fungus with furled edges, a lush mat of moss clinging to a rock, birds, and animals, and insects, the spiky purple petals of an ironweed plant, likely the last of the season. When he picked up a rock from a stream, a pinecone-shaped pebble, tumbled and polished by the moving water with tiger-striped bands of copper and black, and then placed it in my hands as a keepsake, I thought to myself, not for the first time, that George is the most generous man I've ever known.

We followed the trail to the shores of a small lake with shimmering, quicksilver water and the most beautiful scarlet oak. When we stopped beneath its branches, George made a pronouncement. He told me that in a few years, after saving enough money, he intended to buy this land and build a home here. Then he took my hand and pulled a ring from his pocket.

No matter how I tried to explain, to help him see that I would never quite fit into Asheville, and that I loved him too much to take him away from this world he's so clearly a part of, George didn't understand.

I know that Elmer won't understand either, so instead of answering his question, I kiss his weathered cheek, and say, "Goodbye, Elmer. I'm glad I got to know you."

Miss Ida knew of my plans for a quiet departure because I had to settle my bill beforehand, but no one else did. Things had been awkward enough since I refused George; there had even been some arguments, which made life uncomfortable for everyone. A round of goodbyes could only make things worse. Miss Ida agreed and promised to keep my secret.

I'd left the boardinghouse early that morning, before anyone was awake, and had carried the wheat-colored suitcase filled with quilts and a secondhand leather satchel of clothes down the stairs to the waiting taxi, which took me to Biltmore. The driver returned in the afternoon, to drop me at the depot.

I am standing on the platform with my bags at my feet, wearing the powder blue suit I arrived in, and the same silly blue hat, seeing dark purple and tasting anise, feeling the dull ache of regret and hoping the train is on time. It will be easier, I think, once I am on board and heading north. The trees, the mountains, the land of the sky, remind me too much of George. It will be easier to forget when I'm back in the city, surrounded by pavement and honking horns.

A faint rumble beneath my feet says the train is approaching. I peer down the track and spot a puff of steam in the far distance. At the same time, I feel a presence behind me and turn around.

"George. I . . . I wasn't trying to sneak away without—"

My mouth tastes like chalk and my cheeks go hot from shame, because that's exactly what I was trying to do. But not for the reasons George might suppose.

"I'm not upset with you, I just thought it would be easier for everyone this way. But maybe I was wrong." I smile a little. "I'm glad we have a chance to say goodbye."

George shakes his head. He's not smiling but he doesn't seem angry either.

"I didn't come to say goodbye, Adele. I'm here to catch the train. I'm coming with you."

"To Baltimore?" He nods. "George, you can't."

"Sure, I can, it's a free country." He pushes his fedora higher on his forehead. "Anyway, why shouldn't I?"

There are scores of reasons that mostly boil down to one: the fact that George will hate Baltimore. He would be even less understood and accepted by its residents than I was by Miss Ida and the sewing circle. The woods and mountains are his home. He's happy here and George's happiness is everything to me, more important than my own. But I don't know how to explain that. Once again, words fail me. I can't even conjure a color that expresses all the things I'm feeling.

So I throw out my hands and cry, *"Because! You don't even have any luggage!"*

George's eyes crinkle at the corners and he starts to laugh, and laugh, and laugh. The vibration below my feet grows stronger. There is a squeal of metal and a hiss of steam as the train pulls into the depot. George stops laughing, shakes his head, and smiles.

"I can buy new clothes, Adele. And a suitcase to put them in. I can even buy a honeymoon cottage in Baltimore, if that's what it takes for us to be together."

He lifts his hat from his head, steps closer.

"You keep talking about us being from two different worlds. Well, maybe there's some truth in that. So I've got an idea: let's make our own world. It can be here, or it can be in Baltimore. It can be in a ship at sea or at the top of a tree, for all I care. The only thing that matters to me is that you're in it."

There is movement all around us, conductors making announcements, passengers climbing down from the train, others climbing aboard. George opens his fingers and the fedora drops to the ground. He moves closer still and puts his arms around me.

"Don't you see? When I'm with you, I'm already home. You are my world, Adele. You're my everything."

The moment he says it, I know it is truth, the truth we share. When he lifts me from the ground and kisses me, no words are necessary. There is nothing I have to do, or say, or prove to anyone, not anymore.

I am his everything. He is mine. From this day forward and for the rest of our lives, there is only one world: ours.

CHAPTER THIRTY-FOUR

October 2011

I unlocked the door, set the boxes on the counter, snapped on the lights, and was immediately struck by two things.

First, that Yolanda was a genius. Until I saw it for myself, I had no idea how stunning her exhibit design would be.

The walls and front windows had been covered with floor to ceiling, fourteen-foot swathes of black fabric. When she explained what she wanted to do, I thought it would be too gloomy, but she just shook her head. "It's actually going to make things seem brighter because the colors will really pop." And, of course, she was right. Displayed against the black background and under stage lights rented from a local theater, Adele's quilts looked richer and more vibrant than ever.

Most of them were hanging on the walls, displayed along- side posterboards printed with old black-and-white photos of Adele, George, the cabin, the lodge, and the city of Asheville back in the day, as well as appropriate excerpts from the book. I had thought it might be too much, but, once again, Yolanda was right. The posters put the quilts into context, helping to explain Adele's struggles as an artist and a woman, and her growth over time.

But my favorite display was overhead. Yolanda had hung the smaller quilts on black dowels suspended from the ceiling in a sort of circular serpentine. When she asked if I had any fishing line that she could use for the exhibit, I couldn't imagine what she was going to do with it; now I understood. The thin filament hangers were almost invisible, so Adele's quilts appeared to be floating. It was genius. It was magical. She had to have spent every second of the previous three days working on it. I felt a twinge of guilt about leaving all the heavy lifting to her, but somebody had to deal with the book crisis and I'd been the only available candidate.

The second thing that struck me was that there were *way* too many chairs.

I stopped counting at sixty because the sight of them was starting to make me feel nauseous. By the time Yolanda walked in, I'd already folded up the back two rows and stowed the chairs behind the checkout counter.

"What are you doing?" she asked, dumping an armful of grocery sacks onto the counter. "I just put those up last night."

"There's too many," I said, folding another chair. "You don't want pictures of empty seats going up on social media. It makes people think the launch is a failure and the book's a dud. Also, looking out on a sea of empty chairs makes authors very, very nervous."

Yolanda marched toward me and took the chair from my hands.

"Will you stop already? It's going to be fine. People will come in droves."

"Easy for you to say. You're not the one who'll be reading aloud to a room full of empty chairs. Do you know how hard it is to get people to actually show up at a book launch?"

"But it's not *just* a book launch. It's an exhibition opening too."

"Do people show up in droves for those?" I asked hopefully.

"Um . . . no. Usually not, unless the artist is really famous, or has a big family. Don't look so terrified," she said, unfolding the confiscated chair and placing it at the end of a row. "It'll be fine. We sent out three hundred invitations with all the pertinent information and special emphasis on the fact that there will be free food and champagne. People will come," she said with a confidence that, in my opinion, was both unwarranted and naive.

"What if they don't?"

She shrugged. "Then we drink the champagne, build a bonfire with the books, burn the building to the ground, and collect the insurance money. Speaking of books—" she said, raising her eyebrows into questioning arches.

The reason I was missing in action for three days was because we'd had a problem with the printer. Given that our two-year journey from manuscript to publication had had nothing but problems, this wasn't surprising. But it's hard to have a book launch party without books, so when the printer called to say delivery would be delayed due to a warehouse strike, I drove to Indiana and picked up the books personally, or at least as many boxes as I could fit inside the new used van Dawes bought in March.

Dawes, who still loves a road trip, had offered to go in my stead but I said no. Though I don't worry about him disappearing anymore, I still can't make mushroom and cognac sauce, and since our last wedding of the season was on Saturday, the job of courier fell to me.

When I nodded toward the book cartons, Yolanda let out a squeak and clapped her hands.

"Did you see them? Are they gorgeous?"

"Not yet."

She tsked her tongue. "You wanted to wait so we could do it together? Aw. That's so sweet."

"Well . . . the truth is that I had to get out of town before rush hour, so I tossed the boxes in the back and drove straight through. But then," I said, drawing out the words and casting my eyes toward the gallery, "I got so distracted by the absolutely genius way you hung the exhibit that I forgot all about the books." I threw out my arms. "Look at this!"

Yolanda beamed. "It does look pretty good, doesn't it?"

"Good? Are you kidding? It's brilliant!" I exclaimed. "You know, if our publishing venture goes belly-up, you could get a job designing exhibits for museums."

"Yeah, well, let's hope it doesn't come down to that. But the way things have been going lately, you never know. C'mon," she said, turning toward the boxes. "Let's open these babies and see what's what, make sure they didn't print the covers sideways or decide to translate it into Urdu."

She almost wasn't joking. Getting to this day, launching the first book from Loblolly Press, had taken longer, cost more, and been tougher than we could ever have imagined. The actual printing was particularly fraught. When the proofs came back with six of thirty chapters missing pages and the chapter headings in a font called Trattoria Gothic, which looks just as weird as it sounds, Yolanda almost burst into tears.

We each slit one side of a box, then lifted the flaps simultaneously after counting to three, revealing two pristine stacks of the most exquisitely printed and bound books I'd ever seen, with a textured cover that looked like Adele's confetti quilt, the hues perfectly true to the original, and the title *Color of Life* and the credits embossed in a luscious shade of amber . . .

Well, we didn't *quite* burst into tears. But Yolanda blinked and sniffed and I pressed my fist against my mouth and swallowed pretty hard.

The inside was just as beautiful as the outside. The fonts were just what we'd asked for, the margins were even, the spacing was perfect, and all of the pages were there—not one was missing or out of order. The left-facing page of each chapter had a big, beautiful photograph of the quilt the chapter was based on, printed on thick, luxurious paper with just a hint of a sheen. For a few minutes, we flipped silently through the pages, because sometimes there really are no words. It was all that we'd imagined and better than we'd hoped.

Finally, I closed my book.

"We'd better hop to it. I need to unload the rest of the boxes. I only had room for forty cartons, but that should be enough to fill our orders until the strike breaks."

"If it's not, I'd be only too happy to drive to Indiana and pick up more." Yolanda closed her copy and stared at the cover. "I still wish you'd at least put 'with' in front of your name."

Though we'd both weighed in on the title, decisions about the credits were mine to make. Choosing to list Adele as the author and myself as the editor just felt right. Because even though I wrote the words down and polished them up, I still believed they belonged to Adele. Yolanda was bothered because she thinks I'm selling myself short, but she's wrong. I was proud to see the words "Edited by Esme Cahill" on the cover of this beautiful book. Editing is what I do, and I'm good at it.

I took the book from Yolanda's hand. "Come give me a hand with the cartons."

"Let's wait until David gets here," she said, walking around the counter and pulling out the folding chairs I'd stashed away. "He's bringing a dolly to unload the champagne. You should get dressed. It looks like you slept in your clothes."

I had but, at that moment, wardrobe was the least of my concerns.

"A *dolly*? How much champagne did you buy?"

"Six cases."

"Six? *Cases?*"

Yolanda flapped her hand at me. "Stop. It'll be fine. You've heard the old saying, 'If you pour it, they will drink it. And buy books.'"

"No one says that."

"Well, *I'm* saying it. In fact, I'm thinking of putting it on the company logo." She started replacing the rows of chairs, putting the first down with a thump and a smirk. "Go get dressed."

"I hate you, Yolanda."

She kissed the air.

"I hate you too, Ez. Now go."

CHAPTER THIRTY-FIVE

*M*iraculously, they *do* come.

By the time we're ready to begin, all of the chairs are full and a dozen people are standing in the back. Many of the faces are familiar.

Robyn is there, of course. As well as David, and Dawes, and Hannah.

When Hannah came through the door, her face lit up like a sparkler and she bounded across the room and jumped into my arms, squealing, "Auntie Ez!" as if three months had passed since I'd seen her and not three days. She's doing so well and growing like a weed. In another year or two, I won't be able to pick her up. She's also turned into a real little bookworm, for which I am taking full credit. Dawes isn't really a reader. I like him but the longer I know him, the more I realize that my first instincts were right—he really isn't my type.

I take Hannah to Malaprop's on the first Saturday of every month and let her go crazy and get three or four books, sometimes more. Then we walk down the street to Chocolate Fetish and buy a box of chocolate frogs. If the weather is nice, we'll carry the books and the candy to Adele's bench and read until it's too dark to see. Am I spoiling her? Possibly. But her love is for sale and I'm in the market. And after all Hannah has been through, she could use a little spoiling.

Dawes and Hannah aren't the only ones to drive in from the lodge. Vera and her sisters have come, and so has Brian. He made the cut after all and will soon be promoted to assistant manager. Cassie—who we hired to help with banquets because our event business is too much for me to handle alone anymore—is here and so is Jeff, head of maintenance. Even Jamie is here; he graduates from culinary school in the spring and will be starting as our sous-chef two weeks later. The better business gets, the more staff we have to hire. Profits are modest but considering how many people we've brought on, we're doing well. We've already booked twelve weddings, a retirement party, a quilting retreat, and a bar mitzvah for 2012.

A lot of my Asheville friends have shown up—the women from the crochet group Yolanda started and I joined, everybody from the Thursday night book club I started and Yolanda joined, Sylvia Barnett and Sutton (she divorced Martin fourteen months after the wedding but doesn't hold it against me), a handful of old classmates I've reconnected with, and a few of the merchants from the other businesses on Haywood Street. I also see Gwen Blessing, who has written a wonderful novel about a Depression-era widow in Appalachia who makes dulcimers and collects songs. Gwen's book will be our second release.

Looking around the room, I'm touched to see that so many out-of-towners have made the trip. Quite a few of our regular lodge guests are in the crowd, including the Wilsons and Mr. Thayer, whose daughter drove him down from Kentucky. He's widowed now and quite frail, but sharp as ever. When

I greeted him, he palmed me five dollars, winked, and said not to spend it all in one place. Carl is sitting in the front row, frumpy as ever in spite of the agency's success, still wearing his class ring and a too-short rayon tie.

Oscar is here, but that's not unusual. He shows up every couple of months for a week or two, partly to write but mostly to see Robyn. They've gotten past the giddy stage and Robyn, thankfully, has stopped murmuring about how handsome he is. But they don't seem to have tired of each other. Oscar's book did really well, made all the bestseller lists. His next book, *Suspended Animation*, will be released in May and is already causing a buzz. Judging from the size of the crowd and the number of unfamiliar faces I am seeing, I suspect word of his presence has gotten around. After Oscar agreed to introduce me this evening, Yolanda listed him as emcee on all the invitations.

While I'm standing with Oscar at the side of the room, waiting for stragglers to find a place to park themselves so we can start, I notice a man in the fifth row. I've never seen him before but there's something about him that looks familiar. That might be wishful thinking on my part. He is tall, slim, has sandy hair, gorgeous, turquoise-colored eyes that I notice even through his glasses, shoulders that are broad but not too broad. He is, in short, exactly my type.

When he catches me staring, I dart my eyes away, turn to face the wall, and whisper to Oscar out of the corner of my mouth, asking if the guy in the fifth row is one of his fans.

"Which guy?" he asks, craning his neck and scanning the crowd in a far too obvious way.

"Tall, sandy hair, glasses. Do you know him? Don't point!"

"Who, that one?" he asks, pointing. "Nope. Never saw him in my life. Do you want me to go over and ask his name?"

I cover my eyes with my hand.

"No. Thank you."

"So, listen," Oscar says, "when I get up there and introduce you, is it okay if I call you Half-pint?"

"Is it okay if I spike your champagne with arsenic?"

Oscar grins. "Okay, so I'm taking that as a hard no. But listen, Ez, there's something else I want to talk to you about. Now's probably not a good time but later could we—"

Yolanda approaches, interrupting his request and rubbing her hands together. "So? It's almost seven o'clock. Are we ready?"

"Not quite," Oscar says. "Esme wants to know who the guy in the fifth row is."

Yolanda turns around, cranes her neck. "Which guy?"

"Oscar, don't point!" I hiss but, of course, it's too late.

Yolanda turns back to face me. "As a matter of fact, I do know him," she says, sounding more than slightly smug. "*That* is Ryan Chrysanthemum, head of the botany department."

I unhinge my jaw. "Shut up. He is not."

"I told you he'd be perfect for you," she says in a chirpy voice. "Do you want me to introduce you later?" I nod mutely. "Consider it done. But first, let's sell some books. Oscar? You ready to do this?"

Oscar strides purposely toward the podium. The crowd, which had been getting restless, starts to applaud. When my stomach begins to knot, Yolanda puts her hand on my shoulder, then leans down and whispers in my ear.

"Hey, Ez. Guess what? We did it!"

I squeeze her hand and grin. Yes. Yes, we did.

"Know something else? This is going to be one of the best nights of our lives."

. . . NO WORDS ARE necessary. There is nothing I have to do, or say, or prove to anyone, not anymore. I am his everything. He is mine. From this day forward and for the rest of our lives, there is only one world: ours.

When I finish reading and look up from the page, applause hits me like a roll of thunder.

It's obviously a hometown crowd, but their enthusiasm is genuine. I answer questions from the audience, filling them in on what happened after the kiss. I tell them how George actually did get on the train, how he and Adele went to Baltimore to visit her mother for two weeks and get her blessing. I tell them how Jimmy, who owned the pool hall and thought of George as the son he'd never had, died shortly after and left a small bequest that, together with all George had saved, allowed them to buy the land and build those four cabins, the first structures in what would, indeed, become their own little world, a world they delighted in sharing with others, a legacy they passed on to Robyn and me and which, though of course I don't say that out loud, I plan to pass on to another generation someday, if not a child of my own, then perhaps to Hannah.

When the questions are finished, I force a frowning Yolanda up front so the audience can applaud her too, then we thank everyone for coming, and I push through a crowd of well-wishers to the table in the back of the room and start signing books.

Dawes, David, and Oscar walk around with trays of champagne and platters of hors d'oeuvres. Somebody turns on the music, our preselected playlist of songs from the 1940s including tunes from Glenn Miller and even Spike Jones. I sign piles and piles and piles of books. The final count will be close to two hundred, because many folks are buying multiple copies as gifts. More than one booklover jokes about how I'll need to ice my arm that night, and my hand actually does start to ache after a while. My face starts to hurt too, but only because I am smiling so much.

So many interesting people come through the line. I can't spend as much time talking as I'd like because other people are waiting, but I hear more than one intriguing story about Asheville back in the day. One man tells me that he's working on a book based on the life of his great-grandfather, a doctor who emigrated from Switzerland in the 1890s and ran a tuberculosis sanitorium. I give him a card and say I'd like to read the manuscript when it's ready.

Ryan Chrysanthemum approaches carrying five copies of the book for me to sign.

"They're Christmas gifts. I come from a long line of voracious readers. Oh, could you sign that last one to Chris? That's what everybody calls me." He chuckles. "Chrysanthemum is kind of a crazy name. Say, I was wondering, there's a reading at the bookstore on Saturday afternoon. Would you like to go? Maybe grab lunch after?"

I give him my card too, and we make plans to meet. He walks away, carrying his pile of books. Yolanda comes up behind me to replenish my supply, and whispers in my ear, "Hey, Ez? You might want to get a tissue, wipe that little bit of drool off your mouth."

I elbow her in the ribs, but discreetly, and greet the next reader.

The last person in line is Robyn. She slides a copy of the book toward me. It feels weird to sign a book to my mother but she insists.

"Adele would be so happy about this, and *so* proud of you. But there's something I want you to know, Esme. I'm proud of you too. And I always have been. Even when we weren't getting along, I was always proud of you. Jealous, sometimes," she admits with a shrug, her eyes a little wet even as she smiles, "but always proud."

When I think about how things were between us not even three years ago, I'm in awe of how much has changed. I can't say that I was always proud of Robyn, but I am now. And I genuinely like her, which is perhaps even more surprising. When I tell her, Robyn throws back her head and laughs and says, "I know, right? Who'da thunk it?

"Here's something else I hope you'll like," she says, and stretches out her hand like a monarch giving a peasant permission to kiss the ring. The diamond on her finger is *huge*!

"Wow! Oscar?"

She bobs her head and beams, suddenly looking ten years younger.

"He asked me last week but I didn't want to say anything until after your book party. I know he's been divorced four times, but I've never been married. If we add them up and divide by two, I figure we're not too far off the median for people our age."

Her math seems a little off but she looks so happy that I don't say anything.

"Besides," she reasons, "this is the first time Oscar's marrying someone closer to his own age."

This part, at least, is accurate. Oscar and Robyn are both about nineteen years old, at least emotionally, so I have every reason to believe they'll do well together.

There are things to work out about where they'll live and who will take over for Robyn at the lodge if she ends up spending a lot of time in Sag Harbor, but these are topics for another time. I hug her, then get up from the table and go looking for Oscar.

"Can I call you Dad now?"

"Only if I can call you Half-pint."

I laugh and hug him. "Congratulations, Oscar."

Oscar raises his champagne glass a few inches and inclines his head slightly.

"Congratulations to you, Miss Cahill."

SIGNING ALL THOSE books was wonderful.

But for me, the best part of the evening comes later, when the signing is done and I can go into the gallery and see the exhibit or, more accurately, see *other* people see the exhibit. I stand in the background, watching their faces as they wander slowly from one quilt to the next, taking the time to read the posterboards, or discuss the quilt with a friend, or to simply stand before my grandmother's art for a long, long moment, taking it all in with silent appreciation.

Seeing Adele finally receive her due is the most satisfying thing about this entire long journey and, quite possibly, the most satisfying moment of my life.

An old woman with a cloud of snowy white hair, deep wrinkles in parchment-thin skin, and a little too much rouge on her cheeks approaches with shuffling steps, clinging to the arm of another woman about thirty years her junior. We've met before, while I was doing some additional research on the book. It's Liz Reynaud and her mother, Betty Rae, who lived at the boardinghouse with Adele and George during the war.

"Mother has something she wants to say to you," Liz tells me.

Betty Rae was short to begin with and time has made her

shorter still, even shorter than me. When I lean down so I can see her face to face, her blue eyes are brimming.

"I wanted to tell you that I'm sorry," she rasps as tears spill over onto her cheeks. "I wish I could tell Adele but I can't so I am telling you: I am so sorry. We made fun of her work and I know that hurt her. But we just . . ." She pauses, attempting to collect herself.

"We'd never seen anything like that before, not in those days. Please, forgive me. We didn't understand what we were seeing or what it was. We didn't know what *she* was."

I swallow back the thickness in my throat, lean down even closer, and close the old woman's trembling hands in mine.

"It's all right, Mrs. Reynaud. It's all right. There is nothing to forgive. I don't think she knew what she was either. I'm not sure she ever knew. If she had," I say, lifting my head to take in the glorious serpentine of color and life above us, "all this would have happened a long, long time ago."

I AM ALWAYS going to be a planner, the kind of woman who swoons over a good spreadsheet and adds stuff she's already done to her to-do list just for the pleasure of crossing items off. And why not? There are worse things than knowing what you want from life.

But here's the deal . . .

Everything worthwhile takes longer than you think, trust me on this.

You can work hard, and you should. Because even the most spectacular failure serves its purpose, setting you up for the success to come. And as long as you learn, no lesson is never a waste. But the stuff that really matters tends to come with a built-in timeline that's usually a secret and almost always different than yours.

But it's worth the wait, believe me.

Or don't. Either way, it is what it is.

The next morning, I take my coffee and my sewing basket out onto the porch and sit in the rocker with the sun on my face and the song of birds in my ears, stitching hexagon patches. I've got a hundred now, almost enough to make a wedding quilt for Robyn and Oscar. But I'm not in a rush. For the first time in my life, I'm not waiting for anything to happen. I am savoring all I have and all I am in this moment.

And when I lay aside my patchwork and give my full, precious attention to the goldfinch perched among the leaves of Adele's scarlet oak, I know that the things that matter most are mine at last, with more to come.

Much more.

ACKNOWLEDGMENTS

Wonderful readers! Without you, I wouldn't be able to do this work that I love. To show my appreciation, I have some gifts for you.

Visit my website, mariebostwick.com, and click "Esme Extras" under the "Goodies" tab for book club discussion questions; a letter explaining the facts and inspiration behind Esme's story; a peek into Esme's world, with suggestions and travel tips for your next visit to beautiful Asheville, North Carolina; and even a few Esme-inspired recipes! (Caramel cake, anyone?) Thank you so much for spending time with me and Esme. I hope you enjoyed the trip!

MANY THANKS TO . . .

Lucia Macro, for her editorial insight, encouragement, enthusiasm, vision, and patience above and beyond the call of duty.

Liza Dawson, my literary agent, for her advice, counsel, and ability to say exactly the right thing at exactly the right moment.

Asanté Simons, for keeping the editorial ducks in a row, the plates spinning, and the author on track.

Kathie Bennett, of Magic Time Literary Publicity, and Ashley Hayes, of Uplit Reads, for all the woman hours and brain power they devote helping my books find their audience, as well as the occasional nudging of the sometimes spotlight-shy author.

Linda McDonough and Adam Kortekaas for their dedication and expertise in the nuts and bolts of all things website, blog, newsletter, and social media, and for making things run smoothly so I can focus on the only thing I'm really good at—writing.

Betty and John Walsh for cheerleading, for careful reading of crummy first drafts, and for eagle-eyed attention to typos and missing words.

Staff of the Buncombe County Special Collections in the Pack Memorial Library for assistance and guidance in researching the history of Asheville and the surrounding area during the Second World War.

The archivists of the National Gallery of Art, for assistance in researching artwork stored at the Biltmore estate during the war.